EMPIRE OF LIES

J.L. BECK

Copyright © 2023 J.L. Beck

Cover design: Haya Designs

All rights reserved.

No part of this book may be reproduced in any form or by any electronic or mechanical means, including information storage and retrieval systems, without written permission from the author, except for the use of brief quotations in a book review.

BIANCA

Blinking my eyes open, I stare up at the popcorn ceiling as the shock from my father's confession still rattles me.
Callum murdered Mom.

It's not like I expected or even hoped to wake up this morning with anything else on my mind. The sort of bombshell Dad dropped on me last night isn't something a girl forgets.

It makes no sense. No matter how many times I thought over the situation while nervously cleaning the house last night—because I needed to do something with the energy churning in my gut after I put Dad to bed— I couldn't figure out an answer to the single most important question that kept coming up. The key to everything.

Why?

Why would Callum want to murder my mom? Outside of being my mother, she wasn't anyone special—just your everyday average person. Nothing my father told me would lead me to believe she had anything to do with his business. They didn't even know each other—Tatum and I hadn't even met until middle school, which was well after Mom died. My frustration mounts. I can't figure out a way to connect them to make it make sense.

My muscles ache, and I groan as I sit up and throw my arms over my head to stretch. Why did I bother trying to sleep? I spent the majority of the time tossing and turning. I might have gotten a few hours of fitful nightmares, yet no sleep. The nightmares mostly circulated around mom. Before today, I dreamt of her once every few months or so.

They'd always been dreams of ordinary, everyday things like making dinner together or going shopping. I'd wake up and wish I could hug her and tell her how much we both miss her. They were never nightmares. Not until now.

Dad continuously said she died in a car accident when I was eight years old, too young to ask questions. Too busy trying to get over the idea of never seeing her again, of never hearing her voice or smelling her perfume when she hugged me.

You don't question what your dad tells you at that age, especially when he's the only person you have left. If there was more to it and he didn't want to tell me since I was too young, I get it. You don't convey to a heartbroken little girl that some monster murdered her mom.

Thirteen years have passed since then, and not once did the man think to mention she was murdered.

A look out the window tells me his car is still in the driveway. His bedroom door is still closed when I open mine and peer out into the hall. He's in there, sleeping off his drunken state. Until last night, I don't think he's ever been drunk in front of me. Buzzed, maybe, but never that far. Practically falling asleep sitting up at the edge of the bed, talking nonsense. I genuinely want it to be nonsense. A particular kind of nonsense.

Otherwise, Callum isn't just the murderer I fell in love with. He's the murderer who destroyed my childhood and crushed my father's heart in his fist, changing the entire course of our lives forever.

And worst of all, he lied about it. To think he's been lying about it the whole time. Unless he's killed so many people, he can't keep track of the bodies anymore. I guess that's seemingly possible. The very idea makes me shudder in revulsion as I wash up, then get dressed.

Not for work, however. I can't possibly go in today, even if I've already missed so much time. I don't want to lose my job, and I can't afford to, either. Only there's no way I'd be able to sit all day and focus on anything except Dad and his confession.

"I'm sorry," I mumble into the phone, speaking into Sam's voicemail while setting my toiletries up in the bathroom. "I thought I was ready to return by now, but I'm still shaky. I could always log in from my laptop if you need me today, but I think it's better if I try to work from bed." I doubt Mr. Adams will expect me to work, but I do want to leave the offer out there. I don't know how much longer I will be able to get away with this. That's the thing about a situation like this: you don't know you've pushed too far until you've already done it, and somebody's pissed at you. I don't want to be the problem child in the office, and if I'm ever going to get a place of my own, I need to stay employed and keep putting those checks away.

I just can't do it today, is all. And not only because I still have to put a little bit of makeup on my cheek to hide what's left of the bruising from the accident that wasn't an accident. It's a good thing I woke up before Dad and got in here before he could see my clean face. I can already imagine his reaction. He'd never let me leave.

I can't help but feel guilty for lying to my boss as I go downstairs and head straight back to the kitchen. I don't want him to regret hiring me. How was I supposed to know my life would implode around me? I didn't choose any of this.

There isn't enough coffee in the world to make me feel human this morning, yet something tells me we are both going to need it. One thing I didn't have the chance to do last night while putting the house back together was go out for groceries. It was too late, anyway. I would make breakfast if there were anything more than a few takeout containers and a quart of milk in the fridge. Something greasy to help with the way Dad's going to feel this morning.

This sight of the empty fridge is one more concern to tack on with the rest. This isn't him. He spent years raising me by himself, and we never had help in the house. When I was old enough, I started taking on some responsibilities, but it's not like the man forgot how to go grocery shopping. I came home for last-minute visits during college and never found the house in disarray.

Could it really be true? Could this be the big case he's been working on, exhausting himself with? The case he was finally starting to break the last time we were together? And there I was, without the first clue what it was all about.

I must be the worst daughter in the world, because as I fix a pot of coffee, I don't know whether I want this to all be in his head or not. It's sad but true. It might be better to think Dad is losing his grip on reality, for at least then it wouldn't mean I've betrayed him, my mother, and myself by falling for Callum. *How could I be so selfish? Stupid? To think I was falling for the man who ripped my entire life to pieces.*

I can't even blame Callum for it. I walked into this knowing he was no good for me. Hell, that was half the fun.

Footsteps overhead make my stomach flip and my pulse stutter, but I pull it together, sitting at the square kitchen table as I cautiously watch Dad shuffle into the room wearing last night's clothes. "You weren't a dream," he murmurs with the ghost of a smile. There's recognizable pain in his bloodshot eyes, but he leans down to brush a kiss over the top of my head anyway.

"Nope. I'm here, live and in the flesh."

"I hardly remember you coming in last night." He opens the refrigerator door and winces when the light hits his eyes. I could've told him it was a waste of time.

"I helped you to bed." I observe him from the corner of my eye while sipping my coffee, waiting for his memory to clear up. Wondering if he'll remember the things he said.

"I was wondering how I ended up there." At least he's not trying to laugh it off. There's an appropriate amount of sheepishness in his voice. "I'm sorry you walked in on me like that."

When he reaches for a mug from the cabinet, he finally notices his surroundings. "Wait a second, did you clean the kitchen?"

What was the first hint? Being able to see the bottom of the sink? "No, the housecleaning fairy must've visited in the middle of the night," I joke.

"Honey, you didn't have to do that." He sinks into the chair across from me, groaning softly. "I shudder to think of all the questions you must have about how things have been going around here."

"Questions? Worries are more like it."

"I don't need you worrying about your old man." He takes a gulp of his coffee before setting the mug down, his hands trembling. "Things have been crazy at the station. Sometimes I barely have time to microwave a meal before going to bed. I don't always notice when the dishes start to pile up."

Or the dust gets thicker, or the beer bottles line the counter. My teeth sink into my tongue before I can say something that will hurt his feelings. I don't want to do that. No matter how irritated I am, he either doesn't remember last night or doesn't want to admit he does.

It's like being with Callum, in a way. Wondering if I can say what's on my mind. If Dad indeed did forget what he said, what happens if talking about it reminds him? I could pretend it never happened, but I don't know how long I could keep pretending. This will taint every aspect of our relationship, no matter how hard I try to let it go.

His gaze lingers on the clock, and he takes another sip of coffee. "Shouldn't you be getting ready for work by now?"

"No, I'm taking the day off." *Oh, God, he doesn't know anything about the accident or that I missed a week of work because of it. I keep forgetting. It's like my life has become a web of lies and secrets. Keeping track of who knows what, what I can and can't share, is a full-time job in itself.*

It's not like I could tell him Lucas hit me with his car. It was hard enough to admit he cheated on me. This is considerably worse than that, and I know Dad would go after him for it. I can't face that drama right now. *Especially since Lucas is dead.* An involuntary shudder rolls through me and I wipe a hand over my cheek without thinking. It's almost a surprise when my fingers come back blood-free. I'll never forget how warm the splash of blood across my face was before he fell over my legs.

"Not because of me, I hope. I'm fine." Wow, and I thought I was a lousy liar. Maybe it's the hangover he's clearly fighting against. The fact that he seems to be hungover gives me a little bit of hope, strangely enough. He's not too far gone if his body still reacts this way to too much alcohol.

"Actually, in case you missed it, I brought bags with me last night. I was thinking about spending a little time here. Not officially moving in but staying for a bit, if it's okay with you?"

It's almost miraculous, the change that comes over him. A grin splits his face, and the worry creases on his forehead become smaller. "You know nothing would make me happier. I've wanted you home since the day you left." He's not lying. "However, I hope this doesn't mean you're having trouble."

Funny you should mention that. I came here because I was running away from the man you think widowed you. Yes, that's precisely the sort of conversation we need to have at the breakfast table. Or ever.

Time to break out the excuse I had prepared. "Things weren't going so well with my sublet. I have to start looking for a new place, but in the meantime I figured I'd crash here."

"Or you could always stay here, with your old man." He winks before pushing his chair back and going for another cup of coffee. "I wouldn't charge you rent, even when you have that fancy job that pays you so well."

A fancy job I sincerely hope I still have by the time my life returns to normal.

If my life returns to normal.

He's obviously not going to say anything about Mom, and I

haven't built up enough courage to. That's a can of worms I don't feel like cracking open.

It'll lead to so many other questions, too. Like why he never told me how Mom actually died. Would he bother to tell me the details now? Or am I still too young to know?

The aggravation these questions stir in my head gets me out of my chair. "I'm going to unpack my things, since I was too busy around here last night to do it then." I make a big deal about leaning in and giving him a sniff in passing before waving a hand in front of my face. "Maybe you should take a shower, Detective. How are you supposed to sneak up on the bad guys when they can smell you from a mile away?"

"Very nice," he grumbles wryly while shooing me away. "That's exactly where I planned on going." Good. Maybe he can soak his head under some cold water for a while and start thinking clearly.

It's better to be away from him, upstairs in my old room with all the certificates and awards on the wall. I always did like getting a gold star, which is probably why I would be drawn to a man like Callum. He goes against everything I'm supposed to be, everything I imagined for my life back when I was a kid getting an award for never missing a day of school. I was always a good girl, except I'm tired of always doing the right thing. I want to rebel against the person I used to be. The one who was never really seen.

For as long as I can remember, before I knew the specifics of his life and work, I sensed an aura of danger around him. Even now, I can't put my finger on it. The particular light in his eyes; the way he carries himself. He could change the temperature in the room with a single look. He has the power with just the lift of an eyebrow or the tip of his head to the side, and everyone around him falls in line. There's something sexy about that. It draws me to him.

And look where that got me. I should have been less concerned with perfect attendance and more concerned with learning how to read people. I've made so many mistakes.

I'm probably making one now, filling the dresser drawers with my clothes in the house I swore I'd never move back into. My heavy heart is dragging me down. Already, I miss Callum so much it hurts—and I hate myself even more for it since he doesn't deserve my heartache.

That doesn't stop me from grasping at straws, frantic to explain away Dad's beliefs. I can't imagine how he could be right. Callum never does anything without a motive; there can't be one. My mom, the woman smiling at me from a framed photo on the dresser, couldn't have done anything to put herself in his crosshairs. She was good, pure, and devoted to us.

The alternative is Dad driving himself crazy trying to solve what could've been a simple car crash. Not comforting. And if I ask him for specifics, he won't give them up, if only because of my friendship with Tatum.

I wish I could trust either of the men in my life to give me the whole truth. I'm sick of never knowing who to believe, whether I'm being manipulated—for good reasons or otherwise. I sag down onto the bed and stare up at the ceiling. I'm tired of being in the dark, tired of allowing myself to be led astray. If I want answers, there might be only one way to get them. I might have to dig for the truth on my own.

CALLUM

~~~~

It's nothing but a house, though it's not the house that's the problem.

It's that she would rather live in that tiny dump of a house than with me. She'd rather return to the one place she swore she didn't want to be, with a father who suffocates her. All because the idea of living with me is too disgusting for her to consider. The blood in my veins is boiling.

The place is dark except for the light over the front door, illuminating a rundown porch. They've been gone for half an hour, she and her dad. Romero witnessed it—I didn't want to be here in case she recognized me on her way out.

She or Charlie. *That prick.* The man's had it out for me long before our daughters ever met. Even if she didn't notice me parked halfway down the block, he would have. He's got a sixth sense when it comes to me.

All the more reason to get the hell out of here before they return.

"What is taking so goddamn long?" I growl into my phone, staring at the upstairs window I know looks into her bedroom. The blinds are drawn, and any innocent neighbor wouldn't notice the faint glow behind them. They wouldn't be scanning for it in a quiet, peaceful neighborhood like this.

They don't know the big, bad wolf has arrived.

I know what to look for, of course, and every moment that glow persists is a moment closer to Romero being discovered when the man of the house returns. I'd imagine he's working by flashlight, which I doubt makes it easier to get shit done efficiently.

Not my problem.

Romero sighs. "The name of the game is discretion, right? Hiding the camera? Feel free to come in here and do this if you think you could do a better job."

If I didn't need him so goddamn badly, I'd fire him here and now. Nobody talks to me that way. I'm still Callum fucking Torrio.

Callum Torrio, who is now parked halfway down the block on the street the woman he loves grew up on. Waiting for his right-hand man to finish planting a camera in her bedroom so I can at least look at her. I've become addicted to the sight of her, and the past two days without her have felt like hell. I'm addicted to her scent, her touch, her taste. None of those I'll get to have again unless I can convince her that nothing was going on with Amanda. I hate the thought of her thinking what we shared wasn't real.

There's the option of taking her anyway and keeping her tied to my bed until she promises she'll never leave, but that's a bit unconventional, and I highly doubt Tatum would allow it. My only option is to wait patiently, which is not my strongest attribute.

When she left my house, I knew this was where she would end up. She had no other place to go but was so determined to get away from me. Hence it was obvious that she would go straight back to the one place she wanted to avoid. I recall the things she said about Charlie, how he keeps her in a cage. I won't deny the proof that's in front of me.

She would still rather live with him than be with me. I've been through brutal fistfights that didn't leave me aching the way that piece of truth does. There's a pain in my chest, bitter and persistent. She wants nothing to do with me. It pisses me off, yet there's nothing I can do to make her believe otherwise. I've called her a million times, texted her, and tried everything I could to explain the truth to her. Nothing is working. I wouldn't have to go to such irrational lengths to see her if she would only just listen to what I needed to say.

God, she's so stubborn and beautiful.

"Are you getting the feed?" Romero's question stirs me out of my brooding, and just in time. I'm beginning to hate myself for it.

I pick up the tablet and scroll through the app connected to the device. "It's dark," I groan. "How much fucking longer is this going to take? They could show up at any minute."

"My hand was over the lens." He pulls it away, and now the image on the screen is of a girl's bedroom. It's about as big as my bedroom closet, decorated in pinks and creams. The walls are covered in posters of musicians I vaguely remember Tatum being interested in years ago. It would seem Charlie didn't bother taking them down when Bianca moved out. I bet he wants to freeze her in time, the soft innocence of his daughter.

There's not much we can relate to, but I can understand his mindset. There are times I don't recognize the woman my daughter has become. There are still days when I expect a freckled ten-year-old to come running in from the pool, dripping water all over the kitchen floor while digging in the freezer for a popsicle.

"I don't like the angle. I want to see the bed."

"I've already fixed the angle," he informs me in a tight voice.

"Then change it. Fast."

"You know..." The image jerks, giving me a clear shot of his scowling face. "This could all be cleared up much easier and much less illegally."

Illegal. As if we've ever cared about that. "What, you suddenly have qualms about breaking and entering?"

"Breaking. Entering. Installing a camera in a girl's bedroom so you can spy on her. In the home of a detective, by the way, in case you forgot."

"What's your big idea, genius? How would you handle a situation like this?"

"Well, there are many ways, though you could start by trying to talk to the girl. One-on-one."

"Do me a favor and get the job done," I bark into my phone. "I don't pay you to give advice unless I'm asking for it, and I didn't ask for it this time." I did, just only after he started bitching. I have no idea what's gotten into him lately—he usually reserves his opinion except in serious matters. Life-or-death shit.

The past few months have marked a turning point. I noticed it before now, when he had too strong an opinion on whether I should use Tatum as a bargaining chip with Jack Moroni. No matter how many times I swore I had no intention of marrying her off to Jack's son, he wouldn't let it go. When did he grow a conscience?

Romero sighs, smart enough to keep his mouth shut while aiming the tiny camera at Bianca's slim bed.

Telling me to talk to her. As if I haven't tried. As if I haven't spent the past two days crawling out of my fucking skin trying to get a hold of her. Calling, texting, making a horse's ass out of myself by approaching my daughter and asking her to check in, to at least find out whether Bianca is alright, and to tell her how desperate I am to talk.

I have even stooped so low into making a fool of myself in front of my kid—anything, so long as Bianca will give me a chance to explain.

How my ex-wife is a diseased cunt who will stop at nothing to destroy every good thing in my life. How she's dragged her feet for years, refusing to give me a divorce until she gets what she believes is coming to her. *My money*, as much of it as she can get her hands on. As far as I'm concerned, she might as well not exist. If it weren't for the shit she's put me through, I would have gladly forgotten her name by now. She's never been a mother to our daughter. There's no reason for us to interact otherwise.

In my mind, I'm single. Unattached.

Since when does it matter what it says in the eyes of the law? I've never exactly given a shit about that. A glimpse in the rearview mirror reveals my troubled gaze. The dark circles under my eyes, thanks to sleepless nights spent longing for Bianca's warmth and sweetness in my otherwise cold bed. "What's the big deal?"

"What was that?" Romero quips.

I didn't realize I spoke out loud. Now I have to explain myself, something I never do, even in better circumstances. "I said I don't see the big deal."

"About what?" Romero tweaks the camera's position another few inches until the bed is centered in the frame. I can also see part of the bedroom door and the mirror over the dresser. It's as detailed a view as I'm going to get.

"Any of this. You want me to talk to the girl? Fine. Then get her to answer her phone. I've been trying since she left. All because, what? My ex isn't out of the picture completely?"

"That could be." He's speaking quietly, tension in his voice while he fixes the camera's position. According to what he told me, it's mounted inside the top corner of her bookshelves, partly concealed by a stuffed animal. "She's young. She's already been pushed around."

"But Amanda doesn't mean anything. She's a pain in the ass and determined to ruin my life. How is that my fault?" I sound like a whiny little bitch. This is what she's made of me. I've grown into a whiny little bitch, begging for a chance to be understood.

"You never told her about the papers not being signed."

"Why would I?"

"Did you ever think that keeping it quiet makes it look like a bigger deal than it is?"

My anger rises. "Just do your job."

Either he forgets I can see him, or he doesn't care. He shakes his head and rolls his eyes in plain sight. "I'm done. On my way out now."

"Wait," I whisper when a familiar car pulls up from the other direction. "I think she's coming."

"Son of a bitch." Just like that, he disappears, the bedroom door opening and closing. The phone goes dead, too, leaving me with no idea whether he's escaping. I guess I'll know soon enough.

My gaze darts back and forth between the footage on the tablet of the bedroom and the Corolla, whose headlights shut off a moment before the driver's door opens. At that moment, everything else ceases to exist. I don't care that Romero has to sneak out of the house while Bianca and Charlie unload groceries at the curb.

I don't care that a detective would probably have a nose like a bloodhound and would be able to sniff out a stranger's presence. Romero's intelligent enough not to wear cologne or anything that would give him away, except Charlie is a real pain in the ass, determined to fuck with my life. I wouldn't be surprised if he picked up on something being off, no matter how good Romero is at his job.

All of it falls away at the sight of her. How has it only been two days? I feast my eyes on her beauty, soaking it in the way parched earth soaks in the rain. My mouth goes dry, and I forget to breathe, too busy taking in every detail to worry about something like keeping myself alive.

The way she laughs and how she grumbles when Charlie takes one of the bags from her like he thinks it's too heavy for her to manage. At least I know I'm not the only man whose opinion she brushes off.

For one wild, breathless moment, I see myself getting out of the car. Facing her. Daring her to ignore me now. Demanding she come home, where she belongs. With me, in my arms, in my bed. Where I can watch over her, protect her, worship her.

That's all I want to do. Why can't she see that? What do I have to do to open her eyes to the reality of us needing each other?

"Look at me," I whisper as she and her father cross the sidewalk and approach the front porch. "See me. Know I'm here. This is what you've made me do. These are the lengths I have to go to if I want to look after you. Know that I haven't given up. I would *never* give up on you, even if you think you've given up on me."

While Charlie unlocks the front door, she does, in fact, look out over the street. Absently, though, her gaze drifting over houses and cars. She looks straight past me, through me, and I grit my teeth to hold back a roar of frustration. How can I sit here without her knowing I'm right here? Can't she feel me the same way I still feel her? Did I make that little of an impression on her?

With a blink of my eyes, she's gone. The lights inside flicker on and I wait, holding my breath, staring at the house. Waiting for a scream, a gunshot, something, anything.

Instead, my heart leaps into my chest when the passenger door opens. I reach for my Glock out of sheer reflex. "It's only me." Romero ducks into the car and slams the door before leaning back in the seat, panting. There's a sheen of sweat on his forehead. "I cut through two backyards and nearly broke my ankle on a swing set. I'm not as good at hopping fences as I was when I was a kid."

Considering nothing out of the ordinary is coming from the house—no Charlie darting out onto the porch, looking around, nothing out of place—it seems like he made it out safely. "Good work."

"Thanks." He turns his head to look at me, his brow furrowed. "Are we leaving or…?"

Right. We have to go. As much as it tears me to pieces to leave, it's my only option. It won't be enough, watching her or listening to her soft voice thanks to the camera's microphone. I know that now. Seeing her hasn't lessened my craving—just the opposite. I need her more than I did before.

I have to get her back beside me, by any means necessary. And when I do, it's going to be different. No more secrets, no lies. I've learned my lesson.

If it's a choice between keeping things to myself and losing her,

I'll force myself to open up. I'll tell her everything there is to know about me.

However, I will not jeopardize her safety. That, she can't ask me to do.

Deep down right now, it pains me to know she's safer than she ever was with me.

I push the doubt aside before pulling away from the curb, forcing myself to leave her.

It's not forever, I remind myself. We'll be together again, and when that time comes, I'll make it so she can never escape me.

BIANCA

"It's nice of you to stick around to make sure your old man's taking care of himself." Dad finishes unloading the cold stuff into the fridge before standing up straight. He eyes me warily, as if he's trying to figure me out. "However, you don't need to take another day off work to look after me. I'm fine, and you can't afford to lose your job."

"I know." I turn my back to him before filling a pot with water at the sink. It's a relief to be able to loosen my face up a little—it's been more than an hour since we went out for groceries, and I spent the entire time straining to keep my expression neutral. I'm exhausted, and my cheeks ache already. And it's all because I can't let him know what's going on in my head.

"Honey? Did you hear what I said?"

"Hmm?" Turning off the faucet, I set the pot on the stove. "Sorry. I couldn't hear you over the water."

"We'll both head to work tomorrow, and when you get home, I'll have dinner ready for you." He pulls out a pitcher to mix up iced tea, something we always drank with dinner when I was a kid. The first time I ate dinner at a friend's house, the fact that they wanted us to drink water, was horrifying. I thought everybody drank iced tea, the powdered kind from the can.

It always made me feel like I was helping with the meal, pouring the powder and stirring it into the pitcher. Testing the sweetness. Mom would try it after me and give me a thumbs up. *"Thank you so much for being such a big helper."*

Between the constant reminders of her and the fear that I might've betrayed her with Callum, it's astonishing I can get through something as simple as fixing dinner for us. I zoned out a few times when we were at the store and kept trying to add things to the cart after Dad had. *Ugh.*

I have to shake myself out of the distraction gripping me these past two days. Like just now, walking into the house, I could have sworn somebody was watching me. It's ridiculous, really, and just another way Callum has sunk his nails into me. In real life, people don't lurk around in the shadows, stalking girls and claiming it's because they love them. I have to adjust my thinking before I lose my sanity.

It's already bad enough I'm walking a thin line with Dad. Weighing every word I use, tiptoeing around the obvious. The way he let the house fall to pieces along with himself. The things he said about Mom and Callum, which he still hasn't uttered a word about.

I wanted to give him the time and space to do the right thing on his own. I'm not deluded—I didn't think he'd break down and pour the whole thing out, but this is a huge development and she was my mother. *Don't I deserve to know the truth?*

It's a relief when he retreats to the living room at my suggestion and turns on the ball game. I can practice in my head what I want to say once we sit down to eat.

Dad, I'm going to lose my mind if you don't tell me what you meant about Callum murdering Mom. Yeah, sure, that'll work. He won't be completely shocked at all. I'm still unsure if he remembers what he said before passing out. I want answers, but I don't think I can dump them on him like that.

I guess the best way to go is to be gentle. *Hey, Dad, you said a few things the other night, and I was hoping we could talk about it.* I mean, that's normal. It's almost enough to make me lose my hold on the plates I pull out of the cabinet. Callum. Mom. Impossible.

But what if it is possible?

I hate that question. It's the reason why I haven't gotten into it yet with Dad. Unable to come up with a motive, I can't see it being true. Callum wouldn't murder an innocent young mother, for fuck's sake. A flash of bitter disbelief blazes through me, leaving in its wake a horrible taste in my mouth. He's many things, but he's not that sort of a monster.

You're assuming she was innocent.

Stupid subconscious. That could be the reason Dad doesn't want to offer an explanation. It might mean sharing a lot more. I was eight years old—what did I know? So many things could've passed under my nose without me ever noticing. I don't think I could handle having that picturesque image of her shattered, but I have no other option. I need the truth. At the very least I need to know what makes Dad so sure it was Callum who killed her.

By the time the food's ready, I'm not closer to having any sort of resolution than I was before. *This is ridiculous. Grow some balls Bianca!* Since when can't I talk with him? Okay, so he can't know about Callum or about Lucas hitting me with his car or about where Lucas is now… fine, I can't talk to him about most of what's gone on lately.

This isn't the same. We've always been close, but especially over the loss of mom. If there is anyone I can talk to about her, it's him.

"Goulash?" Dad's eyes light up at the sight of what's waiting on the stove. It isn't goulash, actually, just macaroni mixed with ground meat and tomato sauce. One of my favorites from when I was little.

"I can't help thinking about the past," I admit as he fills up a plate. "When Mom taught me how to make that. I'm so glad I had the chance to learn."

"Me, too." He's smiling fondly as he sits at the dining table.

"I feel like she's still here with us at times like this." Heavy-handed? Yes. I'm laying it on thick, hoping he picks up the hint and runs with it.

"It makes me happy to think of you keeping her memory alive."

Fuck. This is torture. He's so happy, eating and smiling, and all I want is to ruin things by bringing up the painful past.

Whatever's happening, it's visibly affecting him. And it's not like I can stay here forever, no matter how much he wants me to. I should at least find out what he's going through if I'm going to eventually leave him again.

It isn't easy to ignore the rush of nostalgia at the first bite, tears threatening to fill my eyes. All of a sudden, I'm a little girl who wants to know why her mom had to die. I swallow back more than noodles before I can muster up the courage to speak.

"Do you... remember anything about when I first got here a couple of nights ago?" I keep my gaze trained on my flowered plate because it's easier than watching the light drain from his eyes. Somehow I know if I look up at him, that's what I'll find. A man empty of life, of joy.

"Not very much. Enough to feel guilty." He clears his throat sharply before his fork clangs against his plate. "Why? Did I say something stupid? You know, you can't trust what a person says when they're drunk. A person's rational thought process isn't there."

He forgets I went to college, though he's probably so deep in denial that he never imagined me going to parties. Like, I don't know what it's like to be drunk. Like, I don't know that a person is far more honest when intoxicated than sober. Rational thoughts make you lie; when you're drunk, the truth pours out.

"Don't bother trying to cover your ass in advance," I warn with a smirk while glancing up at him. "You mean you genuinely don't remember anything? You were in your room, looking through pictures, talking about Mom."

At first, all he does is stare at me. There's nothing angry or malicious about it. More like he can't figure out what he's looking at. "I remember pulling the boxes down from the closet. I'm sorry if it upset you. Sometimes I find myself feeling sentimental."

He cracks a brief grin, lifting his shoulders. "Now you know. Sometimes, your old man gets sentimental and has too much to drink. Or is it the other way around?"

The silence between us drags on. His face falls when I don't chuckle along with him.

"Is there anything you think I might like to know about the way Mom died? Like... I don't know... maybe that it wasn't an accident?" My voice is far more accusing than intended, but I can't stop the emotions from slipping out.

"Bianca—"

"The way you always told me it was?"

"You don't understand." His chair legs scrape over the floor when he pushes back and out of it. He's trying to escape, to run away from the truth, but I can't keep living a lie. I just can't.

I'm out of mine before he can make his escape. "No, Dad. I'm begging you. I need to know the truth. What have you been keeping from me?"

The apples of his cheeks grow red, and his dark eyes narrow. "Did it ever occur to you," he murmurs in a deceptively low voice, "that I have reasons for what I do? For what I share with my child?"

"I'm not a child anymore." My hands slap against the tabletop hard enough to make our glasses shake. "And I can't forget what you said. You told me Mom was murdered. Is that true? Tell me the truth."

The corners of his mouth twist in a smirk that baffles me until he retorts, "Not if you ask the detectives assigned to the case."

"What does that mean?"

"It means the official story is a car accident. It's always been a car accident." Does he know he's rubbing his palms over his thighs? Like they're sweaty. Like he's nervous. My nerves are rattling, so I can relate to that.

I need to do this, even if it feels like I'm pulling the bandage off a healing wound. I'll hate myself forever if I miss this opportunity.

"What's the other story?" I whisper, unsure whether I want the answer.

He draws a deep breath that expands his chest and reminds me what a fit, powerful man he still is. It's easy to look at your dad and see an old man, but the truth is, he's only a year older than Callum. I hate to think of him wasting away, drinking himself to death in a house full of filthy dishes and takeout containers. It'll be worth it if it means suffering through what I'm about to hear so I can help him through whatever he's dealing with.

"The other story." He lowers his brow, folding his arms as his jaw juts out like he's pissed off, bitter. "The other story involves your mother's autopsy featuring a bullet wound to the head. Her original autopsy."

I grip the table edge in fear of falling to the floor. "Original?"

He nods. "As in the first autopsy, before the report was altered."

My hand flails around behind me to grab my chair before I end up on my ass. "And you know that for sure? That the report was altered?"

"I saw the original before the alteration. It disappeared from my desk, and everyone I asked pretended it was never there. All this time, they've been telling me it was never a gunshot wound. They've treated me like I was a poor, hallucinating widower."

"But..." It's getting harder to breathe. My throat seems to be closing, my heart constricting a little more with every beat. "Why?"

"That's where Callum Torrio comes in." His expression softens for the first time since this started, but only a smidge. "I'm sorry, honey. This is why I didn't want you to know. I knew it would hurt because of Tatum, but you deserve to know the truth." He shakes his head. "I should've told you a long time ago, before you two became so close. Nothing good can ever come of that family." He's vibrating with rage so intense the air practically crackles around him. The light hanging over the table casts eerie shadows over his face and hides his eyes when he lowers his brow again. "Callum knew I was after him. That I finally had something that I could pin on him. Watching him get away with his crimes... I couldn't let it go, except the man was Teflon. He still is. Nothing sticks to him."

I shouldn't have said anything. *No, he shouldn't have lied.* How could I have known where it would go?

It should shock me to know Dad and Callum had it out for each other, but I always assumed it had to do more with the illegal wrongdoings that Callum got away with and my father's deep moral compass of taking down corruption. This is much more than I could've bargained for. "He knew? You're sure about that?"

"I wasn't exactly discreet," he snorts. "He knew damn well I've made it my mission to take him down."

I'm starting to see it. I don't want to. I want to close my eyes and pretend it isn't so sharp.

"He put a bullet in your mother's brain as a warning to me," Dad concludes in a grim voice. "I know it must be painful to hear that. I've told myself for years that Tatum is not her father, but it's inevitable that she'll start taking after him as she ages. No matter how good of a person or how different she tries to be from her father, his blood still runs in her veins." His forehead smooths, and he smiles. "Now that I have what I've been looking for, I can finally put all of this to rest."

"And what is that?" I croak.

"The original autopsy. Whoever was supposed to remove the original from the archives didn't do their job very well. Nevertheless, it took a hell of a lot of digging to find it."

Every question he answers only brings up two more. "I don't understand. Who would hide something like that?"

"A dirty cop. There's corruption in the department, there has been for years. That's how Callum manages to skirt prosecution and why your mom's autopsy was altered to keep him out of it. All these years, your poor mother hasn't been able to rest in peace because that bastard is out walking free, doing more criminal shit. Money can make anyone innocent, but the truth is you can't unsee it once it's in front of you."

"Don't do that," I whisper, closing my eyes. "I can't take it." I don't need him giving me ideas about whether or not Mom is able to rest. I might as well ask him to shove a knife into my chest. As if I need more reasons to regret every choice I've made over the past few months. It makes too much sense. I don't want to believe it, but I can't pretend the pieces don't fit together.

All except for one, but I can't bring it up. It's probably the most important piece of all. Callum wouldn't kill an innocent woman. Not to send a message. I know him too well to believe otherwise. *But you aren't supposed to, are you?* And that's why I have to bite my tongue before I accidentally blurt out too much. I can't defend him. It'll look too suspicious.

He wouldn't.

He couldn't.

Even if it was thirteen years ago, he might've been a different man at that time. I refuse to believe this. Even if I've seen how easy it was for him to put a bullet through somebody's head, even if he threatened to hurt me, it was only ever a threat. Every part of my heart aches, telling me it's a lie. My stomach churns violently, and I jump up and stumble to the sink just in time for the drain to catch my vomit. *Oh god.* This can't be true. None of it can. Even if the alternative means Dad's losing his grip on reality.

"I'm sorry," he murmurs behind me once I've finally stopped retching. "I am, honey. I didn't want you to know. The truth is ugly sometimes."

That's one word for it. I'm still shaking when I rinse my mouth out, slumped over the edge of the sink. Dad's been after Callum all this time, while I was busy fucking him. It's too twisted. My stomach lurches again at the thought.

The knock at the front door forces me to stand upright. My heart's in my throat, and I'm suddenly sweaty. *He wouldn't. He couldn't.* It's the worst timing ever for him to show up. He wouldn't show up here, least of all with my father here.

Unless it meant kidnapping me and taking me back to his house. I can't pretend that would never happen. Callum's capable of anything. Even... *no,* he wouldn't do that. He wouldn't murder an innocent. I repeatedly tell myself that and cling to the thought like a life vest, praying it'll keep me above the rising water.

Dad's footfalls signal his walk to the front door—where his sudden, sharp announcement makes me turn to face the open door. "She can't see you right now. We're in the middle of something."

"I want to see her." Instead of a deep, masculine voice, I hear my best friend's voice. The relief that washes over me brings tears to my eyes. "I need to make sure she's okay," she insists.

He barks out a snarky laugh, like she's an idiot for worrying. "Of course, she's fine. Why wouldn't she be?"

"Excuse me, but I'd rather see that for myself."

"Excuse *me*, but this is my house and we're not having visitors right now. We were having dinner." He shakes his head, "Never mind, that doesn't matter. You're going to have to leave," he insists in a firm voice as I enter the room, looking over his shoulder to see if it's really her. If she's really here.

It's not like I don't know her voice. I merely need to see her with my own eyes to be sure. She's standing on the porch with her arms wrapped around her middle, frowning up at my father and wearing a look that can only mean trouble for whoever stands in her way.

"Either you're going to get out of my way," she retorts, "or I'm going around you. She's my best friend and a grown woman, and if she doesn't want to see me, then she can tell me herself."

I hate to break it to him, but she's not going to give up.

Considering her father might have killed my mom, I'm not sure how to feel about it.

CALLUM

"I wouldn't mind going through the motions, if I didn't know it's a waste of time," I grumble on my way through the large glass doors of the lawyer's office. It's no surprise to find so many associates working at this hour of the night, chugging lattes and energy drinks at nearly nine o'clock. Romero and I wait at the front desk while he texts Bob to let him know we're here. The receptionist has gone home, I assume.

"Do you think she's here yet?" Romero mutters, now changed from the dark clothes he wore only an hour ago into a suit that's slightly more in line with a visit of this nature. Nobody would ever know he's fresh off a home invasion.

Another reason to hate my ex with all of me: I want to be home, watching the feed from Bianca's room, not arriving at my lawyer's office for a late-night meeting I'm sure will get us absolutely nowhere.

"Of course she isn't," I mutter in reply, lifting a hand when I see Bob striding our way past a row of offices. "It was her great idea to have the meeting this late, to begin with. Now she's going to make sure we wait even longer for her to show up. This is her MO. If the ball isn't in her court, then she steals it."

At times like this, it's damn near impossible to remember what I ever saw in her. Aside from her looks and her body, what was it? What made me stick around after we fucked and before Tatum came along? Why the fuck did I marry her? What made me believe there could be something real?

It was a turn-on. I had never met a woman like her before. She wasn't satisfied with simply taking my money and leeching off my success. She wanted that success for herself, for both of us. She drove me to be bigger and better than I was, the poor kid whose father still lived and worked in a tiny go-nowhere town.

In some ways, I have her to thank for what I've accomplished, because she encouraged me. Her cutthroat attitude helped guide me to where I am today. I know now there was no love behind that encouragement, no genuine desire for me to be better since she knew I was capable of big things. She wanted it for herself, was all, and spotted a willing tool already on his way up in the ranks.

We were supposed to build an empire together. For us. A life, a family, a legacy.

Unfortunately for her, she couldn't leave well enough alone.

Just like then, tonight is yet another act of manipulation. Bob winces when he reaches us, shaking our hands. "Sorry we couldn't talk her down to an earlier meeting time," he offers. Amazing to think of a time when I didn't know this man. Amazing to remember believing—innocent, naïve as I was—that our relationship would be a short one.

"I've learned to expect the worst from her," I assure him. "I know you did your best."

He looks visibly relieved at my acceptance. I guess working for a known arms dealer with a violent reputation could give a guy an ulcer or two. "Can I offer either of you something to drink?" he asks, leading us back to the conference room. "Amanda and her team are also running a few minutes late." Romero and I exchange a knowing look behind him.

"Did any of her team give you an idea of what she feels is so important that we have to get together at nine o'clock on a Wednesday night?" Romero asks, his eyes sweeping the conference room. An act of habit, making sure everything's safe. I doubt there are many safer places we could be, yet that doesn't stop him from surveying the room, then sweeping his gaze over the buildings on the other side of the windows lining one wall. Bob frowns when Romero begins lowering the shades, although he offers no argument.

"No, only that she felt it was imperative to meet." He offers me a pained, sympathetic look. "Of course, the hope is she's come around."

Yeah. And I still hope Santa Claus will come down the chimney, but it will never happen.

It's five past nine when a team of men in suits come marching toward the glass-walled room, and in the center of the cluster is none other than the venomous snake I made the mistake of marrying at a young age, too stupid to know better. She's sleek, polished, like she just stepped out of a salon. Her blond hair is pulled back into a low ponytail, and her stiletto heels click smartly against the floor when she strides into the room. She's wearing a red business suit, so all the attention is drawn to her.

"Please, have a seat," Bob invites, and I watch with little amusement as the six-person team arranges themselves on the opposite side of the long, shining table in the center of the room. He offers them drinks and a few accept bottled water.

Amanda merely shakes her head, too busy giving me a look I know very well. Smug, almost playful. She's fighting back a smile. The best I can do is show no effect at all. She wants to get a rise out of me like the child she is.

One of her lawyers clears his throat, looking up and down the table like he's making sure his team's ready to begin. "Mr. Torrio."

A single glance at Bob shuts that down. "You'll be addressing me," he informs her team. "I speak for Mr. Torrio."

Amanda arches an eyebrow. "Did you lose your voice?" she

murmurs. "Must be all the screaming you did when I visited you at home over the weekend."

Bob sits up a little straighter. "Did we or did we not agree that neither party would trespass on the other's property without advance warning to the legal team? If so, I didn't hear anything about this."

The stupid bitch. Her face falls when she realizes the trap she stepped in, though she quickly recovers. "I was worried about my daughter."

"Then why do you imply Mr. Torrio would have any reason to scream at you?" Bob counters. "Miss Torrio lives in her own wing of the house. There was no reason for you to interfere with Mr. Torrio."

Her cheeks grow redder with every second that ticks by. Romero, who is seated at my left, snorts softly. I don't. The most powerful weapon I have in my arsenal is a blank face. That gets to her better than any screaming or threatening can ever do. A typical bully, unable to deal with being ignored. The second she gets you to react emotionally, she has you trapped.

"Our client has reason to believe her husband is more motivated to come to a final agreement," another of her lawyers announces. "And if that's the case, it's time to get serious. We've drawn up a new request for a settlement, plus increased monthly alimony payments until such time as Mrs. Torrio remarries."

"Absolutely not," Bob replies without bothering to skim at the papers the lawyer slides his way. "There will be no alimony payments beyond what the judge sees fit to award, and the settlement Mr. Torrio offered back when the divorce proceedings were in their early stages is more than generous. There are also several investments that Mr. Torrio is prepared to sign over, as well as the house in Vail. That was the final offer yesterday and will remain the final offer today. The only way that offer will change is for it to decrease, not increase."

I don't blink, smile, or snarl. I stare blankly across the table at the woman I once believed I loved. Funny, I saw only what I wanted to see. Hell, her ambition was a turn-on. Right up there with her tits, legs, and those lips that had the power of a hoover vacuum. I had no idea how thin the line between ambition and ruthlessness could be, but I knew now.

"If Mrs. Torrio is interested in more money," Bob continues, "she can always sell the Vail property once it has been signed over to her. She can also cash out the investments, though that would be a mistake akin to killing the golden goose. Nonetheless, she is a grown woman and can decide as she sees fit."

The lawyers exchange book's. "Then there is no agreement," one lawyer murmurs, glancing at Amanda for verification. She's seething. Her carefully constructed façade is on the verge of collapse. It's all a mask. Each piece is placed strategically. Nothing about her is genuine; she's only an endless pit of misery and emptiness. Dark, screaming emptiness.

I know that now. I know what it means to be with a woman who possesses a soul. One with genuine warmth and kindness, who gives a shit about the people in her life. Tatum, her father—hell, even Lucas. She even wanted to protect him after he ran her down. She showed more compassion in one single moment than Amanda has in her entire life.

After the woman seated across from me twisted him around her finger and put ideas in his head. She'll never admit it, but she doesn't have to. The flash of guilt on her face when I initially accused her back in my bedroom told me the entire story. Like a child caught doing what they were so sure nobody else was aware of.

It's low even for her. It's not typical for her to do the dirty work. She twisted me up, pushed me to claim more power all for her own endless materialistic needs, then discarded me for other men once it was clear I was over being manipulated. Now, she has this team of clueless assholes doing the dirty work of fighting for more than she deserves.

"You're this determined to screw me over?" Her voice drips with disbelief while she shakes her head slowly. "Are you seriously declining without even reading what my lawyers have put together? To be so stingy and vicious. It doesn't fit you, Callum."

My jaw aches; I'm clenching it so hard. I want to tell her she doesn't know me. Doesn't have the first clue, but even so nothing I say to her will matter.

Bob lets out a bubble of laughter, yet he's a lot gentler about it than I would be. "If you consider the millions Mr. Torrio has offered you as an example of stinginess, it's clear we'll never come to a final agreement. Mrs. Torrio, I've been handling marital disputes and divorce agreements for thirty years, and I've never had a client willingly offer such a generous percentage of their net worth. Mr. Torrio has not once threatened to reduce his original offer. He only refuses to increase it. I'm not your lawyer, but if I could give you a piece of advice, it would be to take the offer."

"So I won't get another red penny." She folds her arms over her chest, arching an eyebrow. "Not a single cent?" She tilts her head to the side, examining me. "I thought you were motivated now?" Laughter dances behind her otherwise empty eyes, and it has the power to raise my hackles. I can't give her the explosion she so visibly wants. Especially in front of so many witnesses.

"You shouldn't—" one of her lawyers cautions, but she dismisses him because she's always ignored common sense.

"Aren't you in a hurry to get me to sign the papers?" she continues, batting her eyelashes at me. Like that would fucking get me to break. "Wouldn't it make sense for you to be free, at least legally? That way, you can move on with your life?"

Romero sits up a little straighter, but a soft growl from me keeps him quiet. She's at a high simmer now, about to start steaming. The longer I sit here, refusing to react, the greater her rage grows. She'll shoot herself in the foot the way she always does. It's only a matter of time.

"It would be wise of both of you to come to an understanding, so you can *both* be free," Bob points out in a firm voice. He's losing control of the situation and he knows it.

"Mrs. Torrio played a large part in Mr. Torrio's success," one of her team points out. "She only wishes to be compensated for that."

"Mrs. Torrio lived an extremely comfortable life while living beneath her husband's roof," Bob counters. "And, by all appearances, lives very comfortably now. Mr. Torrio filed for divorce when evidence of his wife's various infidelities were uncovered—if it wasn't for that, we might not be sitting here now."

He checks his watch, sighing. "And we're wasting time. Either she signs the papers as they stand now, or we start carving up what she's already been offered."

Amanda's nostrils flare while I remain impassive, gazing at her without emotion. "I have an idea," she murmurs, reminding me of a snake preparing to strike. She's fresh out of ammunition, and the only way she knows how to react now is to hit below the belt. "Why don't you give up your little whore, and maybe then I'll sign."

Romero grunts. Bob stammers.

I stand.

There's an evil gleam in her eyes as she lifts her chin, following my progress. I lean in, palms flat on the table. My blood is boiling, raging. I can't believe I ever found anything about this woman attractive. "You would know about being a whore," I snarl. "That's what this is all about, after all. *Money*. The only thing a whore truly cares about."

"Callum…" Bob murmurs in warning.

Romero stands beside me, even as I ignore him the way I am ignoring Bob's voice and the way her team inches their chairs away from her, like they don't want to get caught in the blast.

Amanda doesn't even blink, nor does she look away. "And you mean to tell me she doesn't? What the hell would a young girl want with an old man like you? Typical midlife crisis," she laughs, shaking her head. "I've considered you to be many things, however… I never thought you would go after a girl your daughter's age. How long has it been going on? Was she even eighteen when you started screwing her?"

"You will not say another word!" I slam my hands on the table hard enough that even she jumps, while one of her lawyers scrambles out of his chair and backs away, his back slamming into the glass wall surrounding us. "You don't deserve to talk about her. And you don't have the first fucking clue what we are or aren't. But then again, how would you?" I demand, and Romero grips me by the shoulders, pulling me back before I climb over the table and wring her neck until the light leaves her eyes for good. "You don't understand anything beyond your fucking bank balance. And if you think I won't find a way to make you pay for what you've done to me, and Tatum, you're out of your fucking mind."

"Boss, that's enough," Romero warns and pulls me away from the table. He backs me up to the window, placing himself between me and the evil bitch still glaring at me.

Fuck. I'm not proud of that. All the fighting against playing into her hand, and I did it anyway. She got the reaction she wanted out of me.

"I promise you," I warn, straightening my suit as I sidestep Romero to look her in the eye. "You will get exactly what's coming to you and then some. All of the shit you've put in place will come back and bite you in the ass, and I can only hope I'm there to see it happen."

"Is that a threat?" she asks in a sickeningly sweet voice. "Because we are in a room full of lawyers, and it's not exactly the best time to threaten me."

I grant her a smile that makes her breath catch. The smile people see before they realize they've pushed me too far and there's no going back. "Not a threat, sweetheart. A promise. You're playing with fire, and we all know what happens to people who do that."

"We'd better call an end to this." Bob wastes no time gathering everybody and ushering them out of the conference room. Amanda glares at me, almost pouting as she leaves. Almost like she believed she would have gotten somewhere tonight. Like the mention of Bianca would inspire me to sign on the dotted line.

She never was one for subtlety.

Romero blows out a heavy sigh once we're alone, with Bob showing everyone else to the door. "So much for playing it cool."

"Was I supposed to sit idly and let her insult Bianca that way? I don't give a shit what Amanda thinks about me. She does not disrespect the woman I—"

He lifts his brows yet says nothing, only waiting by the door for me to cool down and give the other team time to clear out of the building before we go. I wouldn't trust myself to do the right thing if I had to set eyes on her again this evening.

I never imagined blowing up the way I did. It isn't me, especially not when there's so much at stake. Not in front of a half-dozen lawyers. Specifically not when it was so clearly what she wanted. None of those things matter, in any case. When it comes to Bianca, all bets are off. There's no predicting what I will or won't be able to endure when she's involved.

The thought of her unravels a deep unsatisfied need. It's only been a couple of hours since I saw her outside Charlie's dump, but it might as well be a lifetime. I crave her, burn with the need to possess her. Only I can't. I can't do anything, not while she's there.

"Let's go," I decide, already crossing the room. "I have things to do at home."

Like watching her. I need to see her, to hear her, to exist even on the fringes of her world because it's better than enduring the emptiness of being without her.

That's all I have to go on. It won't be this way forever. Bianca will be mine again in due time. I just have to devise a plan to get her back.

And I think I know the perfect place to start.

"I know that look." Romero's voice drips disapproval as we step out of the elevator in the parking garage. "You're plotting something."

"And if I am?" I counter. "I pay you to make things happen, not to judge me."

"Just promise one thing." He comes to a stop at the driver's side door, throwing me a fatigued look over the roof of the car. "Promise I won't have to break into a girl's bedroom again."

"This time, I'll be working solo," I assure him before climbing into the car.

Don't worry, Bianca. We'll be together again soon.

BIANCA

The porch light makes Tatum's golden hair gleam as she stands on tiptoes, peering over Dad's shoulder to see me. "Hey," she exhales, and there's a world of relief in that single syllable. The worry lines etched on her forehead and between her brows loosen.

"See, she's fine. You've seen her with your own eyes," Dad snarls. "Now, it's time to go."

"Dad," I groan in dismay. She didn't do anything to him, to either of us. I'm sure his sudden change in attitude hurts her. He's never been anything but warm and friendly with her until now, and while he's angry at Callum, he needs to realize that Tatum isn't her father.

"This is my house," he reminds me, looking at me over his shoulder grimly. "I think I still have a say in who does and doesn't step over my threshold. No matter how she puffs out her chest and throws threats around."

I hope she understands how sorry I am when I wrap a hand around his wrist and tug him back away from the door. "Dad, she's my friend. You've never had any issues with her coming over before." I tug again, and this time he looks at me, and I hope he gets the message when I stare up at him. I can't say it out loud, not in front of her.

She is not her father. She's done nothing wrong.

He can't transfer his hatred for Callum onto Tatum. It's not fair to either of us, and I can't even consider picking between the two of them. I love my father, but Tatum understands the things my father never could.

My father's nostrils flare, and his jaw twitches like he's fighting against whatever it is he wants to say. At least he's fighting against it. That's a good sign. "Fine," he finally grunts. "But this isn't going to turn into a sleepover."

"Nobody said it was." He shakes his head, muttering to himself as he walks away, but at least he's doing that much. Going back to the kitchen, where he'll either finish eating his dinner or start on the six-pack he insisted on picking up at the store.

Something tells me I know which one it'll be.

I can't worry about that now. I haven't even gotten into the drinking situation with him, and I know better than to think he'd do anything except shoot me down for bringing it up.

I turn my attention to Tatum, whose face isn't as red anymore. She still looks shaken. Her angry gaze remains trained on the kitchen doorway until I motion for her to follow me. "Come on. We'll go up to my room." What a shame he had to be the one to answer the door, because having her here is a massive relief otherwise. I don't have to pretend as much when we're together. There aren't as many secrets I have to remember not to spill.

Although now, I have the super fun privilege of having to pretend my dad doesn't hold her dad accountable for Mom's death. I honestly can't remember the last time I went through life without having to remind myself of everything I'm not supposed to talk about. There are so many secrets. If I get out of this with my sanity intact, it'll be a goddamn miracle.

When we reach my room, and I close us inside, she sighs and sort of deflates, then sags against the chair, letting her head droop as she recovers from the sudden nastiness downstairs. "What's his problem? He's never acted like that before."

"Would it help if I said it's not you but him? He's going through some things." I face her with my back against the door, trying to smile. "Hi."

"Hi," she whispers, biting her lip. "You're not mad at me, are you?"

"No! Why would you think that?"

"I've been trying to get a hold of you for two days, and all I got was a single text telling me you were here and you were fine." Her eyes sparkle with unshed tears and there's a catch in her voice.

Right away, it makes me see everything from a different perspective. And I feel like shit about it. She had a breakdown at the hotel, and by the time she woke up at home the next day, I was gone with no explanation.

"I'm sorry." When I extend my arms out, she rushes into them, wrapping her slim arms around me to return my hug. It's easy to think of her as being tough and having her shit together. Like she doesn't really need anyone. I can't make that mistake, not after seeing her fall apart as she did. "It's just... I couldn't take all the other calls and texts. I finally had to turn my phone off. I don't want to block his number, but..."

She's shaking her head when she pulls back. "Okay, that's fine. I just don't want to worry that you'll disown me because of him."

"I would never." Nevertheless, I can see how she would think that, and after everything she's been through, it makes sense. "I've been a shitty friend the past few days, and I'm sorry."

"We're both kind of a mess right now, aren't we?" At least she tries to laugh, even if it doesn't ring true. She's fighting hard to keep it together, that much is obvious.

We both sit on the foot of the bed, angling our bodies to face each other. "How are you holding up?" I ask, touching her shoulder gently. "How are you feeling?"

She blurts out a disbelieving laugh. "You would jump right in and worry about me. You're the one who—"

I shake my head, holding a finger to my lips, glancing at the door. Understanding touches the corners of her eyes, and she nods. "You're the one who had to come here when shit went south."

It's like talking in code, although it's the only way I feel safe. To think, I thought Dad would lose his mind if he found out about Callum before this evening. I had no clue. All I can do is be thankful I was so careful about keeping our relationship discreet.

"I'm fine," I lie. I've never been farther away from fine in my life, except lying is better than admitting the truth right now. "Dad's sort of a mess, though. I'm really sorry he was so rude to you."

She snorts. "Overprotective, as always."

"It's more than that. He's... I don't know. It's like he's unraveling. Here I was, running back for help, and I found him in worse shape than I was."

"What do you mean?"

I mean, he thinks he finally found the evidence he needed to pin my mother's murder on your dad. Sure, why not? I'll just hammer the final nail into the coffin and completely ruin everybody's life. One confession and I'll destroy her relationship with her father, my relationship with mine, and any hope of a future with Callum. I bite my tongue. I don't know how much longer I will be able to keep all of this to myself. The truth is eating me up inside.

"Between you and me, he's been drinking." Her face crumbles a little like she's genuinely sorry to hear it. I know it's disloyal to him, but it's better for her to take his attitude as some kind of drunken rage than to know the truth. If she ever thought Callum did what Dad swears he did, it would break her heart. She's already been through too much. Plus, she already has one parent who has done nothing but disappoint, neglect, and hurt her. I can't take away the one good parent she has left.

"Ugh. How long has it been going on?"

"I have no idea, and of course, there's no point in asking him for the truth. He'll only deny it and say it's not a problem."

"I'm so sorry. But you know..." I can tell she's trying to be kind, like a true friend, choosing her words carefully. "Even you realize you can't actually help him, right? You can encourage and cheer him on. However, you can't stay here forever to watch over him. I know you want to help him, but you can't make him see things for what they are."

"I never said I was trying to make him see things."

"You don't have to." She smirks the way a friend does when they've known you most of your life. "That's just how you are. Kind and sweet. You want to help however you can, but you can't give up your life to do it."

"That really isn't what this is about. I wouldn't even be here in the first place if it wasn't for..." It's not fear of Dad overhearing us that quiets me. I can't bring myself to say it out loud. The wounds of the truth are still fresh. "The way he lied to me. I deserved the truth. At the very least, he owed me that. He should've let me make my own decision on whether or not I wanted to be the other woman. Instead, I was taken by surprise and had to sit there on the bed while she called me a slut. It was humiliating, among other things."

"Do you want me to kill her for you?"

The question takes me by surprise, and a bubble of laughter escapes me. Tatum laughs with me, and the tension in the room evaporates by the time we're both wiping tears from our cheeks and catching our breath.

"You're crazy," I gasp, and all she does is shrug like it's nothing new.

"Seriously, though. She's such a bitch. I'm sorry you've had the pleasure of meeting her."

"It's not your fault. You didn't make her the way she is."

"I wish I had been there. There are so many things I want to say to her." Her jaw tightens, and something tells me her anger isn't only for my sake. She's got more than enough reasons to tell her mother off.

"It's for the best that you weren't," I murmur, shuddering at the humiliating memory. How ugly it was, how nasty Amanda sounded. Callum wasn't much better, even if he had every right. "I've never seen people talk to each other the way they do. It was bad enough without me being part of the reason they were fighting."

"Yeah, it's different since your parents actually loved each other."

Oh, God, it hurts. It hurts so much. She's right. Mom and Dad did love each other. Even when I'd catch them arguing, they were always at least civil. No screaming or name-calling. Looking at Tatum now, I see so much of Callum in her. *Could he?* Does he have it in him to put a bullet in an innocent woman's head, to protect himself?

"Did you know they weren't officially divorced yet?" I ask.

She shakes her head. "I swear to God, I figured it was finalized ages ago." Then she snickers, rolling her eyes. "Big surprise, Dad kept yet another secret from me. I'm so shocked because, you know, that's so unlike him."

I can't muster up a laugh this time, because I know all about secrets. I'm keeping about a million of them myself. "I'm surprised your mom didn't say anything to you about it."

Her jaw tightens again. "What? Talk to me? Why would she do that?"

I figured she might do it to get between you and your dad. I don't have the heart to say that out loud, even if it's what I'm thinking and even if I have no doubt Amanda would stoop that low. Even before her little performance back at Callum's, I didn't exactly have a high opinion of her. Watching my best friend get disappointed time and time again by her thoughtless mom left me with a bad taste in my mouth a long time ago. I shouldn't have been surprised by how determined she was to make everybody miserable.

"Listen to me." The way she grips my hands, it's like she wants to break my fingers. "It's really good that you're here right now. In fact, it's probably the best place for you."

Instantly, ugly thoughts start to race through my head. "What's wrong? Is he okay? Did something bad happen?"

"No, he's fine. I mean, he's a miserable wreck and keeps asking if I can get a hold of you because he's crawling out of his skin without you, but otherwise, he's fine. I'm more worried about her and you."

He did accuse her of knowing Lucas, didn't he? I didn't have much time to think about it then—many other things were going on—but that's something I've pondered while trying and failing to fall asleep. Was she the reason Lucas went crazy?

"She will literally do anything to get what she wants," Tatum continues in a hushed voice. "I could kick myself for thinking she ever finalized the divorce. She knows that once it's over, it's over for good. She won't be able to get any more money out of him. Therefore she's doing everything she can to make him miserable and force his hand. As far as she's concerned, he is ruining her life. To get even, she's going to ruin his."

It's a dumpster fire—the whole thing.

"Do you think I'm in danger because of her?" I can't believe I'm even saying this. I can't believe Callum wouldn't stop to think about what Amanda is capable of. He's so concerned with my safety, protecting me, all that. Why didn't he bother to consider her being a threat?

Especially if he suspected she got to Lucas. It's like every time I turn around, there's another reminder of how he's no good for me. Even if, in my heart, all I want is to go back to him. I miss him with every part of me, every fiber of my soul. Being separated leaves me aching and weak.

Tatum takes way too long to respond. "I wish I could say no and be certain, but right now, I think it's best to lay low. And just know that he really, truly is determined to get her out of his life for good."

"Oh, really?" *Pardon me if I have a hard time buying that.*

"Right now, they're at a meeting with the lawyers. Both of them. He's dead set on putting this behind him so he can be with you."

I wish my heart didn't swell when she said that. I wish I didn't feel so happy. I want so much for it to be true—my entire life has become about him and us.

Something inside me aches when another thought hits me. "Are you sure that isn't what he told you to say? Is that why you're here? Did he ask you to come see me because he knows I won't see him?"

Her head snaps back, and right away, I regret asking. "How could you even think that?"

"I didn't mean it... like that."

"Too bad, that's exactly how it came off." She drops my hands. "No, he didn't tell me to come and say that. He knows better, for one thing. I wouldn't do it anyway, not even if he begged. I waited until he was gone to come here. I don't want him to know since all he'll do is jump on me when I get home and ask me a million questions. I figured you wanted your privacy, and when you were ready, you'd talk to him."

"I'm sorry. Don't be mad at me," I beg. "Please. You're all I have. I can't lose you."

"I'm not mad." She sighs and her shoulders sink. "You're kind of all I have, too. I can't afford to lose you."

"You'll always have me. Even if I've run off for a few days, it's not because of you. I'm really sorry," I add when the pain on her face intensifies. "You don't deserve to be in the middle of this."

"Yeah, well, you happen to be two people I love, even if you both make me want to scream sometimes." She grins, and I know she doesn't mean it. Not completely. "Are you sure you're okay here? I'm serious. If he's unstable..."

"Everything is fine." Now I wish I hadn't said anything, but I needed an excuse for his behavior. Men and their bad behavior. I'm so tired of having to make up for it. "I'm more worried about him becoming his own worst enemy."

"I absolutely can't relate to having a dad like that," she deadpans.

We share another laugh, but this time it's tinged with sadness. "And you're sure you're okay?" I have to ask. "Are you… taking care of yourself?"

She lifts her chin, defiant. Typical Tatum. "It takes more than some egotistical asshole to break me. I wouldn't ever dream of giving him that kind of power."

I wish I could believe her.

I wish I could believe Callum is innocent.

I wish things weren't so broken, and my heart didn't beat for a man I never should've been involved with. I know the truth can set us all free. However, lies are easier to tell. It's not the freedom we seek but the protection our lies offer us. I have to stop hiding behind them. I have to break free, even if I know it's going to hurt.

CALLUM

"What's wrong? Is he okay? Did something happen?"

I tap the screen to pause the replay, then rewind it back ten seconds to watch it again. To savor the change in Bianca's voice and posture when she got the idea there was something wrong here. How quickly she jumped from bitter sadness to concern over me. The desperation edging her words, her breathlessness, it's all somewhat gratifying.

I sit back in my chair with a smile, watching the change come over her again. Does she realize she changed so suddenly, or is she still kidding herself into thinking we're through?

She can run all she wants but can't pretend she doesn't care. At least I know I still have that.

Just as I still have my daughter's loyalty. Am I entirely thrilled she went behind my back to visit Bianca without at least telling me her plan? No, but I can forgive her secret visit since I know she's defending me. While Tatum loves her best friend, she also wants to be sure Bianca knows the truth—at least, the truth as she knows it. There are still parts of my life she's unaware of, and that's by design. I'll never want anything more than to protect her from the ugliness and danger.

Even if she resents me for it. That little joke about her inability to relate to having a dishonest father. It touched a nerve, and I'm still seething more than an hour later after getting home and immediately pulling up the footage recorded by the camera in Bianca's room. I couldn't have imagined I'd find my daughter there, but if anything, she did me a favor. She gave me insight into my little bird's psyche, probably more than she would have offered if I had come straight out and asked.

No, there's no *probably* about it. I believed her when she swore she wouldn't feed Bianca any stories about me. Not my fierce, independent kid. As much as it irritates me, I can't help but appreciate her loyalty.

I have to know exactly what Bianca's thinking, feeling, doing. I need to use any tool at my disposal, because she will not make it easy to win her back.

I hope she doesn't think her stubbornness and a few ignored phone calls will convince me to leave her alone. If so, she should know me better than that. It's the hardest-won victories that are the most satisfying, and I always win. Bianca cannot escape me. She might think she has, but only because I let her believe she could.

Now the clock is ticking. It's past eleven, and knowing Bianca, she'll want to go to bed soon. Especially if she plans on going to work in the morning. I settle back at my desk, a drink in hand, my tie discarded, and my shirt partly unbuttoned. The house is quiet, painfully so. Incredible how the solitude I valued so highly not that long ago, now leaves a bitter taste in my mouth.

All this peace and quiet does is remind me of what I've lost, even when I plan to get it back. Next time, I'll be more careful. I won't give her a reason to run away. If it means honesty, as Romero said earlier, I can make that sacrifice. I can learn to be better, to open up even when I don't think it matters.

I would tell her that, if only she were here. All the promises I would make. If she asked for the moon, I would happily comply, as long as it ended this constant, painful longing. Now that I've had

EMPIRE OF LIES

her, it's the height of cruelty to ask me to live without her. Without her body, her sweetness.

Her goodness. Her warmth and her light.

Her tight pussy gripping me, commanding me when I want to be the one doing the commanding. I'm a man who prides himself on strength, yet the fact is, she *is* my weakness. And while I should be working on removing her from my system, I know it would be a waste of time to even try.

Hence my sitting here, sipping my scotch, waiting for her to return to her room. The more I observe, the better my chance of getting inside her head and finding out what it will take to bring her around.

All I can do is laugh bitterly at myself before taking another sip from the glass. I can tell myself all I want, that this is nothing more than a means of understanding her better. Deep down inside, however, I can't deny the insatiable need to see her. To watch her undress and indulge myself in the sight of her lush perfection.

I sit up at attention when the bedroom door swings open. *Finally.* Did she have to put her father to bed? Resentment tugs in the back of my mind, and I grind my molars, eyes trained on the tablet. So he's been drinking, has he? And she would still rather be with him. It boggles my mind. Was it that bad here? Or is she being the dutiful daughter? Likely, except I'm not about to comfort myself with that idea.

She got scared and reacted emotionally; part of that was my fault. She won't come back until I make things right. I'm not going to excuse myself.

There she is. The tension running through my body loosens at the sight of her. She softly closes the door and kicks off her shoes before sitting at the foot of the bed as she did earlier with Tatum. She sighs, then drops her head into her hands, and I have to wonder if she's thinking about me.

"Do you know you made a mistake?" I whisper, taking in every part of her with my hungry gaze. There's something defeated about her posture, the way she props her elbows on her knees and exhales slowly, deeply. This is a girl with the weight of the world on her shoulders. I only want to take that weight away. Can't she see that? What do I have to do to prove myself to her?

She blows out a long sigh before standing and stretching. I know that look on her face. Plainly visible, thanks to the high-quality camera recording her. It's so clear and sharp I can practically see the pores on her face. She's determined. To do what I haven't the slightest idea, but I'll find out. Somehow, I'll find out what's going on in that head of hers. She can't hide from me.

When she crosses her arms over herself, taking the hem of her t-shirt in her hands, I barely move. She lifts the shirt overhead, revealing a lacy bra I've unhooked before. I can almost feel it under my fingers as I watch, instantly captivated. My own private show, made even more exciting since she doesn't know about it.

Next comes her jeans, and when she bends to pick them up off the floor, I'm treated to the sight of her ass. My cock stirs as hunger flares to life. It's always there, simmering, yet there's no keeping it from bursting into flames now that she's down to a skimpy thong. What I wouldn't give to touch her right now, to have her in my lap. Straddling me or bent over the desk. Yes, I like that better, the idea of her body sprawled across the desk, feet on the floor, legs spread. I would pull that thong off with my teeth before running my tongue between those round, firm cheeks.

She reaches behind her to unclasp the bra and free her tits, and now I have no choice but to lower my zipper and free what's already hard, straining. I could look at her body every day for years, for the rest of my life, and never get tired of it. Nothing will ever quench my thirst.

I take myself in my hand and stroke slowly while she goes through her dresser for one of those night shirts she likes to wear. I'll replace every single one of them with my own. They suit her better than the hottest piece of lingerie ever could. There's something absurdly sexy about how she looks with the hem barely skimming the tops of her thighs, with her tits moving gently beneath the cotton. The taut peaks of her nipples brush against the fabric, and I groan at the thought of touching them, thumbing them slowly. Watching her expression as she dissolves in pleasure.

It's almost enough to make me consider getting in the car and driving there now, breaking in the way Romero did, stealing into her room, and taking her whether she likes it or not.

Deep down inside, I think she'd like it... eventually, anyway. She can't deny how her body needs mine, no matter what her brain tells her. There's always going to be a more profound wisdom beneath the surface.

She still looks miserable when she sits on the bed after pulling back the blanket. "Regretting your choices, huh?" I murmur, stroking myself faster, staring at her legs and wishing I was there to pry them open. "I bet you wish you had stayed now."

Or is there something more? If I could only ask and get an answer. She told Tatum she doesn't want to block my number, which only gives me hope. I can still get through to her. Remind her that no matter what's dragging her down, I will do everything in my power to remove it from her life. No matter what it is.

I fucking killed for her. What else must I do to prove what she means to me?

Her hands land on her thighs the way I wish mine could, and I stroke myself faster when they begin to creep up, almost reaching the hem of her shirt. "That's right," I whisper, panting. "Touch yourself. Make yourself feel good. Envision me touching you. Do you wish I was there?"

My heart is ready to burst by the time she lies back, swinging her legs up onto the bed, then parting them. This is precisely why I wanted the camera angled the way it is now; I have a straight shot of her pussy, still covered by a thin piece of fabric, but only until she peels it off and sets it beside her.

Holy shit. Has it really only been two days since I gazed upon this glorious sight? Since I swept my tongue along her seam and reveled in her reaction. Her fingertips brush the insides of her thighs and I moan, using the cum dribbling from the tip of my cock to lube my shaft.

"That's right, baby," I grunt, eyes glued to the spot between her legs. "Make yourself feel good. Do it for me, little bird. Come for me."

She closes her eyes, arching her back at the first contact with her smooth pussy lips. Her mouth falls open and her head to the side when she strokes her pretty, pink clit. She knows just what to do and I watch, stroking faster, grunting with desire.

That could be me. It should be me.

Her head rolls from side to side, and she pulls up her shirt with her left hand, exposing her heaving tits. She takes one in her hand, massaging, tweaking the nipple until her teeth sink into her lip. She tries to contain a moan but can't entirely, and the soft sound makes my balls lift. That sound, the sound of pleasure. That's all I want to give her.

Her fingers move in a blur over her clit, her touch light, and soon her hips jerk rhythmically while her breath quickens. So does mine, my rasps filling the air, my heart racing while I fist my cock faster while careening toward the edge the way she is.

"Come with me," I grunt, staring at her pussy, tightening my grip the way her cunt would tighten around me if I were inside her now. Goddammit, I want to be inside her. Now, always, forever.

She opens her mouth to moan again, and this time there's a name to go along with it. "Callum..."

Fuck. It's that single word moaning at the last moment before her hips lift, and she goes still, that makes cum spill over my fist and onto my lap. I can barely silence my roar of triumph. The release, mixing with the knowledge that it was me she was thinking of, was me she was imagining working her clit until she came.

There's a wet spot under her ass when she settles back down, and slowly she withdraws her fingers from her glistening folds.

I'm almost dizzy, spent from the force of coming harder than I have in ages. All that pent-up need rushing out of me all at once. I don't care that I made a mess of myself. I don't care about anything but knowing she was thinking of me. Imagining me.

How much longer will she be able to imagine before she breaks down when her body demands the real thing?

I reach for a tissue while she lies still, catching her breath and staring up at the ceiling. She's glowing, at peace, and I gaze at her in wonder while she comes down from her high. There is nothing in the world as beautiful as my little bird when she's just come, all flushed and radiant and spent.

"Callum," she whispers again—but this time, there's a catch in her throat. A tremble in her voice. I watch in dismay as she throws her forearm across her eyes, and her soft sobs begin. Her body shakes from the force, tears rolling down her cheeks.

"No, no," I murmur, shaking my head, dismantling from the inside out.

She can't hear me, of course. I doubt she'd be able to stop herself if she could. She might cry even harder, because I'm the reason for her tears. She rolls onto her side and curls up in a ball, holding a pillow to her mouth to muffle the sound of her anguish.

Anguish, I brought her. This is all because of me. I might not have meant to hurt her, but I did. Deeply. So deep, her body shakes from the force.

And now I have no choice except to watch, just as I watched her come. As much as I want to turn away, I can't give in to weakness. I owe her this much. I will witness her pain and remember it every time I resent her for leaving. Every time I wish I had never set eyes on her, since that would mean essentially freedom from the torment she's putting me through.

"You won't be crying for long," I promise, whispering to her shaking image. "I promise you, little bird. Soon, you won't have any reason to cry."

BIANCA

"It's so good to have you back." Stephanie's smiling from ear to ear, standing outside my cubicle as I finish getting my things together at the end of what had to be one of the longest days of my life.

I feel like a different person than when I walked out of here on my lunch break that last day. I thought I was going to sign a lease. Something so innocent, the sort of thing people do every day. I expected to return to my desk afterward, because why would I think otherwise?

Now here I am, more than two weeks later. It might as well be two years or two lifetimes. Since I last walked out the door, I was hit by a car and rushed to the ER. I spent days in bed, trying to recover. I found out my best friend was being abused by her ex and was then kidnapped by mine.

And now he's dead, and the man who killed him might have also killed my mother.

When I think of it that way, it's no wonder I could hardly keep myself focused today. Everything seems so stupid and pointless. It's not like I had a terrific opinion of my job before this, but now I can't imagine why anybody would want to spend their life sitting here, going over spreadsheets, wasting hour after hour.

Is this what happens when a person realizes they could have died more than once? Is this my big turning point moment where I realize I need to shake up my entire life instead of wasting another minute doing something I hate?

Right. Fat chance of that happening, especially when I'm living with my father. I'm surprised he let me out of the house to go to work, but not very surprised since he still thinks this job is a big deal. Like I made a massive success out of myself sitting in a gray cubicle all day long and slowly going blind while reading over figures until my eyes crossed.

The least I can do is offer Stephanie a smile and hope it looks sincere since it's not like she did anything to hurt me. "You're just saying that because you're glad you won't have to cover for me anymore," I tease her, winking.

"Okay, I'm not going to pretend that has nothing to do with it." Only she gets serious right away, and her smile slips. "Honestly, though. It's good to have you back. You gave us a scare." Girl, you have no idea how much scarier things got.

I know she means it, even if I can't imagine why. I haven't been here that long. I still have to get used to the idea of people genuinely liking me and not just putting up with me because I tagged along behind Tatum, who was always more popular and better at making friends.

"Let's see if I can make it two days in a row." I hold up my crossed fingers and laugh it off, even if inside I'm shaking. I have to do this again tomorrow. How the hell am I going to get through the rest of my life this way?

Especially when all I seem to do is think about Callum all day long instead of keeping my mind focused on work.

Immediately, I stop myself before allowing him to encompass my thoughts yet again, and replace memories of him with those of my Mom. The way she took me trick-or-treating alone since Dad was always working that night. Our Saturday afternoons at the movies. Learning how to bake bread from scratch, though I completely forgot that one after a little while. How she always smelled like flowers, how she laughed—rich, hearty, almost bawdy. Like there was a dirty joke she was just dying to tell somebody. I grin at the reminder of it while walking to the elevator.

She is who I need to be thinking of now. How can I feel otherwise? Aching for Callum is pretty much the same as spitting on her memory. I still don't know for sure whether Dad is right and Callum is the one who killed her, but until I know, I have to at least try to remain neutral.

Which means conditioning myself out of obsessing over him morning, noon, and night.

I'm miserable, but that's how it has to be. I hate this sense of this dark, ominous cloud following over me. Instead of rain, guilt and shame shower me all day long. I can't believe I made it so easy for him to manipulate me.

The parking garage is mostly empty by the time I exit. A few people decided to stay late, but everyone else filtered out a little before me. Even with a backlog of work, I can't bring myself to put in the extra time when I'm so sad, not to mention feeling overwhelmed. It's not like I'm leaving early, anyway. I'm so wound up in my own thoughts, and need to get home that I don't hear the door opening.

Or the echo of footsteps behind me.

I don't see him until he's right behind me, his gorgeous face reflected in the window as I'm about to unlock the car door. Even if I want to scream, there's no time to react. I've barely registered his presence when he clamps a firm hand over my mouth, snaking his thick arm around my waist, before pulling me flush to his muscular chest. Panic grips me by the throat. Is this where his true intentions are exposed and I discover that my father wasn't lying?

God, I hope not. This would be a terrible way to go.

Somewhere in my mind, an alarm goes off, and I finally struggle in his grasp.

Fight. Don't give up.

"Fuck, it's been too long since I touched you. Stop squirming, or I'll end up fucking you against the car door," Callum growls in my ear.

The deep timbre of his voice sends goosebumps across my flesh. Some of the fear and anger have receded, yet that doesn't mean I'm not running away from this psycho the moment he releases me. The car door in front of me opens, and he releases me with a shove, forcing me to crawl across the seats.

My hands slip on the cool leather as I put as much distance as I can between us. I didn't recognize his car parked next to mine. Then again, I wasn't paying attention. *Stupid me.* I should've known leaving the protective nest of my father's house that he would track me down. A man like him refuses to let what he wants slip through his fingers, and apparently, I'm what he wants today. Callum climbs into the backseat casually like he didn't just abduct me. He smooths a hand through his dark hair, and I swallow around the knot in my throat.

No matter how handsome he is, I must remember that he's not a knight in shining armor who was sent to rescue me. He's the villain, only capable of putting his needs before others.

"What is wrong with you?" I demand, my body trembling.

Anger and fear battle it out. I want to punch him in his stupidly gorgeous face and run away. Adrenaline courses through my veins, and I reach behind me, flailing around while trying to find the door handle.

"Child locks," he grunts. "To keep little girls from jumping out of the car when they shouldn't."

I wish—God, how I wish—I could hate him. That sitting this close to him didn't set off a fire in my soul. I wish I didn't want to throw myself into his arms and bury my face in his neck and revel in his nearness. Being near him after days without him feels like I just took my first sip of water after going thirsty for days. My soul is refreshed even if my mind recoils with horror.

I find my voice again while straightening out my blouse with shaking hands. "What the hell do you think you are doing? You can't just show up at my work and force me into your car. There are cameras, and anyone could have seen. Are you trying to get the police called?"

"Do you think this is the first time I've grabbed someone and thrown them in the back of my car?" He lets out a chuckle, and I'm glad he does, even if it terrifies me. It helps me harden my heart so I don't make the mistake of begging him to take me back. I need to be strong, and that would be very weak of me. I have to remind myself that he did not tell me the truth about him still being married and *might* also be my mother's killer.

"I don't care how many people you've thrown in the back of your car. Whatever you want to say to me can wait till I'm ready to hear it."

"That's the problem. I couldn't wait another second. I had to see you, had to see with my own eyes that you're okay." That snide, teasing note calling from his voice is replaced by something that could be mistaken for tenderness.

I know it's not real. It can't be. Nothing about him is real. If it were, he wouldn't have so casually lied to me about his marriage, making me believe what we had was real.

"I'm fine. I'm back at work, living my life. Thank you for asking." I jiggle the handle, glaring at him, pressing myself against the door when he moves closer. The heat of his body radiates through me. If he gets any closer, I risk giving in to him, and I can't have that. "Now let me go. I need to get home.."

He lowers his brow, his eyes like burning embers. I should look away. Only I'd still feel their heat burning if I did. "There's no running away from *us*, Bianca. You're not going anywhere until we talk about this," he rumbles, leaning in close enough that all I can smell is the intoxicating scent of his cologne. *Cinnamon and cloves.*

With him this close, it becomes harder to remember how bad of a man he is, and instead how good he could make me feel.

"See?" With both hands, I shove against his chest as hard as I can, even managing to put a little room between us. Straightening my shoulders, I let the proudness envelop me. His eyes widen with surprise, but it's not enough to keep him from reaching out to place a hand against my knee. I smack his hand away and shake my head. "I have to wonder if you're crazy or just psycho? What would make you believe that I would allow you to touch me after the bombshell that was revealed? How can I trust you? None of this is real. We're not real, and showing up at my work and forcing me into the back of your car will not change that."

Even now, I know I'm lying to myself. Everything about us is real. I just don't want to admit it right now because I'm angry. I've been duped, made a fool of. Everything I know about him, everything that might be true, it all dissolves when I'm with him. Breathing him in, staring into his eyes which glitter with an intensity I've never seen in anyone else's. The way he looks at me, there is nothing like it.

I want him to touch me. I want him to be honest with me. I want him to tell me my Dad is wrong. I want him to make everything go away and tell me it's going to be okay.

Mom. Think of her. Think of the lies and how he made you feel.

"Everything with Amanda can be worked out, though not if you run away from me. I haven't even had a chance to explain things to you." Again, he grabs my leg, and I slap his hand away again. I can't think straight while he's touching me.

"Explain?!" My voice raises, anger raining down on me. "There would be nothing to *explain* if you would've let me decide for myself," I remind him, closing my legs tight while folding my arms over my chest. The last thing I want to do is deny him, for it means denying myself. I have to remain strong, however. Especially when I crave him too much. It would be so easy to give in and think it over later.

"To decide what?" he challenges.

"Why should I allow you the opportunity to explain yourself when you didn't give me the chance to decide if I wanted to be the other woman? You didn't even tell me you two were still married. Do you have any idea how humiliating it was for her to come in and throw that in my face? And there I was, embarrassed, wishing the floor would swallow me up."

"Amanda is no one. Just a conniving bitch trying to break down everyone around her. Don't let her get inside your head."

"She didn't. You did." This time, when I reach for the door handle, he takes my hand and engulfs it in his. A silent reminder that he is much bigger than me and that I don't stand a chance if I try to fight back. "What happened... it reminded me of everything I went through..." I can't even say his name.

"You did nothing wrong. Neither of us did." Callum tries to soothe me, but his words mean shit. If we weren't doing anything wrong, there wouldn't have been a need to hide the fact that he was still married to her. *Would you have crossed that line knowing that, though?* I don't know the answer to that question. I wanted Callum for as long as I could remember except lust grew into something else somewhere along the way.

"Bianca. I'm begging you to understand. The thought of losing you kills me. I can't breathe or think clearly without you. Let's talk this out and work through our problems." His voice is low, almost hypnotic, and already I know he's reaching the deep depths of my soul. My body is awakened by his voice and the nearness of his body. It's pitiful how much I desire him. The crotch of my panties is already soaked, and my core tightens, begging me to give in to him. I want to, badly, but I'm reminded of how heartbroken I am by the heavy thump of my beating heart.

"Who's to say I want to work through anything?"

"Oh, little bird." He leans in, looming over me, one hand on the door, the other on the back of the seat. His arms cage me in. I was already caged. My heart and soul are locked away, and he has the only key.

No matter how much I want to push him away and spit in his face, all I can do is tremble as he lowers his head inch by inch. Moving closer like a cobra readying itself to strike. I watch carefully, ready to push him away or turn my face if he attempts to kiss me, but like always, he surprises me. He swerves at the last second, brushing his lips against my neck instead of my mouth. "It's fine if you want to pretend you don't want me," he whispers, and icy tendrils wrap around my heart. "Pretend all you want. The truth is evident to both of us."

"What truth?" I whisper, closing my eyes, bracing myself like that will do anything to help. I'm already breaking down, melting, all that resolve disappearing in favor of the absolute inferno blazing between my thighs. Thinking with my pussy will only get my heart broken, but Callum has a way of making me forget that as he rearranges my organs.

"Love me or hate me, it doesn't matter. We belong together." He lifts his head enough to look me in the eyes, and I want to give in. God, I need to. I was never going to win, so what's the point in fighting anymore?

"No." My voice is weak, faint, like what's left of my resolve at this point. I have to at least tell myself I tried.

His liquid gaze hardens, going cold all at once. "Maybe I need to remind you of what we have, and the only way I know I can make you feel. I'm not sure what's happened in that head of yours over the last two days, but I already warned you that there was no going back once we crossed that bridge. You're *mine*, and I will do anything I have to do to keep you." His declaration might have been romantic, if it wasn't filled with references that make me appear to be an object rather than a person.

"You don't want a relationship with me." I lean back as far as I can, turning my face away. He doesn't even give me that courtesy as his thick fingers reach out and grasp onto my chin, holding it firmly while forcing me to face him.

"Are you trying to convince me that what we have isn't real or are you trying to convince yourself?" he whispers, his minty breath fanning across my cheek. His dark eyes try to read mine as I put up a solid wall between us. I can't do this with him. "Please tell me you don't think this is a game, little bird?"

"I think it's whatever you want it to be, but that it's not what you assume. You only want to own me, like another business or asset. You don't *actually* want to be with me."

I stiffen at the touch of his free hand against my thigh. *Oh, yes, this is what I need.* This is what I've missed most. His touch—skillful, knowing, like my body was made to bend for him.

"I want all of you," he whispers. "Your pussy. Your mouth. Your mind. Your heart. Every part of you belongs to me. Every inch of your existence is mine."

My hiss of surprise and sudden pleasure fills the car when he caresses the curve of my ass cheek. "Every inch of you," he chuckles before brushing his lips against mine until all I can do is whimper with need. He makes me this way. Helpless. Desperate.

I hate myself for it. I hate him. But more than anything, I hate how right he is.

"The first time I ever touched your pussy, I claimed it as mine." His fingertips dance along the hem of my panties, where they meet the sensitive flesh of my soaked core. My hips jerk on their own, my legs parting as much as the skirt will allow. There's too much clothing in the way. I need it off. I need to let him strip me bare and own me.

No, you need to stop this. But there's no stopping it, no matter how much I want to. This is how it was always going to be. He was always going to hunt me down and claim me again, and I was always going to let him because I am weak when it comes to Callum Torrio.

"Fuck, I knew it." He strokes the crotch of my panties while a

EMPIRE OF LIES

knowing smile spreads across his smug face. "Soaked. Fucking drenched. You only think you know what you want because you're afraid of what it means if you give in. Your pretty pussy knows better. It wants me. It weeps for me, doesn't it?"

I hate him for this, but I swear to god I'll kill him if he stops.

Instead of answering him, I let out a grunt.

"Deny me, Bianca, deny what your heart wants. Fight me if you must, but we both know that nothing else you say matters once I'm deep inside you. You're a whore for my cock and how it makes you feel." He presses down, and stars twinkle behind my eyelids at the sweet, tantalizing pressure.

"You shouldn't," I whisper, even though my heart's racing and my arousal paints the insides of my thighs. It's embarrassing how turned-on by this man I am. "I can't... it's wrong."

"Are you sure you want me to stop?" I hold my breath while he works his fingers under the soaked fabric. His movements don't stop, and I don't know if I could get the words out if I tried. "Scream, my little bird. Somebody in the garage will hear you. Scream, fight, rock the car back and forth." While he speaks, he runs a finger along my seam. "Go ahead. I'm waiting." I gasp when he slips the tip between my folds. His touch is lazy, yet still sends sparks of pleasure down my spine. "If you truly wanted this to end right now, all you'd have to do is scream and prove to me you don't want this."

Bastard. Evil fucking bastard.

Instead of telling him no, and cussing him out, I do the one thing I shouldn't. I crack down the middle and crumble into a million tiny pieces of shame as I tilt my hips and invite him to go deeper.

"Good girl. I didn't think so."

My cheeks burn shamefully even as the heat he's stirring in my core rivals that. That's what I care about most when I hike my skirt up to my waist to spread my legs wider. Being in the back seat is awkward, but I prop a foot on the center console to make room for his broad body, which he settles between my thighs.

"There it is," he mutters an instant before entering me with two thick fingers. "Beautiful. I want to ruin you. Destroy your pretty pussy." I bite my lip to stop myself from moaning. The pleasure ripples through my core, and he scissors his fingers, touching every spot perfectly. "There's what I've been missing. This pussy. My pussy. So tight, and sweet. Fuck I can't tell you how many times I've thought about fucking you in the last forty-eight hours. The thought of never touching you again makes me feral."

I know he doesn't mean it. He's only trying to prove a point. That I'm helpless against him, and I'll let him say and do anything he wants so long as he continues his assault on my body. Fucking me with his fingers, he uses his thumb to roll over my clit. *It's only sex. Nothing more,* I remind myself as he sets my entire body on fire. Flames lick the edges of my skin, promising to turn me to ash.

"Fuck my fingers," he growls against my neck, running his tongue over my throat. His teeth press against my flesh, and he bites against my thundering pulse just as he inserts a third digit. He pounds into me, his knuckles against my tender flesh.

The girth of his fingers stretches me, and while there's a slight bite of pain, it's not enough for me to beg him to stop. The opposite happens. I start to pant. *Harder. Faster.* His thick muscled arm is a blur as he fucks me faster and harder with his fingers. He's preparing me for his massive cock, and I wither against the door, consumed and at his mercy. "Fuck yourself on them. Give your pussy what it wants."

"Oh, fuck..." I can't help it. Not when he talks that way. Not when it feels so good. The car rocks back and forth while I ride his hand, grunting and gasping. Sweat beads against my forehead, and I gasp. My hand wraps around his wrist, my nails sinking deep into his skin. I ride his fingers wishing it was his cock.

I need this. I need to let go of everything I've kept bottled up inside me. The fear and confusion, the distrust and guilt. I put all of it into fucking his fingers the way he orders, because in the end I'm always going to follow his command. I don't have a choice. He owns me.

"Callum!" I shout, and the sound is loud enough to make my ears ring in the tight space. He's punishing me, pumping brutally, his hand slapping against my flesh, but I want it. It's what pushes me to the edge and over, the tension bursting all at once. "Oh.... I'm coming. I'm coming!" I cry, and I'm only vaguely aware that I'm actually crying. The wet tears slide down the apples of my cheeks, leaving me shaking. Pulling his fingers from my clenching center, I watch through half-lidded eyes as he brings them to his lips and licks them clean. His groan of pleasure makes me tremble with fresh desire even though I'm still coming, my insides fluttering with little tremors running through me from head to toe.

When his gaze meets mine, I see something behind his eyes I've never seen before. Hunger, darkness—they're nothing new, but what I see now is almost... eager. Searching. Looking for something I can't put my finger on.

There's no time to put it together before he's on me, tearing open my blouse. I gasp as he buries his face between my breasts, forcing them out of their cups. His animal grunts, combined with his tongue that glides over my hardened nipples, make me writhe and claw at him. I try to peel off his jacket and unbutton his shirt, except he stops me by shoving my hands away. His attention is focused on my body and satisfying himself with me. I try to ignore the way that makes me feel and watch with anticipation as he undoes his pants. The sound of his zipper lowering is almost enough to make me cry again. *Yes, this is what I need.* To be one with him while he's deep inside me, reminding me of the one most important thing: *us.*

Not him, not me, but us together.

I don't know why I ever thought otherwise.

"Mine," he whispers before pulling my thong to the side again. I feel the thick mushroom head of his cock at my entrance. He plunges deep, stretching me the way only he knows. The burn that always accompanies the first thrust slowly melts away, and I arch against him. He wraps an arm around my lower back holding me to him, molding us together.

"I don't know how you could ever deny what we have or share. Not when the evidence is dripping down your thighs, and you're mewling like a cat in heat for me to take you harder."

"Callum!!" I gasp.

The car rocks harder than before, our rhythm quick and rough. The windows fog, but I don't care. All that matters is the tension building in my core. It's deep, throbbing, growing with every unforgiving stroke.

"That's my little bird," he grunts in approval. "My little slut. You're a slut for my cock, aren't you?"

"Y-yes!" I blurt out. I'll say whatever he wants me to, so long as he doesn't stop.

"Only mine. Nobody else's."

"Nobody else's." I'm so close, ready to scream again, clutching him with my arms and legs and inside, where my muscles are starting to clench tighter.

"Because nobody… could fuck you… like this." I shake my head, only because it's true. "Say it."

"Nobody could… fuck me… like this!! Callum, oh, shit!"

"Come for me," he rasps in my ear, grunting. "Give me your orgasm, little bird. Give me what belongs to me."

I do, for there's no way to stop it. The breaking of the unbearable tension and all the sweet, blissful sensations that race through me in the aftermath. I shatter like glass, exploding, my entire body trembling.

"Callum." I moan his name, my nails biting into his flesh while he continues moving inside me.

"That's right." In my daze, I feel his hand taking hold of my throat and turning my face toward his. "Look at me. Look in my eyes." His strokes deepen, and I catch sight of his clenched teeth before meeting his gaze.

"Tell me," he growls through his gritted teeth, breathing hard. "Tell me this isn't real. Tell me what I make you feel isn't real."

The aftershocks of my orgasm are still rippling through me. I know he has to feel every pulse of my muscles as he invades me over and over. I can't lie. This is what he does to me. No matter how I fight, he has a power over my body I can't ignore or pretend doesn't exist.

He smirks when I shake my head. "I know you can't, because you know it's true." His thrusts slam me against the seat and rock the car forcefully, bouncing us up and down. "What we have is special. It's more profound than anything you or I could create on our own. It's us. Together. I will never, ever stop fighting to make you see it and admit it out loud."

I won't. I can't. Even if every crash of our bodies together brings me closer to bliss. Even if I feel more alive when he's inside me than I do at any other time, ever.

"Tell me," he grunts between punishing strokes. "Say it. Say what we both know is true."

I won't. He will not break me.

Even if I want to give in. There's a craving deep in my soul, like a tiny blaze that gets stronger each time he buries himself in me. All I want is to give him all of me. He's who I belong to. Who I belong with.

My nails rake over his shoulders, my legs closing tighter around him, drawing him deeper without consciously meaning to. He's right. My body knows what it needs, and it needs him.

"This tight pussy," he groans, pounding me harder. So hard I whimper–in pain, in pleasure, I'm not sure. Both, maybe, and the pain makes the pleasure even more intense. As if I want him to hurt me. I like it. "I'm going to come. Do you think your pussy deserves my cum?"

"Yes!" I gasp, digging my nails into his ass.

"Prove it. Make me believe you deserve it."

"Please, please!"

"Please... what?" he grits out.

"Please." I lock my legs behind him, holding him in place. "Please, fill me up. Give it to me."

There is no reason for this. It makes no sense. Why do I want this? I only know I do. I do so much. His groaning reaches a feverish pitch, hard and fast like his thrusts, and on the final one he drives deep and stays there. A rush of heat follows his deafening roar, and I have no idea why it feels so satisfying to know he's emptying himself inside me. When he pulls me closer, winding his arms around my back and holding me against his chest—where his heart pounds almost shockingly fast—it feels right. Like I was always meant to be here.

At least until I come back to my senses. The rush of euphoria dies, and I'm left knowing he got to me again. He broke me down against my will. And I loved it.

Disappointment takes root and spreads through me until I can do nothing but push against his chest with both hands. "Let me go," I grunt, pushing again, until finally he loosens his grip. Maybe it's surprise. Maybe he already got what he wants, but either way, he lets go so I can sit up.

"What's wrong now?" he demands in a growl, still hovering possessively over me while I try to pull myself together.

"We shouldn't have done that."

"According to whom?" He runs a hand over my hair, clicking his tongue. "Will you ever stop denying yourself what you want? Who cares what the rest of the world thinks, or if it's right or wrong."

It isn't the rest of the world I care about. It's the fact that I just begged the man who might have killed my mother to come inside me. I don't know who I am anymore. I don't know how to feel.

Stroking my hair, he murmurs, "Don't you know you belong to me? I don't say that lightly. There is no other woman in the world I'd rather be with."

His hand cups the back of my head, his fingers pressing against my scalp as he turns my face toward his. He narrows his eyes, lifting his lip in something close to a snarl. "Much less come inside. I'm not going to waste time fighting the inevitable. I know you belong to me, Bianca. You are mine, and I am all you'll ever need." He trails the fingers of his free hand over my jaw. "When are you going to wake up and realize this, as I'm not going to stop until you do."

The thing is, my traitorous body agrees with him. The slightest touch, and I'm shivering, fighting the urge to melt into his arms. But I can't. I can't betray Mom like that–and until I know the truth, it will always feel like a betrayal.

I manage to turn my face away, shaking off his touch. "No. We're wrong for each other. You're wrong for me. Why don't I get a say in this?"

"Because I know better, and I'm older and wiser."

"You don't, though." I feel him dripping from my pussy as I pull my clothes together, trying to show a little dignity, even though dignified is the last word that comes to mind whenever we're together. "This can't happen again. I don't want it to happen again."

"You know you do."

"Stop telling me what I know!" I snap, and the way he recoils in surprise gives me strength. "I know how I feel, and this makes me feel awful. Rotten and wrong. You can't say you care about me or want me if you don't care that my being with you like this makes me feel terrible about myself. It doesn't work that way."

"Fine, then," he sighs. "Let's talk about it."

"There is nothing to talk about," I insist. "We're nothing. This was only sex and a mistake at that. I'm finished."

On the one hand, it feels good saying what's weighing on my heart. On the other, the hurt touching his eyes and tugging the corners of his mouth downward makes me feel small. I don't want to hurt him, no matter how he's hurt me with his thoughtlessness and possessiveness.

Then, it's like somebody flipped a switch. His face goes smooth, hard. Those dark eyes of his become icy pools of water. "Very well."

Reaching for the door, he flips the lock. "Go…for now. Just

remember, the time will come when you'll have no choice but to face reality. No matter how you think you feel or how determined you are to let the world tell you what you should want, there is one thing that will never happen, and that's me letting you go. I'll spend forever reminding you of how powerless you are against what's between us, until you stop fighting it."

With my fingers around the door handle, I whisper, "Stop trying. You're wasting your time."

The last thing I want is to get out of the car and leave him behind, knowing I've wounded him. My wounds are even deeper, though. Because I can't figure out why resisting him is so impossible. And I can't figure out what kind of person it makes me when I give in again and again.

My head is spinning, and my body trembles from shame and disappointment as I get behind the wheel of my car. He gets out of his car, slips behind the wheel, and pulls out of his space without hesitation.

Leaving me to rest my forehead against the steering wheel and despise myself for making it so easy to break down my defenses.

I can't let that happen again. Not ever, not for any reason.

Because he might know how to work my body into a frenzy, but he also knows how to break my heart with a single glance, and giving Callum any more power over me would be giving him the bullet to kill me.

CALLUM

"Where the fuck is Romero?" I shout down the hall. My voice echoes menacingly, but the pair of guards at the other end only shrug their shoulders uselessly before continuing their sweep of the house. He's disappeared. Everybody has. Leaving without explanation, giving me no chance to stop them before they make their choice to betray me.

I need to stop thinking like this.

This isn't the same as what I'm dealing with when it comes to Bianca. She walked out on me and was callous enough to turn cold when I went out of my way to show her the truth, even if her stubborn little brain wouldn't allow her to accept it. I'm not giving up, no matter what she says. I don't care if she thinks we shouldn't be together. She'll come around to it, and if she doesn't, then I'll make her see it for herself again and again until there is nothing except us in her mind. She's poisoned my mind and has left me questioning everything I was so sure of only months ago.

I no longer know whether I have control over anything or anyone. I have to wonder if it was all an illusion in the first place. Romero never checked in with me today. I went down to his cottage to personally get his ass out of bed, only to find it empty and his car missing. It's unlike him to vanish without giving me a warning or at least a fucking reason. Add to that the fact that he won't answer his phone—it's turned off, straight to voicemail which is very unlike him—and I'm ready to start ripping heads off and shitting down throats.

Doubt lingers at the edge of my mind. He wouldn't defect. He's never been anything but loyal, and I've had no indication otherwise. Outside of his high opinions, he's the same as always.

That leaves one other alternative. I don't want to entertain it, so I won't let my mind wander too far down the path. However, there is the chance of something happening to him. An accident—or not an accident, something deliberate. The idea of making phone calls and checking with our associates slithers its way to the front of my mind. If I did that, I would look like a hopeless asshole with no control over his men. I can't do that, but I won't have a choice if this continues.

I'm sure the shit with Bianca isn't helping things. Questioning myself, looking at everything through new eyes. She's fucking with my head.

For the second time today, I stride down the hall and out through the front door rather than sit and stew at my desk. I catch a couple of my guards avoiding me—they don't want to get caught up in my rage, and it's better for them that they don't. With the mood I'm in, things could get ugly. The one person I consistently rely on, and he has to disappear with no explanation.

This time, the rear bumper of his car is barely visible, jutting out from behind the cottage. I planned to go through his shit and find out what he's hiding, but now I can demand the truth in person. A mix of emotions batters me inside, leaving me bruised and bitter by the time I reach his front door. "You'd better have a damn good explanation," I growl.

Usually, I would give him the time to answer a knock. Today, he's not getting that courtesy. Trying the door handle, I twist it and shove it wide open. At the creaking of the hinges, he bursts from his bedroom, a gun in hand.

He lowers it at the sight of me, leaning against the door jamb, releasing a deep breath. "Since when do you—"

"You have no place to ask me questions. Not when you shut your fucking phone off and disappear the entire day. You're my first in command, and you think you can do whatever the fuck you want without warning me?" I take in the sight of him—the flecks of blood against his starched, white shirt jump out immediately. "I'll give you five seconds to explain yourself."

He sighs again, this time wearily. "Do me a favor."

"Fuck off." I growl, "You're already running on bought time. Give me a reason not to shoot you."

"It's not what you think. Let me take a shower and get changed," he urges, ignoring my threat of death. "I'll be back up to discuss this with you. I'm sorry I forgot to turn my phone back on. I had some business to take care of."

"Your business is my fucking business. Hiding shit from me is useless. I'll find out eventually, and when I do..."

His brow furrows, his eyes darting over my face like he's trying to see whether I'm serious. He should know better by now than to question me. "After everything we've been through? You think I would go behind your back and do something? That I would betray you?"

"You're stalling."

"It had to do with something you handed off to me. I finally got a lead, and after I showered and dressed, I was going to head to your office and tell you about it."

Scanning my memory is no use. I've given him so many tasks that there's no pinpointing which one he could be referring to. "I think I would remember giving you the order to shut your phone off and disappear off the face of the Earth."

"Boss, I didn't do anything you didn't tell me to do. Now, I think that girl is too deep in your head. I hate to see you turn into some paranoid wreck because of her. I made an oath to you, and I haven't gone back on that." he says again when I snarl.

All I can think of is my promise to his dying mother. To protect him and make sure he was safe. He's had more than enough opportunities to betray me. I doubt he will start now. Still, that leaves doubts in my mind. Where the fuck has he been?

"You have ten minutes," I grunt.

But he's right, too. This is paranoia, plain and simple, though I don't know anyone else with more of a reason to be paranoid. Between my vengeful ex and a girl who insists on defying me at every opportunity, I'm starting to unravel at the seams. That's a reality that I can't afford. To crumble would be a weakness, and to show weakness to your enemies is giving them a loaded gun and hoping they don't shoot you. With that in mind, I need to be strong-minded.

I leave, slamming the door behind me, and march back to the house. My vision is red, my heart banging against my ribs, and the keys I'm still holding bite into my palm when I clench my fist around them. He didn't tell me anything about an errand he was running today. Fucking Christ. I'm the boss. *The leader.* The man running the show, and yet I had no idea what he was off doing. I shake my head.

It's time we set a few things straight, such as who calls the shots and who gets paid to follow orders. I've let him get away with too much all because he's efficient, loyal, and trustworthy. I should have nipped this in the bud when he first started offering opinions I never asked for. That's what I get for letting things slide. I know better. You give them an inch, and they take a mile. I need my men to remember who they work for. I need to take back control.

It's all the same, just like how I let it slide when Bianca wanted to spare Lucas' life. Yes, I kept looking for him, but I should have made it my single priority to track his ass down. I should've known there was something else coming up around the bend. I've been around long enough to know the kind of shit an unhinged person is capable of doing, but I did it for her. I told myself it was for the best to make sure she felt like she had a choice in the matter. That's a mistake I won't be making again. Her safety is my biggest priority. Even if I have to do things she won't like or agree with, they'll be done.

At least Romero holds true to his word. His footsteps echo down the hall ten minutes after I've left him alone. He enters my office wearing a t-shirt and gray sweats—also unusual. "We don't have any meetings today," he explains as soon as I raise an eyebrow at his un-business-like appearance. "Plus, I was sort of in a hurry to get here. Someone was threatening to kill me."

I lower myself into my chair and nod toward the pair of chairs across from me. "Talk to me. Make it good, because I'd hate to kill you for something small. You're one of my best men."

He settles in, and now I notice the dark circles under his eyes. It's evident he didn't get much sleep last night. I doubt he went to see a woman. Romero is strict about the woman he sleeps with and never brings anyone back to the cottage. *Ever*. I doubt this has to do with that.

"Like I told you, I got a lead. It came in overnight, and I didn't want to wake you. I thought I'd get everything settled before morning and bring it to you once I had it under control."

So far, believable. "What's it about?"

"I found a certain *friend* of ours. I got a call from a mutual acquaintance telling me he'd be flying in and arriving before dawn." The gleam in his eye tells me how much he looked forward to bringing me the news. "He's currently being watched like a hawk in one of our warehouses down by the river. I went over there to ensure he was as uncomfortable as possible while waiting for you to welcome him back to the states."

My chest tightens with anticipation. "Kristoff."

Romero nods, "The son of a bitch thought he could sneak back into the US unnoticed. He hopped a flight on some asshole's jet."

"How'd you catch wind of it?"

He lifts a shoulder, reminding me how much I don't know and

how fucked I'd be if anything happened to him. "I have my connections, and I made sure to place calls to all the private hangars in the area. He couldn't stay under the radar forever. Eventually, he'd have to come back to get more money from his daddy."

"Let me get this straight." Leaning back in my chair, I study him, and there's no escaping the feeling that I'm looking at him through new eyes. "You went ahead and did this without clearing it with me first? What if I didn't want to take him so soon? What if I had other plans?" I'm goading him, trying to find a reason to be angry when I have none.

"He raped your daughter."

He could have stuck a hot branding iron to my skin, and it would've been less painful than that reminder. "I'm aware of that. But I didn't give you the go-ahead to bring him in."

"I thought when it came to things like this—"

"I do the thinking. Not you. I give the orders, and you follow. You don't come to me after the fact, then announce you essentially kidnapped him." Eyeing him, I add, "Considering the blood on your shirt earlier, I'm guessing he's not in good shape."

Romero hasn't flinched; he's barely blinked. Only his jaw twitch reveals he's fighting against the impulse to argue. "He deserves death, so he should be thanking me that he's still alive. Unfortunately, he needed a little... convincing to behave."

"I should have been the one to do that. It's my right."

"Something tells me you'll have the chance again. He doesn't seem like the kind of guy who learns his lessons the first time." When he reaches up to brush wet hair back from his forehead, I notice his bruised knuckles.

"I can't have you going over my head and making decisions like this. You know I trust you—"

"Trust me? You walked into my home unannounced and accused me of betraying you."

"Says the man who left his fucking phone off all day instead of checking in with me. That's unlike you. What was I supposed to think?"

Color rises in his high cheeks as he leans forward, his lip lifting in a snarl I've seen before—just not while it was directed at me. "You were supposed to think that everything I fucking do is for you and your family and your business."

"You didn't do this for me. You did it for you," I growl.

I saw the look in his eyes when Tatum told us what the piece of shit did to her. It mirrored my own. Romero might seem like a gentleman, but beneath his mask is a bloodthirsty villain waiting to shed his good-guy image. It's how I know he wants revenge for my Tatum, but he can't just make choices that could jeopardize everything I've built.

"Or maybe I did it for her." His eyes widen a fraction before he slams himself back in the chair. He looks downright shocked to admit such a thing. Rather than look at me, he stares out the window while his stubbled jaw tics.

I'm still reeling from that outburst when a soft female voice pipes up. "Did what for who? Who's *her*?"

Tatum enters the room, arms folded, shoulders hunched. I might not recognize her if I knew her any less. Her blonde hair is pulled into a bun on top of her head. Smeared eyeliner is under her eyes. Her oversized tee and black leggings are stained.

Who is this girl?

Her gaze ping-pongs between Romero and me. It seems Romero, like me, has lost his voice. All he does is stare at her, blank-faced. A slab of stone would have a better reaction at this point.

"Tell me," she insists. "What did you do? And be careful how you answer, for I hate to tell you how voices carry around this place. I could hear you all the way down the hall."

Now I know how an explosives expert must feel while handling live ammo. "Sweetheart, why don't you go back to your room? We can talk about this later."

"I'm not a fucking child. If you're talking about me, or anything related to me, I have a right to be present and defend myself." She steps up to the chair Romero sits in, standing over him, daring him to look at her.

He sighs, his eyes narrowing. When it comes to Tatum, there is a weakness that seems to linger in Romero. I can't put my finger on it. "Kristoff flew back into the states overnight. I had your father's men pick him up at the hanger and then gave them the order to hold him so he can be dealt with."

"You what?" She nudges the chair with her knee. Disbelief painting her delicate features. The shock in her voice makes me pause. *What did she think would happen?* That we would let the bastard go? After what he did to her. Not happening. "You did what? I think I'm going to need you to repeat yourself because I can't fucking believe what I just heard!"

"Tatum." I stand, rounding the desk, reaching for her. In true Tatum fashion, she backs away, shaking her head, her eyes feral. Distress ripples off her in waves. I'm tempted to go to her, yet I don't want her to run, regardless of what I said about her going to her room. At this moment, she's fragile and I don't want her to crack more than she already has.

Finally, she reaches the windowsill and has no choice but to come to a stop. She's not at the jumping-out-a-window stage yet. "I don't know why I'm surprised," she mumbles under her breath. "And don't bother lying to me. I know what you're going to do next."

Keep calm. "Sweetie, I just learned about this a few minutes ago. I haven't made any decisions."

"That's bullshit, and we both know it. You decided exactly what you would do the moment you discovered what happened. His days were numbered, then."

I can't stop myself this time and cross the room, coming to a stop in front of her, my arms falling to my sides when it's clear she's not going to let me hold her. "You can't expect me to let this go. I won't apologize for protecting you. You're my daughter, goddammit. I won't let him get away with this, and you shouldn't want him to either."

"It's not your revenge to take. You're not the one he…" She stops in her tracks, her green eyes filling with unshed tears. The image before me makes my heart ache. He did this to her. He took her and made her a shell of the person she used to be; for that, he will wish for death a million times over.

"Listen to me." Out of desperation, I reach for her again, more for myself than for her. My poor girl. I want to take her pain away, her heartache, and the only way to do that is to kill Kristoff.

This time she swings her arms, fighting me off. *My God.* What's happening to her? Finally, I manage to take hold of her arms and pin them to her sides before pulling her in against my chest, using my strength to hold her still, no matter how she fights. "Tatum, sweetie, I want to help you, but you have to let me. I couldn't stop what happened, but I can make him pay for what he's done to you. Let me do this for you."

No matter what she says, he'll pay for what he did to her. I'll lie to her if I have to, but he's not getting away with abusing and raping my daughter.

"This isn't helping!" Her tears soak into my shirt and her body heaves with the force of her emotions. "Don't you understand, Dad? Killing him won't make the nightmares stop. It won't make me forget what he did. Even if I'm not the one to kill him, his blood is still on my hands, and I can't…. I'm not that person. I have enough weight on me. I can't be responsible for someone else's death."

Again, the parallels between her and Bianca jump out at me. That's exactly what she said, that she didn't want to have Lucas' death on her conscience.

"You aren't responsible for anything that happens to that piece of shit. For now, I need you to forget about Kristoff," I add when she starts to argue. "Right now, we need to focus on you. Getting you the help you need. *You* matter more than he ever will."

I close my arms around her, breaking down a little further with every tremble, and choking sob that escapes her. She feels thinner, for fuck's sake. This is not my daughter. This is not who she is. *But it is now.* This is what he did to her; this is what you failed to see. The guilt threatens to choke me.

"I'm going to start calling some doctors—"

"I don't want a doctor!" She shoves away from me with all the strength in her body, enough to break free of my grasp. "There is nothing a doctor can say to me that will make it better. I only want to forget. I can't even sleep to escape the nightmare of my life because his memory haunts me. I close my eyes and he is there, his fingers, his body." The terror in her eyes kills me. "Now I have to worry about this. How am I ever supposed to forget what happened if I know you killed him? If I knew the reason he died was because of me."

"Okay, I hear you." I glance at Romero, though he doesn't notice while staring at her. In all the years I've known him, he's been very in tune with hiding his emotions. Although over the last few weeks, that mask seems to have slipped off. Looking at him now, the rage in his eyes mirrors my own, but beneath that rage is something else, something tender. "I won't kill him. Neither will Romero. I'll let him keep his miserable life. Only you have to do something for me. You have to let me help you get through this. You can't just forget it—or else you would have been able to do so by now. Do you understand what I'm saying?"

Her wild eyes dart back and forth between Romero and me, her head appearing to be on a swivel. "I don't believe either of you. It's just another lie on top of a stack of never-ending lies. If I didn't happen to hear this conversation, then I'd bet he would be dead already."

She's still sharp. Tatum might be broken, but the pieces of her that are still intact are all there. "That's not true."

"Yes, it is. I know you better than that. All you ever do is lie! To me, to Bianca, to everybody you're supposed to care about and want to protect. You lie to protect us. Except you aren't protecting us, you're controlling us. Making choices for us, completely disregarding our feelings. I'm sick of it!" I don't even get the opportunity to speak before she's whirling around, running from the room. Her broken sobs echo down the hall. There's nothing I can do to stop her, but no matter what, I have to find a way to get her through this. I can't lose my daughter. This is merely another reminder of everything slipping through my grasp, and I'm trying to catch them all like grains of sand.

"Please tell me you didn't mean it?" Romero's question is practically a whisper compared to all the screaming I just endured. "Are you really going to let him live?"

Rage simmers in my veins. "As badly as I want him dead, I can't risk hurting Tatum further. This might be the last thing holding her to the ground, and I'll never forgive myself if I was the reason for her complete fracture." I stare out the door into the hall while my temperature rises and my pulse picks up speed. Slowly I turn my head, meeting his concerned gaze. "That doesn't mean we can't draw it out. Just because I won't kill him doesn't mean I won't enjoy every minute of torturing him. By the time I'm finished with him, he'll be begging for death."

"It's what he deserves. I know Tatum doesn't want his blood on her hands, but if we don't end his pathetic life, he could hurt others. I refuse to let that happen."

"Eventually, he'll die, but my primary focus is helping Tatum heal. In the meantime, we make this fucker suffer."

The way Romero's gaze darkens tells me he likes the idea more than ever, but I have to wonder what percentage of what he's saying is true. Sure, he doesn't want Kristoff to do this to someone else, but I fully believe he wants to paint the streets with his blood for a very different reason. Is it possible Romero cares deeper for Tatum than I may have thought? I shake the thought away. No, Romero and Tatum despise each other. This is revenge, plain and simple.

BIANCA

A car door opens and closes outside and my heart lurches. Immediately I fold up the lease agreement I've been studying since I got home, ready to tuck it under the sofa cushion before Dad comes in from dinner with his ex-partner from the police station. He's usually in a good mood after the two of them spend hours swapping old stories, but that doesn't mean he'd be in any mood to know I'm ready to move out again.

I wait, holding my breath. When a minute passes without him opening the door, all I can do is laugh at myself for being so jumpy. I'm an adult, with a job and capable of making my own choices, yet when it comes to my father, it seems I have no choices.

Ever since Tatum was here last week, I haven't been able to stop replaying what she said about me giving up my life. She's absolutely right—it's so easy for me to forget about myself. I can't let my father's problems become my own. He's dead set on hurting himself, drinking too much, and obsessing over making Callum pay for what he may or may not have done. That's up to him. I can't sacrifice everything I want for myself in the meantime.

Guilt clings to my pores at the thought, but I'll have to get over it. I have my own life to live, which means I need to pull up my big girl panties, sign the lease and move out. Of course, I missed out on the perfect place in town, where I was planning on signing before I had second thoughts.

Imagine if I had kept going instead of turning around and crossing the street. How different would everything be right now? Lucas would still be alive. The darkness clinging to me wouldn't feel so suffocating. I guess that's the truth about every choice we make in life. If we had slept in just a few minutes longer or decided to go out for that drink with friends. Every choice gets us to this very defining moment in time, and no matter how much we might want to go back in time and make a different choice, that's not an option. All a person can do is move forward.

I steer my attention back to scanning the contract and wonder if I should get somebody to look at it for me. Just to be certain I'm not being taken advantage of. It's the sort of thing I would ask Dad about, but I'm not ready to share this with him yet. Not until everything's ready to go, and there's nothing he can say or do to stop me.

I hate having to think about him that way, except his already unbearable overprotectiveness is operating in overdrive. Just last night, he told me to call and let him know when I'm on my way home from work. It's as if he wants to make sure I'm not sneaking off somewhere or getting myself into trouble. I might as well be living with Callum all over again.

The simple thought of him makes me ache the way it has the several days since he ambushed me in the parking garage. He hasn't tried to contact me since then, and I should be grateful. This is what I wanted, for him to leave me alone. However, in some ways, it's the last thing I want. His absence makes me crave him more. Callum claims he'll never let me go, that we aren't over, and that he won't stop trying to make me see that we're meant to be. Nevertheless, no matter what happens, I won't be able to forget that he lied to me. Hid from me that he was still married.

If it wasn't a big deal, why hide it?

No, I didn't ask but I shouldn't have to. If he was still married, he should've at least warned me. The more I think about it, the deeper my anger runs. Callum wasn't ever going to tell me, and I need to learn to accept that. I need to make peace with it and move on. It's time for a fresh start.

Does it hurt? Of course. I would rather be with Callum than without him. But not if it means spending the rest of my life in this constant tug of war. Back and forth, never knowing what's going to happen next. It all depends on the mood he's in, and that can change from minute to minute. He's the most unpredictable person I've ever known, and it exhausts me. I deserve better than that. And maybe if I keep repeating that to myself enough times, I'll start to believe it. Time heals all wounds, but a broken heart? That I'm not so sure of. That's not even taking into account the information my father shared with me. If I don't ask Callum about it, I'll never get an answer. Although, the truth terrifies me. *What if he killed my mom?* I don't want to know the answer, but I *need* to know it.

My phone is on the coffee table when Tatum's name flashes across the screen. I haven't spoken to her since that night when she was here, which is unusual for us. We usually talk daily. I hit the green answer key and bring the phone to my ear.

"Hey you. I was worried. I tried to call you like five times, you haven't returned a single call. I figured you wanted space." *No response.* At first, it appears she must have butt-dialed me somehow. All I hear are muffled noises. "Tatum? Are you there?"

"They're going to do it. I know they're going to do it!" Her words slur together, making it hard to decipher what she's saying. I bite my tongue before commenting on her being drunk. My only concern is what she's trying to tell me.

"They're going to do what? What are you talking about?"

"They're gonna kill him, B. They're going to kill him! I'm so sick of the fucking lies! Doesn't he see the impact this could have on me? Doesn't he care that he's hurting me?"

I take a calming breath and push down the anxious feeling starting to form a knot in my stomach. Remain calm, at least for

Tatum. "What are you talking about? Start from the beginning, and take some deep breaths."

"Fuck you!" she seethes.

I can't help but recoil from the bitterness in her tone. "Hey, don't do that. I'm not the enemy here. I just want to help you, and I can't if I don't know what's happening."

"You want to help me? Then maybe convince my lying asshole of a father not to kill Kristoff."

Shit. "Kristoff isn't even stateside, so you have nothing to worry about." Her fear is rational, but she has nothing to worry about with the asshole completely out of reach. *Yet.*

"No, he is. Romero found him. He flew back to the states." A shuffling sound fills the receiver, and then she's speaking again. "That's all he does. Lies. He'll tell me to my face that he won't do it, but then he leaves with Romero, and neither of them would tell me where they are going. I'm not dumb. I'm not a child. I'm tired of being seen as some stupid girl, with a rich father who does bad things!" A bitter laugh escapes her.

She's unhinged, and whatever she drank isn't helping matters. I have to talk her off the edge of the cliff because losing her isn't an option. She's my best friend.

"You said Romero and your father left. Is anyone else home with you?"

"Don't play stupid, Bianca. There's always somebody here, but nobody who actually gives a shit about me. The only reason my father's men care about me is due to him signing their paychecks. Romero, too. He only stays because my father makes him. No one cares about me. Kristoff didn't care either. What's it matter if I live or die?" A sob fills the line.

The sound is soul-crushing, like an animal on the verge of death. I can't leave her like this. She's right. All of Callum's guards might be there, though none of them can help her right now. There's so much going on, but I need to ensure Tatum is okay. The only thing I know for sure is that: Callum isn't there. If I'm careful, I might be able to sneak inside, sober her up, and send her to bed. I'll get an Uber, so I won't have to leave my car where he'll see it. It's a long walk up to the house, however that's nothing compared to being there for my best friend. She needs me, and her father isn't going to stand in the way of me being there for her. As much as I dread going there, I can't abandon her.

"Don't say that. I can't lose you. Just stay where you are. I'll come over, and we can talk through this."

"You... you'll come?" She goes from screaming rage to trembling fragility in the blink of an eye. I'm reminded further of her unstable state. She didn't leave me the night Lucas broke my heart, or the night her father killed him. She's been there to hold me together through all my breakdowns, and I need to do the same for her. Even if it means risking seeing him, I have always loved her way before noticing her father.

"Yes, I'll be there in a little bit. Hold tight." I grab my keys and head out the door, navigating to the app for an Uber along the way. The last thing I want to do is explain to my father what's happening, but I'm a grown-ass woman and my best friend needs me. I'll deal with the fallout later.

* * *

"Do you think they'll do it?" Tatum looks up at me from her bed, finally calm enough for me to tuck her in. I lost track of time, listening to her rant and rave, trying to force water down her throat instead of whiskey. I held her hair back twice so she could throw up, then helped her wash up and change into clean clothes.

She's a mess, and not her usual messy self. This is a new level of breakdown for her. Even at her worst, she's always kept it together, at least on the surface. It's clear she's cracking straight down the middle, and no one seems to notice. It's like she can't be bothered to wash her hair or change her clothes. Even the strongest people have a breaking point, yet that doesn't mean I'm willing to watch her crash and burn.

From the day we met in middle school, she's been the strongest, toughest person I know. Even when I ended up on my ass in a puddle the day I transferred in, with the school's biggest bully standing over me with his fists hanging at his sides. I was scared and confused, especially since Dad made it sound like this new school would be safe, full of rich kids who'd be a good influence. I shudder to think of the overtime he had to work to afford it.

Out of nowhere, a blonde tornado came rushing in, shoving him hard enough from behind that he ended up sprawled on his hands and knees in an even bigger puddle beside me. She held out her hand to help me up, a smile on her face. After that, she took me to the girls' bathroom to clean up, of course not before cursing him out using words I had never heard before.

She was my hero then, and has been every day since. But even heroes need somebody to look after them sometimes. It's easy to forget that.

I brush damp curls away from her forehead and try to smile to reassure her. "If your dad said he'll let him live, that's what he'll do. He doesn't break his promises to you." That's one thing I can honestly say without a twinge of guilt. He never breaks his promises to her. He might be an asshole, a liar, and manipulative as all hell, but he's never not done what he tells Tatum he'll do. One thing about Callum Torrio is absolutely true: he loves his daughter more than anything else in his life.

My attention is brought back to Tatum. Her eyes are puffy and swollen from crying, and a stray tear rolls down her cheek. "I would never forgive myself if he killed him. He doesn't get that. You know he's all fucked up with the way he sees things. It's revenge. He wants to hurt him for hurting me, except he doesn't understand. He doesn't realize I just want to forget him. I can't do that if I'm reminded that I'm the reason he's dead."

Yes, I do know. I know too well. "He'll keep his promise to you."

It's the only thing I can say that wouldn't be a complete lie.

From what I managed to piece together over the past couple of hours, Kristoff landed and Romero grabbed him. I can't pretend to be sorry. The son of a bitch deserves everything he gets. For Tatum's sake, I hide my relief that he's not running around free to ruin somebody else's life. I only wish that didn't make me feel like I'm no better than Callum. I have no right to criticize him if I'm going to be glad he got his hands on Kristoff, no matter what that bastard did. There's the way good people act, and then there's the way Callum acts. Forgetting that would be a grave mistake.

"Shhhh, sleep." I lean down to kiss her forehead. "And don't worry about Kristoff. He'll be fine." That feels like a blatant lie, mainly since it is. Knowing Callum, he'll find some way to keep his promise while doing whatever the hell he wants to do. I saw the murderous rage in his eyes when he looked Romero's way back at the hotel. There was no misinterpretation. As soon as the truth was revealed, Kristoff's days were numbered, and even though it would hurt Tatum, I'd never stop him if I had the chance.

Men like Kristoff don't change. I'd be surprised if he didn't have another girl already, somebody he could use and hurt. It might be wrong to think this way, but Callum would be doing the world a favor by killing him. The justice system won't do anything, even with Callum strong-arming them. Kristoff's parents aren't as wealthy as Callum. But they have money, so they don't care. You can't make someone who thinks they can buy away every problem, see the damage they have done.

I stay lying beside her. I'm unsure how much time passes, but it's not long before she sleeps. Her soft snores fill the room, and I check to ensure she has plenty of water and ibuprofen by the bed before tiptoeing out of the room. I'll wait until I'm at the end of the driveway and maybe even a little further down the road, then I'll request a ride back to the house. I need to get out of here before Callum shows up. I've already remained too long, and every passing minute prompts me that I'm pressing my luck.

None of that really matters, not while knowing how badly Tatum needed me. I wish I could stay and spend the night with her. Only that would also mean explaining to my father where I'll be, and that's another train wreck waiting to happen. I don't need him pulling up in a rage, threatening Callum. Things would be so much worse if he showed up here. The kind of worse you don't come back from.

Yet another thing Callum lied to me about, or at least neglected to mention; there's absolutely no way he didn't realize my father was hunting him like a gazelle. Trying to pin any crime he could on him. He didn't ever bring it up. I mean, on the one hand, I can see why he might want to spare me.

"Hey, Bianca, your father's dead set on putting me behind bars. Let's fuck."

It's not exactly the best use of foreplay. Then again, perhaps I would have thought twice about getting involved with him if I knew exactly why my Father never seemed keen on Callum. It's no secret he walks on the wrong side of the law. Intuition always told me he did sketchy things for a living. The bombshell my dad dropped on me obliterated everything I thought I knew. The fact that my Dad was utterly aware of it and determined to stop him takes things to a whole other level.

My father's obsession with making Callum pay isn't just unhealthy, it's terrifying. If he were to discover I'm here, that would be the ultimate betrayal after the knowledge he shared with me. I won't choose between Callum and my father, especially when there is nothing to choose. Callum and I are nothing, and my father wants revenge for something he has yet to prove Callum did. Trying to wrap my head around it makes my temple throb. To think I was complaining not too long ago about how simple my life was.

Sorry fate, I've changed my mind. Please make things normal again.

My steps are quiet as I slowly descend down the hall. Tatum doesn't have a private entrance, although I can see why her father wouldn't want that either. He needs to at least know when she's coming or going. Control in every aspect is his thing.

The tiny hairs on the back of my neck rise with every step. I'm looking over my shoulder every few strides. I'm not sure why I'm so paranoid. He hasn't been here the entire time, and I have no reason to fear him. He's never hurt me, and he wouldn't, but that's not what this is. The fear I have isn't for him. It comes from falling for him. I'm weak where he is concerned, and if I want to leave with my heart intact, I need to make sure I stay strong and firm, because the second he touches me I'll become putty in his hands.

I need to know all the facts. If he's responsible for my mother's death, or whatever's actually going on with him and Amanda. I can't allow anything to happen. He says she's nothing, but why aren't they divorced yet if that were true? I have to remind myself that we're nothing. That what we've shared never should have happened. Just a few more steps. I turn my attention back toward the door. My shoes slap against the floor, the sound echoing through the house. The door is in sight. I'm seconds away from escaping.

The heavy foyer door opens, and I freeze mid-step. Suddenly I feel like a mouse caught in a trap. Callum steps inside, his features hidden in the dim lighting. I stare at him, drinking in the image of the man in front of me. His high cheekbones, perfectly sculpted chin and nose, with thick lashes that frame his green eyes. My heart hammers in my chest, and I curl my hands into fists to stop myself from reaching for him.

What you shared wasn't real. Think of your mother. Remember, he doesn't want you. He wants to keep you, like a trophy.

No matter what I tell myself, none of the things hit home. The appeal they should have on my conscious thoughts wholly misses the mark. It's hard to remind myself of anything except the way he makes me feel when he's standing before me like a Greek god, ready to head off into battle. He lets out a feral growl as he slams the door closed, his gaze sweeping the room almost as if he can sense me standing there.

Our gazes collide. It's a cosmic affair. I forget how to function, forget that he is the villain in my fairytale. He pauses, his entire body becoming an impassable iceberg. I try to ignore how his eyes drink me in, the way his tongue darts out over his bottom lip.

Be strong. Even as my heart tells me to go to him, my brain screams to me of the pain he's caused me. If I had only been a couple of minutes quicker; another choice I made that led me to this very time. At this moment, staring at the last person I wanted to see and the only person I wanted to see at the same time. They're both him. I can't escape, no matter how I try.

"Bianca." I shiver at the way he says my name. His voice sounds like he swallowed glass chips. It's gruff and thunderous. I hate that I can't get a good read on him. Nobody has the power he has over me. Nobody has ever looked at me the way he does, like he's willing to burn the entire world down to keep me at his side. A man who would kill and destroy anything between him and what he desires, is a very dangerous man indeed.

"I—" Any pitiful explanation I was about to offer gets put on hold when I finally notice the red splotches on his clothes. *Blood.* It's on his shirt and gray slacks and dried on his knuckles. Fear and satisfaction fight for control. All I can do is hope he's dead.

"Did you kill him?" I ask, my voice brave.

"Are you sure you want to know the answer to that question?"

Do I? "Tatum will never forgive you if you lied to her, but then again, if Kristoff valued his life at all he wouldn't have hurt her the way he did."

Callum tilts his head to the side, regarding me, and I can't lie the threatening look he's got going on makes me want to climb him like a tree. The blood on his hands, the feral look in his eyes. The deep tone of his voice. Fuck, I have to stop letting my hormones run the show.

"Why are you here? The last time we talked, you told me to stop trying, to let you go. Now you're in my house. Did you change your mind? Are you finally ready to admit what we have is real?"

Of course, he would go straight to us. The man is insufferable. "I didn't come here to see you. Tatum called me. She was drinking, and I was worried. The last thing she needs in her state is to be alone."

"There are two guards at each entrance and exit. She wasn't alone."

He takes a step towards me, and I take a step back without thinking. If I let him get close to me, then he'll touch me, and if that happens, I'll shatter all over again and forget that he is the enemy in all of this. Even if part of me knows deep down he's not the one that killed my mom. That my father is wrong. I have no proof. It's merely my intuition, and when it comes to him my thoughts are always skewed. Callum makes me question everything I thought I knew.

"Your guards are paid to protect her, yet no one can protect her from herself. Don't leave her alone. I'm worried something will happen, and I can't bear the thought of losing her."

"And you think I can? She's my daughter, Bianca. Everything I do is to protect the people I care about. You included."

"You don't need to protect me. I'm not your problem." I cross my arms over my chest. I need to leave before he traps me with his body and makes me admit truths with his fingers and cock. I can't do this, not until I have more information.

"That's where you're wrong. You're not just my problem. You're the fucking air I breathe, and every day that passes where you aren't by my side is one where we both suffer. Stop this nonsense."

I can feel my resolve breaking, crumbling with every word that passes his lips.

No. I can't do this. I can't let him manipulate me.

"Look, I need to leave. There's nothing for us to talk about. I've said everything I need to say. I've asked you to stop. Please don't make me get the police involved." I'm not sure where the last bit came from. It's not like I'd actually do it, and I doubt it would do anything to stop him. Nonetheless, I need to try and appear serious.

The laugh that fills the air is bitter, unhinged. He crosses the space between us in a second, his hands sink into my hair and he wraps the locks around his fist. My scalp stings, but my traitorous body ignites under his touch. I want him to teach me a lesson. I want him to prove to me he wants me. I want this to be *real*.

Tilting my head back, he stares down at me, his frame pressing against mine. I can feel every delicious inch of him. My scalp throbs, the pricks of pain zipping straight to my core. "Let's get one thing straight, little bird. Nothing will stop me from possessing you. Not your father, not the police, not some fucking piece of paper telling me I can't come near you. I will gladly go to jail if it means I get to touch you, fuck you, kiss you, and claim you. No one can keep you from me, not even yourself. Don't tempt me to prove to you how much you want me. We did that last time, and I'm sure you can remember how that ended." The smirk on his beautifully smug face makes me burn with rage.

"You're absolutely psycho." I try to tug out of his hold, only his grasp on my hair tightens and the pain causes tears to prick at my eyes. "This isn't a game, Callum. Why can't you respect my wishes? I don't want you. I don't want to do this. You lied to me, you hurt me."

With his other hand, he traces my cheek. His touch is a match strike meeting kerosene. "Believe it or not, I wasn't trying to hurt you, little bird. I wasn't lying to you. The only one lying right now is you. I know you think I don't see it, but I can see you're afraid. Of what we are, what all this means."

I grit my teeth because his words are hitting a little closer to home than I'm comfortable with. "I'm not afraid, and I'm not lying. Delusional and crazy is what you are."

He doesn't appear to believe me, not in the slightest, "Delusional and crazy, huh? I guess I must be seeing things then because you're trembling with need even now. Your knees are wobbling, and I bet your pussy is weeping for my cock. You're ready to be fucked, though you aren't ready to face the truth. What a shame."

"Let go of me. I'm done with you and whatever game you're trying to play."

"This isn't a game. However, if it was, it doesn't end until I say it does, little bird."

"You're a despicable man, and you need to let go of me. I have to leave," I hiss through my teeth, trying to ignore the way his touch makes me feel.

"Do you truly want me to let you go?" he whispers, his hot breath against my ear. "Or do you want me to prove to you once again who owns this body? Who makes that pussy quiver? Who's cock belongs to you?" I shiver, my body already betraying me. If he slid a hand into my leggings and pressed against my pussy he'd discover what a traitorous liar I am.

"Let me go." I try to strengthen my voice, even though it's nothing more than a whimper once the words come out. I do my best to remain strong, but then he does exactly what I was thinking. Keeping his grasp on my hair firm, he uses his other hand and slips it into the waistband of my leggings. *Oh god. I'm going to implode.*

His fingers drift lower and lower until he uncovers the proof I've been trying so hard to hide. A grin tugs at his lips, and he traces the seam of my pussy through the thin fabric of my thong. I hate him. I love him. I want to murder him, but I never want him to stop touching me, either. *What is wrong with me, and why can't I escape the hold he has on me?* He's a killer, a manipulator, a very bad man, although none of that seems to matter when he touches me.

"What a beautiful fucking lie." His fingers graze my clit, and I'm so turned-on a cry of pleasure escapes my parted lips. He's right where I need him, just not close enough. Arousal starts to coat my thighs, and my panties are beyond soaked. I'm embarrassed by how turned-on I am, but there is no escaping the truth. I want this man more than dignity, more than anything bad he could ever do to me. "Your panties are soaked. I can feel your arousal on your thighs, and..." His nostrils flare as he breathes deeply while his skilled fingers slip beneath the fabric, grazing my bare pussy. "I can even smell it in the air." His pupils dilate, and my heartbeat picks up speed. "Nonetheless, you lied to me. In fact, you continue to lie, refusing to face the truth. Which makes you a bad girl, and, well, bad girls don't get rewarded, my little bird. They get punished."

I don't know what that means, but I also don't care. I'm too far gone. I can't comprehend what is happening. All I know is I can't let this end yet. With a growl, he releases me. Perhaps it had been his grasp on my hair that caused all the rational thought to leave my brain. For as soon as he stopped touching me, I remembered that I needed to go. It feels like he's giving me a secret option. His eyes watch me like a hawk watching its prey.

"LOSE THE CLOTHES. Take off your leggings and thong. I want your pussy exposed and at my mercy." It's an order, not a request, and I can't deny the way my nipples harden at the gruffness of his voice. Still, I'm frozen in place.

Make a choice. Fuck him or tell him to fuck off.

I already know what I'm going to do, and so does my body. Without thinking, I slip my fingers into the waistband of my leggings. Slowly I peel them down my legs and kick them off at my feet. Callum regards me for one brief moment and then smiles.

"Good girl. Now get on your knees. It's time for your punishment."

Leaving as an option, the hell it still is. The door is right there. I could grab my leggings, put them back on and rush out of the house. I could make the safe choice. The one that doesn't put my heart in the crossfires of heartbreak. I could do a lot of things, but what I actually do is the opposite of everything I'm thinking.

Giving into the lust, the need for Callum's undeniable touch, I do as he asks. The second my knees kiss the cold floor, I stare up at him, loving the approval that reflects in his eyes. Callum is many things; a monster, the devil in reincarnation, but right now, he is *mine.*

CALLUM

I was trying to give her an option without saying it flat-out, and now she's on her knees at my feet like an obedient little girl. I'm not sure I would've let her walk out of here if she had tried; nevertheless, it feels like progress on my part. My cock is hard as concrete, and there's nothing more that I want to do than fuck her right here on the floor, but I have a point to prove.

If I'm to win her back, I'll have to use her one weakness against her. *Her body.* I feel like an asshole for doing it this way. However, she's beyond reason when I'm not touching her, and there's no way I'll ever let her go. Reaching for my belt, I undo it. The sound of the metal clanking makes her pretty blue eyes widen a smidge more. I tug it free and hold it in one hand. She looks at the leather instead of me, and I can already picture her conjuring all kinds of thoughts.

"What are you going to do? Spank me?" Her voice quivers, and I wonder if it's from fear or arousal. Probably the first guessing from the way fear licks the corners of her gaze.

I don't want her to be afraid. I want her to be liquid in my hands. Pinching her chin between my fingers, I force her to look at me. "While spanking you seems very tempting right now, I get the feeling it would be nothing but a mere reward for you. So I have something else planned. Tonight I'm going to show you who owns you." Her delicate throat bobs as she swallows and I release her chin, taking the belt into both hands.

"Put your head down," I order, and she drops her head forward almost instantly. *Fuck.* She's so submissive when she wants to be and stubborn every other time. I bring the belt around her neck and listen as an audible gasp meets my ears. I don't say a word, letting her draw her own conclusions as I fasten it around her neck, ensuring it's snug but not so tight that she can't breathe. The leather presses against her slim throat, and with nothing more than a tug, I'll be in complete control. I pull on it gently as soon as I'm finished, forcing her to look up at me.

Desire shimmers in her blue eyes when they meet mine, and she looks like a damn masterpiece naked from the waist down. Her lips are plump, her pussy exposed, all with my belt around her delicate little neck.

"Let's go," I growl. My own desire for her makes it difficult for me to follow through on what I want to do. She looks exquisite, and I want to thrust my cock deep inside her. She goes to push up off the floor, but I smirk and press a hand to her shoulder. "No, little bird. You'll crawl for me while I hold onto the belt. Then when we reach the bedroom, I'm going to fuck your pussy until you beg me to stop."

"Oh god," she whimpers, still doing as I instruct. I tug on the belt, guiding us down the hall. It takes every ounce of fucking strength inside me not to put an end to this and take her from behind, ending both our misery for release. I grit my teeth and remind myself that the wait will be worth the reward. Tugging the belt harder, I make her move faster. A breathless mewl escapes her and the sound goes straight to my cock.

"Keep up, little bird. You don't want me to fuck you out in this hall. Anyone could come out and find you like this. Do you want that?" It's a lie. I would never let anyone see her like this, much less let them watch me fuck her. I'd cut their eyes out of their skulls before allowing that to happen, except what she doesn't know won't hurt her. Moving faster, her hands slap against the stone floor. I smirk, staring down at her pussy, watching as her arousal coats the inside of her thighs. It's beautiful how her pussy drips for me.

"Would you really let someone see me like this?" she asks, almost breathless.

All I can do is smile, "Of course not, little bird. There are no guards inside the house at night, and if someone did happen to see you in this position they'd never live to tell a soul."

"Good," she whispers in reply and continues to let me guide her to the bedroom. I notice the small trail of liquid that seems to follow her. She's so turned-on she's making a mess of the floor.

"You're making a mess of my floor. Maybe we should turn around and I can have you lick up this mess you're making." She doesn't reply, and I pull on the belt tighter, enjoying the harsh breath she takes.

"Please, Callum, please fuck me. I'm dying." Her begging is adorable, but I'm not ready to give in just yet.

"Keep crawling. Let's go into the bathroom." Of course she follows my demands, her movements quicker now. She's desperate for my cock, and I can't blame her.

By the time we reach the bathroom, I'm close to blowing my load. I'm barely restraining myself. Tugging on the belt, I force her to stand. Her legs are shaky, although she manages when I grip her by the hip to steady her. "Put one leg up here. Spread yourself wide for me. I want to see *my* pussy, and how turned on being my pet makes you."

"Yes, please. God. I swear if you don't fuck me soon."

"Shhh," I growl into her ear and watch as she lifts her leg onto the marble counter, displaying her swollen pussy. She's so turned-on, her clit is engorged. I'm not surprised. I've played back in my mind how easily I made her pussy squirt back at the club.

I tear off my clothes and shove them to the floor, not caring that I've ripped fabric or buttons in the process. Grabbing onto the belt once more, I wrap it around my fist, once, then twice, forcing her back against my front. She's teetering right on the edge of the marble, barely able to stay put.

I meet her gaze in the mirror. "Look at you. Look at what I do to you. Do you see it? Do you see how bad you want this? How bad you want me? Yet, you deny what we share. You deny that I want you and that I want to be with you. Does this look like a man who doesn't want you? Does this look like you don't want me?" Her blue eyes shimmer, and I wonder if she's going to cry. I don't want to break my little bird, but I also need to prove a point. I need to prove that she is mine, and that we're one.

I'm never letting her go, so she needs to accept that fact now.

"Callum, this isn't about us," she groans.

"Oh, but it is, little bird. It's always been about us. We both know what this does to you. How it feels, letting me touch your body." She lets out a strangled moan while the skin of her cheeks and throat start turning a pretty red color as I pull the belt tighter.

"There's nothing more beautiful," I whisper in her ear, peering into her eyes in the mirror, "than watching you melt into pleasure. It's happening right now. Your eyes darken, and your lips part so you can breathe."

"I need more than this," she whispers, closing her eyes, softening against my chest.

"More?" I know what she means, but rather than giving her what she wants, I let my fingers slide through her slick heat to circle her puckered asshole.

Her body goes stiff as I pepper kisses along her throat until she loosens up. "Tell me you want me to take your ass." Now that she's good and slick, I begin to probe deeper, toying with her. Seeing how far she'll let me go. When she whimpers, I sink in up to my first knuckle. *So tight.* "Tell me. Say... Callum, I want you to fuck my ass."

"No," she whispers, shaking her head. "It would hurt too much. I don't want that."

Still stubborn.

"But what's pain without a little pleasure?" I whisper, nipping at her ear. "It's okay, little bird. I don't have to take your ass tonight. There is always tomorrow, or months from now. Soon enough though, I'll take your ass, Bianca. And when I do, you'll be begging me to do it."

She lets out a guttural moan as I tease her ass, and I wonder how much of it is anticipation running underneath her fear. I'm vividly reminded of how difficult that first thrust inside her pussy is, and the thought of her tight ass struggling to take my cock as well excites me. So tiny and fragile. The fact that I could so easily break her, but I choose not to.

"You've been bad, which means you must be punished," I tell her. "Unfortunately, none of my methods have worked so far, so instead of denying you what you want, your punishment should be making you see how easily your body betrays you. It knows how bad you want and need me, yet somehow you deny yourself that."

My cock is hard as steel, dripping with excitement against her ass. Soon, so very soon. First, I'm going to make her beg for it.

"I'll show you again and again," I promise. "Even if I have to fuck you every single day, every hour of the day, during my meetings, bouncing you on my cock while I'm on business calls. I'll do it. Nothing will thrill me more than filling you with my cum, and watching it drip down your legs. Even if I have to tie you to my bed, feed you, and bathe you, I will make you see that we are real and that you are mine."

"Please!" she gasps. "Fuck me, please! I'm dying!" Her juices coat my knuckles, and I fuck her ass faster, the single digit pumping inside her.

"Beg for it. Beg me to fuck you, and maybe I'll give us both the relief we want."

"Oh, god. Callum. Please fuck me. Please."

I look down to where my finger disappears inside her ass. I can't wait to see my cock there. "Shit, the way your ass takes my finger, squeezing it so tightly, your slick pussy gushes over my palm. You're such a good girl, Bianca. I can't wait to replace my fingers with my cock."

"Callum!!!" she cries, and her nails dig into the counter. Every muscle in her body tightens like a bowstring that's ready to send an arrow sailing right into my heart.

"You want my cock, baby?"

"Yes, give it to me. Fuck me. I want your big fat cock inside me. Please," she begs so prettily. I can't wait any longer, not with her writhing against me. I pull my finger from her tight ass. The scent of her musky arousal fills my nostrils as I take my leaking cock into my hand. I stroke it, using the pre-cum as a lubricant, before I bring it to her entrance. With one deep stroke, I'm inside her.

"Ohhhh." There's nothing like that first stroke with her, where she struggles to take my entire length. I love knowing that she's never been with a man as big as me. She pushes up onto her tiptoes before settling back down again. Her legs tremble, a low moan releasing from between her parted lips that rises in pitch each time I slam against her.

I punish her with my cock, taking her hard and fast. "Look at me," I pant, tightening the belt until she does as I say. "Mine. You're mine. Don't you dare look away, or I'll stop fucking you." With every stroke, I break her down further, leaving her helpless.

When I bend her forward to give myself room to play with her ass again, she almost howls, jerking her hips, meeting me thrust for thrust.

"You think this is good?" I demand, pumping my finger into her ass in tandem with my cock. "Soon, I'm going to use a plug on you. I'll get this tight hole ready for my cock by stretching it out."

She whimpers—then, all at once, the fluttering of her muscles turns into tightening, clenching, as it massages my shaft. Her greedy pussy wants to milk me, but I hold back, pushing through the impulse to let go. Fucking her through all of it while she moans helplessly, the orgasm stretching on and on until she loses her breath.

"My beautiful little bird." I pull her back again, holding her close, and watch as tears slip down her cheeks. My beautiful, fragile little bird is so easily broken, and so entirely mine. Her eyes bulge wider the tighter I cinch the belt until her skin goes from red to purple, and a rattling noise stirs in her throat.

All at once, I let go of the belt and she sucks in a ragged breath while I pull my cock that's dripping with nectar from pussy. "On your knees," I order. She's still gasping and shaking but offers zero resistance as I push her to her knees in front of me. "Open that pretty mouth. Nice and wide for me."

She gags at first when I plunge in all at once, hitting the back of her throat. Her tears wet my hands as I take her face between them and fuck her throat until her weak gagging and the slapping of my wet balls against her chin fill the room. "Do you want me to paint your face with my cum?" I ask.

The way she moans in response leaves me panting. *Made for me. She is made for me.*

"So close... So close, Bianca..." She holds on to my thighs with both hands, saliva dripping down her chin, coating my sack. Doing her best, she works her tongue on the underside of my cock until the weight in my balls can't be ignored any longer.

The tingling at the base of my spine explodes into sheer bliss as I pull out and take aim. "Get ready." I only have time to grunt before splashing her tongue and swollen lips with the first sticky ropes of cum. My ears ring, my chest rising and falling so rapidly I swear it's about to explode. If it does, at least the last sight I'll enjoy will be that of my cum painting her beautiful face. By the time I finish, she's dripping with it, and there's never been a more beautiful sight in my entire life.

She's still on her knees when I remove the belt. Then I wet a hand towel at the sink. She doesn't say a word as I help her to her feet, steadying her when she sways slightly. My touch is gentle now, careful as I clean her. Our eyes meet, and she immediately turns away, touching something deep inside me. *Did I hurt her?* Had I been too rough? I was sure to take care of her, ensuring she enjoyed everything. I might have been a little delirious, but I would've known if she wasn't into it, right?

After pulling on shorts, I walk back out into the hall to grab her leggings. She still won't look at me, even as I help her step into them.

"Won't you at least say something?" I finally ask. It's apparent that something is weighing on her now that everything's over. She's thinking clearly again.

"I don't know what to say," she whispers. Her voice is hoarse, husky, and I wish she would say more. The sound only reminds me of how wholly I controlled her. I have to keep her here tonight. I need to talk to her; I need to hear her raspy voice in the dark. I can't let her go now.

I'm about to open my mouth to ask her to stay, when she says, "I'd better go."

That's it. No explanation, no apologies.

All I can do is fight my natural instinct that tells me to order her to stay, no matter how much I need her. What I truly need more is for her to want to be here. "I see," I sigh heavily. "Don't let me keep you."

Her brows draw together for a split second—like she can't believe I would let her go without a fight. When I offer nothing else of a response, she backs out of the bathroom, still watching me like she's expecting a sudden change of heart.

Remember, you are trying to do this the right way.

Yes, and that's the only thing keeping me from demanding she gets in my bed and stays there. I force myself to remain in place while her soft, rapid footsteps fade to silence. I hate this. Hate letting her go and watching her leave, however it's a necessary evil. I can't have her if she doesn't want me, even if keeping her is the only way I can continue to breathe. If my little bird refuses to be mine, I guess I'll have to get used to death.

Because without her, death appears to be the only option.

BIANCA

"You know, we haven't been out for another happy hour since that first one, where you bailed on us."

It isn't until I realize everybody's staring at me that I tune back into the conversation in the break room. It seems I've developed a bad habit of tuning out things that bore me, and nothing bores me more than small talk being exchanged around the coffeemaker. It's either grin and bear it or not get a refill of coffee, and I *need* all the caffeine I can get my hands on today.

"Are you talking to me?" I ask on a nervous laugh.

Todd rolls his eyes. "No, I'm talking to the other coworker who bailed in the middle of a happy hour the first time she ever came out with us."

"You honestly need to let this go," Stephanie sighs while I sputter in confusion. "I swear, you are worse than a dog with a bone when you make up your mind to be pissed off about something."

Todd snorts. "I'm not pissed. I'm just saying we were all worried."

You didn't come off so worried about me.

Sometimes I wish I had the nerve to say the things that pop up into my head. If I remember correctly, he and everybody else were busy having a good time, slamming back drinks and dancing, while I was upstairs with Callum, watching from the one-way glass in his office as we were… the muscles in my stomach tighten. This is not the best place to think about that. It's bad enough that I've been fighting memories of last night all day long.

"I'm still here, alive and well. I'm sorry things went as they did." I make a big deal of checking the time on the microwave before anybody starts demanding specifics on what happened that night. It's been weeks, for God's sake, only Todd can't seem to let it go. "I need to get back to my desk."

I'm starting to think Todd might have a tiny crush on me, which is a shame. Maybe if I didn't know Callum existed, things would be different. That's a little difficult, since he does exist, and therefore no other man will ever measure up.

It's like living a double life sometimes. Going through my days as an average twenty-two-year-old working her first real, grown-up job while spending her nights as Callum Torrio's slut. It's precisely how I feel today. I'm more than a little ashamed of how easy it was for him to twist things around until he had the upper hand, bending me to his will.

Out of all the places I feel like being today, seated at my desk with an inbox full of spreadsheets to review has to be at the bottom. I might be here physically, but mentally I'm on another planet. Nothing could matter less than whether somebody put a decimal point in the wrong place or didn't use the correct formula to calculate interest.

In my head, I'm in Callum's house. Crawling on my hands and knees. Watching in the bathroom mirror while he fucks me hard enough to hurt me, maybe not physically but emotionally. Inside, in my chest where my heart is, he has peeled back the layers, refusing to let me see anything except him and me. It's amazing I can still walk after what he did to me last night.

My cheeks flush every time I think about it, meaning I've sat here all day looking like I have a sunburn. I can't get him out of my head, but since when is that anything new? It's times like this I wish I knew the magic spell that would break me free of his grasp.

At the same time, to be free of him would destroy me.

I would have a challenging enough time staying awake and alert if I wasn't already fighting for my life after a night spent tossing and turning. I worried Dad would be waiting for me when I got home. Thankfully, however, he was already in bed.

At least his bedroom door was closed, though a light shone from underneath telling me he was inside. I figured it was better to stay quiet and tiptoe through getting dressed for bed rather than disturb him. His night with Ken must have been an absolute rager if he didn't have it in him to fling the door open and demand a full play-by-play of the evening.

Instead of being tortured by his questions, I tortured myself for hours, wrestling with a sense of betrayal. What would Mom think if she knew I just got home from fucking a man not only old enough to be my father but also the man Dad blames for her death? What kind of person does it make me that I'm willing to have sex with the man, knowing how much Dad hates him?

I can't spend the rest of my life living like this. Forever torn between wanting Callum and feeling like I'm being disloyal to my parents. It's not that I don't believe Dad's theory about how Mom died—I'm willing to consider a lot of things, but seeing how far off the rails he seems to have gone, I can't help wondering how much of it is in his head.

No matter what, he believes it, and that's bad enough. It involves everything he does now, along with the certainty of Callum's guilt. Until I find a way to prove he's wrong, he will never accept the two of us together. How am I supposed to be happy if it means cutting him out of my life, which I would probably have to do? How am I supposed to choose between the man I love and my father?

By the time I fell asleep, one thing was clear: I had to prove he was wrong, which meant figuring out how much of what he was saying was true and how much was what he wanted to believe.

Now that I'm here, all I can do is stare blankly and wonder where the hell I should start.

"Are you okay?"

My head snaps up at the sound of Stephanie's voice. She's standing at the entry to my cubicle, leaning against the wall with her arms folded. I can't tell if she's concerned or judging me. "Yeah, why?"

"For one thing, I've been standing here for a solid minute, and all you did was stare at your screen without moving. Second, you seem spacey."

"Oh. Yeah, it's been a long... summer," I finally conclude with a shrug.

Then I wince, dropping my voice to a whisper. "Is it obvious? That I'm spacing out?"

"No, I'm not trying to freak you out. It's the kind of thing the person who sits in the next cubicle notices." She sets her coffee down on my desk before perching on the corner, like I invited her to or something. "What's up? Is everything okay?"

A lie is practically tumbling out of my mouth before I stop myself. Lies have become so much a part of my life recently I hardly have to think about them anymore. I don't want to be a habitual liar. That's not me. It also doesn't mean I have to tell the whole truth, either. There's an entire range of possibilities in between.

"My dad's been upset lately," I mutter softly enough that she has to lean in closer. It's bad enough I'm about to do this without letting other people overhear. "The anniversary of my mom's passing set him off, and I got to thinking just how little I truly know about her accident."

"Oh, sweetie. I'm sorry." She pats my shoulder a little awkwardly. I can't blame her. I just dropped something heavier than the usual office gossip on her.

"When you walked over here, I was reflecting on that. On how I don't know anything about how she died. I was eight, so it's not like I was too little to understand what death meant. He must have deliberately kept things away from me, which has only made me more curious." Biting my lip, I ask, "Is that morbid?"

"Hell, no!" she whispers back. "It's natural. Normal. Your mom died, and you don't know anything about it. That would drive me crazy."

"I was wondering how to find out more information, although I seem to be drawing a blank."

"Have you looked up her obituary? What about reports on the accident?" Her forehead creases. "Sorry. I probably should've asked what kind of accident it was?"

"Car."

"They might have written about it in the paper—especially since your dad is a cop. Isn't that what you told me before?"

"Yeah, that's a good point."

"Was it when there would've been articles published online? Like, not so long ago that there wouldn't be websites?"

I snort, "How old do you think I am?"

She shakes her head, grinning, "Okay, right. Have you ever thought of Googling her name?"

Well, since she put it that way, I feel kinda dumb. "No, I haven't. I'll start there."

"I'll leave you to it—and, uh, pretend you aren't doing this on company time." The big wink that follows makes me laugh since she's the queen of shoe shopping on her laptop when she should be working.

Once I'm alone again, I enter *Jessica Cole* into the search engine. Turns out there are lots of women with that name. After scrolling through the first results page, I add *car accident* into the search bar.

I definitely wasn't prepared for this.

The first result comes with an image attached—a big, vibrant, full-color image of a mangled car. I let my eyes fall closed. I don't want to look. *I can't look.* Instantly I remember why I never Googled her name, even when the idea occurred. She was dead, and nothing would change that, so why would I force myself to look at something so awful? It was hard enough being without her. I didn't need another reminder of her not being here.

Now, I'll never forget the sight of the car with its tail end sticking out from where she ended up in the woods. I've imagined it so many times, yet nothing could have prepared me for the sight.

Slowly, I open my eyes again. It was raining that day, and the cops clustered near the car wore ponchos over their uniforms. From the angle the photo was taken, I can see the deployed airbag. The car door is wide open, so I imagine her body was already removed when she was shot.

There's nothing left to do except click the link to the article from which the photo originated. It's from the local paper published a day after the crash and doesn't tell me anything I didn't already know. Mom was thirty when she died—the mother of a young girl and the wife of a detective. As I read on, I find out that they blamed the crash on the weather. *It was raining.*

The road could have been slippery, and I highly doubt people only just started driving like assholes the second a drop of precipitation fell from the sky. It's possible somebody swerved, or she might have even swerved to avoid someone or an animal. Things like that occur all the time. I shudder to think of how often they do.

The front of the car was folded like an accordion when it hit that tree. I wonder how fast a person has to be going to crunch the front of a car that way.

"I swear, you drive like a grandmother."

I can hear the way Dad used to tease her whenever she was behind the wheel. He hated riding as a passenger when she drove since she drove so much slower than he did. *"I have precious cargo onboard."* She'd wink at me in the mirror as she'd say it.

Mom would've been driving slower, especially if it was raining hard, though somehow she was moving fast enough to crush the front of the car on impact.

My hands start to tremble, and I can barely minimize my browser window. I can't have it sitting right out in the open in case somebody walks past—even more I can't sit and stare at the car any longer. It makes my head spin and my heart race as a cold sweat clings to the back of my neck.

Why would she be driving that fast in the rain? Cars used to fly past her on the highway—I recall hearing horns blaring so many times, where every so often, somebody would flip her the bird as they passed by. I learned a few filthy words during those car rides, mainly from the frustrated drivers as they passed. It was never enough to make her speed up.

Granted, I wasn't in the car with her that day. She might have had less of a reason to creep down the road. Being cautious was her thing. Constantly double-checking the locks on the doors and windows before going to bed. Asking if we made sure everything was turned off before leaving the house. I asked Dad about it once, and he shrugged it off. Some people are extremely careful because they know how thoughtless others can be.

Once she was gone, he became the cautious one. Actually, he became downright paranoid. I'm starting to understand why. All it took was a few minutes of internet sleuthing, and I was concocting all kinds of stories. How maybe she had to speed up to outrun somebody. Or perhaps another car forced her off the road.

My imagination is running away from me. Drawing these conclusions will not get me answers, although there's no denying how much more interested I am in Dad's theories than I was before. Still, even though I can imagine the car being run off the road and Mom's terror when it was happening, there is something I'm having a difficult time visualizing.

Callum, sitting behind the wheel of the other car. Him stepping out of the car and walking over to my more than likely crying mother, standing beside the car and firing a bullet into her head.

He's many things to a lot of people, but he is not the man who terrorizes and murders an innocent woman. I refuse to believe that, I can't. No matter what my feelings are towards him, and no matter what my father thinks it's not an option, because that would mean I've been sleeping with my mother's murderer and I don't know if I could survive that truth.

CALLUM

"Don't forget, you have a meeting with Sebastian Costello later today," Romero tells me as he glances up from his tablet. "He told me he has some news about the missing shipment."

The shipment. Those fuckers. "Tell me he knows where the fuck it went?" I grunt, grinding my teeth at the reminder of the loss. A shipment of that size doesn't just disappear.

This is a nice distraction from where my thoughts currently were, being held captive by a brown-haired, blue-eyed woman. Like always, thoughts of her are there, constantly lurking in the shadows. She's a poison without a cure, and I'm addicted to every hit I get from her. Everything has been fucked since I received word that one of our cargoes was being overtaken and armed men were removing the shipments.

"He hinted at having a possible lead," Romero replies, nostrils flaring. "I don't know if that's a good or bad thing. It could mean he's the one responsible, and he's just fucking with us."

"Or it could mean he knows something we don't. First things first, I want to meet the kid. Get a feel for who he is." From everything I've heard, Sebastian Costello is a natural up-and-comer in our world. Have always respected his father, Salvatore, although I found him to be a bit soft.

He was tough but always preferred to settle disputes with as little violence as possible. I never had the chance to meet his son. I knew he would eventually pass on the reins, but when he got sick, business between us stopped.

If the rumors are true, Sebastian is nothing like his father. Violence is merely another way for him to get what he wants.

Romero slides a file my way, and I open it immediately, my eyes drinking in the information. The contents are as I confirmed. "He's suspected in at least half a dozen hits and has continuously managed to beat the rap. He's the oldest of three siblings, and his brother is just as unhinged as him. He's got a temper and is very ambitious. Prior to the old man's passing, he convinced him to renegotiate a bunch of deals that were made years ago–in his family's favor. From the looks of it, he's grown tired of leaving money on the table."

There's a photo of him paperclipped to the inside of the folder. I've known a lot of kids like him; lean, chiseled face and dark eyes that emanate hunger. Wrath. Ambition. "And he's being open about all this? No secrecy?"

"Nope. He wants the word to spread so people know he's not fucking around. At least in the underground operations."

I nod, already liking him. Straightforward. Honest. He's not afraid to show people what happens if they cross him.

Romero sneers, "In other words, he's coming here today pretending he wants to help, only essentially he wants to renegotiate."

"Maybe. But if he can help put a stop to this bullshit, I might consider it. The percentage loss would be worth it, being that we're bleeding out money every day that the shipment is not found." We exchange glances. "However, that's only if it works in our favor."

My phone rings, and my heart clenches in my chest. *It won't be her, it never is, but I always remain hopeful.* Bianca's reintroduced me to the concept of hope. I wish I could tell her, but I can never find the words I want to say when she's actually in front of me. Forever, that more profound, darker desire wins out. Then I make mistakes. Where she's concerned, I'm a raging lunatic. Obsessed and unhinged.

Speaking of mistakes... "This is the fourth or fifth time I've noticed her calling," Romero observes when he sees Amanda's name flash across the screen.

"Typical. The less attention I give her, the more she wants."

"You never know." He stands, shaking invisible wrinkles from his slacks before crossing the room. "She could be calling to tell you she signed the papers." The way he chuckles as he enters his office tells me he knows how unlikely that is.

No way in hell did she waste this much time only to turn around and sign the papers. Whatever game she's playing is long, and it doesn't end with her signing a damn thing. She would rather continue dangling this over my head, fucking with my life.

"Did you sign the papers?" I demand upon answering.

"Wow, hello to you, too." She has the nerve to sound wounded after all she's done.

"Can we skip the pleasantries? I think we're past that bullshit now, wouldn't you say?"

"Oh, forgive me. Sometimes I forget how busy and important you are."

"Don't act like you care if I'm busy or not. You've called me more in the last couple of days than in the last two years. What do you want?"

"Maybe I wanted to accept accountability in the way things unraveled the last time we met at Bob's office," she murmurs. "I let my feelings get the best of me, and that was wrong." I roll my eyes. Somebody on her team must've told her how stupid she made herself look. Told her that she had taken things too far and that she was not doing herself any favors by behaving as she did. Now, I get the apologetic act she's putting on.

"I'm not the one you owe an apology to." My short nails dig into my palm when I recall how she talked about Bianca. A woman so far above her in so many ways, I don't have time to get into it.

"Yes, well..." She laughs softly. "I hope you don't expect me to feel warm and generous toward the child who is fucking my husband. I don't care whether or not she knew about the status of our divorce. I think it's a good thing she ran off. She should really try to find a boy a little closer to her own age."

Calm. Restraint. I have to be smarter than I was at the lawyer's office. For all I know, she could be recording our conversation. I wouldn't put it past her, honestly. "That's no longer any of your business, Amanda. My relationships, who I fuck or don't fuck, are none of your business. Now, if you'll excuse me, I have more important things to do than—"

"I'm sure you've heard the old saying you'll attract more bees with honey than with vinegar."

I swear to God, the way this woman thinks... I could get a migraine trying to decipher her word games.

"Why do I want to attract bees?"

"You know what I'm saying," she huffs, "I want to be friends."

This duplicitous, stalling bitch. It's enough to make me bark out in laughter. "So that's your newest tactic? You want us to be friends. Let me guess, you think if we are friends, I'll be more likely to give you everything you think you deserve. Is that it?"

"Of course, you would say something like that. Always looking further than necessary into things. To you, everything is about keeping what you think you deserve."

Think I deserve? The audacity.

"It is what I deserve, being that I worked for it."

"Oh, really? You worked for it?" Venom drips from her laughter. "Tell me, Callum, does your little whore work for all the dollars I'm sure you pay her?"

My jaw clenches so hard I swear I can feel my teeth cracking. I refuse to play into her hand. I cannot give her what she wants. All this push and pull, God damn it, she makes it impossible. Since the very beginning, she's known precisely which buttons of mine to push.

"Tell me something. In your life, what have you ever worked for? You couldn't even be bothered to be a mother to the daughter you wanted so badly, much less a decent, faithful wife. All you've ever known is how to use people in order to get where you want to be. So spare me your sanctimonious bullshit."

"I'm just saying. Maybe I'm not the only sanctimonious one."

"Then why would you want a cent from me, considering your feelings about how the money came to be?"

She sputters, and I can practically see how red her face must be by now. She never wastes time stepping into a trap she set herself.

"You've taken up enough of my time. From now on, unless it has something to do with our daughter, I would appreciate you communicating through our lawyers. I have nothing to say or share with you." Before she has the chance to continue talking, I end the call and toss the phone onto my desk.

Once again, she leaves me wondering what the hell I ever saw in her. I'm starting to think there won't ever be any hope of getting rid of her, but I have to try. Particularly if I ever want to have anything meaningful with Bianca.

* * *

SEBASTIAN COSTELLO IS YOUNG—HE turned twenty-five a month ago. He comes off as cocky, but I see it as more of a front. A way for him to convince you he knows what the hell he's doing before trapping you. His usual expression would appear to be a smirk since that's most of what I've seen from him since he entered my office, taking the leather chair across from me. Romero, as always, lingers near the window. Holding his tongue as expected, all the while watching closely with his keen, experienced eyes.

Sebastian shakes his head when offered a drink. "I prefer a clear head when discussing business." This little shit, posturing in front of his elders. I wasn't much better at his age. In comparison, he's got an advantage over me; he was raised in this dark world while I came into it in my late teens. I have no doubt his father groomed him for leadership from the day he was born. It's what happens in crime families. The men are set up from birth to take over the family business and the women are merely pawns, set up in arranged marriages and used as bargaining chips.

However, Sebastian is not the only one with experience. Unlike him, I have actual, real-world knowledge, not the sort of experience that's attained while sitting on daddy's knee or playing in his office while the grown-ups talk.

"I understand you've come with some information you think would benefit my business," I ask gruffly as a lead-in. It's a breadcrumb. I won't take it any further. I want to see how he handles this without any help from me.

He nods, looking at a carefully blank-faced Romero before swinging his gaze back to me. "There's been much talk in certain circles about the hijacking of your shipment." He smooths down the front of his silk tie, obviously wanting to up the tension by pausing.

"Okay? Who's responsible?"

"Let me ask you something." Sebastian tilts his head to the side, studying me. "Who would benefit from stealing that shipment of weapons?"

"Who wouldn't?" Romero counters.

"Not financially," he replies with a wave of his hand. "We're not talking about the business side alone."

"Jack Moroni," I growl. Unsurprisingly, it is the first name to pop into my head.

The corners of his mouth twitch. "Word travels fast in the

underbelly of the city, and everyone heard about your unfortunate dinner from a few weeks ago."

Instantly my heart begins to race while my chest tightens. My lungs can't seem to get enough air into them. That night took a grisly turn shortly after Bianca lodged a fork in Dominic Moroni's hand.

Now is not the time to get distracted.

Shaking it off, I ask, "Well, what was said?"

Now he wears a full-blown smile—it reminds me of a shark, if anything. Sharp, white teeth merely waiting to pierce into my skin. Eyes nearly as black as the gleam of his hair. "There's plenty of people who would like to meet the girl who had the balls to stab that stupid son of a bitch in the hand. But that's just it. Word has spread, and nothing bad has come of it. Almost everyone who's heard the story finds it hilarious. A case of someone getting what they deserve. So for Jack, it's become personal. He wants to hurt you. You've embarrassed him. His family. His name's sake. It's all anyone is talking about."

"Ahhh." Everything he's saying makes sense. I have no reason to believe this kid would lead me astray—and it isn't like I couldn't get confirmation of his story. "Are you assuming that means Moroni would be stupid enough to hijack my weapons?"

"It's not an assumption. His son told one of my men. He thinks he's smooth," he continues, scoffing. "He's so sure his daddy won't let anybody make a fool out of him. That sort of stupid, childish bullshit."

Eyeing him, I speak with care and purpose. "It was my understanding that your family always worked closely with Moroni and his crew. Has that changed?"

Rather than waiting for me to lead him in the direction my thoughts are going, he picks up the hint. "My father did. He didn't like Moroni or respect him, but felt it was more wise to be a friend rather than foe. Violence was never his thing." The glimpse of what I catch in his eyes reminds me of a psychopath barely holding onto themselves. There's the real Sebastian.

"And under your leadership, things are going in a different direction?"

"I can't stand the son of a bitch," he shrugs, "I never could. Plus I am not, how do I say it, the diplomat my old man was. With all due respect to his memory, I miss him like crazy, but he ran things very differently than I do."

"Of course." I appreciate his candor, even if the disapproval on Romero's face says otherwise from his perspective. Probably because I try to fall on the side of the diplomat since there is no point in letting a slip of the tongue earn me an enemy.

"I guess that brings us to the bigger question." I make it a point to grin as I look him up and down. "Why are you here? I understand hating Moroni is a common factor, yet is that all there is? Are you trying to honor an old relationship or are you looking to get something else out of it?" I feel the need to be open and honest with him.

"Bottom line, I have a cache of weapons and the means to keep them coming. You have the means of transporting them. I think we could arrange a deal that would benefit both of us. It would mean your buyers are getting what they want. At the same time, it'll increase your cash flow while I expand our operation. My father was never interested much in this portion of the business, although he was old school. He was very intelligent and a respectable leader, but he didn't have the vision it takes nowadays to keep up with changing times. I'm not leaving money on the table anymore. I hope I can count on you to partner with me."

I appreciate his honesty, and I'm never one to overlook the opportunity for a profitable deal. Still, I withhold judgment, mulling it over silently while Romero waits for my answer. I don't think he trusts this kid, and I can understand why, but again, Romero isn't in charge.

Yes, Sebastian is young, but he's hungry. He wants to succeed, and it's undoubtedly noticeable. I can't possibly pass up the opportunity to work with him.

"Send me the specifics, and I'll look it over," I vow, standing and extending a hand. "And as a gesture of good faith, when I recover my missing shipment, I'll be happy to offer a percentage to you in thanks."

"I appreciate the gesture. Please let me know if there's anything I can do to help in the recovery efforts." He shakes my hand, his grip firm, before turning to Romero and offering him a shake as well. The momentary pause as Romero sizes him up isn't lost on me. "I have men that aren't afraid to get their hands dirty if you need the assistance. I simply want to help."

I nod, and Romero shows him to the door. As soon as he's gone, I pour myself a generous amount of scotch. Tough kid, rough around the edges even with all his posturing in that suit and expensive haircut. Certainly somebody I'd prefer to call an ally than an enemy. When Romero returns, he immediately launches into the earful he's dying to give me.

"We didn't need him to tell us it was Jack. I think it was obvious from the beginning that he's behind this shit."

"Did you pay any attention to that kid?" I sip my scotch, shaking my head. "That is someone we want as an ally. He thinks he's doing us a favor, and in a way, he is."

"How so?"

"He came in here as a gesture of friendship. He wants us to know he intends to make good on the relationship I had with his old man. That's extremely valuable." Then I lift a shoulder, grinning. "And it means more money in our pockets if we can work out a deal. It's a win-win all around. The more guns we sell, the happier I am and the happier our clients are."

"You're the boss. I see your point, we want him on our good side. I'm warning you, in any case. I've got a strange feeling about him. There's more to him, and I don't trust him. It's too soon, and he's far too cocky."

"Then why the fuck do I trust you?" I call out after him.

He's smart enough not to say a word. We haven't gotten into our disagreement over Kristoff, but I really can't get on his case about it again. Specially when I had so much fun beating the shit out of that son of a bitch. I didn't stop until he begged me to. Stopping was the hard part. I didn't want to, but I also promised to be back. Now I have the pleasure of knowing he's waiting. Wondering when I'll return. Dreading the idea while also maybe wishing I would get it over with and kill him.

It's almost enough to get me hard.

The buzz of an incoming text stirs me out of my reverie as I imagine Kristoff bleeding out on the cold concrete. Not that there's any suffering too extreme for him after what he did to my daughter. Death isn't even enough at this point. I look down at the screen and find a message from Amanda. Once again, she cannot help but remind me that she exists. So thirsty for attention. I regret ever giving it to her.

Amanda: Remember, it would be in your best interest to give me what I want.

It took her that long to come up with such a pitiful retort? She's not the opponent I thought she was. But if it wasn't for her—her cruelty, her lies, her greed—I would have the one person beside me that I crave most. I would finish my final meeting of the day, then find Bianca wherever she is in the house. I'd bend her over the nearest flat surface and fuck her senseless just because I could. Always having her presence to look forward to, her smile, her laughter. *Her love.* She might never have spoken the words out loud, but I saw it in her eyes. It shined brighter than anything else.

She was beginning to love me, if she wasn't already there.

And now she's gone, willing to run over if Tatum needs her, but not if I do. She would rather run away from me. She would prefer to blame me for something outside my control.

That's what's on my mind while I type out a quick reply.

Me: The only reason you're still alive is our daughter's exis-

tence. **If not for her, I would have rid the world of you long ago. And I still can, so don't tempt me.**

I send the message and return to my scotch, mulling over my Moroni problem and imagining all the ways I could make his life miserable for deciding to fuck with me. I might not be able to punish Amanda in the way I'd like to. I also can't seem to get Bianca out of her own head. It looks like Moroni's going to have to bear the brunt of my anger. Eventually, everybody will remember who they're fucking with and just what the Torrio name means.

BIANCA

There's meatloaf in the oven and mashed potatoes being kept warm on the stove. I even bought Dad's favorite ice cream on the way home. It's pretty lame, except it's all I have. It's the only weapon at my disposal to bring my father around for an actual conversation with him about Mom. The promise of a good meal, something it seems like he misses out on when I'm not around. He's been a stranger the past few days, coming home late and leaving the house early.

The only evidence I have of him being here is the dishes in the sink every morning and a damp towel on the bathroom floor. He's been treating this place like a hotel, and me the housekeeper. I think the worst part of all is that I don't mind. The least I can do is take care of him, since he's doing me a favor by letting me stay. I won't be here forever. I have every intention of leaving. I'll have to either piss or get off the pot soon regarding that lease, but I will sign it. I only asked for a few days to work on a few things and the landlord was more than happy to agree.

All that's left is getting it through to Dad. Part of me wants to pack up my things and go without saying a word—he hasn't given me the respect to show his face and refuses to even clean up after himself. After all that, do I actually owe him an answer on where I'm going? I might do it if I knew he wouldn't come looking for me. Although I know him well enough to know he won't let it go. I'd rather get this out of the way now than face drama down the road.

I sent him a text, telling him I'd be making dinner tonight, asking him to come home right away. He sent me back a single letter: *K*. Do people not understand what it does when they send that single letter? Maybe he wants me to feel anxious.

Until I'm sure he's being wise about how he conducts this investigation of his—and not running himself into the ground while he's doing it—I can't in good conscience leave him here alone. I simply don't have it in me.

My cell buzzes on the counter, and I glance over at it while heating the gravy. Seeing Callum's name and that it's a text he sent makes me tremble. It's been a couple of days since we last were together at the house, and I've welcomed the silence since then. What is there to say? I'm still angry with myself for making it so easy for him to do whatever he wanted, no matter how much I enjoyed it.

Curiosity won't let me leave the phone where it is. No matter what I tell myself, I'm not strong enough to ignore his message. The phone almost falls from my hand before I can open the app to read the entire message.

Callum: You win.

Okay. If he's deliberately trying to goad me into responding, it worked.

Me: Win? What did I win?

Callum: You gave me the silent treatment long enough to force me into texting you first. How are you?

How am I? I doubt there's enough time to type out my response before leaving for work in the morning. There's been plenty of time to think—obsess—over every moment we spent together that night and all the reasons why it will never work between us.

Me: I'm wondering why what I want and need never matters to you.

I doubt he was expecting that.

I can't believe I said it—and now that I have, it's like a dam has burst. My thumbs fly over the screen.

Me: I might as well be with Lucas all over again. He used to say and do things all the time that hurt me. Except in this case, I'm not being cheated on. I'm helping you cheat on the woman you're still married to. No matter how often I tell you we can't do it anymore, you still find a way to push me into it. I hate myself for that. You've made me hate myself.

Callum: That's the last thing I want. I don't know how to say it to make you understand. She means nothing to me, and the only thing keeping us married is the fact that she hasn't signed the papers. You are not the other woman. There is no one else.

Easy for him to say.

Me: I am. Can you at least see how hypocritical this makes me look? Breaking up with Lucas for cheating on me and then turning out to sleep with a man who is still married to his wife.

Callum: I'm not married. We haven't lived together for years.

Me: Semantics. You made me feel like a slut that day at the house, and I can't forget the shame I felt. I was the whore in your bed, but worst of all, I was the last one to know. I didn't get the chance to make a choice.

Callum: You're right. I'm the one at fault.

Somebody catch me, I may faint from shock.

Callum: I should have told you instead of assuming it didn't matter.

I should put an end to this before Dad gets home, except there's heat spreading in my chest, anger and indignation and shame fighting to be heard.

Me: And then, when I need time to work things out and try to protect myself from getting hurt more, you tell me I deserve to be punished. How does that make any sense? How am I supposed to want to be with you when you treat my feelings like they don't matter?

My heart's thumping madly by the time I send that, and every moment I spend waiting for a reply makes breathing more difficult than before. Finally, the blinking ellipsis tells me he's typing a response.

Callum: What can I do to make it up to you? Whatever it takes, I'll do it. All that matters is making things right. I'll do anything to get us back to where we were before–because no matter what you say now, we both know what we have is real. I want it back. I want you back for good. You can't deny how we need each other, and you know in your heart there's no ending to this. Why fight what's bigger than both of us?

I wish he didn't make so much sense. I wish I didn't want so much to give in. It would be so easy and would feel so good… at least, at first. Until he ultimately makes me regret it.

But maybe it will be better this time. You don't know unless you try.

Me: I need to finish getting dinner ready, but more than anything, I need to think about things.

I don't care if he thinks it's sudden, cutting off the conversation like that. It's much better to end things abruptly than to let Dad see how flushed and shaky I am, thanks to this conversation. I'll think about it all later when I'm alone with nothing but my thoughts. A quick splash of cold water on my cheeks helps cool me off, and a few deep breaths slow my racing pulse. Not that it matters once I hear Dad's key in the lock of the front door. Right away, I get that sick feeling in my stomach, like I'm at the top of a roller coaster's highest point and about to go over the edge. Since when do I feel that way about my own father?

Since he became so damn unpredictable.

That's the simple answer. Right now, he's rumpled, messy. His button-down shirt is a little wrinkled, and his hair could use a combing. At least he's here and can walk a straight line, so I hope that means he's sober. I think he's been stopping at the bar every night rather than doing his drinking here, in front of me.

"Just in time," I chirp from the kitchen as I open the oven door. "Meatloaf's ready."

"Smells good." Almost like he's surprised. I force myself to smile through it.

"You've been putting in some long hours lately. Should I be worried?" Does it sound like I'm teasing? I hope so, even though I'm not. I hate feeling like I'm walking on eggshells, but eventually, the truth has to come out.

"Why would you have to worry about me?"

"All these late nights and early mornings. You've been so scarce lately–of course, I'm going to worry about you." I set down the pan and remove the potholders from my trembling hands. "Are you sure you're not overdoing it with your investigation?"

"I knew there had to be a reason for you to do this." He waves a hand over the table I so carefully set. "What's this, an intervention? Do you think I'm taking this too far, too?"

Too? It makes the skin on the back of my neck prickle, that word. "Why? Am I not the only one who knows?"

He steps beside me, his eyes stern, and now I can smell the liquor on his breath. *Jesus Christ.* It's six-thirty, and he's been drinking already. "You will not do this. You don't get to ambush me in my own home. Did you think making me dinner would change things?"

I set the meatloaf down in the center of the table before turning to him, hands on my hips. "What is with all the anger? What did I do to you? All I care about is you, and whether you're taking care of yourself. Excuse me if I'm a little concerned, but you've given me more than enough reasons to worry. Look at yourself. I can smell the liquor on your breath. Do you realize that? What is going on?"

A brief flash of shame crosses his face, but his expression soon hardens. "I thought I made it clear enough already. My entire goddamn life, all of it revolves around this. Making that bastard pay for what he did to us. Why can't you see that everything I do is for you?"

"Doing what?" I demand, throwing my hands into the air. "Staying out until all hours of the night and getting drunk? How is that supposed to help me in any way? If it does anything, it makes me worry more."

He slams himself into his chair, snickering. "You can't be too worried."

"What does that mean?"

He purses his lips and lifts his brows, tapping his fingers against the tabletop. "If you're that concerned, why are you going behind my back and looking at apartments?"

Oh, my God. That's what this is about. I'm not sure how he knows anything. Nevertheless, he is a detective. I guess he has his ways.

"Since when was it ever a secret that I would find an apartment and move out?" I finish putting the mashed potatoes in a bowl and leave them on the table, even though my appetite is now gone. I'm too busy looking back over my actions, trying to figure out what clues I dropped along the way. It shouldn't be a surprise. It's not like I was going to live here forever.

"Ever heard of being honest?"

"How can I be honest with you when you're never here? And since when is your daughter, an adult and a college graduate with a good job and a steady income, not allowed to find a place of her own to live in? Do you realize how many parents wish they could be in your shoes? Never once have I leeched off you. Never once have I expected you to do anything for me. I would think you'd want me to flap my wings and leave the nest."

"Yeah, well, I'd prefer you didn't." To my surprise, he takes two slices of meatloaf and heaps a mountain of potatoes onto his plate.

When he picks up his knife and fork, I sigh in disbelief. "Why is that, and would you mind giving me your attention while we talk about this?"

"Which is it? You want me to eat my dinner, or do you want to talk about this? Can't we do both? I'm starving."

"Okay." I suck a deep breath into my lungs and release it slowly, not that it does much to calm me down. It's how I have to be, or else this is going to evolve even further, and fast. "Exactly why do you think I need to stay here?"

He shrugs while pouring ketchup on his meat. His gaze refuses to meet mine. "How else will I know you're safe? You, of all people, should understand how dangerous the world is. How many things can go wrong. Anything could happen. You could be driving to work one day, completely innocent, and end up dead."

"That could happen to anybody at any time. You can't expect me to stop living my life just because you know how bad the world can be. Death happens. It's inescapable."

"We both know you flirt with danger a little too much. Letting yourself be associated with that family is bad news."

This again. I'm about to stab myself in the eye with my fork. It will never stop, and I don't expect it to, however the constant reminder of Callum is not what I need right now. Isn't it bad enough he already plays a part in every thought I have? I either spend the day wishing I could be with him or regretting the last time we were together and hating myself for making it so easy for him to get to me. To do whatever he wants. To make me beg him for it. Nonetheless, here my father sits, unwittingly throwing that in my face.

I have to fight off the anger threatening to leak into my voice. "Tatum is my best friend. That's not going to change, no matter how you feel about her father or what he may or may not have done."

"May or may not have done?" He slams his silverware on the plate and pushes his chair away from the table before launching himself out of it. The overhead light swings, making shadows dance across his face while he leans in.

I have to force myself to face him head-on. No cowering, no shaking, no tears. "Dad, you can talk about evidence all you want, but unless you have it and it's indisputable, you still don't know for sure that it was him. It could have been anybody! Walking around saying you have evidence when you don't, is illegal."

All he does is scoff, but that's okay because it gives me time to recall what we initially discussed. "How did you know I was looking for an apartment? Did you just assume or…?"

"I didn't have to. You left a lease agreement on the coffee table a few nights ago. When I was out with Ken, remember?"

I shouldn't react, only there's no stopping it. My shoulders slump, and I close my eyes. I could kick myself for being such an idiot. "I didn't mean to do that."

"I didn't think you did," he snorts. "You're way too secretive for that."

"I'm not trying to be secretive." It's a lie, probably an obvious one, judging by how he laughs.

"Anyway, you don't have to worry about it now. You won't be moving into that apartment or any apartment until I say so." With that, he plops back down in his chair and digs in like a man who hasn't eaten in weeks.

I stare at him as ice forms in my veins. "What do you mean? Why won't I be moving in?"

With his mouth full, he grunts. "I called them today. Told them you weren't interested."

There's no way to make myself believe this. It's too unhinged, even for the man sitting across from me. One I hardly recognize. How can this be my father? Sure, he was always overprotective to the point of driving me crazy, but he never did things like this. "How could you do that? How could you make that decision for me?"

"I know better. Eventually, you're going to see that. I know what you need, and what you need is to be home."

"You don't know the first thing about what I need. In fact, I'm thinking you never did." It's my turn to push back from the table, only this time, I won't sit down and gorge myself. My throat is so tight I doubt I could swallow a single bite of food. Despair and bitter rage battle for control while I shake beside the table.

"I know far more than you. You're just a kid."

I can't blink back the tears that fill my eyes. "I'm not a kid. I'm a goddamn adult and I can't believe you would have the audacity to cross a line like that. How could you? What gives you the right to decide where I live or what I do?"

"Maybe this will teach you to be honest and not hide things from me." He's reprimanding me like a child. Whatever made me think I could get through to him. Whenever I think I'm getting ahead, he dumps a bucket of ice water over my head to show me how little I know. It's clear as day that he's losing his mind.

"You want me to treat you like an adult?" he continues, spearing a piece of meatloaf on his fork before popping it into his mouth. "Then you need to act like one, which means realizing the importance of staying away from that friend of yours and her father. I'm sure the apple doesn't fall far from the tree. She can't be trusted."

"That's rich, coming from you. If there's anyone that I can't trust, it's you! Look at what you did!" Anger pulses deep in my veins, and I walk out of the room before saying something I inevitably regret later. The only place I can escape to is my bedroom, so that's where I go. Another second in that kitchen with my father, I might not be able to come back from the things I'd say.

I don't get it. I can't understand what's going on inside his head. What would make him believe that was a rational thing to do? How did things get this far, from adoring overprotectiveness to flat-out insanity? My heart's pounding so hard I feel dizzy. I have to scream into a pillow or else risk breaking down in sobs.

This is a nightmare. My conscience is getting to me–all the lying had to wear me down eventually. I'm going to wake up any second now and feel a rush of relief. Nope. No such luck. I'm very much awake and very much trapped. I want to call the landlord, but I don't want to look like a complete loser while attempting to explain why my father would do what he did. It's pointless now, anyway. I'm sure they filled the vacancy.

I grab my phone and call the one person my father doesn't want me to have anything to do with. Lucky for me, she answers right away. "Hey, what's up?" Her voice is a little flat, lacking its usual sparkle, although she sounds better than the last time I saw her.

Everything pours out—except for his comments on her, of course. She can't know about that any more than she can know what he thinks Callum did. By the time I'm finished, I'm wheezing and on the verge of tears.

She blows out a long whistle. "Wow. He's absolutely lost his fucking mind."

"I know, and I have no idea what I'm supposed to do."

Here I am, sitting on my bed, a hand cupping my mouth and the phone speaker. I might as well be a teenager again, venting to my best friend about how mean my father's acting. It's like we're both reverting, and I don't know how to stop it. Actually, I do. I know exactly how to stop it. I was trying to, and then my father ruined it.

"I wish I knew what to say. I guess I know how you feel, sort of. You know how protective Dad is of me."

"I do." And more than ever, I wish I was with him right now. I need somebody to hold me and understand what I'm going through. I'm so desperate and needy that I want him with every fiber of my being, no matter what he's done to hurt me. I'm alone, and I hate it. I can feel the darkness circling me like water going down a drain.

"Mhm, I have an idea. Let's run away again. For real, this time." I'd think she was kidding if there wasn't actual enthusiasm in her voice. She sounds clearer than she did when she first answered, too. "We could leave, and I mean really leave. Go to a different state. No one will be able to find us. We could start totally new lives, be completely different people. Haven't you ever wanted to start over? In a new place with a different name where no one can ever find you?"

The hope in her voice is like a punch to the gut. She's that eager to run away from her problems. I won't deny it; it's tempting. The idea of running away, hiding, putting everything behind us. I'm so caught up in the notion that I'm even about to ask her where she thinks we could go, when something stops me.

Common sense.

"That didn't work so well last time, did it?" I point out, my heart plummeting.

"Okay, so we learn from our mistakes and do it better this time."

I flop back on the bed, staring up at the ceiling, knowing she won't like what she's about to hear. Unfortunately, part of being a good friend is telling your friends the things they don't want to admit themselves. "Nobody ever gets anywhere by running away. In the end, your problems catch up to you, and nine times out of ten, they're worse than they originally were."

"But—"

"No," I whisper. "We can't run, Tatum. Not this time. I'm tired of running away—I mean, I ran here, and look what good that's done. I'm trapped all over again. I can't keep jumping out a window because the room's on fire without knowing where I will land. I need to stop reacting and start being proactive. There will be no more running away."

"So, what do we do?"

I hate it, but there's only one solution. "I think it's time for both of us to stand our ground and work our problems out. I think it's time we face these things head-on."

"I don't like the sound of that. My idea sounded better. Yours sound much more rational."

I laugh into the phone. Tatum's always had a way of breaking the ice. "That's because it is. Pull on your big girl panties. It's time for us to take back control."

CALLUM

Anyone watching me as I sit behind my desk, scanning emails, would imagine I'm present. Working, focused, and managing my empire. In other words, they would never think I'm fantasizing about a particular young woman who owns my every thought, dream, and breath.

There are times when my thoughts of Bianca are so vivid I would swear she was here in the room with me. I can smell her perfume, as if she's walking past me. Light and fresh, so powerful I can almost believe I can be young and fresh, too. Like she has the power to wipe away the ugliness and darkness surrounding me.

I shouldn't have touched her, tasted her while she was here, on my desk. For now I can't get the image out of my head. All I can see is the arousal that gushed from her, pooling beneath her ass, her writhing and moaning. She was helpless to my touch.

My dick is so hard it aches. So fuckin hard, I have no choice but to run my hand over the straining bulge and consider taking it out to elevate the pain. I rarely give in to temptation in the middle of the day, not when Romero or anybody else could come walking through the door, but if I don't find a way to release the tension, I'm going to explode.

What I wouldn't give to hear her whisper my name while I undo her with every sweep of my tongue. While every pump of my slick fingers makes her muscles flutter and tighten... I'm barely able to stifle a groan of mixed desire and discomfort. It'll snap in half if it gets much harder.

The ringing of the desk phone shakes me out of it enough to identify the double ring that makes it an internal call. The words *Front Gate* flash across the narrow ID screen before I pick up the receiver. "Henry? What's the matter?"

"There's police on the way up to the house."

Looks like a painful erection is the least of my worries. I jump from the chair and carry the phone to the window, expecting cruisers and flashing lights to be trailing up the driveway. Instead, all I find careening up the winding road is a single, dark blue Acura.

When a pair of my guards hold up their hands, signaling for the driver to stop or at least slow down, they have no choice except to jump out of the way as the car barrels past them. *Fuck.* I grit my teeth and slam the phone into the cradle. Marching into the hall, I let out a sharp whistle to signal for Romero to follow. He has to jog to catch up to me, his footfalls echoing loudly on the polished wood.

"What's going on?"

"Trouble." I round the corner into the entry hall. The front door is directly ahead of us. Voices carry from the outside, with one belligerent voice rising above the others. It's male, and he's full of rage. I clench my hands into tight fists. What idiot would be dumb enough to show up here screaming obscenities?

"Are you sure you should go out there?" Romero asks when I touch the doorknob, his voice bordering on concern.

"Yes, however be on the lookout. This is my house, and I won't stay inside to hide from some asshole trying to ambush us." Nobody in an Acura is going to get the jump on my men. There's a reason I pay them like I do—besides, if the guy were really that dangerous, they would have already taken him down.

I'm not sure what I expected when I opened the door, but

nothing could have prepared me for seeing a familiar face on the other side. There's a wall of armed men standing between him and me. He's red-faced, snarling, with his shirt only half tucked in and an empty bottle of *Jack Daniels* lying on the ground near his car door. It probably fell out when he opened it. Fuck, this is worse than I thought.

"What the hell is going on?" I demand once I've taken in the scene.

I wave a hand, calling off the guards. Charlie looks different. I used to recognize the man he was. The version before me bears a slight resemblance. He's put on a few pounds and is not as polished or put together as he used to be when we had to see each other at an event, like the girls' graduation.

Nonetheless, he would stare holes through me back then, too. Similar to the way he is now. It goes to show that a person can change physically, but their hate for you can never dissipate.

"Charlie," I fold my arms across my chest, slowly looking him up and down, "you look like shit."

"Shut the hell up," he snarls, his voice slurring. "I don't want to hear your bullshit."

"That's very rich of you as you fly up my driveway, rushing towards my house like a bat out of hell while nearly running down two of my men. In what world do you live in where you think that is acceptable?"

Another question lingers. How did he get past the front gate? I imagine he flashed a badge and knew the right things to say. Either way, I'm going to have a talk with Henry.

My men eye me wearily, waiting for my command. It would be effortless to nod my head only once and be rid of this obstacle forever. It's a tempting thought. Getting him out of the way and allowing my little bird to live her life unencumbered by her domineering father.

Unfortunately, it's not an option, nor will it ever be. I shake my head slightly, but enough that they know to stand down. He's no threat—at least, not to me. He's too busy hurting himself by the looks of it.

"Why don't you explain to me why you're here?" I suggest in a cool voice. Let him rant and rave. It's not me that's making a fool of myself. Nothing is saying I need to sink to his level of childishness.

"Gladly." He's bleary-eyed, swaying on his feet. *Drinking this early in the day?* It shouldn't come as a surprise after what I heard Bianca tell Tatum. He's made a real mess of himself, this man who's spent so much of his life thinking he was superior to me. I can't pretend there isn't a sense of gratification in seeing him this way. Watching him sink to new lows.

It's almost laughable that this is the man who thought he could take me down. What a sad joke.

He lifts his lip, his narrowed eyes glittering with rage when they lock on mine. "*You.* You and your daughter. All these years, I knew you were no good for her. Nothing but a bad influence. That's what I told myself at the time. I only wish I had the backbone to nip this shit in the ass. But..."

He lifts his chin defiantly. "I told myself she needed people in her life. Friends. She had already lost so damn much, and it's all thanks to you!"

I touch a hand to my chest. "Thanks to me?" He's not making any sense, not even close. I can barely keep up.

"And then I have to sit here and watch her make these mistakes. Every minute she spends in your presence, she moves further away from what's right."

He swings his arms wide enough that my men have to back away, and I don't think he notices. His gaze never wavers from mine. "How can you convince a kid to do the right thing when they see all this? I let her get closer to your daughter, and this poison seeped into her. I bet she sees how you live and thinks this is what she wants. I bet she wants your world. She wants to live like your Tatum."

Pain pinches his features. "Now you've ruined her. I barely

recognize her anymore. This is your fault. Once again, I'm reminded that I should've killed you years ago."

"That's right, detective," I encourage with a laugh. "Say it out loud, with witnesses all around us. You wanted to kill me years ago. What, you didn't have the balls to go through with it?" I'm goading him, my own anger bubbling to the surface. I hate the way he treats Bianca. The way she feels responsible for him.

Beneath my anger, rational thinking tells me he knows about us. That's what I'm gathering from his speech. *Did she tell him?* No, she couldn't have. Even if she didn't, how else could he have found out?

"I'll show you some balls right now, Torrio. Don't you fucking test me." He points at me, his arm trembling. "If it weren't for you, everything would be different. But that's what you do, isn't it? You take what's good, and you destroy it. Rip it apart, piece by piece, until it's just as ugly as you are on the inside. You're a destroyer, a locust! You take, and you take, except you add nothing to the world. All you do is *destroy lives*. Orphan children. You spill blood, and you collect the money."

"Are you finished?" I can only shake my head. "Why don't you try pulling yourself together, Charlie? Maybe when you do, it'll be easier for you to see why everything in your life is falling the fuck apart. Or would you rather be weak and continue to blame your fuck-ups on everybody else?"

"You're my only fuck up," he snarls. "Letting you go. The fact that you're breathing right this second."

"Listen." I hold my hands up, palms facing outward, as I work to remind myself who I'm looking at. This is her father. She loves him. She wouldn't want this. "I have nothing against you personally. Even when I knew you were knocking yourself out trying to pin a charge on me, I said, I get it. The man has a job to do. I even respect it. And the only reason I could, was because I knew you'd never be able to make a charge stick. I'm too fucking smart for that. Still, I didn't rub it in your face. Nevertheless, here you are, driving up to my house, writing checks you can't hope to cash. Are you sure this is how you want it to be?"

A tear escapes his eye and rolls down his cheek, sparkling in the sunshine. "You ruined my daughter!" he bellows.

Ruined her? "If she wants to be with me, she can be. She's a grown woman who can make her own goddamn decisions. She doesn't need her daddy telling her what to do anymore."

When his face falls, and he takes a staggering step back as if I've hit him, I realize my mistake.

"Be... with you?" he whispers, shaking his head. "No. No, that's not true."

"That's what I said." *Fuck.* There's no taking it back now. It's painfully obvious he did not know about us, and I just spilled the whole can of beans.

My men back away, clearing their throats, looking at the ground while Charlie stares holes through me. He's drunk, his brain drifting, although not slow enough that he can't put together what he heard. "She's been with you? You... have been together?"

I shouldn't continue. I should send him on his way and hope his drunken state will cover up the memory, but what's the point? He's going to find out, eventually. I'm not hiding my relationship with Bianca from anyone. I don't give a fuck what anyone thinks. She is mine, and I will scream it from the rooftops if I have to.

"Yeah, that's exactly what happened, and she's a grown woman. She can decide to be with whomever she wants. Believe it or not, your approval is not needed when it comes to her happiness."

"How could you?" he whispers, backing away and retreating to his car. *Good, let him go.* If he's lucky, he'll wrap the damn car around a tree and put himself out of his misery. He would spare his daughter a lot of pain in the process.

"What?" I call out after him. "Tell me what is it that's pissing you off? Is it that you can't face the truth that your daughter's a grown woman? What the hell are you even here for, Charlie? What did you think coming here was going to accomplish? I can't force Bianca to stay away from me, and I won't try."

He slides into the front seat, one foot still on the ground—then quickly emerges, the metal of the gun in his hand shimmers in the light.

"Boss!" Romero moves like lightning, placing himself between Charlie and me while my guys rush toward him.

"No, no!" I shout, waving my arms over my head to break things up. "No, let him feel like a man. He just found out he doesn't have control over his daughter. He needs to feel like a big shot again. I wouldn't dare to take that away from him."

"You sick son of a bitch!" He's shaking so hard I doubt he could aim if he tried. I bet his vision is doubling by now because he keeps squinting and blinking. Surprisingly, he made it here in one piece. "First, you took my wife, and now you're taking my daughter. When will it be enough? How many more lives do you need to destroy?" He's so stricken, so defeated, I wonder for a second if he's going to put the gun to his own head.

Romero peers at me over his shoulder. "Do you know what he's talking about?"

"I don't have the first idea." I wave him to the side, in any case. I'll be damned if I hide behind somebody else, especially when it comes to this broken-down shell of a man. "What the hell are you talking about? I did nothing to your wife. We never met."

"No," he moans. "No! You're a fucking liar! Is this how you sleep at night? I always wondered about criminals like you. How you can look at yourself in the mirror every day without letting the guilt eat you alive. I wonder how broken you must be to walk through life knowing all the pain you've caused others."

"That still doesn't explain what you're talking about. What makes you think I did anything to your wife?"

"Don't play stupid. You know what you did!" he bellows. "You fucking killed her! You took her from me. One single fucking bullet to her head, and she was gone. It meant nothing to you, but to me…

she was my person. She was a mother and a wife, but more than anything, she was innocent! She was everything to me, and you took her. You fucking took her." His voice cracks, and he crumbles, releasing a ragged sob, allowing one of my men to disarm him easily.

That's what he thinks happened to his wife? Now I have to go back through my memories. Has Bianca mentioned her? Did Tatum? I do remember back in the day when the girls were young; there was a time Tatum mentioned Bianca's mom being in heaven. If I recall correctly, it was a car accident. Perhaps Charlie knows something I don't, or maybe he's delusional.

"Charlie." My voice is lower now, drained of some of the outrage he's stirred up. "I'm still not sure what you think I had to do with your wife's death, though I assure you, it wasn't me. If somebody put a bullet in your wife's head, it didn't come from my gun. That's not how I operate."

"Bullshit!" he barks. "Everything you say is a lie."

"Look, I had no reason to kill your wife. So what, is that why you were after me? Get in line. I can't tell you how many times I have dealt with cops and even the feds on my ass. Do I go around killing their wives? No. Never the innocent. You might not believe it, but I do live by a code. Killing innocent people, especially women, that's at the top of the list. I had nothing to do with it, and I'm sorry you think I did. I could have set you straight a long time ago."

"Stop. Enough with the lies and delusions. The only person you're fooling is yourself. I know your type. You think you're a good man. Only you aren't. You're a scourge on the earth, and now you tell me you're fucking my daughter. All you'll ever do is hurt her. You're going to ruin and drag her down, and I'll be damned if I allow that to happen."

"None of those things are true. I love her!"

Shit, again. Something about this asshole has me confessing to things I never intended. "I love her," I say again, calmer this time.

I'm sick of denying it, anyway. "I don't want to hurt her. That's the last thing I want. She means the world to me, Charlie."

"I don't believe you."

"It doesn't matter whether or not you believe me. It's the truth. We both can love her."

"You took… everything…" He staggers, then drops to one knee. I look at Romero and jerk my chin, signaling for him to help the poor bastard up. It's not like me to feel sympathy for somebody like him. A person so hell-bent on fucking up my life and showing up at my house to stick a gun in my face. It doesn't really matter what I think or want, not when he's Bianca's father. I'm not going to kill him. I love her too much to do that. I never intended to admit it out loud, not yet. However, everyone knows now. There's no point in hiding the truth, anyway.

"Get him home," I order Romero, who helps Charlie to his feet. "One of you guys, follow them in Charlie's car."

"You can't have her! You can't!" Charlie yells after me, and I turn away from them to walk back towards the house. I briefly catch him fighting with Romero, but he easily subdues him. I walk the remaining way into the house.

Now he knows. Fuck, he knows the truth. I drag a hand through my hair, hoping he doesn't lash out at her. Maybe I should warn her, but then again, I would have to explain how he came to know in the first place. Everything will spiral, and she'll ask questions. The idea of causing her pain… I don't want that for her. Maybe we'll both get lucky. He's so drunk there's a chance he won't remember any of what was said when he wakes up. I trust Romero to do the right thing by him, and I'm sure he'll be unharmed when he comes to.

There's something else on my mind now, something that refuses to go unnoticed now that it's been brought up. Why does Charlie think I killed his wife, and what would make him assume I would do something like that? Part of me thinks it involves needing someone to blame, but it could be something else. His wife's been dead for years. He can't honestly believe this whole time I murdered her, right?

A more significant question comes to mind, then. Does Bianca know what her father thinks? Did he tell her? Is that one more reason she wants nothing to do with me? It's almost too much to handle all at once, the questions and implications and possibilities.

Above all of it, one idea rings out the loudest.

Finding out who fired that fatal shot might go a long way toward setting things right.

BIANCA

I force a smile as I step up to the desk in the lobby of the police station. How long has it been since I stood right here in this very spot? Thinking back to the last time I was here, I think I was twelve or thirteen and so excited and thrilled about visiting my dad at work.

Back then, he was important, a higher-up. Funny, I never would have guessed that everything would change less than ten years later. Excitement would become embarrassment; a sadness encompassing me as soon as I walked through the double doors. Being here now, everything is different. I'm here to help my father, not to visit him. He's no longer the hero I worshiped as a little girl. Not anymore.

I wrinkle my nose upon my first deep breath into my nose. The place reeks of stale coffee. The tiled floor could use replacing, and the fluorescent lights… well, fluorescent lights never do anyone any favors. It makes us all look washed out and gaunt. I try to ignore the lingering stares as I stand waiting. A handful of random people are in molded plastic chairs, probably waiting to see an officer.

An officer behind the desk steps forward. He assesses me, then frowns. I can understand why, sort of. I don't look like any of these people. I'm dressed for work since I came straight from the office. "Can I help you?"

"I was hoping I could see Detective Ken Miller?"

"Sure, and you are?" he asks, so bored it sounds like he's about to yawn.

Most of the people in these types of jobs are overworked and underpaid, so I force myself to bite back a sarcastic reply at his dismissive tone. "I'm Bianca Cole. He used to be my father's partner. I was hoping I could say hello."

"I see." He nods toward the chairs. "Have a seat. I'll call him and see if he has a minute to see you."

I turn around and walk towards the chairs before I sink into one. I chew on my bottom lip anxiously while tapping my ballet flats against the floor. Dad would absolutely murder me if he knew I was here.

Paranoia skates down my spine, and I find myself peering around the room, half-expecting him to pop out of one of the offices any second. It's bad enough that he's been blowing up my phone all day, telling me we need to talk *ASAP* but never explaining what we need to talk about. There's no guessing what it could be that has him coming unglued.

As if on cue, my phone buzzes again, glowing brightly in my purse. I don't even bother to look at it, and instead ignore the call in favor of going back to looking around, nervously wondering if maybe this mistake will blow up in my face.

It's been two days since the showdown in the kitchen, but it feels like weeks. My father's been impossible to talk to since then and essentially nonexistent. I never even saw him yesterday—I'm not sure he ever came home after work. I know his tactic is to ignore me, to try and punish me for being an adult and having a life that isn't centered around him. It's how he is, how he has been since my mom died, but it can't be that way forever.

It's why I'm here now. Ken might have more insight than Dad would ever give me. Plus, the two of them got together less than a week ago, so they might have discussed my mother's death or Callum since that's mainly the person at the front of his mind all the time.

It's not even two minutes before a familiar man comes striding down the hall, his heavy footfalls bounce off the linoleum, and his lips turn up into a smile once he recognizes me.

"Bianca, is that you? How is it even possible? The last time I saw you... goodness. You were just becoming a teenager." Ken's dark hair is graying a little, and the laugh lines around his eyes are deeper than I remember them ever being. None of that matters though, because he still has the same friendly smile that always made me feel safe when he'd visit the house. Back then, he'd ruffle my hair. Now I'm a bit too old for that.

"Yup, it's me. Just a little taller." I chuckle.

"Careful. You're going to make me feel like an old man."

"Sorry," I cringe, "However, it is nice to see you." I hug him briefly before he motions for me to follow him. While we walk, I notice a few curious glances from the officers we pass, though no one says anything; they all go back to their business. Ken walks us down to the row of offices along the back wall. He steps inside, and I walk past him, sitting in the chair in front of his desk.

"Can I get you something? Coffee or soda?"

"No, thanks. I don't want to take up too much of your time."

He's like the former version of my dad: put together nicely, clothes freshly pressed, face newly shaved. I glance over the framed photos on the table behind him. His wife and kids. I remember them a little, catching fireflies on summer nights after one of our dads grilled burgers. Life was different back then. Easy. Peaceful. Sometimes I miss it.

Right away, he sighs. "I bet I can guess what you're here for, and trust me when I say it's not how I wanted things to go down. I did my best to speak up for him. I truly did."

Oh no. I get the feeling more is going on here than even I know.

"Okay, so I feel kind of stupid admitting this, but I don't know what you're talking about."

His brow creases with confusion. "I assumed... never mind. Let's back up and start from the beginning. What's going on? Why are you here?"

"Well, I know you saw him last week. Or at least, he told me he was supposed to see you."

"Yeah. I saw him," he confirms. Nothing about the manner in which he says it gives me an inkling of what happened.

"He told me about his investigation." I don't mean to sound condescending or judgmental, I can't help it. There's a definite change in my voice when I say it, and I can't be bothered to cover it up.

His jaw tightens as he leans back in his chair, squeaking beneath his weight. "That damn investigation of his. I've never seen a man so consumed with something in my entire life."

I let out a sigh of relief. "Okay, good. You know about it."

He snorts, shrugging his broad shoulders. "Yes. In fact, that investigation is why he lost his job."

The floor falls beneath my feet. *Wait. What?* I wasn't expecting that. I'm not even sure I've heard what he said correctly until I play it back in my mind. Even then, I have to ask him to repeat it.

"What did you say?" The words are a squeak, the sort of sound a scared little mouse makes.

His gaze widens. "Okay, that's what you meant when you said you didn't know what I was talking about. He didn't tell you?"

"No. He didn't tell me. I had no idea he was fired."

"Kiddo, look, I'm sorry." His eyes dart over my face as he stands and rounds the desk. "It was a few weeks ago."

Weeks? That means he's been leaving the house and pretending to go to work for weeks. "I... I... I need..." The room really needs to stop spinning, that's what.

My lungs burn. I can't breathe. I can't even think. I feel like I don't even know my father, and in a way I guess I don't. This side of him, at least. This obsessed, crazed side of him was something I never knew existed, and now it's costing him everything.

"Hold on. Let me get you a bottle of water. Stay put."

I'm not going anywhere. Not on shaky legs or when I can hardly take a normal breath. *Fired.* How? He loved his job so much. That only seems to open another door of questions.

Why didn't he tell me? I can feel myself spiraling down a vast dark hole. He's been lying to me all this time. I don't even know what to do with this information. Like how could he go on pretending he was working this whole time? If he's not going to work, where the hell is he going? What's he doing?

Ken reappears and presses a cold bottle of water into my hand. "Here you go, and as I said, I'm so sorry. I figured he would've told you by now."

I take a sip and try not to spill, thanks to my shaking hands. "I apologize. I'm just… shocked. I can't make sense of it. How? Why? What happened?"

Rather than return to his chair, he perches on the corner of his desk and sighs. "As you said, he had his investigation."

This damned investigation. "Right. He told me about it, everything he *thinks* happened."

"That's all I ever heard about for a long time." He strokes his jaw, and I can see the pain in his eyes. It rings through his words just as plainly. The two of them were so close, like brothers—I used to call him *Uncle Ken* when I was too young to understand we weren't actually related. "Your mom.. Jessica. He'd always go on and on about finding the proof and revealing who killed her."

"He never told me how she died? He has all these theories, and I don't know what to believe."

"You know what he believes, though, don't you?"

I nod slowly as the lump in my throat won't let me speak. "He thinks Callum Torrio did it."

He nods, his expression stern and severe. "And do you know why?"

"Because he wanted to put him in jail?"

"Wanted to? He was obsessed with the idea. Still is, if I'm being honest." he mutters, shaking his head. All the light has drained out of his eyes, and now he just looks like an older man with the weight of the world on his shoulders. "Your dad is a great man, except that once he gets something in his head, it's impossible to change his mind. He becomes ensnared in this vicious place of needing to solve the crime himself."

"Yeah, I know." *Do I ever.*

"So, he sees this guy, Callum Torrio. Everybody knows he's an arms dealer. Everybody knows he's dangerous. The sort of stuff he was doing was pretty much what you'd call an open secret. The difference between your dad and the rest of us, was he just couldn't let it go. We understand you can't win them all. Besides, there are people out there who are far worse than Callum. People who make it a lot easier to pin charges, gather evidence, and secure witnesses. Torrio's like Teflon. You can't get anything to stick to him, nothing worth prosecuting, for the most part. Your dad didn't get that. Didn't see that what he was doing was causing more harm than good."

It's wrong, so wrong, how the faint pride warms me inside when I hear that.

That's not the kind of thing to be proud of, Bianca.

"I can't tell you how many times and by how many people he was asked to back off. It got to the point that he was wasting time and company resources. He'd be here well into the night, making phone calls, pestering potential witnesses. Ultimately, he got demoted after he tried to stage a raid on one of Torrio's businesses without bothering to obtain a warrant."

I thought it couldn't get worse. "Are you talking about when he went from lieutenant then back down to detective?" That makes sense why he was demoted so suddenly.

He nods slowly. "I hated to see it happen. We'd been partners for years by then, and I considered him one of my closest friends, if not the closest. He was the youngest lieutenant in the department—there was no telling how far he could've gone. The potential was endless." His shoulders slump. "But even I couldn't get through to him. Nobody could. There I was, thinking the demotion might shake him out of things. Like he would finally learn his lesson, step away, and return to doing the job he was supposed to do."

"Then your Mom...." He winces and trails off, giving me an apologetic look.

"It's okay. I've come to terms with it. You can say it."

"Well, that's it. You lost your mother, and he only spiraled from there. Don't get me wrong," he continues when I groan, "things didn't necessarily pick up until a few months ago. I don't know why. He hadn't mentioned anything in a long time. He was doing his job, working hard, and I had hope that he would be promoted again. It had been so many years, you know? But then... I'm not sure what happened. Maybe the anniversary of her death set him off again."

Yes, the anniversary did pass a while back. Funny how I forgot, but then I was getting ready for graduation, filling out job applications and sending my resume out. I had so much on my plate, not to mention a boyfriend who was getting sloppy, staying out until all hours and not even bothering to devise a decent excuse. In other words, I had a lot on my mind.

"And then I graduated," I whisper while my heart sinks lower into my stomach. "Maybe that's what did it, pushed him over the edge. Me getting older, graduating, and then the anniversary passing. He was lost before, and my absence only made it worse."

"Whatever the reason, it was like he was possessed all over again. Soon after, he was only coming to work to use our resources. He wasn't here to do a job anymore, and everybody knew it. He wasn't even making an effort to hide it. I tried to talk to him about it, but I might as well have been talking to the wall."

All I can do is shake my head, fear and disappointment slithering through me.

"What do you think, Ken?"

"You mean, what do I think happened to your mom?" My head bobs up and down as I brace myself. Whatever he says, I can handle it.

It's obvious he's fighting to say the right thing before he shrugs. "I think your dad is lost. When we got together last week, I felt like I was looking at a stranger. He was manic and so sure he had finally found the missing piece he'd been searching for. Supposedly, he found the original autopsy report that said your mother died from a gunshot wound to the head."

It feels like all the puzzle pieces are aligning. Possibly my father was telling the truth, after all. "That's what he told me too. Do you think it's possible?"

"Between you and me, kid, there isn't a department in this country that doesn't have at least one bad cop in it. It's just the kind of thing he's talking about... It's conspiracy-level stuff, and truthfully, I can't imagine that. I mean, what he's describing would take a lot of coordination—a huge cover-up. Falsifying autopsies, destroying evidence. It would be much bigger than some cop being paid under the table."

"How can he be so sure of it and claim he found the original autopsy, then?"

Ken lifts a questioning brow. "He says he did—but I haven't seen it. Have you?"

"No." The buzzing from my phone—again—makes me want to scream. My hand trembles as I run it through my hair and hope my head doesn't explode from all this information. "I really don't know what to think. You're telling me he lost his job, and somehow he's gone all hours of the day and night. I don't know how to help him or even what to believe. I can only imagine the trouble he will get himself into trying to solve this case."

"I know. I want to help him, too. There's no insight to give him when he insists on pushing his conspiracy theories. My hands are tied as it is. He doesn't have many friends around here anymore, and he made enemies of the friends he did have when he started throwing around accusations of cover-ups and dirty cops."

"Oh, God, no." Someone will need to give me a shovel to get out of the hole he's dug. "I'm so sorry. I know it isn't my job to apologize, but I feel like I have to."

"I understand. I've felt the need to apologize more than once, myself." He stands, sighing heavily, and I also take that as my cue to stand. "I'm sorry to be the one to tell you about him losing his job. I wish I could be more helpful."

"No, you've been plenty of help, believe me. Without this visit, I'd think he still has a job." And now, I want to go through his finances to make sure he has the money to support himself and keep the house. Jesus, now I'm back to parenting my parent.

As if you ever stopped.

"Don't, you know, tell him I told you." He winces, looking sheepish. "I know how that sounds, but your dad can be a little over the top, and while he hasn't been himself, he's still a brother to me."

"No worries, that would mean admitting I came here in the first place, and he would lose his mind if he found that out." Impulsively, I give him another hug, and it reminds me of everything Dad could've been if he hadn't unraveled. A detective, who the others look up to, somebody who hasn't wrecked his professional reputation.

"Take care of him, kiddo," he murmurs, patting me on the back. "Please take care of yourself, too. Don't get too wrapped up in this. You've got your own life to live." He pulls back and holds me by the shoulders, his lips broadening into a smile. "And remember, no matter what, he's always been so very proud of you."

"Thanks." I don't say anything else as he shows me to the door again. I can't speak. I can barely walk. I'm too busy concentrating on holding back tears. I have to find a way to get through to him. There has to be a way to help him get his life back on track. Otherwise, I'll be forced to watch him slide into poverty all because he couldn't tell fiction from reality.

As I walk the long hallway, I pick up on the curious gazes of more cops. It's not difficult to imagine them having secrets. Resenting me for being here, if they even know who I am. I wonder if it's possible Ken could be wrong?

Could one of them have covered up what happened to my mom? I don't know. Nonetheless, the more questions I unearth, the more answers I lack. A part of me also wonders if I, too, am beginning to unravel at the seams?

CALLUM

"Now, everybody knows," Romero announces.

Yes, I have no doubt Romero's right. The men I employ are tough as nails, although that doesn't mean they won't gossip like a bunch of women when given the opportunity. They only need a pitcher of mimosas, and you'd think they were at brunch.

"Who cares if they know?" I hold his gaze as I stand outside his cottage. Nightfall makes it difficult to read his expression.

"I guess I'm just wondering if we're ready for the repercussions it will bring. Her father showed up here with a gun yesterday, and you let him go. He essentially got away with threatening you without a hair on his head being disturbed."

"What was I supposed to do? Yes, he came here looking for a fight, but the guy was at risk of hurting himself more than me." Folding my arms, I stare carefully at him, trying to get a read. There's a reason we're having this conversation here versus inside the house, so close to the others with big ears and even bigger tongues, ready to speak to the wrong people.

"I just don't want any of the men spreading rumors that you're going soft. Not for a girl, not for anyone. It's bad enough..." He blows out a long breath, staring out over the grounds. "It's bad enough that one man is working with Amanda."

Shit. I must've spaced that. I remember Romero bringing it up, but we've had so many things going on.

"What's the plan with that? Why haven't we found out who it is yet?"

"It's not as easy as you think. If any of them think they're being questioned or watched, we'll lose the opportunity to catch them. At this point, they're all guilty until I can prove otherwise."

It's hard to believe things have come to this. Amanda's found a way to fuck with every aspect of my life. I hate to imagine one of my men, whom I've trusted up until now, going behind my back and working with that viper. Now, I have to prepare myself for the possibility that one of my men might have reported what went down yesterday.

"I'll leave you to come up with a plan of attack. One way or another, we'll find the snake in the grass. Even if we have to force him to tell us."

In the meantime, there was no hysterical phone call from Bianca either, so I trust Romero left Charlie in decent shape back at the house. I'm sure he couldn't have been much fun to be around when he finished sleeping it off, so not getting a phone call seems strange. The idea of her living with the fallout irritates the living shit out of me. She deserves better. I need to find a way to put this to rest for her sake, if for nothing else.

"Are you going to tell her?"

"I can't."

"She deserves to know. It's her fucking father, after all."

"I realize that, but... no, he wouldn't hurt her. He loves her too much. Besides, he's not crazy, even if his actions make him appear that way."

He releases a derisive snort. "You've got much more faith in the guy than I do."

"He's obsessed and out for revenge. Imagine loving someone

with your entire heart, and something happens to them. They're shot and killed. Taken from you and your child. It's traumatizing, especially if you don't believe what happened, to begin with. What the police tell you is enough to drive you to insanity. The only problem is Charlie's trying to get even with the wrong man. I didn't have a damn thing to do with that woman's death. I can see how he would want to blame me for it, but it wasn't me."

The thought of something like that happening to Bianca makes my stomach churn. Suppose someone hurt her or tried to take her from me. There would be nothing to stop me from losing my mind. I'd kill, destroy, and burn the world to the ground. In more than one way, Charlie and I are the same.

"This is a new leaf of understanding that you've turned over," he points out with wry humor.

Yes, because of her. This is what she's done to me. I don't know what to do with my conflicting feelings. There's no black and white anymore. I don't know whether I should be grateful to her for that or if I should hate her to my dying breath. Nothing is simple now. She's changed me more profoundly than even Tatum's birth could manage.

"Either way, it'll hurt her to know he pulled a weapon on me, and I don't want her worrying about how I might retaliate. It's better to let it go for now and hope he's not stupid enough to show up here again."

"Do you think he would? I hope not, although there's no telling when you're that bloodthirsty for revenge."

"I don't know, but we'll cross that bridge when we get there."

Nothing's been settled by the time I wave him into his house before turning back to mine. The singing of crickets and the occasional flicker of light from fireflies catch my attention yet have no calming effect as I march across the courtyard. There's so much hanging in limbo now: Bianca, my daughter, whether my ex will throw Charlie's appearance in my face. She would be stupid enough to do it, too.

What do I do about it all? That's the question. I could rummage through phone records and see who's been contacting her. I suppose that's the rational idea. As for Tatum, she's been quiet the last few days, ever since Kristoff returned. Other than that first night, she's kept to herself. Except when I see her around the house, she does seem to be in better shape. At least showered and in clean clothes. I have to take that as a good sign. I can't push her, though, or else I might risk her regressing. I've been having Romero keep watch of her just for safe measure. I can't lose her.

My life has become one big minefield. I never know where to step.

Of course, my other concern is Bianca. I see her face in my mind's eye as I walk through the house. I used to imagine this home, full of life. Nights like this, with so much weighing on my mind and so much pain in my heart, it seems more like my men are guarding my tomb. I can't remember the last time my thoughts went so dark, but I can't shake them off.

There's a man out there who believes I killed his wife, who came here yesterday intending to kill me in retaliation. The woman I love lives under his roof. A woman who goes out of her way to avoid me, who refuses to see what we have, the love that we share. I can't even keep her here with me. How will I ensure she is safe?

Fuck, Bianca is wreaking havoc on my mind and body. Destroying me from the inside out. Chipping away at the old pieces of me, causing something new to grow in its place. When I reach my office, the light aroma of vanilla hits me first.

I smell her before I see her. She's seated in my chair, her feet up on the desk. She's holding a glass of whiskey in one hand, leaning back and staring up at the ceiling. Her dark russet brown hair hangs in thick waves over her shoulders, and her full mouth is pursed in thought.

Incredible, the number of reactions a person can have all at once. Joy floods me, followed by relief. She's here. My arms ache to hold her as my hands stir to reach out and touch her. It's been days since

I've last touched her skin. Even now, I have to wonder how I've lived this long without the feel of her skin, the smell of her hair, and the touch of her soft curves beneath my fingertips. As always, there's that hunger burning low in my gut, threatening to unleash itself.

To take, to claim, to own every last bit of her.

No. Not this time. I cannot let that impulse be the only guide. She'll shut down instantly and build a wall between us. For once, I have to be stronger than my baser instincts.

"What are you doing here?" I ask gruffly. "And how did you get in without me knowing?"

At this rate, I'm going to have to post someone at every fucking window and entrance.

"I still have a key that I never gave back to Tatum, because I figured..." She looks down into her glass as if her thoughts consume her.

She's still wearing her work clothes, I see, hours after she would have left for the night. It's late, which makes me wonder where she's been. The question disappears as I drink her in, her skirt rides up thanks to her position, and her bare legs make my mouth water. I force myself to look away before I can react with my cock rather than my brain.

"You figured you would live here?" I prompt.

"For a little a while, that's what I thought." She takes another sip, then exhales. "Anyway, you can have it back if you want." I can't get a proper read on her.

Brushing the comment aside, I loosen my tie, then remove my cufflinks before rolling up my sleeves. I feel her pensive gaze on me as I walk over to the bar. "I'm assuming you're here to talk." There's a pause, and I continue since she doesn't respond right away. "It must be a pretty heavy conversation if you needed a drink beforehand."

"This isn't a game, Callum." She sounds tired. It isn't easy to control my curiosity when all I want to do is take her into my arms.

I want her to be mine, but I need her to admit what we have. For her to see that this is real.

Looking at her, I want to tell her that whatever's weighing her down, I'll take it. I'll carry it. She only needs but ask.

"Nobody ever said it was." After pouring myself a drink, I turn to face her, noting her somber expression in the light from the desk lamp and the worry lines between her brows. I expected fear to shine in her blue eyes, yet there's none.

Bianca's worried, yes, but she has resilience right now. A hardness. Looking at her, I see a woman who's been through more than her fair share and is so fucking tired. That vulnerable edge, that touch of weakness I saw in her weeks ago, is nowhere to be found.

Have I broken her?

Have I lost the woman I love before I've even had the chance to confess it to her?

Uneasiness coats my insides. I need her softness. I need her vulnerability. It's my life's blood, and it's nowhere to be found. What's happened to her? I can feel the change even in the days since I last saw her.

"I've got some questions," she redirects before guzzling back the rest of her drink and placing the glass on the desk. She doesn't let go of it, though. Choosing instead to spin it, staring at the prisms of light thrown off by the ornate engravings. "And I think you hold some of the answers I need."

"You know me, I'm nothing if not helpful."

She pins me with a stony stare. "I told you, this isn't a game."

"Who said it was? You're the one who found your way into my home, barged into my office, and made yourself comfortable. By all rights, I should have you removed."

Where did she park? How did she get inside without me noticing? There are so many questions to which I get the feeling I won't get answers. That's not what she's here to discuss.

"But you won't, will you?" The coldness seeping from her hits me like a wave of ice. This is all wrong. This isn't the Bianca I know, the Bianca I desire.

"Try me. You go from telling me nothing between us is real, that it's only sex. Fast-forward to you showing up, and suddenly you want to talk." I watch her as I sip my whiskey, which may as well be water since I can't taste it. Every fiber of my awareness is trained on her—her reaction, that unnerving sense of calm hanging over her.

It's the calm before the storm. A beautiful fucking storm that I will gladly let rip me apart.

The glass goes still, her delicate hand clenched tightly around it. "I didn't come here to talk about any of those things, and certainly not us. I will ask you something, and all I want is the truth. After everything we've been through, I deserve that much."

"Okay, what do you want to know?"

She hesitates, then licks her lips before bracing herself. "Did you kill my mother?"

Goddamn him. Of course, he fucking told her. That sick, pathetic son of a bitch. Bringing his daughter into this, twisting her up in his web of lies. I have to keep my expression neutral, because the other option is to let the mask slip free and show my real feelings, which won't get me anywhere. The absolute truth hangs on the edge of my tongue. I want to spill the beans about the way he showed up here, drunk and raving, accusing me of shit.

How unstable he is and how he can't be trusted. I want to tell her he has no idea what he's talking about and that he's lost his damn mind. As much as I want to shake her out of whatever grasp he has on her, I can't bring myself to do it. I cannot be the one to bring her that intense pain. It's better if she hates me and thinks I'm the villain who took her mom away.

"You'll have to be more specific," I mutter, lifting a shoulder. "You know I've got plenty of notches on my belt. The faces all tend to blur into each other. You know, you kill one, you've killed them all."

"You son of a bitch." I duck in the nick of time as she sends the glass sailing across the room. It lands somewhere over my head, smashing against the wall at my back. Pieces of glass fly in every direction. "What is wrong with you? Why would you say something like that? I should fucking kill you! Hell, I wish I could!"

Yes. This is how I need her. Emotional, burning with rage, ready to break.

Hot, blazing satisfaction burns through my veins while I launch myself across the room, taking her by the arms even as she tries to throw punches. I pull her from the chair and drop her ass onto the desk. "You wanna kill me?" I snarl, so close our noses touch. "You only wish you had the balls to get rid of me that easily."

She snarls at me, her teeth clenched. "Yes! Yes, I do! I fucking hate you!"

"Then, by all means, little bird." Reaching behind me, I take hold of the Glock, pulling it from my waistband and placing it on the desk. "Do it."

Her eyelids flutter, her already flushed cheeks turning a darker shade of red. "What?"

She's shocked, it's obvious. She didn't expect me to put a weapon in her hand.

"You heard me." I force her legs apart with one of mine, wedging myself between her thighs. She bats at me with her hands even as I take hold of her wrists, squeezing hard enough for her to suck in a pained breath between her lips. I don't want to hurt her, but I need to prove a point. "It's clear you're a big bad monster now, and you already said you want me out of your life. Well, the only way to do that is to stop my heart from beating, and the only option you have is to put a bullet in me right now. Some come on, get it done and over with."

"Stop," she whispers. "Don't push me."

"Who's pushing who?" All at once, I release her, holding my hands up in surrender. "I won't fight back. Go ahead. You're strong and determined. And you hate me. It's an easy enough task. Take the gun." When she hesitates, I snap, "Do it!"

She recoils, eyes wide, but she still reaches for the gun. She takes it in her hand, a hand that's trembling, though not so much that she can't lift it and aim it directly at my heart.

I look down at the steel, then at her. "See, that wasn't so hard, was it?" I already know this could go bad, however I have to believe she feels the rippling energy between us too. I have to believe that her heart beats in tandem with my own. "Well? All you've got to do is squeeze the trigger, and it'll all be over. You'll be free of me, little bird."

"I should..." she seethes, her body trembling so hard, she can't keep the damn thing still.

"No, you look at me," I bark when her gaze drops down to my chest. Taking a handful of her hair, I wrap it around my fist and pull her head back, forcing her to look me in the eye. "You don't come into a man's house and make a threat like that if you're not willing to live up to it. Got it? In that, let me promise you something. You will never have this opportunity again, so if this is what you truly want... If you hate me so much that you want me dead, and you wholeheartedly believe I did it. Go ahead. Kill me."

The gun still shakes, so I wrap a hand around it, holding it steady before pressing my chest to the muzzle. The action elicits a gasp from her, and she stiffens. Her teary eyes widen further, terror shimmering back at me. Even now, I savor that look, knowing I can bring her to this point. There's nothing as pretty as when she cries. Well, except when my cock is in one of her holes while she's doing it.

"You've already blasted my life to pieces and invaded every fucking part of me. I can't think because of you. I can't do the things I know I need to do, for they'd hurt you. You may as well end my worthless life here and now, Bianca, considering without you it doesn't mean a fucking thing, anyway. And if you would rather snuff me out than work through this, be my guest. I don't know how much longer I can endure the torment of loving you, anyway."

Her baby blues dance over my features, her mouth gaping open.

"No, don't do that," I whisper, leaning closer, gritting my teeth as the steel digs into my flesh. "Do what you came here to do. Pull the fucking trigger, Bianca. You won't ever get another chance."

"I... I..." A tear escapes her eye and rolls down her cheek. Another soon follows, then another. Her brows draw together, pain etched in her features. "Don't make me do this."

"I'm giving you what you want." Still holding her hair, I run the fingers of my other hand over her flushed cheek. "I'm always trying to give you what you want. Can't you see that? If this is the last thing I can give you in order to make you happy, at least I'll die knowing that I gave it to you. So take it. Take my life. Put a bullet through my heart." Running my thumb over her bottom lip, I whisper, "You already own it. Put me out of my misery, for that's what this is without you. Misery."

BIANCA

I'm dreaming. I have to be. If I'm not, then I somehow have to sort all of this to make sense and I don't know if I can do that. He can't mean what he's saying. This is just another game, another test. It's his way of finding out whether I'm for real. Pushing me the way he always does.

Nonetheless, he sounds like he means it.

When he says he loves me, it sounds real. I want to believe it. No, I *need* to, or else what was all of this for? I know what this is, except I'm afraid to believe it. That's the problem. It could be another game. Another level to the mental torment he puts me through. Will I shoot him if he says he loves me? And what if I did? Where would that get him?

None of it makes sense, but then again, nothing about him ever has.

"Pull the trigger," he whispers, the fight draining from his voice. He sounds sad, like he's giving in to the inevitable.

"You know I won't." I still grasp the butt of the gun without taking my finger off the trigger. "I can't."

All that leaves is the two of us staring into each other's eyes, both of us panting, and I don't know what to do. I don't know what to think. I didn't come here for any of this. "I only want the truth. That's why I came here. I need to figure everything out, and I can't keep running away from my problems, hoping they'll disappear."

I'm tired, so tired.

"You want the truth?" In a flash, he takes the gun from me and sets it aside, then buries his other hand in my hair. He's cradling my head in both his hands now. "I told you the truth. It's the only truth I know. You've destroyed me—and the worst part is, all I want is more. More of you. More of us."

He leans in, pressing his forehead to mine before a shudder runs through him. "Look what you've done to me."

What I've done to him? There's not enough time to go through everything he's done to me. The way he's turned everything upside down. Made me hate myself. Left me questioning who I am. My loyalties and what I will and won't stand for.

What I'm willing to let somebody do to me.

How many times I'll come back for more.

Similar to right now, sitting on this desk, the man forces me to put a gun to his chest. All the while, I simply want to strain the extra inch and press my lips to his. I want to kiss him as hard as I can. I crave the sensation of my lips bruising under his.

"Bianca..." He pulls back just enough to peer into my eyes. "I need you. Don't make me beg for this. Please."

His hands slide over my neck, then my shoulders. I can't pretend my flesh doesn't tingle beneath his touch. His fingers press into my skin when he can no longer hold back the desire. His need to claim me is just as strong as my need to be claimed. It's like a veil has been lifted, and I can see everything that used to be so foggy.

When his head darts forward and his mouth covers mine, I melt like ice under a flame, clawing at him like a wild animal. This is the only time things make sense, when he's kissing me. When his hands roam my body and memorize every inch.

He works my thin cardigan over my shoulders, then loses his patience and yanks it off along with the tank top underneath.

Pulling them both off over my head, he buries his face between my breasts. The slight scruff of his beard prickles against my skin. The way he grunts while peppering kisses across my throat and collarbone as I grind against his thigh that's still wedged between my legs.

How is it always like this? We're explosive together. It takes nothing for him to light the match and set my soul on fire. Every kiss, every touch makes me crave more. I can lose myself in him completely, and that's what I need most. To lose myself and forget everything else.

"That's right," he mewls, panting, before sliding his tongue under my bra to lap at my nipple. A moan rips from my throat. "Fuck, I've waited so long for this moment, Bianca. It's been torture waiting for you. Hoping you see it."

He presses firmer against my pussy and I grind further down on him, frantic to ease the tension that only gets worse with every touch. Reaching behind me, he unclasps my bra and tosses it aside before pushing me back flat against the desk.

"Made for me," he murmurs, his huge hands cupping my breasts. His touch has the power to turn me to ash, to burn me to embers. He's right. I was made for him. That's the only way to explain how my pussy instantly floods at the slightest brush of his fingertips. The musky scent of his cologne. The sound of his voice. I was made for him—and he was made for me.

"Let's see if you're dripping yet." The sudden tearing sound and pinch at my hips tell me that he ripped my thong clean off me, and now cool air brushes my bare pussy. It's such a contrast to my overheated skin that a delicious shiver races through my body.

I lift my head to watch him lower himself to his chair and wheel closer to the desk. I'm exposed, a willing victim in this dangerous game of love that we share.

"Look at the way it quivers," he marvels, his voice low and thick with desire as he gazes down at my pussy. "Every time your muscles tighten, more of that sweet nectar drips out of you, painting your thighs. How am I supposed to resist this?"

"You aren't."

He lifts his gaze to mine, smirking. "You're right. I'm not, and I won't. I'm going to make sure you drown me." Fingertips dance along my slit, spreading me wider. "What do you think, little bird? Do you have enough of this sweet nectar to put me out of my misery?"

"I think if you keep talking, I'm going to…"

Before I can finish, he's diving deep, his tongue lapping at my clit, and it's a spark to a roaring fire. I can only groan, lifting my hips to meet the violent strokes of his tongue. He flicks my clit back and forth, alternating between sucking and licking it while two of his thick fingers press inside of me.

Oh god. The thick digits stretch me, and when he scissors them, my eyes nearly roll to the back of my head. Every cell in my body, every inch of my flesh, burns with the intensity of the sun. His fingers move in and out of me fast, my arousal dripping down his entire palm with every slam of his knuckles against me.

"Yes… oh God, Callum. Don't stop." The words rush out of me as I rise higher and higher. I can feel the orgasm building deep in my core, the muscles tightening.

Goodness, if he stops this time, I'll truly kill him. One more thrust of his fingers and a lap of his tongue, and I explode. There's nothing to do except scream in relief as the wave breaks and rolls over me, pulling me deep into the undercurrent. Blissful shivers wrack my body from head to toe. I'm a victim of his vicious pussy eating skills.

"Mmm…" I open my eyes and look up across the length of my body at Callum. He pulls away, bringing the fingers that were just inside me to his lips. He licks them clean, wearing a blissful expression the entire time. "I'll never get enough of you."

Like he wants to prove his point, he moves back between my legs, burying his tongue in my pussy to lap up what's still flowing from me like a river. It takes seconds for him to make me burn again. My nerve ends sizzle, and the tension that just eased starts to build again.

I'm consumed with the desire to touch him. I reach down and wind my fingers through his hair. "Callum..." I moan his name while lifting my hips.

I offer myself to him, grinding against his face when the pressure from his tongue isn't enough. Whenever we're together, he turns me into this greedy, needy slut. Unable to think about anything but *more*. His rumbles vibrate against my slick, throbbing flesh as he runs his tongue from my asshole up to my clit and back down again, circling my tight asshole before applying just enough pressure to make me cry out.

"Yes! More!" I barely recognize the sound.

Another broken animal sound tears itself from my chest when he pulls my hands from his head and stands. He tears off his shirt and pants while I lie back, trying to catch my breath. The man standing before me is the epitome of gorgeous. He's beautiful, perfect, right down to the intricate ink decorating his smooth skin.

Mine. He is mine.

And he wants me. His cock is rigid, the tip dripping pre-cum, giving away how badly he needs me, yet he shoves my hand away when I reach for him. *Always in control.* All I can do is smile. He pulls me up, turns me around and guides me back down to the desk until I'm lying on my stomach with my ass in the air.

"Your ass is perfection, little bird, and I can't wait to fuck it."

"Maybe someday, we'll see," I tease, which earns me a slap to the ass. The sting ripples over my skin but inevitably only turns me on further.

"Oh, it will help. I'm fucking this ass, no matter what. I'll be the only man who's been there, so it's mine, baby."

Whatever response I had is lost to me when he presses the head of his cock against my entrance and works the thick head into me. "Shit." I gasp. There's never been a sensation like the way he stretches me. The pleasure becomes uncomfortable when I feel pressure against my asshole that leaves my nails scraping along the wooden desk. *Jesus.*

"Shh," he whispers, working his dick deeper into my pussy while probing the tight ring of my ass with his thumb. Something warm and wet hits my skin–his saliva–before he resumes gently fucking my ass with his finger. Slowly he loosens the tight ring of muscles, and I relax into his touch. My nerve endings crackle, every part of me consumed by how he works my body over. I might as well be clay in his hands.

"My dirty girl," he chuckles once I become accustomed to the sensation and push back against him. There is no pain this time. Only pleasure, deep and dark, and so, so good. "You like having your ass and pussy taken at the same time. Is that what you're trying to tell me?"

"Yes… yes!" I moan, working him the way he's working me, giving back the pleasure he so generously grants with every stroke and slap of skin on the skin when he drives himself balls deep inside of me. He's so deep it feels like he's piercing my soul.

"I'll have to get you some toys," he grunts, quickening his pace. "Have you walk around with a buttplug inside all day to get you good and ready for my cock. Fuck your pussy with a dildo while I take your ass with my cock. Would you like that?"

I'm so caught up in the pleasure coursing through me that I miss the question. My scalp stings when he fists my hair in his hand and yanks my head back. "Would you?"

"Yes!" I sob, and it's true. The thought amplifies the heat and brings me closer to the edge. "Yes, please! Take me. Use me."

"It's so easy to make you beg," he chuckles, his breath against my ear. "The things I want to do to you, little bird. You have no idea. I love seeing how much you enjoy my cock, and how fast you fall apart when I'm inside you. You become such a slut for my dick when you're needy and racing for the finish line."

The words are degrading, yet they hit their mark and send me leaping towards the finish line. I want the release; I need it so badly.

Every conscious thought is focused on that single goal as my body works for it, my muscles clenching around Callum's pounding dick until... until...

"Yes! Oh, God, I'm coming! Yes!" My cries dissolve into frantic gasps for air while Callum picks up his pace. His hips press against mine, and he punishes me with every thrust, almost like he hates me. Fuck, he takes me in such a savage way that the desk moves with each thrust.

"Your pussy squeezes me so tightly, little bird. I don't think I could pull out of you if I tried. Not when my cum belongs inside you. Always inside you."

All I can do is smile against the desk and let him use me. A moment later, he explodes letting out a roar of pleasure. I feel his hot seed pumping inside me, thoroughly warming me. The idea of him losing himself in me. Losing control.

"Fuck." He pulls out with a groan while all I do is remain weak and trembling, lying there. At least, my body is. I wish there was a way to come so hard a person could forget everything bothering them. It's not possible. Once I come back to reality and everything comes into focus, I'm reminded of the shit storm that is my life.

I blink back the tears that are shimmering in my eyes. I will not cry. I can't. I need to be strong. Callum notices immediately as he helps me stand, because why wouldn't he? The concern carved into his handsome features is the polar opposite of the dark, seething animal he was moments ago. "What is it? Did I hurt you?"

I can only shake my head. "No, that was... great. Better than great. It's just..."

He's going to hate me for ruining the moment. I just know it. Who wants to deal with a teary girl after something as great as what we just shared. Things are already so tenuous between us, and I did hold a gun to his chest earlier. Now, I'm unraveling into an emotional wreck.

"Come here." He presses back into his chair, holding his arms out for me to sit in his lap. I hate how fast I climb up into his lap, feeling vulnerable. It's like only his strong arms have the power to keep me from falling apart.

He cradles me against his chest for a short while, rocking me like a small child. I melt into him, the feeling of his warm skin against mine, the heavy thump of his heartbeat in my ear. For a second, I can forget about who killed my mom, what's wrong with my father, and the battle between Callum and me. The only thing I feel in this singular moment is content. Joy.

Callum, of course, has to pop that fictional bubble with a sigh. "We can avoid it all you want, but we both know you came here to discover who killed your mom…"

"I know, and I haven't forgotten it." No matter how much I wish I could. I raise my head from his shoulder, studying his blank expression. "Somebody killed her, and my dad thinks it was you. He has this entire scenario made up in his mind. It's insane, but it's also hard to believe that it's completely made up."

"The loss of those we love can affect each of us differently. When we lose someone we love without an explanation, the brain is forced to devise a logical explanation, which means putting the blame, especially something like thinking your spouse was murdered, onto someone else." He gives me what could pass for a guilty look. "No matter what, I can see why he'd think I was responsible, but he doesn't know me. Not truly. He knows what the media and his peers know. He knows what my rap sheet says about me, but certainly, he believes what he wants to."

"But it wasn't you?"

I can't believe how much I'm hanging on to his response right now. This could mean continuing together or ripping my still-beating heart out of my chest.

He scowls, shaking his head. "I swear to you it wasn't me. I had no reason to kill your mother. That isn't how I do things—murdering innocent women to get a point across?" A look of disgust twists his features into something ugly. "That's not me. Believe what you want about me otherwise, but that is one thing I need you to believe."

I want to believe him. I need to believe him. Part of me knew all along that it wasn't him, even as uncertainty makes a person believe in anything that might seem like a rational answer.

"If you didn't do it, then who did?"

He runs his fingers through my hair, distracting me from the fear of discovering the truth. "Honestly, Bianca, if I knew I would tell you. Sometimes, things like this happen, and there are never any answers. If all these years have passed and there hasn't been a conclusion reached, maybe it's time for him to try to heal. For both of you."

"It's not me that I'm worried about."

He takes my chin into his hand, smiling softly. "Of course, it's not. You're never worried about yourself."

"Don't do that." I jerk my chin away and try to ignore the hurt I leave behind. Now is not the time to break down or get off-topic. "This isn't about me, though even if it was, I'm not some angel. You don't need to tell me how good of a person I am. Yes, I'm worried about my father, nevertheless he's not the only one who needs an answer. I want to know the truth too. Was my mother shot? Was it an accident? He said the original autopsy included a gunshot wound to the head. I mean, I guess that would've been what killed her, but if that's true the autopsy was changed. He swears there's an original report and told me he found it."

"Do you believe him?"

That is the big question, and because it's too important to fire off a thoughtless answer, I take a second to give it actual thought. *Do I believe him?* Nobody else seems to. They must know something I don't. Then again...

"I guess it's easy for people who don't know him as well as I do to write this off as a grieving husband grasping at straws after all this time," I muse. "Trying to make sense of something that doesn't make sense. I can see why they would want to dismiss him right away, but I know him. He's my dad, and well, he might be a little cracked. However, I also know he wouldn't make this up. I don't think he would keep pushing this hard, or putting this much effort into something that wasn't real. He believes he's right. And he's already..." I hate admitting this, but I want Callum to know how serious this is. "He's already lost his job because of it."

Somehow, that statement awakens him. The mask of concern falls away in favor of complete shock. "They fired him? After all the years he put in on the force?"

"Yeah." I frown. "He didn't even tell me. I'm sure he's thought about it, although it can't be easy. My guess is that he's too ashamed to tell the truth."

"This is way worse than I thought," he murmurs, staring into space like he's talking to himself.

"He doesn't know that I know. I only found out today. I haven't been home yet." A shiver ripples through me, and I draw my arms around myself. "I'm not looking forward to going home either. Am I supposed to tell him I know? Or do I wait for him to tell me?"

Callum pulls me close again—gentle, protective, and right away the tension building in my muscles starts to dissolve. I can breathe easier with my head against his shoulder.

His lips brush my ear before he whispers, "If I could take all this away, I would. Those aren't just words. I would rather you not have to go through any of this."

"I believe you." I can't help but nuzzle his neck, breathing deep, looking to pull as much of his scent into my lungs as I can.

"I think for now, the best thing to do is wait for him to come to you. If you confront him—and anything will seem like a confrontation, no matter how kind and concerned you come across—it will only worsen things. Right now, from the sound of things, you don't want to make it any more difficult than it is."

"That's true."

His arms tighten around me. "Outside of that, I want you to know that I swear to you on my life that I did not have anything to do with your mother's death. I'm going to find out what happened though, because seeing you so broken up and hurt kills me."

"You don't have to." Even if my heart does soar at the possibility. If anybody has the resources, it's him.

"I'm not saying it just to say it. I mean it. I have every intention of figuring this out."

"Really?" I almost can't believe the emotion that wells in my chest. It's all-consuming. The idea of not having to handle this mental load alone is overwhelming. I didn't understand until now, really, what a strain it's been. How lonely it is to carry a secret all by myself. I don't have to be alone anymore.

"We're going to make it through this, I promise." Callum's lips brush against my neck and I sigh, fully content.

For the first time in days, I have faith. I can allow myself to believe this could end. That maybe, finally, Dad can have the closure he needs. "Please," I whisper, tucking my head under his chin like he can protect me from the world. "I'm afraid that if he doesn't find out the truth, it will destroy him, and then he won't have anything left to live for. Not even me."

The truth of that statement pierces my heart with a dull knife.

I can't lose my dad. I've already lost too much.

Callum's hold tightens, dragging me from my thoughts, and while I'm afraid of the uncertainty of what may happen going forward between us, I've never been more content in my life, cradled in his arms. And it makes me believe that we might have finally found our way back to each other. Against all odds.

CALLUM

I have prepared for meetings with highly violent, volatile men and felt less pressure than I do now, putting together a tray of food and coffee in the kitchen for which I plan to bring up to the bedroom. Bianca was asleep when I left her there, sprawled out on her stomach, her hair fanned out across the pillow. I could have laid there for hours watching her. Soaking in her soft sighs, the rhythm of her breathing, and the way her brow would sometimes wrinkle. Like even in her sleep, her troubles follow her.

Today is a new day, and I hope, as I gather breakfast with Sheryl's help, that between last night and this morning I can convince my little bird that I'm committed to taking as much of her troubles away as I can.

"I take it Miss Bianca is back?" Sheryl's eyes twinkle as she fills up a platter of muffins, fruit, and cheese. "This is what she likes best for breakfast."

"I'm sure she'll appreciate your thoughtfulness." So do I, but it's unusual being in this situation. Almost embarrassing. Like getting caught by a parent. I must remind myself she's my employee, not a disapproving guardian. No matter if she likes to act like she is occasionally.

As I set off with the tray, my gait is lighter than it's been in days, even if I slightly dread what's coming next. We concluded things well last night, and I couldn't have been more relieved when she agreed to spend the night. I didn't want to send her back home to him. I know he would never hurt her—of that, I'm certain—but it's still not a welcoming environment.

Whether or not it's right, I need to protect her from returning to a hostile situation. I know I can't save her from all of the world's evils any more than I can save my daughter, though I'll be damned if I don't try.

She's still asleep by the time I return, still on her stomach with one knee hitched up and off to the side. The blanket barely covers her ass—the most innocently erotic thing imaginable. Even when she's asleep, everything about her reaches something in me.

Rather than pulling the blanket back and waking her up with my tongue, I set the tray on a chair near the bed before sitting beside her.

"Hey, Sleeping Beauty." I lean down and brush my lips against her cheek, temple, and bare shoulder. Slowly she starts to awaken, a little bit at a time, sighing drowsily as she does.

"What time is it?" she mumbles, though most of it is muffled by the pillow she buries her face in when sunlight touches her open eyes.

"It's past nine o'clock." I gently brush a stray hair away from the side of her face. "You slept like a rock."

"It's Saturday," she grumbles. "Ever heard of sleeping in?"

"Ever heard of burning daylight." I run my lips down her arm and watch as goosebumps erupt across her skin. "I couldn't wait another minute for you to wake up."

She rolls over, her mouth curving up into a smirk. "Were you lonely?"

"You can't keep yourself away from me for days at a time and expect me not to take advantage of having you here." The fact is, though, it was almost a lonely experience, as much as I enjoyed the chance to watch her sleep. She's someone whose presence I can't imagine ever growing tired of.

There's never an end to the questions I want to ask, the stories I want to tell, or the skin I want to touch and kiss. I'm an explorer who finally found what he sought amid a long, rough, almost deadly journey. Now I'm supposed to find a way to cope when she wants to sleep in; I don't think so.

"It just so happens I should get up now, anyway." She stretches her arms over her head while she purrs like a cat.

"Hungry? Sheryl made sure to send me back with some of your favorites."

"Muffins? Is there brie, too?" The excitement in her voice makes me smile. Here I am thinking I was the only person who could make her eyes light up like that.

She sits up, pulling up the blankets, while I tug the tray and settle in beside her. I almost can hardly believe the man I've become—one who eats breakfast in bed with a woman and can't imagine being elsewhere. I can practically imagine us lying here on Sunday mornings, reading the paper and maybe listening to music while we talk. It's enough to be with her and bask in her presence. I can hardly recall what life was like without this sense of peace and rightness.

However, things are still looming over us. It would be so easy to pretend everything's fine, that we worked it all out. To gloss over the reason she came here last night and the questions she had. Yes, I promised to help her, and I will, but that isn't the end. Not even close. And if she doesn't trust me, if she's hesitant to believe in me, that's nobody's fault but my own. I have to face it. If this is going anywhere—and I need it to, more than I've ever needed anything—I have to be the man she needs.

"So." Once I've had a little coffee and feel the gears turning in my brain, I set the cup back down to pick out a fresh blueberry muffin.

"So?" She lifts an eyebrow before popping a strawberry into her mouth.

How do I do this? I'm navigating uncharted territory without a compass or map. "Does this mean no more running away? Or am I going to be forced to endure life without you again?"

She's suddenly very interested in her coffee, staring down at it while cream swirls in a cloud. "It depends."

"On?"

"On you." She throws a glance my way before averting her gaze again. "I'm sorry. I'm just being honest."

"I understand that and accept my role in what's happened before now."

Again with the arched eyebrow. "Really?" Even though I deserve it, there's more than a healthy amount of skepticism in that. If we're going to make anything out of this, I have to accept the truth and be honest with myself. I usually am, sometimes to a fault. I don't deny my negative or less-than-savory qualities.

"Yes. Really." When all she does is frown at her coffee, I add, "I want to be together, to be one. You know this. I've told you this numerous times when all you kept doing was insisting we were nothing more than sex."

"You have an interesting way of showing it."

"I've made mistakes. I can admit that. But part of relationships is finding a way through that, right? I'm not exactly great at it, but I think that's what you're supposed to do."

Finally, she sets the coffee aside in favor of frowning directly at me. "This doesn't feel like a relationship? Because up until now, from where I'm sitting, the most we've had is sex."

"We both know that's not true."

"I mean, we can't replay the footage like Sunday night football, but I can tell you, the most we've ever connected is through sex. That has been the bulk of our relationship. Are you trying to say you want more than that? More than me being an item you proudly display on your shelf?"

She won't be satisfied until she's crushed my balls. At least I can say I knew she wouldn't make it easy. I know better now. She deserves this. Deserves answers and honesty.

"Yes. I want more than that. I want you. I mean, do I want to give up the sex? Not on your life." We both chuckle, which I take as a good sign. "But I know in the deepest part of my heart that the sex wouldn't be nearly as good if it wasn't for you. You were always missing from my life all this time. I don't want to go back to living without you. That is just something I'm unwilling to do."

She goes back to her food, picking at it again, pairing a piece of cheese with a grape. "I want to be together, too, but it can't be the way it was before."

"What do you mean?" At least I know she's willing to be more honest with herself. No pushing me away, pretending there's nothing between us. I can work with this.

"The control stuff. I won't be caged—and I told you that before."

"And I told you I want you to be safe. I want you protected from all the shit in the world. I've seen too much of the world's ugliness and almost lost you to it. You can't expect me to turn a blind eye and risk your safety."

"There's a difference between wanting me to be safe and controlling every aspect of my life. It isn't a relationship if I don't feel free to go where I want, to see who I want, or talk to who I want." She looks downright pissed, staring me in the eye. "I want to be able to go somewhere and not wonder if I'm being tracked or followed."

"If you weren't tracked, I wouldn't have found you at that cabin."

Right away, I regret my response when she winces. Why don't I kick a wounded animal while I'm at it? "I didn't mean to throw that in your face."

"Sure, you did," she whispers. "That's how you found me. How you saved me."

Silence fills the space between us while she picks at the rest of her muffin. "I don't want that anymore," she whispers. "Promise me."

Every word takes effort to pry from my mouth. "I promise you. No more tracking."

"I need to feel like you trust me."

"I get it." *It's the rest of the world I don't trust.* That's the last thing she needs to hear after having Charlie for a father. No doubt his work tainted the way he raised her, not to mention how his wife died. The hair on the back of my neck stands at the thought of her. I set Romero on the task of digging up information the day Charlie showed up, and as far as I know, there's been nothing yet. The woman was innocent, the way her daughter is.

"So you'd back off with the following me and tracking if we were together?"

"If?" The word stirs uncertainty in my gut. "What do you mean by *if?*"

Her head tips back until it rests against the headboard. "You know how I told you that my dad thinks you killed my mom—and even though I don't believe you did it, he does." Her chin quivers before she adds, "It would kill him to know we're together."

He already knows, little bird. It's on the tip of my tongue, prepared to tumble past my lips and throw our entire conversation on its head. It might be easier for her if I break the news of Charlie's visit and my awkward confession. However, remembering why I haven't told her about it yet, sets me straight. I don't want her to know the condition he was in at the time, and there's no way to avoid it. A sober, sane man doesn't barrel their way onto my compound and pull a gun. Not on me. Bianca would, of course, rightly assume his condition.

All I know is that he hasn't told her yet. He might be too embarrassed to admit what he did. If that's the case, I'm not going to shame him.

There's nothing to do other than hold my tongue about it. "He's a grown man. He'll have to handle it eventually."

"Not until he's got proof of who killed Mom." She wraps her arms around herself, sighing. "Until then, there's no way it won't look like I'm a traitor who's, you know, spitting on Mom's grave."

The soft whimper does something to me. It twists me up inside, causing me pain, and gives me no choice but to put an arm around her whether she wants me to or not. Judging by the way she leans against me, tucking her head under my chin, I think she wants me to. It's a good sign. I have to take whatever good signs I can get.

"I told you last night, and I'll say it again." I brush my lips against the top of her head. This precious, beautiful creature trembling in my arms. Trusting me. Needing me. "I'm going to find out who did it. We're going to get through this."

"What if you can't? The cops couldn't all this time." Then she scoffs softly. "There could also be dirty cops around. That's another one of Dad's theories too."

Again, I bite my tongue. He's not wrong. There's a reason charges don't stick to me. I cover my tracks. There are more than a handful of cops around town who buy their kids Christmas presents with the money they earn on the side. Money that comes from me.

Nevertheless, I didn't make the order. I might not be the only game in town. Our so-called friends in the department might be working additional overtime, taking whatever money comes their way regardless of where it's coming from. It obviously doesn't explain why an innocent woman died, but some of these guys don't operate under anything resembling a moral code.

"Anyway, there's still another problem, and I can't let it go." I know what's coming before she lifts her head, eyeing me warily. "Your wife."

"My ex-wife," I groan.

"Your soon-to-be ex-wife."

"Very soon," I vow, touching my lips to the tip of her nose. "I'm working my ass off, trying to convince her to sign the papers. Rather, the lawyers are. We aren't supposed to contact each other, but I have faith in my team. They'll get it settled."

I hook a finger under her chin and tilt it so our eyes meet. "You are not the so-called *other woman*. You are the *only* woman. She hasn't been anything to me except a pain in the ass for years."

When that doesn't seem to be enough–for the light in her eyes has dimmed–I add, "I understand your feelings about it. I do. The only reason Amanda is still my wife is her refusal to sign the divorce papers. Right now, that's the best I can offer, although I won't stop until she signs them. I don't want to stay married to her or be with her."

Still, she frowns. "I'm asking a lot from you, aren't I?"

"You're worth it. Every bit and more." I wish I could find the words to make her understand I'd move heaven and earth if she asked me to.

"I'm worth having some freedom once this is all cleared up and we can be together for real? Out in the open?"

My mouth has a bitter taste at the thought, but I fight through it. This is who she needs me to be. "The last thing I want is to clip your wings, little bird. You deserve to fly, and I won't be the one who stops you."

The light radiating from her smile makes the sacrifice worth it. I'll have to keep the memory close to the forefront of my mind, since the idea of letting my little bird fly goes against every instinct I have.

I have her in my arms, happy and as content as she can be, under the circumstances. I suppose her happiness is worth the sacrifice. Having her body close to mine, knowing she wants to be here and wants a future just as much as I do, is as close to contentment as a man like me deserves.

BIANCA

It's incredible the difference it makes when you wake up in a house where you don't have to dread what you'll find when you go downstairs.

I hate thinking that way, especially since it's the first thing that goes through my head when I open my eyes on Sunday morning. This is the second morning in a row I've woken up in Callum's bed, only this time, he's not waiting with a tray full of food. He warned me he'd be busy with work today, but that's fine. I could use a little time with Tatum, anyway. I've been so wrapped up in my own shit, I haven't been as good a friend to her as I could be.

I allow myself to think of my father briefly. I wonder how he's doing? Lately, it seems like he's more interested in avoiding me than anything else, and now that I know the truth about his job, I understand why. The less he has to see of me, the easier it is to avoid answering questions. At least he finally stopped blowing up my phone. He did send a message overnight.

Dad: At least let me know you're ok.

I shake my head. He decided to text instead of constantly calling. If he's willing to do that after years of scowling when I've tried to convince him he'll get a hold of me a lot faster if he texts, that means he's desperate to hear from me and because I'm not a totally heartless person, I respond right away.

Me: I'm fine. I hope you are, too.

Hopefully, he understands that even if I texted him back, it doesn't mean I'm ready to come home. Going home is a terrible idea, but something I'll face eventually. All we'll end up doing is rehashing the same argument, and I don't know how long I could go without throwing his lies in his face. I don't want to hurt him, even as I might not be able to control myself in the heat of the moment.

BEFORE GETTING OUT OF BED, I roll over and press my nose to Callum's pillow. It smells like him, and I smile. It doesn't make me a total weirdo to smell his pillow, does it? If so, I don't care. It's such a joy being with him and allowing myself to be happy. I only wish there wasn't this nagging sense that it would all disappear. My happiness always does.

Now. That is not what today is about. I can't let myself get all dark and twisty—life gives me enough of a reason to do that as it is. Before heading to Tatum's rooms, I stop in the sun-filled kitchen for something to eat. Sheryl smiles before waving me in for a vanilla-scented hug.

"It's good to have you back."

"It's nice to be back. And thank you so much for the muffins yesterday. I might've missed them more than anything else."

"I have some more ready and waiting for you." In fact, there's a breadbasket sitting on the granite countertop that she was in the middle of placing muffins inside when I came in. "I've added a few for Miss Tatum, along with a pot of peppermint tea that I was going to take to her."

"Peppermint tea?" She's usually more the matcha latte type. "Is she sick?"

Sheryl pats her lower belly and winces. "She's feeling rather miserable. I normally brew her a pot on her first day."

Oh! I wince, as well. "Makes sense. I can take this to her room for you. I was already headed there anyway."

"Thank you, and be sure to come back for lunch if you're staying the day. I have some delicious pears and cheese I was going to add to a salad."

"If I wasn't already going to stay, I would now that I know what's for lunch."

Her soft chuckle follows me out of the room. She's such a sweet lady and reminds me greatly of what I've missed all these years without Mom. Just having a woman in the house makes a world of difference. Not that Dad didn't do his best, there are just certain things only a woman understands. Like how a girl wants chocolate muffins and peppermint tea when she starts her period and feels miserable. There's the warmth I've missed, too, a feeling of being nurtured.

I can finally put my finger on it, all because a kind cook showed me her maternal nature. Dad was always there for me in his own way, but there wasn't that warmth. He was the rule maker, his word was law, and while I could always go to him with my problems, his solutions usually involved wanting to get in the middle of things and solve them himself.

He wasn't equipped to simply pull me into his lap for a hug, stroke my hair or ask if I wanted to go to a movie and get some ice cream. I can't believe that Callum would ever take that from me, or from any kid for that matter. I know him well enough to know how he operates.

He always knows exactly what he's getting into—he researches, he plans, and he would undoubtedly know my mom had a child at home. He had a daughter my age when I was eight years old. He wouldn't take a mother from a little girl his own daughter's age. I am unable to believe it otherwise. Not only because I don't want to, but because that's just not the man he is.

Once I reach Tatum's wing, the sound of screams makes me trot with the tray balanced precariously. Only when I reach her room do I realize she's in bed watching a horror movie on her laptop.

"I would ask you how you're feeling, but I guess I have a pretty good idea." All I can do is offer a sympathetic frown as I set the tray down on the bed, then climb in next to her without asking. When you've been friends as long as we have, you don't have to ask.

"I needed to watch other people being as miserable as I am." Ahhh, and at this particular moment, a girl is getting beheaded by a guy carrying a chainsaw. I guess we've all had days like that.

"You want some tea?" As soon as I pour some into the mug, the aroma of mint fills the air.

She accepts it, holding the mug in both hands and inhales the steam with her eyes closed. "I don't know if peppermint tea is enough to soothe these monsoon-sized cramps. I feel like hell."

"I'm sorry. I feel bad now, 'cause I was about to ask if you wanted to go to brunch."

All she can do is cringe. "I'm in no shape to go out in public. It feels like something's kicking me to death from the inside."

"That's fine with me. We can hang out here. It's been a while since we've been able to just kick back and not do anything." The last time we tried, we ran away and hid out in a hotel. It wasn't exactly a feel-good sort of day. I spent the whole time missing Callum and wondering how long it would be before he found us while talking Tatum off a ledge of despair. I take the spot beside her.

For a while, it's enough to eat chocolate muffins, drink tea, and watch a pretty brainless movie. Actually, the longer it goes on, the more obvious it is that I needed something like this. I can turn my brain off for a little while and focus on something with no stakes whatsoever.

And all throughout, I get to have my best friend with me, even if it's apparent she's in utter misery. "Where's your heating pad?" I ask when she groans and curls into a ball. "I'll grab it for you."

"I honestly don't know. Maybe the bathroom closet?" On my way across the room, she asks, "So, does being here mean everything is okay?"

What a loaded question. I'm glad she can't see my face as I open the closet door. Taking a deep breath, I close my eyes and then answer. "It's complicated."

"So *no*, in other words."

"I didn't say no." The heating pad is in here, after all, but I hesitate before pulling it out and closing the door. Here I am again, having to remind myself what I can and can't say.

She doesn't know about my father's theories. It would hurt too much to know what my father is accusing hers of, especially with her hormones all over the place the way they are now. Yeah, I'm not doing that. I'm sure she wouldn't believe it, although she may wonder why my father does, and then there goes opening another can of worms.

Instead of telling her about that, I offer a shrug while returning to her side and plugging in the heating pad at the nearest outlet. "It's messy. You know that. He's technically still married, and then there's the age issue. He's technically old enough to be my father. So those two things right there make everything very awkward. And let's face it, your mom is sort of vindictive. I'm not going to flaunt the two of us being together if there's a chance of her retaliating somehow, you know? It's just not worth the trouble."

"Nevertheless, you two are actually together? Right?" I wish I could know how she feels about that. She sounds relatively neutral, but she won't look me in the eyes, either.

"Do you want us to be?" I ask while climbing back into bed.

"I want you both happy, and if that means being together, then yes."

"I think we're closer to that now than before, if that makes a difference."

"It does." She places the pad across her lower abdomen, then pulls the blanket back up to her shoulders. "It's nice to know things can work out for some people."

Do not engage.

If she's not going to bring Kristoff up in conversation by name, I won't do it, either. Maybe she's trying to open the door for discussion, but I don't think she's ready. It will only make things worse. Instead of launching into a speech about how he wasn't worth the time, anyway, I scroll through *Netflix* to find another movie. "Are we going with horror again? Oh, maybe we should pick a serial killer documentary?"

"That doesn't sound like a bad idea." She burrows deeper under the blanket before adding, "Bonus points if it's about a woman who killed a man for fucking with her while she was on her period."

"Are you kidding? I would start a *Go Fund Me* for her legal expenses."

The sound of her glee leaves me smiling. "I swear, if men had to go through a period just once, there'd be a pill to magically treat the symptoms within a year."

The sound of a man awkwardly clearing his throat gets our attention, and we both look up from the laptop to find Romero hanging in the doorway. His expression is painful, telling me he probably heard what we just said.

"Since when do you sneak around on this side of the house?" Tatum's voice hasn't as much energy or bitterness as I would expect, but she still sounds annoyed.

"Is it sneaking when the door was open?"

I shrug when she shoots me a dirty look. "I had my hands full, remember? I didn't even think about it."

"What do you want?" she asks him with a sigh, sitting up.

"I was passing the kitchen, and Sheryl asked me to check on you. She wanted to know if you needed more tea."

"Actually, since you're here, yes, the pot is empty." She holds it out to him, and he crosses the room, almost tentatively, to take it from her. I wait for the obligatory comment about him being her servant or for him to call her a spoiled brat, but it never comes. Their usual banter is missing.

"Do you, um, need anything else?" He stands tall but doesn't necessarily look at either of us, more like through us.

"Can you convince my uterus to stop hating me so much?" Tatum asks.

All he does is shake his head and walk out of the room.

I can't help bursting into laughter, even if I feel bad for him. "I swear. Men."

"They grow up hearing how shameful and disgusting periods are," she sighs, shaking her head. "What can you expect?"

The man supervised the clean-up after Callum blew my ex-boyfriend's brains out. I'm sure that's not even the worst thing he's ever witnessed. Though somehow he can't stand the thought of a natural biological process taking place? Surely it's not the period part that bothers him, and more of the who the blood is coming out of instead.

"I'm glad you're here, even if things are complicated," Tatum murmurs, resting her head on my shoulder as the documentary begins.

"I love you, Tatum, and regardless of where your father and I are in our relationship, you are and will always be my best friend. So, I couldn't find a show about a murderous menstruating woman, but I did find one about a serial killer who married wealthy men before poisoning them."

"Ooh, yes!" she exclaims.

A few minutes later, Romero returns. He taps on the door before walking in, carrying a pot of tea in one hand and a pill bottle in the other. He tosses the bottle of pills at her, and she catches them in the air, before handing me the pot of tea. "I went out and got these from my place. You probably shouldn't tell your father I gave them to you, but I thought they might stop your uterus from killing you."

She reads the label, and I know I'm not imagining the faint smile that touches the corners of her lips. "What, you don't think my father would like knowing you're giving me narcotics?"

"Don't start, Tatum. I can take them back as fast as I gave them to you." Only he doesn't. He's too busy hiding a smile as he leaves the room.

What the hell did I just witness?

If I didn't know better, I would think they were, dare I say it... friends. Exactly how much have I missed when I wasn't here? I will probably keep my questions to myself, since I'd more than likely get an eye roll from Tatum if I asked. Romero is a locked safe when it comes to sharing personal information, so there's no point in asking him.

After a bit of contemplation, she takes one of the pills, and within twenty minutes, her eyelids droop. "I'm so tired. I should have cut it in half," she mumbles, sliding down until her head is nestled against the pillows.

I grab the cup of tea from her hand before she spills it on herself. "Maybe this is just a sign that you need some rest."

"And there I was," she whispers, sighing as she rolls onto her side. "Thinking things were supposed to get better once I went on the pill. The doctors lied. My uterus still hates me."

"It worked for me. Everyone's body is different."

She snickers, her eyes closed now. "Yeah, what a surprise. I'm different."

I would tell her maybe she just needs a different pill, but she's already drifted off to sleep. As I'm lying beside her, it suddenly occurs to me that I can't remember the last time I had my period.

Of course, being on the pill means it comes regularly. As soon as I hit the fourth week of pills. But even though I've been taking them religiously—I even carry a pack in my purse just in case, which is good in situations like this weekend when I haven't been home—I haven't had a period in... I search my brain trying to line up dates.

EMPIRE OF LIES

Five, maybe six weeks. I don't usually track it since I know when to expect it according to where I am in my pack.

Panic bubbles at the surface of my brain. Okay, deep breath. It could be nothing more than stress... right? Bile rises in my throat. There's a hand gripping my heart. Gripping the muscle tightly. My chest hurts. Dear lord. What if... *No, it's impossible.*

Right away, I pull out my phone and go straight to Google. I type in *'Can stress affect menstruation'* in the search bar. Yes, it's possible, and perhaps that's what I subconsciously chalked it up to. All the stress I've been under.

I wish that made me feel better and made me believe further that it's not possible. However, any time you have sex, you're putting yourself at risk of pregnancy. Still, the chances of it actually occurring has to be low, right? Even if I missed a pill, it's only one. I'm sure it's possible, but is it probable? With my luck, sure it is. All these years of being careful, it would be like me to accidentally get pregnant at the worst possible time in my life.

That might not even be the problem—something *else* could be wrong with me. Maybe I'm not pregnant at all, maybe I'm just sick. There I go again, freaking myself out until I can hardly breathe. The easiest way to know is to make an appointment with a doctor as soon as possible. Otherwise, I'm going to go crazy searching the web for information until I convince myself that I have a brain tumor.

Forcing steady, even breaths into my lungs I settle back against the pillows. It's probably nothing, anyway, plus I won't get anywhere on a Sunday afternoon. Not unless I want to go to the ER, and that's not worth the money or explanation. I try to focus on the documentary, yet no amount of trying gets the thoughts to go away. My brain is like a tilt-a-whirl, spinning around and around. How can I have a hundred different scenarios running through my head all at once?

And some of them—such as what my dad would do if he found out I was pregnant with Callum's baby—are way uglier than anything I've seen so far. Even worse, yes, Callum and I have discussed having a baby. I know he wants a child with me, but talking about having a baby and having one are two different things. With everything hanging in the balance, I'm not sure our already fragile relationship can take the weight of something that big. Moreover, I'm not sure I can take the weight of something that big.

CALLUM

*B*ianca is here. Safe. Secure. It amazes me how that knowledge makes me feel. Being aware of her presence calms me. It allows me to think clearly, focus. All because I don't have to worry about where she is, what she's doing, or if she's safe.

And if I want to see her, I can find her.

All the more reason to keep her here permanently.

One thing at a time. One step after another. Soon I'm going to make this a reality for both of us. I just have to get through a few things first.

"What took you so long to get back?" I ask Romero once he returns to my office. "You were supposed to be getting coffee." And here he is, with empty hands.

Hands which he looks down at before shrugging. "Right. Sheryl sent me on an errand to grab some tea for your daughter as soon as I walked into the kitchen."

"Is she sick?"

"In a manner of speaking." When I raise my brows, he waves a hand. "Womanly stuff. She'll be fine. Sorry, I was distracted."

"It doesn't matter." I rotate my laptop to show him what I've been looking at. "The report you brought me is the sanitized version Charlie was talking about."

"That's what they gave me. I asked for all the information they had on the autopsy. *All* of it."

I'm almost disappointed in whoever was behind this. "They weren't even smart about covering things up, were they?"

"What do you mean?"

"Read over the report. Carefully. Tell me, what did they miss?" I sit back in my chair, watching his eyes scan the screen. He's typically good at picking up on the minor details. Then again, he may not have read over the report before giving it to me.

In my mind, I can't help but wonder how they get away with this. It's obviously a cover-up—a copy-and-paste version. Which tells me the people Charlie went to about this either didn't care to check out the woman's autopsy report, figuring they were dealing with a grieving husband trying to come up with someone to blame, or they knew exactly what they would find and were more interested in convincing him to let it go.

"The wounds to her head." His eyes meet mine, his brows drawing together. "They didn't change the diagram."

"Exactly." The report mentions a pair of small wounds to the back and front of her head and a crushing blow to the chest, like she hit the steering wheel too hard when she crashed. Cause of death: blunt force trauma.

However, the diagram of the body, where the person performing the autopsy marks the wounds on the corpse, features an injury to the back of her head that corresponds to a matching wound on her forehead. Holes, to be more specific.

"It's obvious they were in a hurry," he concludes, sitting back in the chair, tenting his fingers beneath his chin. "What if they knew Charlie had already seen it and had to swap it out right away before anybody else saw it?"

"I guess they didn't get to the medical examiner before the autopsy was conducted." On a hunch, I Google the name on the report. The first result confirms my suspicions. "Well. Isn't that a coincidence?"

"Let me guess. The medical examiner is dead."

"According to this article, within two weeks of filing the report." Romero's jaw drops. "Get the fuck out of here. I was kidding."

"I'm not." Clearing my throat, I read aloud. "A tragic accident involving faulty gas lines took the life of a respected medical examiner, along with those of his wife and two daughters, in an overnight explosion which leveled the family home." I blow out a heavy sigh, shaking my head.

"Jesus Christ," he mutters. "I wonder if Charlie knows that."

"Now tell me this isn't all connected somehow. What are the odds?"

"It's possible."

"Possible? It seems pretty damn apparent to me."

He lifts a shoulder. "It could also have been an accident. Those things do happen all the time."

"It could've been what happened, yes, although for all those things to occur within the same time frame. That's more of a coincidence than anything."

"It's too big a coincidence to be overlooked, for sure. I'll give you that." He winces before standing and pacing the room, looking everywhere but at me. "I just want to make sure we don't go off half-cocked. I know you want this to be true for Bianca's sake, only let's not jump to conclusions."

"I don't think it's too big of a jump."

"It could be." He rubs his hands together, walking in quick, short steps. "It's obvious the report was altered. Probably by some ignorant dipshit. Like a rookie they didn't have to pay very much."

"See, that's the thing. Charlie knows there are guys on the payroll in the department. There will never be any convincing him he's wrong about his theories because that grain of truth is at the center. So if that's true, any other scenario could also be true."

"Right. So unless there's evidence either way..."

"He will never let this go, which means he will always be after my ass, meaning he could potentially make life a living hell for me, but most importantly, for Bianca too."

"What can he do if he doesn't have a job? He couldn't manage to make a charge stick when he was a detective."

"There are other ways to fuck with a man's life. Such as careening into his compound and pulling a gun on him." And making sure I can't be with his daughter without her suffering pains of guilt. Eventually, he will tell her he knows, and there's no guessing how that will turn out.

The thought is enough to make all my instincts flare, the desire to lock her away so she doesn't have to face him. Wouldn't that make things easier? Wouldn't that make it better?

Of course, it wouldn't. Not in the long run. I told her she could have space and freedom, and I meant it. Unfortunately, I can't change my mind whenever it suits me now. I fucking hate this.

"Okay." He comes to a stop behind his chair, gripping the back of it with both hands. "What do we know? We know she had a round hole in the front and back of her skull. What else?"

"Not much else at the moment, but you're going to change that. I want a full file on her. Past employment, where she went to school, parent's names, siblings. And if you can get your hands on any other reports surrounding the accident, I want to see them."

"Do you think she crossed someone, so they put a bullet in her head? I mean, is it possible she had a gambling problem no one knew about?" He's trying to pick out a needle from a haystack. There's a reason this crime hasn't been solved yet, and not just due to the cops who were paid off. There's no apparent reason to kill her.

Romero stands up straight, sucking in a surprised breath. "Why does it have to be her? Why does she have to be the problem?"

"I don't—"

"Wait… what if whoever killed her… What if they were after Charlie?"

"Well, that's what he assumes," I remind him. "That this was a message. Kill the wife, get through to the husband, him."

"That's not what I'm saying. What if they were literally trying to kill Charlie instead of her? They could have expected him to be with her. Followed her from the house, then ran her off the road. It's possible, isn't it?"

"And they didn't know there was a woman in the car and not a man?"

"I don't fucking know," he snaps, not bothering to apologize as he normally would. "My point is, just because it wasn't us doesn't mean it wasn't somebody else who worked with us at the time."

Now he's got my attention. "Somebody who wanted to take the pressure off of us because he was stirring shit up, and their association with us could get them caught up in the investigation."

"Exactly. I mean, how many associates do you work with? How many deals have you put together over the years? It could have been any of them."

"And, of course, if he ended up blaming anybody, it would be me," I muse. "Since he wasn't after them, per se."

"In the end, it might scare him away. Thus it wouldn't blow back on them."

"And if it didn't scare him away?"

"They knew he had a wife," he murmurs. "What else did they know about him?"

I can't bring myself to entertain the thought. What if it had been Bianca? A man, cruel and cold-blooded enough to murder an innocent woman, probably wouldn't back away from the idea of killing a kid.

"Fuck me. I'm actually pissed I didn't think of this sooner."

"Yeah, well, you're not a complete fucking animal like some of these people." I can't disagree. Profitable animals, animals I would rather have on my side. Animals, though, nonetheless. And at the end of the day, an animal will do whatever it takes to survive.

"That would've been... let's say we go back fifteen years, maybe sixteen." There's a headache brewing, and I rub my temples hoping to fight it off. "I'll have to go back through names. Contracts."

"What happens after we put the list together?"

Good question. "We need the list first. Then we'll have to do some deeper digging and make some phone calls. One way or another, we'll find out who killed Charlie's wife and hopefully be able to give him some peace."

"Part of me worries that it's too late for peace."

I look up at him and grimace, "I really fucking hope not." Otherwise, a future with Bianca will start to disappear like grains of sand through my fingers.

I've never believed in ESP or telepathy or any of that, but there are times when I think it might be possible. Just maybe.

Prime example: the soft knock at the door. It's like she heard me, felt me thinking about her. Worrying about her.

"I'm sorry. I didn't want to interrupt." Bianca steps into the room, offering a shy smile. I wasn't aware of how dark the room was until she stepped into it, lighting up everything around her. My heart swells, and my breath quickens. Mine. She is mine.

"Sheryl made lunch—and she told me you never had breakfast." She arches her eyebrow, paired with a smirk. Scolding me without speaking. "Can I bring you some food?"

"Better yet." Pushing my chair away from the desk, I stand, forcing a smile. When, in actuality, I want to apologize for having unintentionally pulled her family and future into my world long before she ever made friends with Tatum.

I'm sorry the ripples of my actions spread so far, to the point where they brushed against her in the worst way.

No, I don't know this for sure. *Not yet.* Although it feels right, somehow. It makes sense. Even if I'm not the one who pulled the trigger, I'm still inadvertently responsible for her mother's death, which kills me.

"We could have lunch out on the patio," I suggest. "It's supposed to be beautiful today. I mean, if Tatum wouldn't mind missing you for a little while."

"Oh, she's sleeping." She glances at Romero, and I can't place my finger on it, but it seems a silent message appears to be passing between them. I wouldn't say I like it, but there isn't really a reason to dislike it. Fuck. I'm being irrational.

"Right. I heard she wasn't feeling well."

Romero stands, nodding to both of us. "I'll be in my office, if anyone needs anything."

Yes, he has plenty of work to do now. Work involving the girl whose blue eyes light up when I reach for her, steering me back to this moment where we are alone. I hold her close and remind myself that she's here and mine.

Until she finds out the truth. No, she wouldn't reject me. I know her heart too well. I need to believe that, so I hold onto the hope as tightly as possible.

She wouldn't reject me.

She told me she loved me.

I have to hold onto that.

"I truly am sorry to have interrupted your work." Still, she's beaming up at me, arms around my waist. "Nonetheless, I do like the idea of having lunch outside. A little sunshine and fresh air would do you good. You can't spend your whole life behind your desk."

My scowl leaves her tipping her head to the side. "What's wrong?"

"It's just, you know, I didn't get into this so you could nag me." I can barely get it out without snickering, and her scowling makes it hard not to laugh.

"Very funny. Somebody has to take care of you."

"That's supposed to be my job. Taking care of *you.*" *Yes, because you've done such a great job of it so far. Look what you did to her.*

"Maybe I like getting to look after you. Ever think of that? A relationship goes both ways. You care for each other equally. "

I still grumble, if only for the pleasure of making her eyes sparkle when she gets mad. "You want something to look after? I'll get you a puppy to smother with attention."

It only lasts a second, the way her forehead creases and her eyes dim. Shit. All my joking has struck a nerve. Her thoughts went elsewhere. "You know I'm joking," I murmur before kissing her forehead, smoothing out the wrinkles. "I'd love nothing more than your attention for the rest of my days."

"I know." Even as her smile isn't as bright as it was before. "I'm just hungry–and somebody kept me up until all hours of the night, so I guess I could use a nap too."

I only growl at the memory. Here she is, unaware, teasing me with love in her eyes. All I want, all I'll ever need. The weight of possibly being the reason her life crumbled, the reason her father went off the rails, and the reason she no longer has a mother sits heavy on my heart. Her life could've been better than this, more than this.

Her smile fades into a look of concern. "Are you okay? You seem troubled."

"It's been a long morning." I can't tell her. She cannot know. I don't know how to say it to her if, and when, I find proof, but that time isn't now. It might be a selfish choice. Nevertheless, I just got her back. How am I supposed to hurt her again with the truth? I can't let it happen. I can't take it. I couldn't cope with losing her love, not when basking in it brings me more joy than anything ever has. Losing her isn't an option.

Standing on tiptoes, her soft lips press against mine so sweetly. "Let's get you out of this room. Some Vitamin D makes everything better."

"I'll give you something that starts with a D," I tease.

"How did I know you'd say something like that?" She winks before taking me by the hand and giving me a playful tug. "Come on. I'm hungry. And I like the idea of having you all to myself for a little bit—while we're both clothed and talking."

It would be perfect if not for the feeling that she won't want me, alone, clothed, or otherwise, once I dig up the truth about how her mother died. I want to believe she will, though there's no predicting how the heart will react.

After all, I couldn't have predicted her holding my entire world in her hands one day.

BIANCA

Breathe in. Breathe out. Breathe in. Breathe out. Get it together. Only I can't hear anything but the roaring of blood in my ears.

"Wh-what did you say?" I can barely hear my voice. "Sorry. I'm..." Can't find the words. Can hardly breathe. I'm going to hyperventilate if I don't calm down. Deep breaths. Slow, deep breaths while the pieces of my life that just shattered all around me drop to the floor in a million fragments.

I walked in here, knowing it was possible. I even knew it was a better outcome than if I was sick. I won't lie, I was still hoping for something simple, like stress.

Fate had other plans. *Now comes the actual stress.*

"Based on your reaction, this is a surprise." The doctor pulls off his gloves and tosses them into a trash can while I lie here, dressed in this thin paper gown, with my feet still in stirrups. He indeed said what I thought he did, didn't he? My ears aren't playing tricks on me.

I'm really pregnant.

He pats my hand before rolling away on his wheeled chair to type something into his computer. "Now, if you require any counseling, we do have staff who we can happily schedule you to see someone. If that isn't of interest to you, we also have other options we can discuss. You need to make the choice that is best for you."

Do I need counseling? What other choice would I make? I can't understand anything this man is saying, and even if I could, I don't know what I would say to him. I can't think or string words together right now. My tongue is heavy, making it hard for me to speak.

By the time he's finished typing his notes out, I manage to find my voice. "How could this have happened? I mean, I know how it happened," I quickly mumble, my cheeks burning. "But I've been taking my birth control pills consistently."

"Sometimes, it happens that way. There are a number of reasons why your pills may have failed. Have you been on any type of medication? How has your health been otherwise?"

I shrug. "It's been fine, I guess."

How am I supposed to remember? I'm still alive, so I guess well enough for my heart to keep beating. All I can do is stare at this man and wait for the news to sink in.

It hasn't yet.

Not even close.

He offers a sympathetic little smile. "I understand. These types of things are the reason birth control can never be viewed as one-hundred percent effective. No matter what, you have plenty of time to make a well-thought-out decision.

"Thank you." The fact is, I have a difficult time thinking that far into the future. I am barely able to think past this moment, and my lungs seem to be shrinking, refusing to accept the oxygen I'm providing them. *I'm pregnant.* There is another human growing inside me. A human that is made up of both Callum and me. It's both wonderful and terrifying.

The doctor leaves me to get dressed, which I do on autopilot. How can I think of anything but the life growing inside me? It wasn't supposed to be like this. There was supposed to be time to plan and decide. I guess that was a childish assumption. These things happen all the time. It just never occurred that it could happen to me. Yes, I know the risk of having sex, but I was already taking all the steps to protect myself.

Panic spears me while I'm halfway through zipping my dress, my hands trembling. *Oh, my God, what is Callum going to think?* Sure, he's been saying that he wants me to have his child since the beginning, though he didn't say right away. Not, like, immediately.

Not while my father still hates him and thinks he killed Mom. Not when we are finally getting back to normal. This is not the kind of situation I want to bring my child into. My child, who I hadn't even dreamed of yet.

I'm going to be sick.

Breathe in. Breathe out. One thing at a time.

There's no option. I have to tell him the truth. That's all. We'll get through it together. He did say he wanted a baby, so there's hope in that. This doesn't have to be a bad thing; full of apologies and explanations. It can be a happy announcement.

The doctor wants to see me for an ultrasound in a month or so, I head to check out at reception and make the appointment. It's like I'm a robot, doing what needs to be done on the surface while trying like hell not to freak out on the inside. That can't be good for a baby—all the stress. Good Lord, I already have to think for the two of us. This is insane.

A baby.

I'm going to have a baby. It's so surreal that I don't know whether to laugh or cry. It's so weird.

I wonder if everybody in the waiting room can see my shell-shocked expression for what it is as I make a beeline for the door. How many girls have left this office feeling as I do now? I should've asked Tatum to come—no, on the other hand, I'm not sure I want her to know yet. I don't want anybody to know.

Right now, I can be happy about it. It's our secret, mine and the baby's. And until the rest of the world finds out, I can feel about it in any way I want to.

How do I feel? Scared as hell. I'm a little disappointed that it has to happen this way with so much drama surrounding us. I want to be happy. I want to have hope.

I'm having a baby.

I'm in such a rush to get to my car for one peaceful moment and think about all the revelations when I bump into another person. Shit. I lift my gaze with an apology on the tip of my tongue, only it never slips off. Not when the individual on the receiving end is the last person to deserve an apology. Amanda sneers at me, her gaze dragging over my body, judging me.

"Look who it is."

"Amanda, I'm not in the mood for you." Like I didn't already have enough on my mind. Like she's not part of the reason for the friction between Callum and me.

"Now, who could you be here to see?" She removes her sunglasses, giving me a sharper view of her narrowed eyes. The woman is pure evil. It rolls off her in waves; icy, cold waves. "You look too healthy for the cardiologist."

What a fucking bitch.

"Look, I need to go."

"No, wait. This is fun." She steps in front of me, blocking my way, still scanning through the list of doctors with offices in the building. "Dermatologist? You're young, although you know how men are. They like us to look our best. Wouldn't want crow's feet to get in the way of your happy little relationship." She makes it sound ugly, and shameful. As if I should be embarrassed for loving Callum.

"Are you enjoying yourself?" I ask, tipping my head to the side, studying her with utter disdain. I'm so tired of her shit. She's scared. Of what? The world? Getting old? Getting hurt? Maybe all of it. Who the hell knows?! She turns it all into bitterness and hatred that she likes to project onto everyone around her.

Her glossy lips curve up into a snide grin. "A little."

"I guess age is nothing but a number, since clearly you have the maturity of a teenager." I can't even believe I'm standing here, entertaining her.

"Hmmm. OB/GYN?" she mutters, arching an eyebrow. "No need to confirm or deny it. I can read you like a book." I shake my head, ready to snap, when she continues, "Let me guess. He made you get an abortion."

The hair on the back of my neck stands on end even as I refuse to let her see what she's doing to me. A person like her feeds off the pain they inflict on others.

"You have no idea what you're talking about."

"Oh god, no. Not at all. Keep telling yourself that. I was only married to the man for years. I know nothing about him. Nothing at all." She folds her slim arms, sneering. "You act like I don't know the man. Like I didn't waste years of my life with him."

"And yet you keep wasting your time on him when you could have been free by now, so do you really want to be free, or do you want to stay relevant in his mind?" I cross my arms over my chest to stop myself from punching in her stupid straight nose.

She smacks her lips together, "Let me do you a favor, honey."

"I don't need anything from you."

Her eyes move back and forth like she's making certain no one else will overhear us. "He doesn't want to be tied down with a baby," she whispers. "So if he hasn't forced you to do it yet, he will soon enough. Mark my words."

"Sure, because explain to me why I should believe a fucking word that leaves your mouth again?"

"He didn't stay with me, and I had his daughter. What makes you think he's going to stay with you?"

"Let me ask you something," I counter, hands on my hips. "What does it feel like to lose? Because that's what this is about. You lost, and you can't handle it. Just like you can't handle the idea of him moving on with somebody younger than you." I look over at the list of doctors in the building. "You're right about one thing. Men like to keep their women young, so maybe you should head over to the dermatologist. You'll give yourself more wrinkles if you keep worrying about things that don't include you."

She huffs out a staggered breath, and this time when I advance forward she steps out of the way, letting me pass. At least she's smart enough to let me go.

After that encounter, my hands are trembling, and I feel a little sick to my stomach. Don't know how much more of her I could've taken before I started to cry from sheer rage. Never would I say it to Tatum, but she's lucky her mother didn't have a presence in her life. I would hate to think of my best friend ending up like that bitch. Shaking my head, I try to let the things she said go. There are so many cracks in the foundation of my and Callum's relationship that it's not hard to think she might be right. All her appearance did was strengthen my doubts and fears.

That someday he won't want me anymore—I mean, this is going to change things for us. What if he only wants the fun, sexy parts of being together? Babies change everything. Your body, hormones, sex. *What if she's right?* I hate her so much, more than I ever have. The pebbles of doubt become boulders with every step I take.

My original plan was to return to Callum's after work today. However, that was before I made a last-minute doctor's appointment. Now, I'm not so sure that's the place I want to be. I doubt I'd be able to keep from blurting out the truth the second I set eyes on him. I'm not like Tatum. I can't pretend everything is okay. I could hardly do it yesterday, when I only suspected I might be carrying his baby. The thought of doing that again now that I actually know the answer is exhausting.

Before thinking twice, I pull out my phone and fire off a text to him. I don't want to disappear, but I need time to gather my thoughts.

Me: I need to stop home. I feel bad, want to check on Dad, plus I need more clothes.

I wish so much that I was going home for support. That I had a parent who I could run to when feeling scared and unsure of the future. Why do people like Amanda exist? She adds nothing to the world. I doubt happiness is possible for somebody like her. She's too broken, too caught up in the things she doesn't have.

The closer I get to the house, the bigger the pit in my stomach grows. I hate that this is my reaction to seeing my father. Shouldn't going home to your parents be somewhere between warm and welcoming? It should be a refuge. A haven of safety. That's not what home with my father is. It's anger, resentment, and sadness—none of which I need right now.

My clammy palms grip the wheel harder while I fight off another wave of nausea. Maybe it would be better to go back to Callum's, after all. *No. I can't do that.* I don't trust myself. My father's the safest option. If anything, he'll avoid me like the plague, while Callum most definitely won't.

I pull into the driveway and notice my father's car is missing. Relief floods my body. I wonder where he's been going, how he's passing the time without a job. I wish we could be open with each other, but he's already proven to me I can't trust him. I hate all the secrets between us, but there's no other option.

Sliding the key into the front door lock, I brace myself against what I'm going to find inside. Did he go right back to the way things were before? It's probably better for me to assume he did, so I'm not shocked by the disarray I'll soon be greeted by.

A sigh of relief fills the otherwise quiet space when I find the house pretty much in the same shape I left it. Could use dusting, and the dishwasher needs to be run, but it's evident he's been keeping on top of things. It might not mean everything's better, but he's making an effort. That counts for something.

I lean against the table. What I wouldn't give to sit down with my mom right now. I was too young to have any serious life issues when she was still with us, but of course, when you're a kid, what seems silly as an adult is a very big deal. Like finding out my best friend didn't want to be my friend anymore back in second grade. I came home crying, and Mom made hot chocolate and set out cookies. She sat with me, listened to everything I had to say, and made me feel better by being there. Her mere existence reminded me I was going to be okay, even if it didn't feel like I'd be okay.

I run my hand over the back of the chair that used to be hers, and I close my eyes and try as hard as I can to imagine that feeling of security she so effortlessly brought to life.

What advice would she give me at this moment? I'm fresh out of college, trying to start a career, and involved with a man I love, even if it's not easy. His ex-wife has me questioning everything I thought I knew, no matter how I try to forget her nasty warning. I already know the answer.

I'm being dumb.

I'm wasting time, come to think of it. Valuable time in an empty house.

I run my hands through my hair. There's nothing I can do about the baby. I'm already pregnant, and that's not changing. I have to tell Callum, soon. The other issue is finding out the truth about my mom's death. So far, Dad hasn't given me any proof or evidence of his claims. What if there's something here at the house? He doesn't have an office anymore, at least not one outside these walls.

Seeing the locked basement door makes a light bulb go off in my head. I shouldn't, right? Then again, he shouldn't have called the landlord and told him I wouldn't be moving in. Not that I'm trying to be vindictive. I'm only trying to remind myself that he has never valued my privacy, so why should I respect his? Nothing else really matters. I have to see for myself what he's so sure about.

With my heart in my throat, I dig through the kitchen junk drawer before finding the spare skeleton key that's always been in there. I can't shake the sense of betrayal as I use it to unlock the door to his home office. This is important, however. I have to remember that. It's bigger than all of us.

He might be holding evidence that implicates the father of my child.

I flip on the light before slowly walking down the creaking

stairs. The room smells like stale coffee and fast food. Then I understand why once I catch sight of the stack of empty bags and wrappers in the wastebasket next to his overflowing desk. I am about to open the window over the old filing cabinets, when the sight of what's mounted behind his desk turns the blood in my veins arctic.

"Oh, my God." At first, all I can do is stare, open-mouthed, breathless. I've never seen anything like this outside of a movie or on TV. The corkboard is covered in pictures and printouts. Some have sticky notes attached to them, covered in his illegible scrawl. It's like he's been building a map of all the possible individuals involved in Mom's death.

There are pictures of Callum he must have gotten from old surveillance—he appears to be ten or even fifteen years younger in some of them. Pictures of the house taken from the street, photos of his cars. The outsides of some of his businesses. I recognize the club and the restaurant where we ate with Jack Moroni.

My stomach turns when I spot a photo of Tatum. What does he think she has to do with anything? Why would he involve her in this? How much of it has to do with Mom now, and how much does it have to do with me? Where is the line in all of this?

He wouldn't give me an answer even if I asked. This is not the work of a man with a grip on reality. Tears well in my eyes when I think of him down here, all alone, obsessing for hours, without a lead or end in sight. Trying to connect the dots when there is no connecting them. I can feel his frustration in the air. The energy of the room is heavy and desolate. How lonely all of this must make him feel.

The sudden buzzing in my dress pocket makes me jolt, and my strangled cry rings loudly in the small space. I expect it to be Callum, who right now is just below Dad on the list of people I don't trust myself to speak to right now. Trying to pretend I'm not shaken up after seeing all of this. He'd know something was wrong immediately.

Thankfully, it's neither of them. The caller ID instead reads:

Police Station. Well, that's not any better. With my heart in my throat, I whisper, "Hello?"

"Is this Bianca?"

I recognize his voice, deep and full of concern. Shit. "Ken? What's wrong? Did something happen to Dad?"

"Not yet," he mutters, almost whispering. "Although something's going to happen if you don't get down here right away."

"I don't understand," I ask. I'm already on my way up the stairs, turning out the light and making sure to lock the door. He can't know I found that, not until I know how to feel about it.

"Someone needs to come and get him and take him home before he gets himself arrested."

"Wait, he's there? At the station."

"Yeah, and if he keeps up his shit, he'll end up in a cell. I'm doing my best. No one wants to hurt him, but he needs to leave."

"I'm on my way." I grab my purse and hurry out the door, barely taking time to lock up. "Please, try to keep him calm until I get there."

"I'll do my best," he grunts. "However, I can't make any promises."

CALLUM

The light inside me seems to dwindle without my little bird beside me. The anticipation of seeing her after a long day of work gets ripped out from underneath me by one single text. The bloodthirsty asshole I am pushes to the forefront of my mind.

What is she doing now? Why doesn't she want to come back here tonight, and how am I supposed to accept that without wanting an explanation? I understand that she's worried about her father. She is constantly worried about him, but she needs to be careful, or she'll never be able to stop worrying about him. He's always going to give her a reason to be concerned. I'm reminded all over again about the dynamic of their relationship. She's his parent, even when he should act as her father.

No matter how much I grind my teeth and fight to force away the suspicions and questions, there's no holding them back. The dam has burst.

Fear grips my heart in its meaty fist. Is he telling her everything he knows? The thought that even with all my promises and vows of honesty, she's going to think I'm still keeping things from her. *Damn it.* I should have gotten out in front of this. Once again, it will look like I am trying to keep things from her for my own gain.

Every gulp of whiskey goes down smoother than the one before. I can't remember the last time I got drunk—buzzed and tipsy, sure. That's the thing about me. I like control. A man as powerful as me can never have a vice that he can't control, and I've always prided myself on knowing when enough is enough. Tonight, I seem to have lost sight of that mark.

That doesn't stop me from getting up and pouring another drink once I've drained my glass. I'm fucked. Completely lost without my little bird. She's made a mess of me. If only she had come back tonight. I wouldn't have to live with the dread of what he might be saying to her at this very minute. The ground beneath us is so fragile to know her father may be planting lies in her head. If not lies, then theories and assumptions. He's always assumed so much about me. Never knew who the real me was—to be fair, I didn't want to know him, either.

She sees him plainly, that much I know. She sees how far he's fallen, and is skeptical enough not to take his accusations at face value. *Isn't she?* The unknown terrifies me. I guess this is what it's all about, as miserable as it is. *Trust.* It's never been one of my stronger qualities. That's what happens when you've been burned time and again so many times you lose faith in people. Not only in women, though women haven't proven themselves trustworthy to me in the past. It's anyone that has the power to take what I give them and rip it apart.

Bianca wants freedom. She wants my trust. *I want her.* It doesn't take a scientist to figure out the formula. If there's any hope of having and keeping her, I must meet her halfway. Will any of that matter though, once the truth is out? Once she discovers I told her father about us? I should've given her a heads-up.

There isn't enough whiskey in the bottle to blot out that question, which echoes in the back of my mind. Will this be the final lie that breaks us forever?

Every tick of the clock is another moment he could be filling her head with lies about me. More than ever, he'll want to keep us apart. He's going to be dead set on hurting us. Hurting me, most of all. I shouldn't have pussed out like I did, telling myself it was for the best, that it would hurt her to hear what condition he was in. *When will I ever learn?* Honesty is easier, even if it hurts the other person to hear.

It's dark now, the grounds quiet. My empire, one built on blood. The blood of the innocent and guilty alike. If Bianca's mother is one of those innocents, who's to say how many others might have flown under my radar all these years? I stare out the window after grabbing the bottle of whiskey from the bar, knowing I'll need it again soon enough.

Was any of this genuinely worth it? If I lose her, I might as well give it all up. I don't know how I can continue to breathe, much less continue running my business, if I lose the promise of her love.

"How long have you been drinking?"

I turn away from the window, glass in one hand, bottle in the other. Romero's watching from the doorway. His gaze falls on the bottle, then the glass. "Were you planning on leaving any, or did you want to empty the bar all at once?"

My heart takes off despite his arrogant attitude. He's the other person I've been waiting for, and it took him long enough to return. "Don't worry about that. Did you get it?"

"Yeah. I got it."

I lift my brows, waiting, but he's too busy staring at me. "Hand it the fuck over. Christ, what are you waiting for?"

He doesn't move. He just stands there, watching me as I walk to my desk, waiting to read the report I sent him to obtain. I am still determining exactly how he did it. As usual, he didn't give me many details. Plausible deniability. "You kept me waiting for hours as it is."

"Sometimes, these things take maneuvering. I can't barge into the police station and throw a wad of cash at somebody. There's stipulations, negotiations, rules."

He approaches the desk, studying me rather than doing what I've ordered. "How much have you had to drink?"

"I told you—"

"I know what you told me. I'm asking for an answer of *how much*?" He eyes the bottle I set on the desk, scowling. "And this isn't me scolding you, but we both know this isn't like you."

"You're wasting my time."

His gaze snaps away from the bottle and lands on me again. "How's Tatum been today? Have you even gone to see her? Checked in on her? Or were you planning on drinking yourself to death in this room?"

My vision is starting to blur. I have to get this over with and get him out of here before I lose complete control. "Spare me the bullshit lectures and give me the report, damn it."

He shakes his head slowly, his mouth set in a firm, disapproving line. "She needs you, too. You realize that, right?"

"Since when is this any of your business? Since when do we get into personal shit?"

"Well, allow me to apologize beforehand. However, I can't just stand by and watch you fall to pieces. What, did you decide to take a page out of Charlie's book and give your liver a workout?"

"You know..." I stand, forgetting the drink for the time being. "This is something I've been wanting to talk about for a while now. I keep telling myself to let it go, but I've obviously let this thing go on way too long."

He says nothing, only pulling back his shoulders and lifting an eyebrow.

"Who gave you the idea that you get to talk to me that way?" I ask. "Somewhere along the way, you lost sight of who's who around here. I'm your boss, Romero. I call the shots. You do as I say and don't question my authority."

"It was a fairly simple question," he murmurs. Let him pretend all he wants—I see his jaw tightening and the spark of light in his eyes. "I was only asking how your daughter is doing."

"You want to know why I'm not with her right now instead of waiting for you to give me the information you were supposed to bring hours ago."

"No," he counters. "I would like to know why you're allowing this obsession to get in the way of the rest of your life. You know, Tatum still needs her father."

"And who the fuck are you to tell me that?" I round the desk as he stands his ground, lifting his chin like the defiant son of a bitch he is. "You know, I could hire plenty of other guys to do your job. Maybe that's it. Maybe I went too far, giving you the idea that you were indispensable. No one's indispensable in this world."

"I realize that."

"Then you're either very stupid or arrogant as fuck. Probably the second if you're still going to stand here and defy me."

"Being arrogant has nothing to do with. We both know it."

"Don't tell me what I know."

"You told your daughter you would do everything in your power to help her. Aside from keeping that rapist bastard in a warehouse so you can torment him, what else have you done? Have you taken her to a doctor? Have you spoken to her about what she's been through?"

"You saw how it was the last time I tried that. What should I do? Tie her down to a chair and question her until she begs me to stop?"

"I've seen you do worse for less."

That's it. That's where he knows he went too far. He clears his throat but keeps his head high. He's a proud asshole, and I want to knock him down a couple of pegs.

"What the fuck does that mean?" I whisper.

His jaw works. "I think you know what it means. If you truly wanted to help her, I mean really truly, you would find a way to get through to her. You'd spend time with her. Except you haven't even tried. Because you're too busy obsessing over Bianca."

"Don't you dare—"

"I'm not trying to criticize the thing you two have. Only, it's like nothing else matters."

"Because nothing else does, goddamnit."

"Not even your daughter? You know," he mutters, eyes narrowing. "She already has one parent who tossed her aside. Do you want to make it two for two? You're on your way."

"Get the fuck out of here. Get out of my house, get out of my compound. Go!"

"I'm not going anywhere, because you don't mean it."

"Now you're going to tell me what the fuck I mean?" Blinded by rage, I break yet another of my glasses by throwing it at him. He ducks easily and doesn't even flinch when it shatters behind him.

"What the hell is going on in here?"

We both turn in time to watch Tatum dash into the room, flushed and breathless, in her pajamas and slippers. "Why are you screaming at each other? I could hear you from the kitchen!"

"Go back to the kitchen," I mutter, glaring at the traitor in front of me. "Go, now."

"No. You're not going to send me off someplace else. I'm not a teenager anymore."

Fuck I can't deal with this right now. My head is spinning as it is, and I might have to kill Romero before the night is over. Of course, she chooses this precise moment to defy me. "For once, would you listen when I ask you to do something?"

Romero shakes his head. "This isn't her fault. Don't take it out on her."

I grit my teeth and clench my fist. I can feel the blood rushing to my head. "Don't tell me how to treat my daughter. She is mine, not yours."

"I'm not anybody's!" Tatum shouts, crunching broken glass beneath her slippers as she charges across the room and puts herself between us. I'm the one she's glaring up at, though, and I hate it. "When are you going to get that through your head? People don't belong to other people. I am your daughter. I am not yours to order around or push aside when you don't want me to see or hear something. I'm not a little girl anymore."

"I realize that," I growl.

"Do you? I've barely seen you or spoken to you in days. You're in here all the time, most of the time with the door closed. You're not eating, and here you are, reeking of whiskey. This isn't like you. This isn't my father."

My head is going to burst if this goes on much longer. "I don't need this right now. I don't need any of this!"

"What don't you need? For somebody to look you in the eye and tell you you're spiraling?" She even nods toward Romero. "And since when do you throw things at him? What is happening to you? It's like suddenly you've turned into a different person. I don't understand why, but I do know you can't alienate everybody just because you're going through something."

"Tatum, you don't know what you're talking about."

"Are you sure about that?" Romero pipes in.

"And you can take your opinion and shove it up your ass," I bark.

"Listen to yourself!" Tatum pleas, getting in my way before I can lunge at him. I don't know what I planned to do once I got my hands on him. I only know I need to shut his fucking mouth. "Dad, stop. Just stop and think for a second. If you weren't drunk, you might actually hear yourself and know you're making a big mistake."

"Don't worry about it," Romero growls, reaching into his pocket. "I've said everything I have to say, anyway." Without breaking eye contact, he tosses what looks like a memory stick onto my desk. "There. There's what you were in such a hurry to get. You're welcome, by the way."

With that, he turns away, leaving without a word. He doesn't go to his office, either—I have half a mind to tell him to pack his things once he gets to his cottage. The arrogant prick. I should have set him straight a long time ago. I should punch him in the face. It would make me feel better, at least momentarily.

"Wait," I say to Tatum when it looks like she's going to follow in his footsteps.

"Dad, trying to talk to you when you're like this is useless. I'm not going to waste my time or yours." The ache in her voice punches me right in the chest.

Fuck me. I might as well be Charlie now, with a daughter who pities him and doesn't see the point in trying to get through to me. I don't move for a long time, staring at the open doorway. The house is deadly silent. The only sound I can hear is the pounding of my own heart.

I'm alone.

Without Bianca, without my daughter, without Romero.

The thought of him makes my hackles rise. The smug little prick. He knows I need him, or else he'd never get away with half the shit he says. I should cut out his fucking tongue for being so disrespectful. Who is he to give parenting advice? He doesn't have the first clue what it takes to raise a child. What it feels like to have part of you walking around in the world, walking face-first into shitty decisions. Knowing you can't stop them, you can't take on their pain to spare them—no matter how much you wish you could.

Add to that a stubborn, smart kid like mine. She's always known her own mind and done exactly what she wanted. She'd cut off her nose to spite her face if it meant proving me wrong. Why would she listen to anything I say when I could barely convince her to get a check-up after learning what Kristoff did to her?

Somehow, Romero has the balls to stand before me and act like he gives a shit. Am I now supposed to believe he's packing his shit and calling my bluff? Is that supposed to scare me?

He'll be back. They all will be. They have to be. Because what's the point, otherwise? Standing here, alone, surrounded by spilled whiskey and shattered glass, a man could be forgiven for wondering if this is what his entire life has come to. It's only me and drunken regret and the memory stick I was in a frenzy to get my hands on and now dread opening.

It sits on the desk, taunting me silently, holding ...what? My salvation? My death sentence? That's what it would be if it led to Bianca leaving me for good. No less than a death sentence.

It makes me eye the USB, the dread building in me, while I circle the desk. There's no going back from this. Whatever I find here, I can't pretend it doesn't exist. What could it be? What information could it hold? They say the anticipation of death is worse than death itself—I wholeheartedly believe that now.

What if I pretend this never happened? That he never found the report? Pathetic. What am I, a child? Still, there's no shaking the question. *What if, what if.*

Fuck it. I might as well get it over with.

I insert the drive into the port on my computer, my stomach knotting. Now I'm regretting all the booze since it's now sloshing around in my gut.

On it are the reports taken by detectives who handled the case. Descriptions of the scene—the skid marks on the road, black paint on the car's white rear bumper that suggested another car forced her into the woods, where she collided with a tree. Partial footprints near the scene, but the ground was already wet and muddy, thanks to rain falling at the time of the crash.

Nobody thought to investigate the paint on the bumper or the footprints? And now I see where Charlie's rage comes from. Why he feels so betrayed. It was his wife, his own fucking wife, in that car. And, according to the statement he gave the investigator, who he probably considered a friend, there was no black paint on the bumper when she took the car that day.

If anyone would have known, it would be Charlie, because it was his car she was driving.

I lean in, squinting, enlarging the print. *According to the victim's husband, the victim drove his car that morning, dropping him off at work while her car was in the shop for an oil change.*

"She was driving his car," I whisper, reading it again. If I wasn't sure before, I'm sure now. The truth can't be unseen, even with all the whiskey in my system.

Whoever did this thought they would find Charlie behind the wheel. They had already done their homework and knew which car to look for, unaware he wasn't the driver. It was a stormy day, probably cloudy and dark, so the falling rain might have made it difficult to identify who was behind the wheel.

"Son of a bitch." Sinking into my chair, I close my eyes while the world spins out of control around me.

They were after him, because of me. Our involvement. It's a textbook plan. Whoever did this knew he was trying to pin something on me. They wanted him quiet, for good, before he came too close to uncovering anything. Or worse, pinning something on them. I have no solid proof, although it doesn't matter. I know this game. I've seen it enough times.

The problem is, now that I have this information, I'm stuck. What the fuck do I do? Do I tell the truth or pretend I know nothing? Selfishly I realize that it might save my ass, but not in the long run. No matter what, Bianca will be heartbroken and worried for her father, which would mean misery for us. That's not even mentioning the promise I made to her.

On the other hand, we could just as undoubtedly be miserable if I tell her everything and she decides she can't look at me another second. Even if she chooses not to end it, why would she want to be with a man who is the living, breathing reminder of the ending to all the good in her life? Her mother may as well be a cautionary tale of what happens when you accidentally brush against a dark web of greed and lies.

Look what happens when you come too close to evil. You don't have to know that evil exists in order for it to close in on you and whisk you away from everyone and everything you love.

It makes sense now—all of it. I understand Charlie more than I'd like to admit right now. I lean back in my chair and stare up at the ceiling. I've drank so much today that I shouldn't even be able to make sense of anything, except nothing can sober you up like the truth.

Before, I was looking through muddy water. However, now I can see clear as day, and it's astounding. If they could do this to her mother, who's to say they couldn't do it to Bianca? It's a terrifying reminder of how dangerous my life is, and how utterly stupid it was to tangle her up in it.

Fuck, no matter what, I need to find out who did this and put them down like the rabid animal they are. It's the only way to balance the scales and protect what's mine, and even if Bianca chooses to walk away, I'll know at least I did everything possible to protect her. All I can do is hope and pray that I can keep everything together before my entire empire crumbles to the ground.

BIANCA

I hate walking into situations without knowing what to expect. After Ken called me, at least ten different scenarios were running rampant in my mind. The entire drive to the station, I white-knuckled the steering wheel, praying it wasn't as bad as my imagination was making it out to me.

Please, don't let this be too bad. Please. I can't shake the mental image of overturned desks and bullet holes in the walls from my head. He wouldn't go completely off the rails like that... would he? I wish I was confident enough to believe my own thoughts, but I'm not. My father is determined to get to the bottom of this and has nothing left to lose.

I climb the stairs leading up to the enormous glass doors, my heart pounding into my throat. At least the glass is intact, so I'll take that as a good sign.

The air is thick and heavy as soon as I step inside. Right away, the cop behind the desk cuts me off, "Excuse me, Miss, do you have an appointment." I halt in my tracks and scan the station for Ken.

Across the room, Ken spots me from the back corner, near his office. "Let her through, Tim." With a reluctant shake of his head, Tim steps out of the way and I walk around him. I sigh and swallow around the knot that's forming in my throat. *Okay.* Everything looks like it's in one piece. No desks overturned, and no bullet holes. Things already appear better than I thought they would be. Snickers and whispers resound from across the room. Don't they have anything better to do than sit here and gossip? All I can think is: *Which one of you screwed him over?*

My teeth bite into my tongue. I know better than to lash out with words. It won't change their opinion, anyway. They could be watching me right now, knowing what they've done. A couple of plain-clothed officers—detectives maybe, I don't know—mutter to each other while following my progress.

Ken waves me over to him while his gaze sweeps from me to his office and back again. "I managed to convince him to quiet down," he mutters out of the corner of his mouth. "Told him it was either that or I'd have to throw him down in a holding cell."

He grimaces like the thought makes him uncomfortable. I guess that would be rock bottom; to end up where you've placed so many people before.

Through the office door windows, I can see half of my father sitting in the chair behind Ken's desk, his hands behind his back. "You restrained him?" I whisper, horrified.

"I didn't want to, but I was running out of options," he says while throwing a bitter look toward the door. "It was the only way I could ensure he wouldn't try to log into the network from my computer."

"That makes sense." Even if I hate it, I can tell he does, too. This can't be easy for him after all the time they've known each other.

Still, before I can set foot in that room, I need to know what I'm up against, "What happened?"

Ken blows out a sigh, shaking his head. "Came into the station ranting and raving. Throwing accusations around, yelling like a crazy person about blood-money and murderers. When they tried to apprehend him, he swung at a couple of the guys. Luckily I was here and was able to step in and take over."

"Which guys?" I scan the room, except what am I hoping to find?

A few black eyes, perhaps. It's wrong, though a big part of me hopes he got to hit at least one of them. Even if it's awful for my father to behave this way, to lash out and act irrationally. Someone in this station helped cover up my mother's murder.

"None of that matters. I called you because I need you to calm him down and get him home before this escalates any further. Do you think you can get through to him?"

Goddamnit, Dad. All I can do is shake my head. "I don't have a choice, do I?" And that, I think, is what sucks most of all about this. I *don't* have a choice. I can't remember the last time I did. It's either help or allow them to throw him in a cell.

I feel like a mother getting ready to scold her misbehaving son. Still, after everything he's put me through lately, I can't seem to push away my remorse for him. I'm just one more person telling him he's mistaken, and he's heard so much of that already.

This is not the place, however. There are too many eyes here. I don't want to buy into all of his theories and go down the rabbit hole with him, but I can't pretend there isn't uncertainty in my gut that gets bigger the longer I stand here. There's an energy of resentment that coats the air like heavy smoke.

I want to help. I don't want to encourage these people. The muscles in my stomach are tightening. I'm walking a tightrope as I open the door, then pull the blinds over the window. Ken will understand my need for privacy.

"Christ." My father's eyes flutter closed, his head falling back as soon as he realizes it's me. "I don't know what I expected, although it definitely wasn't you."

My resolve breaks at the sight of him and the sound of his frustration. Everything I was thinking of saying, all the measured calm words, they're nothing but an afterthought. "Nice to see you too, but it doesn't appear like you're having that great of a time." I pause, walking around the desk to be right in front of him. "What did you think you would accomplish by showing up here?"

It's like we're on some twisted crime show, only he's sitting on the wrong side of the desk—and he's restrained, like the criminal. "Isn't it bad enough that you lost your job? Now you show back up and start spouting off shit and making a scene?"

His eyes fly open. "You know?"

"Yes, I've known for days." Maybe I shouldn't have said it that way, nonetheless at least it's out. "And I don't care if you're upset. I was worried about you and needed answers. Little did I know there is much more that I need to worry about."

He only sighs. "I don't need to be lectured."

Funny. I expected him to be this blubbering, slurring mess, but he's as straight and sober as I can remember ever seeing him. There are dark circles under his eyes, but the eyes themselves aren't bloodshot. They're clear, focused. He even shaved today. He still looks unhealthy—he's lost weight, his skin is ashen, and his clothes are starting to bag on him. Thankfully, he's sober. However, more than anything... he's tired and at his wit's end.

My heart hurts for him. That's what leaves a tremble in my voice. "Dad. I know... I know you're trying to do everything you can to bring justice to Mom, but this has to stop."

"How?" There's as much pain in his voice as in mine. "How do I stop myself? Because trust me, baby, I would love for this to end. I just... I need somebody to tell me how to overcome it, since I can't do it. I can't. I know your mom would want me to. Only I can't. Every time I consider letting it go, this voice at the back of my head reminds me that someone is getting away with all of this."

"There are other ways to do this. But coming here? Accusing people?"

"I had to shake them up somehow."

I can't believe I'm about to say this. But to say anything else would be disingenuous and might do more harm than good. It's challenging to go against what good sense tells me I should do.

I've been heeding to good sense for too long, anyway. And look where it got me.

"Listen to me," I whisper. "If you honestly think somebody here covered up what happened to Mom, do you think the best thing to do is put the attention on yourself? To make a scene? Now more people are going to be asking questions."

"No," he scoffs. "They'll dismiss it and call me a joke. Like they have been for forever."

"I understand, though I need you to think with your head and not your heart. For your own safety."

His gaze tone turns accusingly, "You're not going to tell me I'm out of my mind?"

"I can't possibly tell you that you're crazy, not even if it feels that way. You're entitled to feel how you want to feel. All I have to say is if what you're saying is true, then you need to be careful. Not draw attention or make a scene. I want to help you however I can."

"I wish I could believe that," he murmurs before sighing in that 'disappointed dad' way. "There's no point in lying, Bianca. We both know that's not true."

"What do you mean?" I ask, confused.

"Don't we?"

"You're going to have to stop speaking in riddles."

"I know. I know about everything."

Like a guilty child, immediately, my thoughts go to the baby as guilt threatens to consume me. I grip the edge of the desk to balance myself while my knees threaten to crumble beneath me. "What? How could you know about that?"

His eyebrows shoot up so far, so fast, they look like they want to leave his head. "He didn't tell you? I thought for sure that was why you didn't come home."

Straightaway I know we're talking about two different things. Now I'm more puzzled than ever. "If you're referring to Callum, he told me nothing. I have no idea what you're talking about."

"Huh. I wonder why..." He shrugs like it doesn't matter anyway. "Your old man made a fool of himself, again. I was certain the asshole would tell you right away. Surely he'd never miss the opportunity to make me look like an idiot."

"What did you do?" I whisper over my growing horror.

"I just want to know why? That's all I want to know. Of all the men in the world, why did it have to be him that you chose?"

"He... told you?" Shock ripples through me as I drop into the chair behind me.

"It was a mistake. I'm not proud of myself for going to his house." He looks down at his lap, his jaw twitching. "I wasn't thinking."

"No. Tell me you didn't." This gets worse by the second.

"I did. And I'm sure it's a house you're very familiar with by now." Not missing the subtle hits he's making. He meets my gaze from beneath his lowered brow. "More familiar than ever."

Guilt wells up in my chest before I realize what's happening. I should've known he would turn this around, but how could I have known he knew? The truth is I had no way of knowing, not unless Callum... he should have warned me. Damnit.

Instead of collapsing under shame, I force myself to steadily meet his gaze. "We are not doing this," I hiss through my teeth. "You're not turning this around on me, making me feel guilty. I could easily walk out of here and let Ken throw you into a holding cell the way he would have done if he didn't care about you so much."

Folding my arms across my chest, I can't help but smirk. "So, what's it going to be? We can talk about things, but you will not shame me. I'm an adult, and I'm tired of being treated like a child by you."

"Tell me why. Why him?"

"I'm still not sure what you're talking about."

"You know what I mean. He told me he loves you, yet I don't understand why you chose him. He's a bad man. The things he's done and will continue to do. You could do better."

"He told you..." *He loves me?* Said it out loud? To my father? Either my head's going to explode, or my heart's going to burst.

"Also said that you are a grown woman and can make your own

decisions." He scoffs, shrugging. "I know you're a grown woman who can make your own decisions. I just wish they were the right ones."

"So let me get this straight." Since I don't know whether to be pissed, laugh, or cry. "The two of you had a conversation about *us* without me knowing about it."

He nods. "I figured he'd told you already."

"When was this?"

"Friday. I'm not proud of myself. I went to the house, as I said, and I... I was enraged. I wanted to kill him. And then he told me that you were both together."

My heart sinks when his eyes start to well with tears. "Why? Don't you know who he is and what he does? Do you know how dangerous he is? He's the enemy, Bianca."

"I... yes, I do know." I'm not sure what to say. I had only wished to share the news of Callum and me with my father someday, only mainly in my dreams. "It doesn't matter what you think of him. I care about him too much for it to make a difference. I can't entirely agree with some of his actions, though I can't stop him either."

"Even when you know how dangerous being with him is?" A tear rolls down his cheek, sparkling in the overhead fluorescent light. "I want better for you than that. Hell, you deserve better. Does it not bother you that he could get you killed."

Did Mom think being married to a cop would get her killed? God, I can't believe that thought even entered my mind. It's too cruel. I'll chalk it up to how long of a day it's been. At least I didn't say it out loud. That's the kind of thing I could never take back.

"Sometimes, you make a choice, and that's it. But the thing is, with us, there is no choice. Believe it or not, I tried very hard to do what I thought was right and stay away from him. Except I can't. I just can't do it. And I'm tired of fighting against what I want. I never wanted you to find out," I admit, and he snorts, rolling his eyes. "I knew you would feel this way. And I don't want to hurt you, Dad. I love you. I wish this could all be over for you. I sincerely do."

"It will never be over," he insists, shaking his head. "All this time, knowing there had to be more to it, that I couldn't be the only one who knew. I've been carrying this around inside me for years. I just can't do it anymore. I need to know what happened, and nobody wants to tell me." He looks toward the covered window, his voice going tight, strained. "Nobody wants to help me."

I have never seen somebody so alone. Weighed down. Gaslit to hell and back by people he was supposed to trust. "You are sure you know what you saw? You're certain, a hundred percent, that there was more to it?"

"Yes, damn it." He pleads with his eyes, with the pain chiseled across his forehead, in the corners of his eyes. "I know. I saw it."

"Then I will. I'll help you."

"No." He shakes his head hard, his voice firm. "Absolutely not. It's too dangerous."

"Stop." I stand, and this time I round the desk to put my hands on his shoulders. Right now, he's as close to my real dad as he's been in weeks. It's so much easier to talk to him when he's like this—level-headed, calm. "I'm already part of this. They're all going to know that I know what you're thinking, just because I'm here right now. If you're worried, I'm not afraid, Dad."

"You should be."

"I'm not. I will help you as much as I can, though there's one thing you have to understand. Callum didn't do it. I know," I quickly add when he opens his mouth, "that's easy for me to say, and it's true. However, I know he wouldn't murder an innocent woman to save his own skin."

He blows out a sigh. "He did seem stunned when I confronted him about it. Like he didn't have any idea what I was talking about." With a snort, he adds, "I might have been drunk, but I've questioned enough people over the years that I know how to read a face."

Of course, he was drunk. "Then you believe him?"

He eyes me, his lips set in a thin, disapproving line. "Once he came clean about the two of you, I saw how serious he was about making sure I knew he cared. He said he would never hurt you, and I'm not dumb. He could have gotten rid of me pretty easily if he was guilty and didn't want you to know."

"Wow. That's the most reasonable thing you've said... in a long time."

"I had a lot of time to think about it." He gives me a sheepish expression, "No matter how many times I went through it, I couldn't force myself to be all right with this. Then I reminded myself that it's your life, and I don't want you to be afraid to tell me things."

He thinks that, but how would he feel if I told him I'm keeping a secret right now? I can't even think about it. Not now.

"From now on, we'll both try to be better about that. Okay? And you will not under any circumstances come back here ranting and raving and throwing punches. I'm serious, Dad. It's too risky. I'll try to be careful, but you must also be careful. Okay?"

"Okay." He eyes the door warily. "I'll do my best, but it doesn't change my stance. I know someone out there had a part in covering it up."

"I know," I whisper, bending down to press a kiss against his forehead. "And we're going to find out who that person was, but we're going to be smart about it. You are not alone in this anymore." He releases a strangled sob that leaves me fighting back sniffles, but the moment passes without either of us blubbering.

Ken comes in as soon as I knock on the door, and after he makes Dad promise to behave himself, he uses a pocket knife to cut the zip tie around his wrists. "Straight out the door," he mutters, and Dad nods. I'm sure by now, all he wants is to go home and try to put this behind him. I know that's what I want.

The car ride is quiet. Then within an hour, we're home, with Dad fed and showered. He's calmer, almost peaceful. Like all it took was hearing me say I believe him, to soothe the ache in his chest. "Good night, Dad. Everything will look better in the morning. I promise."

"I sure hope so." He mumbles and makes his way to bed.

I couldn't agree more. Now the only thing left to do is deal with my own problems. In a way, it's easier to focus on him than to turn around and handle my own shit.

What am I going to do? I'm a wreck. Between the baby, my dad, and everything else. The idea of staying here isn't appealing. I want to be with Callum, but he isn't my favorite person right now, either.

He could have told me. He should have told me. I deserved to know. If I go to him, I'm sure he'll give me some bullshit about wanting to protect me or something along those lines. I'm so tired of everybody thinking they know what's best for me.

What I need more than anything is to feel safe. I need that more than I ever have—one hand drifts down to my belly, where our baby is growing. We both need safety, security. I know this, and the idea of telling him still has me in knots. Maybe it's not fair of me to be mad at him for keeping things from me when I intend to keep this from him, at least for a little while. Until I can get a feel for how he'll take it.

That thought only leads me to others.

What happens if he doesn't want the baby?

Could Amanda be right?

He told Dad he loved me. Callum wouldn't have said something like that, much less to my father, if he didn't mean it. I hate that everything is hinged on hope, but it's all I have. Hope that everything will work out for the best. Hope that my father will find happiness again, and hope that Callum won't abandon me when he discovers I'm pregnant.

CALLUM

What was that noise?

My eyes fly open, my heart racing out of my chest. There was a noise somewhere in the house. Unless I dreamed it—I didn't even know I had fallen asleep.

Passed out is more like it. Sitting in my chair, alone, where I ended up after I cleaned the mess on the floor. The thought of Bianca returning to the house and seeing that mess haunted me. I couldn't just leave it, yet I also refused to have anyone else do it.

And it was a brief respite from the blame I heaped on myself once the worst of my drunken stupidity passed. I should've been there for my daughter. I should have been the sort of father she could come to when Kristoff first started hurting her–since I doubt it started in Europe. I should've been there for her in these past weeks, insisting we find her a therapist, all of it.

Somewhere along the way, I lost sight of my priorities. I've had the rest of the night to sit here and hate myself for it before passing out.

My heartbeat slows once I'm aware of my surroundings. All is well, minus the fact that I'm alone. It's no one's fault but my own. Once again, I fucked up everything.

I pull out my cell and check the time. It's nearly midnight. My heart sinks at the lack of a text from Bianca. Hopefully, she's okay. I should text her, ask her, except I'm sure she must've gone to bed by now. It doesn't really matter. I don't deserve an update, which only makes me more convinced that Charlie's turning her against me.

She loves you, you idiot.

I need to get my shit together. I'm spiraling and not as drunk as I was earlier. I can't blame it all on the whiskey, even if my brain is still foggy. That's not an excuse. I can't turn this into a capital offense. I cannot continue making the same mistakes. I'm stronger than this. Better than this.

My eyes are dry, tired, and I rub my knuckles over them while trying to work up the energy to get out of this chair and go up to bed before I pass out again. I'll hate myself for it in the morning otherwise—my neck is stiff and aching from the awkward position I left it in for a couple of hours.

I let my hands fall into my lap with a sigh—only to find a mirage forming before me. That must be what it is. I'm either still asleep or imagining things because there is no way I'm looking at my little bird, the love of my life, standing in front of me, wearing an expression of worry.

"Callum? Is everything okay? What happened tonight?"

"Is it really you?" I whisper, my voice thick.

"No, it's my evil twin sister." She snickers, her gaze swinging around the room. "What happened, and why does it smell like a distillery?" Before I can respond, she walks over to a window and opens it, allowing in a soft breeze. I'm not surprised it smells like a distillery; I did cover the floor in whiskey.

None of that matters now. Not the destruction I caused. Not the things I did or said. I can't get over the fact that she's here. That she came back. Whatever her father said to her wasn't enough to make her hate me.

"How many drinks have you had?" she asks, turning in my direction.

"Enough."

She eyes the empty bottle in the wastebasket, her mouth curving into a frown. "Are you trying to kill yourself? Because there are quicker and cheaper ways than drinking a ten thousand dollar bottle of whiskey."

"Don't you know by now?"

"Don't I know what?"

"That you're the only person who has the power to kill me. The only person I would even let try."

She offers a sad smile, her blue eyes roaming my body. "I don't know. You look like you're trying hard enough yourself." She's not lying. My hair is disheveled, my shirt untucked and hanging open. I don't allow anyone to see me like this, especially not her. It would make me weak in the eyes of anyone else, but I don't care. Not right now.

"You came back," I whisper.

"There's nowhere else I'd rather be."

Her words stir a deeper longing in my chest, and I can't help but reach for her. I need to touch her, feel her in my arms. "Come here. Please. I need you." I can't bear to let another moment pass without touching.

She came back. She's here because she wants to be, needs to be, and needs me the way I need her. The way I need oxygen to continue breathing, the way the sky needs the stars, and the flowers need rain. Without thought, she walks into my waiting arms, crawling onto my lap. My vision is still blurry, but I can't mistake that she's still wearing dress clothes. "Long day?" I whisper, sliding a hand over her leg, then up her back.

"The longest on record." She sighs.

"Is everything alright?" I ask, stroking her back.

"Better now." She buries her face in my neck, and I close my eyes, welcoming the sense of peace that washes over me. She's here. I'm holding her; this is real. She came back to me.

A string of silent moments passes before she lifts her head again, looking at me, looking through me like only she can. My heart's so full I don't know what to do. I don't know what to think. There's no way she could comprehend the hold she has over me. The power.

I can't go another second without kissing her. She tastes like coming home. Her full lips part willingly, easily, but I go slow. Savoring. I was so sure she would turn against me. I didn't know until now how confident I was. Every kiss is rain on parched desert earth, and I take one after another, helpless in the face of my need for her.

"Hold on." She shakes her head a little, turning her face away. "We need to talk."

"Okay?"

"I know you told my dad. About us."

Damn it. I should have known it wouldn't be that easy. I was always going to have to fess up, and it only makes sense that now would be the time. "I did, and I'm sorry. It came out before I could stop it."

"Did you ever think that maybe you should warn me first? Give me a heads-up? So I would know what to expect from him?"

"It's complicated. I wasn't trying to keep it from you." It still is—more than ever. The memory stick is still inserted into the drive, a reminder of the invisible barrier between us. A barrier only I can break down by finding and killing the bastard who took her mother away from her.

"Everything is complicated. All the time. I can't remember the last time something wasn't complicated." She frowns. "But it would have been nice to know ahead of time. Talking to him is like trying to talk someone off a cliff's edge sometimes. He's irrational at best and even more so regarding me."

"I'm sorry. Really, I am."

"I thought we said we'd be honest with each other going forward."

She has no idea what honesty looks like. What opening that box would do to her. The impact it would have on both of us. I want to give her that, but selfishly I don't because that might mean losing her. "Bianca... I didn't want to hurt you, and that's the truth. When he showed up, he was in bad shape. I figured he wouldn't want you to know."

Her brows draw together, and she sighs. "I know. You couldn't tell me he knew about us without divulging the situation. I get it. It just honestly bothers me when I'm the last to know something."

Her soft, silky hair slides through my fingers when I tuck it behind her ear. "I'm sorry for making you feel that way. The whole time you've been gone today, I cursed myself for not coming clean with you."

"Hey, it's okay." She assures me with a tentative smile.

Stroking her cheek, I ask, "What happened? Did he give you shit? Threaten to kill me?"

"Surprisingly, no. He's unhappy, but he didn't blow up as I expected."

"I'm... I'm glad he didn't lose his shit."

"Why did you tell him?" She bites her lip, an unknown emotion lingering in her eyes. "Did you do it to hurt him?"

"Absolutely not. At first, I thought he knew, and that's why he was here. I blurted it out before I realized he didn't know. He only wanted you to stay away from Tatum, and me, by extension. It was too late when I realized we were talking about two different things."

"Shit, this is a mess." She studies one of my shirt buttons, staring at it so intensely I would think she's never seen one before. "Is it true... what you told him? That you love me?"

"It's true. I did say that."

Her head snaps up, her blue eyes piercing mine. "Did you mean it?"

The hope shining in her eyes is an arrow going straight through my chest. "I don't say things I don't mean. And if you actually have to ask me that, I haven't done a very good job of showing you how I feel."

She blinks as if she's confused. "You've done a pretty poor job of it lately, now that you mention it."

"I accept that, and I'm sorry. This isn't all about control or ownership," I murmur, tracing the curve of her jaw, the line of her throat, and then down her collarbone. "You're mine, and you'll always be mine, but how I feel about you is at the center of everything. I want us. And if it means having to tell your father, even while knowing how he feels about me, then that's what has to be done."

"I'm just shocked. It's a huge risk for you."

"No, it wasn't." I run my thumb over her bottom lip, teasing the softest sigh from her. "I would walk through fire for you. I would burn the world to ash, lie, cheat, steal, kill. I'd do anything for you. Anything you ask, it's yours. I will find a way."

"I think I'm scared."

"Of what?" All I can imagine is the sort of fear Charlie put in her head.

Instead, she manages to surprise me. "I'm worried that eventually, things are going to get real."

"And you mean to tell me they aren't real now?"

"Of course they are, but what happens after all of this? When the fun wears off? Will you still want me when I'm not... you know, forbidden fruit?" A soft laugh escapes her, like it's all a joke, but even in my inebriated state, I feel her uncertainty—the hard, frightening edge.

"I'm a lot of things, Bianca," I start, while linking my arms around her back to pull her against my chest. "I've made mistakes, God knows, but I'm not stupid and definitely not naïve. Things change, people change, and time is a bitch, though I refuse to let you think for one minute that my feelings for you could do anything but deepen with time. Nothing's going to change how I feel about you. I will only ever want you more with every day that passes and every beat of my heart."

Taking her hand, I place it over the spot in question, her skin touching mine. "It's yours, completely. Just like every inch of me. All of me. And until the day I stop breathing, Bianca, I will want you. Only you. Nothing will ever change that."

She surprises me when she sits up straighter while rearranging herself in my lap. "What are you doing?" I ask when her fingers start undoing my belt.

"What do you think?" Her blue eyes glitter with mischief, and she wears a shy grin while opening my pants and reaching inside my boxers. My semi-hard cock instantly goes rigid at the touch of her fingers. "I'm going to fuck you. That is, unless you don't want me to?"

This is different. Sitting back, letting her take control. She only gets up long enough to slide her panties to the floor, then hikes her dress up to her hips and gives me the briefest, teasing glimpse of her bare pussy before straddling me again. I'm burning with desire. The temptation to lay her flat on my desk and devour her pussy until I'm starved of oxygen claims every thought in my brain, but somehow I manage to stay seated, curious to see my little bird flap her wings.

Rising up, she guides my thick head to her sopping entrance. There's something ridiculously erotic about watching her do this. Letting her take control, own me.

Her expression transforms into pure bliss, and her eyes flutter closed as she slowly eases herself down onto my length. Her wet, tight heat swallows every inch of my cock down to my base. Fuck. I look down between where our bodies join. I want to watch her tits bounce as I thrust deep inside her, owning her with my cock, claiming her as only I can.

Her mouth falls open, and her breath quickens before she settles in with a soft groan.

"This is all I'll ever want," I whisper, caught between the sensation of being gripped from head to base by her tight muscles and my fascination at watching her take what she needs from me. "To be balls deep inside you, watching your face change as you take every inch of my cock like the good girl you are."

I run my hands up her thighs, over her hips, gripping them firmly while she rolls them in a slow circle, grinding hard against me. I grit my teeth at the pleasure that ripples through me.

"That's right," I grunt, "use my cock. Fuck me, make yourself come. I want to feel your pussy strangling my cock."

"Oh, my God," she breathes, her head rolling from side to side, while she lifts herself up and down, riding me slowly, coating my balls with her juices that drip down my cock. When I reach behind her, fumbling for her zipper to get her out of this dress, so I can see her perfect tits and taste her nipples, she shakes her head.

Opening her eyes, she whispers, "Just like this. All I need is to feel you inside me."

I growl but settle for fondling her ass, stroking her cheeks, molding her flesh while she works herself into a blissful frenzy.

"That's it. That's my good girl. Fuck me, Bianca. I'm always shocked by how well you take my cock. Like it was made for you." I take a handful of her hair and pull her in, my lips devouring hers the moment they touch. Every sweep of my tongue, every nip of my teeth against her full, juicy lips, leaves her moaning into my mouth, guttural sounds that make my balls lift in anticipation of the way she's going to milk every drop of cum out of me. Her tiny nails sink deep into the flesh of my chest, the sting of pain an afterthought. I'll go through anything to keep her at my side.

"Look at me," I rasp, our hot breaths mingling. "Open your eyes. Look at me, Bianca."

Nothing could prepare me for the rush of heat and feebleness that races through me like fire when I gaze into those blue eyes. Eyes I've left full of tears, eyes that have radiated faith and trust. Eyes that are now full of lust, yet there's something deeper flickering in those endless pools of blue.

Something that leaves me exposed. Wide open. It hits me with all the force of a train and is almost enough to make me stop her, to stop all of this. It's too much; I don't know what to do with it. The feeling of her staring into my soul, seeing all the fractured pieces. All the dirty, ugly parts of me.

"Come with me," she rasps, driving herself down. Her ass slaps against my thighs, the sound filling the room as her strokes turn faster, and harder. Every downward stroke rubs her clit against my base while I move inside her. "Please, Callum. Come inside me. Fill me with your seed."

The way she begs is so fucking pretty that I have no choice but to thrust my hips up, pushing deep inside her, my cock hitting the back of her pussy with every penetrating stroke. Our frantic gasps for air fill the room like I'm filling her, stretching her, making her moan my name in helpless abandon.

"Callum... oh god," she whimpers, and I grip her closer, owning her, imprinting myself on her while I continue to jackhammer into her tightness. Her muscles grip me like a vice, and her entire body tenses. Then like a bomb, she explodes, rippling with pleasure as a million tiny muscles massage me, drawing the cum from my balls.

"Fuck, baby, you make it impossible for me not to cum when your pussy squeezes me so hard," I grit through my teeth while trying to elongate her orgasm.

"Callum," she purrs, pressing her face into the side of my neck, burrowing against me like a kitten. Then, the moment her lips touch my throat, I explode. The first spurt shoots from my tip into her hot, pulsing core. I swear I cum forever. On and on it goes, until our combined juices drip from her while she lies against me, gasping for air, warm and trembling and so very mine. Nothing is going to take her from me. Nothing and no one. She's the other half of my soul, the thing that keeps my heart beating.

As badly as I want this moment to remain, I need to get us into bed where we can continue. Snaking a hand between our bodies, I lift her gently and zip my pants before standing and gathering her in my arms, cradling her against my chest.

"Where are you taking me?" She wraps her arms around my

neck and tucks her head under my chin. Now that she's come, she's loose and relaxed, her voice thick.

"To bed, of course. Unless you wanted to sleep in the chair."

Tonight, I'm going to hold her while I sleep. I'm going to hold her because I need to remember, even when I'm not awake, that she's with me. That she's still mine. Even if the fear of what she will soon discover has me terrified to tell her the truth. No, I wasn't the one to kill her mother, but the associates I worked with did. I can only hope she'll forgive me because living without her is no longer an option.

"Callum... I love you." She whispers against my skin, and my heart lurches in my chest.

I don't know what I would do without her by my side. My queen, my love. And I never want to have to find out. I gently place her on the bed and take her face into my hands. Her blue eyes are hazy with sleep. She's content in my arms, and I love the way she looks at me like I'm the keeper of her world.

Pressing my nose to hers, I breathe deeply, "I love you too, and I'll do anything in my power to make sure you see it and feel it every day. I need you by my side, with me through it all. There is no me without you, Bianca. I hope you see that."

"Always." She whispers and then presses her lips against mine, making everything else around us dissolve into the air.

BIANCA

At first, I don't know what's happening when I feel light pressure against my temple. Once, twice. Ugh, something keeps touching me. I try to shrug it off, since all I want to do is sleep. My body is limp with exhaustion, and I'm so comfortable. It feels like the bed has molded itself around me. I burrow deeper against it, hoping for sleep to grip back onto me and pull me under.

It's the soft, deep chuckle in my ear that brings me back to the present. My lips turn up at the sides as Callum pulls me close, making me the little spoon to his bigger one. His strong arms wrap tightly around me, and I bask in the warmth of his body heat. Now I really don't want to get up, ever. Never. I could happily spend the rest of my life wrapped up in him and these amazingly soft sheets.

Too bad my anxious brain has other thoughts. "How are you feeling?" I whisper, just in case his head's about to split open after all the drinking he did. I'm surprised he even has the energy to kiss me, which is what woke me up in the first place. His soft, tender strokes against my temple and ear.

"Surprisingly well," he murmurs between kisses. "You are the ultimate hangover cure."

"I don't know about that." I can't believe he feels okay, although I do believe he would try his best to make it seem that way for my sake.

"Do you have to go to work today?" he asks. When he strokes my arms, his fingers trailing over my breasts, I instantly wish the answer was no. I wish I could stay here forever. Connecting the two of us. It's the most natural, crucial thing. I haven't felt this good, this right, ever.

It's unfortunate what being an adult has turned me into. "I'm afraid I've already missed enough workdays."

"If I had it my way, you wouldn't have to worry about going to work."

"I know, but your alpha tendencies get slightly out of hand. I sort of like having a say in my own life sometimes." Even if it sucks having no choice in getting up and facing the world when it's the last thing I want to do. Especially now, with the first rays of dawn's light streaming through the window. Everything is hazy and golden outside, and everything in this bed is peaceful and sweet. One of those perfect moments you want to capture to hold and try to freeze, so it never changes.

Sadly it never works. All we can do is try to be where we are when we're there. Allowing myself another minute, I close my eyes and melt into his arms, smiling at the kisses he keeps raining on me. "You're going to rub your lips raw," I finally point out with a soft laugh.

"I would rather rub your lips raw."

Immediately, heat flares in my core. The only thing stopping me from inviting him to do that is knowing I have to go back home to get dressed for work. I should have known better than to think I wouldn't stay the night once I got here. I wasn't thinking clearly.

The reminder of how real life exists outside this bedroom makes my heart sink. Not because of the baby itself but because of everything that accompanies pregnancy. It would be the simplest thing if

I told him right now—it would seem almost poetic in a way, considering the baby might have been created in this very bed. And with Callum in such a soft, gentle, romantic mood, he has a better chance of taking it well. Of being happy.

Just do it, then. He deserves to know.

I open my mouth, ready to blurt it out. Only, I can't find the words. You'd think it would be easy. *I'm pregnant. I'm going to have your baby. I don't know how it happened, but it's true.*

And then there are all the unspoken feelings that go along with that. *Please, love me anyway. Please, love our baby. Let's do this together.*

I'm a coward. I can't bring myself to say it. I guess it doesn't have to happen right away, this very minute, but I have to tell him soon. Eventually, he'll be able to realize it without me breaking the news—even now, at this very moment, he's running his hand over my stomach, teasing me, acting like he's going to dip lower. His touches have the power to make me late for work, make me wish for this to never end. My stomach's not going to be flat forever.

"I have an idea." I roll onto my back, gratefully accepting his kiss. I would never have imagined him being this sweet and loving. It's almost like a reward for hanging on all this time, refusing to give up on him. On us.

"You're going to stay in bed with me all day?" he murmurs, nuzzling my neck. "Yes, yes, I think that is an excellent idea."

"I was thinking more along the lines of taking a shower together. I'll do that here, but then I have to run home and get dressed."

"If I ever say no to that offer," he growls, nibbling my neck until I have to stifle a moan, "I want you to get me checked out by a doctor, because obviously there's something wrong."

I can't help stroking his scruffy cheek when he lifts his head, grinning. The way the sunlight hits his eyes makes them gleam and sparkle. He has the face of an angel—dark angel or not, it doesn't matter which. He's absolutely handsome. I wonder if the baby will look like him.

"Why are you smiling?" he whispers before kissing the tip of my nose.

"I don't know. 'Cause I'm happy."

"That's how I want you always to feel. Happy."

"It's not possible to *always* be happy," I point out, still stroking his face, his dark russet brown hair, memorizing every fleck of light in his green eyes. "Or else we would never appreciate it, right?"

"That doesn't stop me from wanting it for you, for making it happen. You deserve nothing but happiness."

"A few minutes ago, you kissed me awake. If that's not happiness, I don't know what is."

He closes his eyes, groaning. "And you expect me to let you out of this bed after saying something like that?"

"Come on." I give his ass a playful smack before wiggling out of his embrace, as much as I really don't want to. "We'd better get moving before I do something stupid like let you convince me to stay."

"Oh, no, we wouldn't want that." He reaches for me, but I manage to get away. However, I'm barely on my feet before he scrambles off the foot of the bed and throws his arms around me. My laughter rings out as he lifts me off my feet and carries me into the bathroom. He's like a little kid—playful, silly. Is this the effect I have on him? Do I make it so he feels safe to show this side of himself?

"What's wrong?" he asks after returning to me once the shower is running. "You have a funny look on your face."

"Not a thing in the world," I assure him. "Everything is perfect."

The curve of his lips is soft, and before we step into the shower, he takes my face in his hands and kisses me. Those tentative lips of his own me, stealing the air from my lungs. The sweet taste of whiskey still lingers on his tongue, but I don't mind. I sink deeper into his embrace, clinging to him. He is the stormy sea, and I am the cliff's edge. The circumstances in which we meet are always different, yet no matter what, we're always linked. I can see it always being this way. This simplicity of being together, of being content because I'm here and he's here and we don't have to hold back. Nothing is standing in our way—no more secrets or lies.

Well, almost nothing. He doesn't know about the baby, and he doesn't know about the run-in with Amanda or her stupid comments that may or may not have made me second-guess things. She doesn't matter. I don't want to think about her now, or ever. I close my eyes once I step under the warm spray, willing myself to let all thoughts of her wash away.

"Just think." Callum steps in behind me, and I turn to him, wrapping my arms around his waist while the water runs over our skin. "If you lived here all the time, we could do this every day." His perfectly sculpted body molds against mine. For an older man, he sure does have the physique of a twenty-year-old.

He genuinely is like a little boy trying to get his own way. And I love him for it. Nevertheless, I have to at least pretend to be stern. "Are you trying to convince me to move in with you?"

"Is it working?" he counters with a devilish smile that makes me weak in the knees.

"You know how much I love this. Being together."

"But..."

"But it's not fair to say things like that when we're both naked in the shower."

"Oh, sweet Bianca. You know I don't play fair." His grin deepens, and his dimples pop out. "Why would you pay rent someplace else when you could live here for free?" As I open my mouth, he adds, "Don't talk. Just stop and think for a minute. You wouldn't have to worry about your dad anymore." He groans, his rock-hard cock growing between us. " I think I'm losing my mind because I can't believe I actually mentioned him while in this position with you."

"Yeah, not very sexy." I grab a loofa and put some soap on it. He takes it from me and begins running it over my neck, chest, and shoulders. There's nothing sexual about his touch, though it warms me from the inside out. Is this what it would be like, the two of us together all the time? Both of us, just vaguely horny, morning, noon, and night?

"However, my point stands." He definitely slows down while he is soaping up my tits, and I'm not about to tell him to hurry up when it feels this good. We really don't have time for things to go any further, though, not if I want to make it home, to get myself ready for work.

"There are still too many complications." I sigh. He lets out a low growl and I place my hands on top of his, stopping him from washing me further. I stare into his eyes, needing him to understand that I mean what I'm about to say. "I know it makes you unhappy to hear this, and It makes me unhappy too. Nonetheless, it's not the right time. It would still feel wrong. I know it's what we both want. That we're adults, but there's too much in the way."

"I know." He wears a sad smile and shrugs before continuing to clean me. "Can you blame a man for trying, especially when the woman he wants looks like you?"

"I'd think you were in need of a doctor if you didn't try to use sex to get me to agree to something." I smirk.

"Wait until I have access to you all the time. There won't be any stopping me from fucking you on every surface in this house."

Immediate guilt knots in my belly. *Nothing but a baby.* Once the truth is out, everything will change. I should tell him, I really should. Only I still can't make the words come out. Fear makes them turn to ice blocks on my tongue.

I'm afraid this will all disappear if I burst our bubble by discussing a baby. That's the kind of thing I can't take back. There's no pretending this isn't happening, so I have to get comfortable with being uncomfortable.

I also need to have a little more faith in him. He's the one that told me he wanted a baby. There's no way his feelings have altered, not when his emotions have deepened. The words Amanda spoke linger at the forefront of my mind. I know she was being a vile bitch and trying to get back at me, but I let her get in my head, anyway. There's no one to blame for that but myself. A leopard doesn't change its spots, and I knew Amanda was this way, so why am I shocked by anything she's said?

I'm sorry, little baby. I just want us to enjoy a few minutes together without any big drama before breaking the news. That's all.

"Turn around," he whispers, and I do, leaning against his broad, firm chest before he starts massaging shampoo into my hair.

"Oh, my God, that feels good..." I'm practically swooning, my scalp tingling, and my knees going weak. When I reach out behind me, taking hold of his hips for balance, his sexy chuckle ignites a fire deep in my belly.

"Careful, now. You'll wake up the beast, and we both know what happens when you do that." As it is, I feel him twitching against my ass, and the temptation to wrap a hand around his cock is almost too much to resist.

"If I didn't know better," I whisper, "I would think you're trying to get me fired."

"Who, me?" There's a devilish tone to his voice.

"Yes, you old man."

"Old man?" He snickers. "If I recall, it was you who was begging me to stop last night because you couldn't take it anymore, so who's old?"

"Fine." I giggle, and he finishes shampooing my hair before pulling the shower head free and using it to rinse the strands.

"No, to tell you the truth, this is nice. Thank you for reminding me."

"Reminding you of what?"

He tips my head back gently, and I go with the motion, sighing when the water hits my head. There's something almost erotic about letting him care for me. "You reminded me there are ways to be with a woman that doesn't involve my dick," he murmurs. "Being with you has reminded me of so many things I have forgotten. Or maybe I'm only becoming aware of these things because I see you in a different light, and you're nothing like anyone else I've ever been with. Either way, know that the sex is fantastic, and I'll forever crave your pussy. Needing it like my body needs oxygen. I enjoy your company, talking to you, touching you, and being together, and I've never had that with anyone else."

I'm stunned to silence by his confession and still thinking about it by the time we're finished, and I'm toweling my hair and he's shaving at the sink. I never imagined teaching him anything—he's supposed to be the teacher, the guy who's seen everything. There's so much more to him than I thought. More than Amanda knows, I'm sure. He's a better man than she could ever fathom.

Like an onion, I have slowly peeled back the layers of who he is.

"What are you thinking about?" My head snaps up, and I find him smirking at me in the mirror. "It seems like you're lost inside your head. Are you sure you should go to work today?"

"You are incorrigible." I leave the bathroom and put my clothes on in a hurry. Not only because I need to get out of here but because the longer I stay, the higher the chance of me spilling the beans. This is why I wanted to avoid him in the first place. The urge to hurl out the truth consumes me. I want him to know, except every time I go to tell him my brain forgets what words are.

I've just finished dressing in yesterday's clothes—without my panties, which we must've left under his desk—and pulling my wet hair back into a bun when a knock sounds against the bedroom door. Callum strolls through the room, still wearing only the towel around his waist, and opens it enough that I can see Romero standing out in the hall.

He appears annoyed, his eyes cold.

"Yes?" Callum's chilly response surprises me.

"There's something I need to discuss with you." His eyes meet mine briefly over Callum's shoulder before glancing back at Callum.

If looks could kill, I'd be dead twice over.

"Can it wait?" Callum snaps. The tension between them is thick enough to cut with a knife. This is awkward. What the hell is going on?

"Sure, although it's important."

"I need to go, anyway," I murmur, tapping Callum on the shoulder while trying to give Romero a smile at the same time. It's like the temperature just dropped twenty degrees.

"Give me a few minutes, and I'll be downstairs." He closes the door before Romero can respond, then gives me a confused look. "What?"

"You tell me," I whisper. "What gives? Did something happen between you two?"

"What happened doesn't matter. I don't want you worrying about me." I can feel it. The wall that he slid between us. It makes me want to shake him. If he had the first idea of how frustrating it is to hear that, to be dismissed when I'm concerned, he might think twice about acting the way he is. However, discussing it right now isn't an option. I don't want to start our day off with a fight.

"I'm going to have dinner with my Dad tonight," I say to him, standing on my tiptoes to give him a kiss. "There are still a few things I want to talk to him about, so I don't know how late it will be. I might just stay there."

"Let me know?" He's gentle as he takes my face in his hands. "You know how I worry about you."

"I do." And I love him for it, even if it's infuriating sometimes.

His jaw clenches, and his features draw together in a pinched, pained expression. It seems for a second like he's going to say something, but he only sighs while his shoulders sink. "Go on, then. Make me miss you all day."

"Oh, stop. I'll be back. I can only go so long without you." I smile.

Romero has already gone downstairs by the time I leave the room, and when I check the time on my phone, it leaves me rushing down the hall and out to my car. It feels almost traitorous not stopping to say hi to Tatum before I go, but then she's probably still asleep anyway. I wish I had time to leave her a note. At this rate, I'll barely have time to grab anything to eat before heading to work.

And I have to eat, don't I? It's no longer about me. It's about the tiny life growing inside of me. "I promise," I whisper once I'm in the car and rolling down the driveway. "Whatever happens, baby, I'll make sure it's the right thing for you. No matter what, I'll put you first."

CALLUM

There is nothing quite like the morning after a fight. Especially when the sight of the person you fought with brings everything back into perspective in bright, brilliant color. I only wanted to savor those last few minutes with her, but Romero's exquisite sense of timing fucked the whole thing up. It's enough to make me grind my molars as I march down the stairs. No doubt he wants a continuation of last night's bullshit. Little does he know how disinterested I am in what he thinks about my parenting skills.

Instead of waiting for me in the office or his own, he stands outside my office door. His body language screams tension: head down, cracking his knuckles, practically vibrating with nervous energy. He may even be talking to himself under his breath.

He looks up upon hearing me coming and clears his throat. "I thought you might want to clean up what you left in here last night."

"What the hell are you talking about?" I shove the door open and walk into the room to confirm I hadn't dreamt of cleaning up the glass and whiskey mess I made, even as drunk as I was. What the hell is he… it's then I notice what's caught his eye. Bianca's panties are still on the floor where she left them.

I'm quick to snatch them up and tuck them into my pocket. "Okay, Grandma. You can come in now."

"Excuse me for trying to be a respectful gentleman."

All that earns him is a grunt. "You're back to being respectful? That's good to know."

Instead of taking the bait the way I almost hope he will, his frown deepens. "I, um..."

Contrary to what I told Bianca, I feel like fried shit after trying to drown my liver in whiskey. I don't have the energy for a rehash right now. "Out with it. You said things you shouldn't have said last night. I wasn't at my best, either. However, I think from now on—"

"This isn't about that," he insists, cutting me off before I've had the chance to finish. Considering he knows how much I wouldn't say I like being interrupted, this must be big. Either that, or he's insanely stupid.

"What the fuck is it, then? You've caught me on a day when my patience is even thinner than usual."

"It's about the call that came in from Kristoff's father. He's starting to worry about his kid."

Fuck. No wonder he looks like he would rather eat razor blades than have this conversation. I sink into my chair with a sigh, rubbing my temples against a worsening headache.

"Kristoff. I almost forgot about him."

"Unfortunately, we don't have the luxury of doing that."

"And whose fault would that be?"

His jaw tightens as he lifts his chin. "We've been down this road already. I did what I felt needed to be done–and you've kept him in the warehouse all this time. We could have dismissed this as a mistake, a mere mix-up."

He's right, as much as I hate to admit it. I've had fun making that bastard wish he'd never been born. I won't pretend otherwise. "Let's be honest with ourselves. It was over as soon as you picked him up at the hangar. There's no taking that back."

He accepts this without flinching. "He'll expect a callback. In this guy's eyes, his kid is still Tatum's boyfriend."

Shit. "I can't have him reaching out to her and dragging her into this mess."

"That's exactly what I was thinking."

"Which means I need to put out this fire before it gets out of control." And to think the morning started out so well. One of the nicest I can remember. Don't I know by now how fleeting such moments are?

"Here. I wrote down his number." He fishes a slip of paper out of his jacket pocket and slides it across the desk. "Call him before he calls Tatum."

I bristle at the almost condescending tone–I don't need him to remind me what's at stake–before picking up the receiver of my desk phone and dialing the number. Jefferson Knight picks up on the first ring, and the tension in his voice jumps out immediately. "Callum. Thank you for returning my call."

I exchange a look with Romero. "Of course. I understand you're concerned about Kristoff. What's the matter?"

"Has he been in contact with Tatum? I attempted to reach her earlier but didn't get an answer."

I never imagined feeling grateful for her penchant for sleeping in. She doesn't need this man in her ear spewing dog shit. "I wouldn't know. Her relationship isn't my business." Romero barely stifles a snort, earning a sharp shut the hell up look from me. "Is something wrong? Is he in trouble?"

"I haven't seen him since the day before they left to go on the trip."

Hmmm. Strange. "Tatum did mention that he said he was going to stay behind for a couple more weeks.." After sponging off her for weeks and brutalizing her for... I shudder to think how long. I must remind myself that this is not Kristoff I'm speaking to. Sure, the son of a bitch raised a rapist who's suffering at this very minute, even though we can't always control what our children do.

"He should've been home more than a week ago. I have no way to contact him, and I don't have the first idea who he was with after Tatum went home."

"He's young. Maybe he's still out exploring." It makes me a proper asshole, feeding lies to a fellow parent, yet something like this was bound to happen. He was never satisfied with his position in life, always wanting more. Willing to latch onto anybody who could help him live the lifestyle he wanted. A professional user. If not me, somebody else was bound to get tired of his bullshit and put an end to his miserable life.

"For this long, without saying a word or reaching out to me?" The desperation rings in his voice. Soon he'll be panicking. "When can I talk to Tatum? I'm sure she knows something. If not, what perhaps his plans were, or maybe who he went off with?"

"Jeff, I didn't want to bring this into it, but Tatum gave me the idea when she returned home that things had ended badly between them while they were on the trip. Hence her coming home alone." From the corner of my eye, I catch a glimpse of Romero turning toward the window. "I don't know if she'd want to discuss Kristoff's whereabouts even if she had the first clue about them–considering she's been home for weeks. I doubt she'd be able to offer much insight on who he's spent his time with lately."

"Are you saying they broke up?"

"I wouldn't put words into her mouth, though it seems that way." Jeff's sputtering comes as no surprise.

"That doesn't sound like him. He was crazy about her."

My hand clenches the receiver, tight. *Crazy.* What a fitting choice of words. "Who's to say what happened once he met new friends while they were traveling? Tatum seemed satisfied to let things go. I'm sorry to be the one to break this to you, and I'm afraid questioning her on this would only reopen old wounds. From the way she made it sound, though, he was enjoying himself out."

"He was supposed to fly home, damn it."

"Do you have confirmation he returned?" Romero looks over his shoulder at me curiously. I have no doubt he covered up all traces of that prick, but it's the sort of question I'd ask if I was nothing but an innocent third party.

"No," he mutters. "I swear, if he gets caught up with a group of Eurotrash kids, I'll lose my goddamn mind."

I force a chuckle while envisioning the miserable, bleeding wreck I left behind after paying him a visit. "I wouldn't be a bit surprised. Observing that flashy lifestyle is tempting. You have my word. If I hear anything, you'll be the first to know."

"Thanks, Callum. And please wish my best to Tatum."

Right. I'll be sure to extend it.

By the time I hang up, there's no question of what must be done. Romero's hard, stony expression tells me we're on the same page.

It's time to pay another visit to Kristoff and find out how eager he is to continue living.

* * *

"How is he today?" I eye the closed office door tucked into the corner of one of our warehouses. There's no evidence of his presence elsewhere—the stacked crates and pallets of merchandise waiting to be moved are the same as ever.

The pair of guards seated in front of the locked door exchange glances before shrugging. "Pissed off," one of them grunts. "Always asking for shit."

"Like a smoke or a walk outside," the other explains. "Not so much the past day or two, though. I think he figured out it's not doing him any good."

Romero releases a bitter bark of laughter. "This fucking kid has some balls, thinking he can ask for anything. This is a five-star hotel with room service."

He's a survivor, or thinks he is. He believes he can talk himself out of any situation, probably because he's had to do it countless times to infiltrate a world that doesn't belong to him. How did I not see through him before this? Because you never paid enough attention to your daughter's life. If anything, this twisted situation has taught me the difference between hovering protectively over her and playing an active role in her protection.

I'll be damned if I thank the prick behind the door for showing me the light.

The guards move aside, allowing us to enter the room. It's narrow, dimly lit, and rank with the stench of body odor and excrement. The bucket in the corner reveals the source of the latter stench, while the pathetic lump tied to a wooden chair is the source of the former.

The button-down shirt he's wearing is now dried with bloodstains and sticks to his skin in sweaty patches. His dark hair hangs in greasy strands in front of his face, concealing most of it. Romero growls like an animal as we approach, but Kristoff refuses to lift his head.

"Don't play it up," I murmur, stepping in front of him. "You won't get far using the victim act. Not with me."

Slowly he stirs, his breathing ragged. "Mr. Torrio, please…" His voice is thick, and his speech is slightly slurred due to the missing teeth he has now. The gash I left on his lower lip hasn't healed well, either. Looks like it might have become infected, and the sight pleases me more than it should.

"I didn't give you permission to speak." What do I do with this pathetic wreck? I can't trust him to keep his mouth shut any more than I could trust him to keep his dick in his pants and away from women.

"I, for one, would like to know what he has to say." Romero removes his suit jacket and drapes it over the back of another chair, then begins rolling up the sleeves of his shirt.

"I still don't understand why I'm here. Why are you doing this to me?" Kristoff's dark, bloodshot eyes dart back and forth between us. "Please, someone explain to me what happened because I only know you think I did something to earn this."

Finally, his gaze lands on me and stays there. "You can't keep me here forever. My father will come looking for me, especially when you have me here for no reason."

"Don't fuck with me." His head snaps back in the wake of my snarl. "You know what you did. Every fucking time you chose to hurt my daughter, you earned another few hours in hell. Pissing and shitting in a bucket, bleeding and bruised. You put yourself in this very fucking place, so don't sit here and play the victim."

"What? What did I do to her?" Fresh sweat beads on his ashen skin.

"Listen to this," Romero sighs. His irritation is getting the best of him. "I figured he'd be smarter."

"I didn't," I grumble. I hope this isn't his defense. Feigning ignorance? He's had a week to figure this out. Couldn't he come up with anything better?

"Honestly, I don't know what you're talking about." It's the tears swimming in his eyes that turn my bitterness to rage. He has the nerve to cry after what he's done. To make himself a victim. "I love Tatum. I–"

A backhand from me silences him, at least for a moment. He's not intelligent enough to keep his mouth shut permanently. "Don't you dare say that again," I warn. "Not ever. I know what you did. She told me everything."

"What are you talking about?" he manages to get the words out once he lifts his head. His cheek glows red now, in contrast to his sickly complexion. "What did she tell you? I didn't do anything to her."

"She showed us the bruises." Romero's fists are clenched at his sides, his chest heaving. Each breath becomes heavier than the last. We've done this together numerous times, but there's something different about Kristoff. A personal edge to it. "She showed us what you did and told us about the rest. About the way you forced her… how you fucking raped her. At this point, you should be thankful you're even alive!"

"What?" He suddenly sounds a lot sharper, clearer. "I didn't. I would never do that."

"If you didn't do those things, then what you're saying is she lied to us, right?" I demand, grabbing a handful of greasy hair and pulling his head back until we're eye-to-eye. "That's what you're telling me? That she's lying. That her having a mental breakdown in my arms had nothing to do with you? Her constant nightmares? That the reason she's been a shell of her former self had nothing to do with you? Men like you are pathetic, and if you haven't used your pea-sized brain yet and put the puzzle together, that's why you're here, you miserable piece of shit. Now stop wasting the last few minutes of your life lying."

"The last…" Tears spill over his lashes and pour down his cheeks. "No. No, you can't. Please, I don't deserve this! You can't kill me, please! I'll do anything!"

"I'm sure you would promise me anything if it meant keeping your pathetic life," I observe. The Glock in my waistband practically burns my skin; I'm so eager to wrap my hand around the butt and pull it free. This could all be over so quickly. I'd never have to hear his lies again.

"My father…" His breathing is quick, erratic. "He's going to find out, and it'll mean trouble for you. You're screwing yourself by doing this."

"Is that supposed to frighten me?" I ask on a sigh.

"I… I don't know what she told you." Wracking sobs consume his entire frame as he shakes from head to toe. "It's possible that there was a misunderstanding, and if so, I'll take responsibility for my part. I know I was drinking too much while we were on the trip. I tried some drugs. Honestly I didn't know what I was doing!"

Leaning down, I scream in his face the words ringing in my head. "She said it started here! She thought the trip would make things better!"

Shoving his head away, I wipe my hand on my slacks. "You let her buy you gifts on my dime. She thought she might be able to keep you happy that way. And you let it happen, then hurt her anyway. You are less than shit. It would make more sense to kill you and donate your organs. Your life might mean something, then."

"Please!" He's gone straight to blubbering, his nose running, blood dripping from the corner of his mouth thanks to the love tap I gave him. "I didn't mean anything!"

Now that he's sweating, his stench is worse than ever. There's a particular sort of acrid odor to sweat born from terror, and it fills the small room until I have to back away. "You meant plenty," I counter. "You took advantage of her in every way possible. Nobody gets away with that."

"She... she wasn't totally innocent!" he blurts out. "She picked fights and threw tantrums and pushed me until I couldn't take it anymore!!"

"And that means you can hit her? Hurt her? Leave your filthy fucking hand prints on her?" Romero seethes.

"No... I just... As I said. I wasn't thinking. I'm sorry... please. Just let me go, and you'll never hear from me again. I'll disappear."

"Oh, you'll disappear alright!" I growl, shaking my head. I don't know what to do. I want to kill him, but I made a promise to Tatum.

"Look, my father is going to come looking for me soon, and when he does..."

"What?" Romero interrupts him, getting right in his face. "What is your daddy going to do to get you out of this? I can only assume he'll be happy to hear what you've done. How you raped and abused a woman, causing her despair, making it impossible for her to sleep at night. Maybe we should give your father a call right now and see what he has to say?"

Kristoff grits his teeth. It's obvious Romero's words have hit their mark. "Did you not hear me? I already told you she was part of the problem. She's lucky all I did was bruise her a little bit after everything she put me through. Her pussy wasn't even that good anyway."

"I'll fucking kill you with my bare hands," I snarl, walking towards him. The air is electrified; I can feel the energy inside Romero, and I know he's going to snap. All at once, he pulls something from his back pocket. The overhead light makes the steel of his switchblade gleam. Before I can stop him, Romero's hand moves in a slash motion and the blade is in Kristoff's skin.

Romero jumps back in time to avoid being sprayed by the blood from the gaping wound in Kristoff's throat. At first, I'm too shocked by this sudden turn to react. I can only watch, wordlessly, while Kristoff gasps and gags as the life drains from his pathetic body.

I pull my attention from the dying man to eye my trusted right-hand man, the stained switchblade still gripped tight in his fist. He's a man possessed, his eyes seeming to glow as they drink in the sight of an agonizing death.

"By rights, that was my job," I mutter once Kristoff's head drops forward, his body limp.

"I'd say sorry, but I couldn't stand another second of him blaming her for a choice that he fucking made." He looks my way, satisfaction gleaming in his eyes. "Sue me if you want."

I can't bother to be mad. It's what was going to happen either way. "We need to clean this up."

"Leave it to me." His gaze swings back to the dead man in the chair. "It's what I do best."

Before I turn away, I catch sight of him spitting on the corpse.

BIANCA

"You know, you don't need to do this."

I turn away from the stove, wooden spoon in hand. "And you don't need to say that again. I've already told you I want to make dinner."

"I'm not your responsibility. As much as I love your cooking." Dad shoves his hands into the pockets of his jeans, shrugging. "I'm the one bumming around without a job. I should be making dinner so it'll be on the table when you get home from work."

"How do I put this delicately?" I can't, and there's no holding in the laughter that bubbles up at the idea. "You make a mean bowl of cereal. But otherwise…"

"Hey! I've gotten better with time," he cuts me off.

"I'll have to take your word for it."

"Very funny." He goes to the fridge and pulls out a head of lettuce. "Do you think I'm incapable of making a salad?"

"I guess we can give it a try. I mean, what could go wrong?" He rolls his eyes, but his sheepish grin goes a long way toward loosening what was left of the anxiety I've been fighting all day. I feared how he might act tonight and whether he'd pick an argument over

Callum. So far, he's avoided the subject, and I'm not going to press the issue. I'm not a child, and I don't expect him to magically drop his resentment and suspicion.

He hasn't threatened to lock me in my room, so I'll take it as a good sign. Now if he knew about the baby, that's a different story. I wish I didn't still feel the rush of guilt that twists my stomach as it has been doing all day. I'm walking around with a tiny little secret that will get much bigger soon. I wish I could envision Dad being happy and welcoming his grandchild with open arms. Maybe he will, eventually, but I'm not naïve. It will take adjustment, time, and a lot of patience.

The aroma of garlic fills the air by the time I pull buttery bread from the oven. "Sorry it's nothing more impressive," I offer while saucing the pasta.

"Are you kidding? I don't need anything fancy."

It must be the relief of not having to lie anymore about work that makes him seem younger, less like there's something weighing him down. Not that he's going to forget about Mom—neither of us could. He's more like the dad I used to know, however.

"How's work treating you?" he asks as we eat. "You have said little about it."

"It's work." When he lifts an eyebrow, I shrug. "I mean, I'm glad to have a job, and everyone there is nice, but there's nothing interesting about it."

"Well, if it was always fun, they'd call it 'play' instead of work, right?" What a Dad thing to say. I'd usually roll my eyes and pretend to gag, but right now I'm happy to be having a normal conversation with him.

For the first time in forever, it feels like we're having a normal meal.

That is, until there's a knock at the front door.

Dad lowers his plate in the middle of taking a second helping, shrugging as he wipes his mouth on his napkin. From my chair, I can see straight through to the front door, even though the curtain hanging over the glass pane minimizes whoever's out there to a featureless lump. "I'll get it," he murmurs, halfway through the room. I turn in my chair to watch him walk to the door, which he opens slowly. His entire body tenses all at once.

"Oh. Hello." I still can't see who's there, though the strain in his eyes when he looks at me over his shoulder tells me this isn't a welcome visit. He doesn't step back to give them room to come into the house, either—no, it's like his body expands, like he's blocking the way.

My thoughts instantly go to Callum. He knows better than to show up here, especially unannounced. *Tatum?* Maybe.

"Charlie, hello. I'm sorry to drop by unannounced—we both are."

I recognize the woman's voice, and the sound of it—plus the emotion, the tears, the way it quivers—makes my stomach drop. *Oh, God, no. Not this. I can't do this.*

"It's just that we don't know where else to go." Yup, I know the man's voice, too. After five years of dating their son, I would know Lucas's parents anywhere.

I almost forgot about him. How could I forget?

Again, Dad throws an apprehensive expression over his shoulder, and I don't know what to do. I never told him anything about Lucas—I'm not supposed to know what happened to him. As far as I know, he's living his life, doing his thing.

Damn it, I'm not prepared for this.

I have to force myself to push through my jittery nerves and shaky legs to leave the kitchen and venture into the living room, as if I am not absolutely terrified of what's about to happen. I have to be strong. I have to.

"Sarah, Josh, I'm not sure what you expect me to do." Dad is still blocking the doorway with his body, but now I see Lucas's dad. God, it looks like he's aged ten years since I last saw him. They took me out to dinner a few days before graduation, so it hasn't been very long.

I have to pretend I don't know why. How could I have practically forgotten about him? Then again, what's the alternative? I can't spend the rest of my life obsessing over what happened, either. I didn't do anything wrong.

Except for pretending nothing happened.

"Bianca," Josh says my name like a saving grace which makes his wife stand on tiptoes to get a look at me. "When did you last see him? Did he reach out to you or say anything?"

"I..." I swallow around the lump in my throat. "No, I haven't seen Lucas in weeks."

"You are aware they broke up," Dad announces.

At least he finally moves aside, giving them room to enter the house. I thought Josh looked bad, but Sarah is a wreck. Her hair looks like she hasn't washed or even brushed it in days, pulled back in a tangled ponytail, while the old college T-shirt she's wearing is stained and torn at the collar. Like it's something she would wear to clean the house. Before now, I've never seen her appearance less than impeccable, even if she was dressed casually.

"No one reached out to you?" Josh blinks rapidly, his gaze bouncing from me to Dad and back again, while Sarah barely stifles a whimper. "I'm not quite sure how to say this."

Maybe it's instinct, but Dad moves closer, pulling me inside his side. "What is it?"

Sarah turns toward her husband and presses her face to his chest. Josh takes a hitching breath. "Lucas... they... he committed suicide."

I lean against Dad, who stiffens in surprise. "My God. Josh. I'm so sorry." All I can do is rely on Dad to keep me standing upright. Let them think it's because I'm surprised and overwhelmed by shock—it's better that way.

Really, it's the way Sarah weeps against her husband's chest. It's the agony running like a thread through Josh's words. I can't take this.

"You're sure he said nothing to you?" Sarah turns to me, and it must be the guilt that convinces me there's blame in her swollen, bloodshot eyes. "Did he give you any idea of his mental state?"

"Bianca, honey..." Dad's grip on me tightens. "Do you need to sit down?"

This is killing me. I'm going to die here and now. All I can see when I look at them is their son on top of me, holding me down on the bed, the crazy look in his eyes, and all the insane things he was saying. About how we were meant to be, about how Callum ruined me.

Before he held a knife to your throat. He was going to rape you. He could have killed you.

I need to remember that before I break down in front of these poor people and tell them everything their son did. Hell, it's not like it would help them. Finding out their son went insane before he died.

"Here. Let's sit you down." In the back of my mind, it occurs to me that Dad now has a reason to take care of me. And I let him do it without question, my head spinning, my stomach tightening to the point of pain. I think I'm going to vomit.

"We're sorry to come in and announce it this way," Josh says.

"Do you two need to sit down? Sarah, can I get you some water?"

Sarah scowls despite Dad's kindness. "What I need is to know what happened to my boy. He did not kill himself. That is not something Lucas would do. I'm his mother! I know my son!"

Do you? No matter how much I want to, I would never say that out loud. It's not her fault what happened to him. But I have to wonder if either had the first idea of what he was going through. They couldn't possibly, or else they might have been able to help him.

"Exactly what happened?" Dad asks Josh. "What were the circumstances?"

"I found him at our cabin." He's struggling to keep himself in check, his voice shaking. God, Lucas looked just like him. I want to look away and close my eyes so I don't have to stare at him anymore, but I must resist the impulse. It's clear from the way Dad rubs my back that my reaction—silence, shock—is convincing. I don't want to blow this. The baby. Callum. My own life. Everything hinges on this.

He found his son at the cabin. His own father found him.

"He would not have shot himself. Never!" Sarah insists. "You know that, right?" she asks me, eyes darting over my face, desperation heavy in her voice. Like she needs me to agree. Like it's the most crucial thing in the world that I agree with her.

"I... I really don't know," I whisper, looking to Dad for help. Never once did I think to prepare myself for this.

"To be fair," Dad murmurs, speaking slowly, "the two of them broke up weeks ago. There was no reason for Bianca to know his mental state." I nod, so grateful that he's here. "But he did come here in hopes I would convince Bianca to... I'm not sure what. Take him back, maybe?"

"How did he look?" Sarah asks, breathless.

"Like himself. He seemed fine—I'm sorry I can't be more helpful."

"Our son was not suicidal," Sarah insists.

"He did seem distraught," Dad points out in that same low, slow voice. I wonder how many victims and families he's had to talk to over the years, using that same calm, measured tone. "Though I know that doesn't give you any peace. I'm sorry. I wish there was something I could say to take this pain away from you."

"I'm so sorry," I whisper. "I'm so sorry this happened."

"Well," Sarah barks, running her fists under her eyes to catch her tears, "maybe if he didn't feel abandoned, this wouldn't have happened."

"Sarah," Josh whispers. "Don't do that."

"I'm just saying. If he was distraught, we all know why."

Maybe I should be glad she's not flat-out accusing me of putting the gun to his head, but she might as well be. All I can do is reel in horror with my tongue too tied to speak.

EMPIRE OF LIES

"Now, wait just a second." Dad holds up his hands, his features hardening. "This is a terrible tragedy, and truly, you have my deepest sympathy. I can't imagine what you're feeling at this moment, but to stand here and imply Bianca was at fault for ending the relationship is cruel and unfair."

"That's not what we think," Josh insists.

"Don't speak for me," Sarah whispers. "He started going downhill after the breakup. He stopped going to work. He was supposed to take over the gym, and he lost interest. Don't tell me it was only a coincidence."

"Sarah, breakups happen all the time," Dad reminds her. He's not so gentle anymore. His tone has a firmness, a command I haven't heard in ages. "You're not the first grieving parent to want to lay blame for what happened to their child on someone else. Nevertheless, it's unfair to hold Bianca responsible. Breakups happen."

"Honey, we should go. I'm... not even sure why we came," Josh murmurs. "We were just hoping, I don't know, that you could tell us something."

I can't hold back the tears anymore. They run down my cheeks and clog my throat until all I can do is shake my head at first. "No," I choke out. "I'm sorry. I really am. I didn't want... I mean, I would never..."

"It's alright," Dad whispers, stroking my hair before turning back to them. "I'm sorry, but there is nothing we can do to help. Truly, I wish there was."

"Can you investigate?" Sarah asks. The hope in that question sends fresh tears rolling down, dripping off my chin faster than I can catch them.

"I've taken a leave of absence," Dad explains. "However, I can make some phone calls. I want to manage your expectations, though. If the ruling was suicide, I'm not sure what else can be done."

It's just like with Mom. Only this time, I'm the one who knows the truth, and I'm the one trying to gaslight this poor couple into believing the story Romero and Callum came up with. How can I sit here, knowing the truth, knowing what happens when the truth is concealed, and pretend? It would kill Dad if he knew I'm sitting here, watching them suffer, when I know everything. He'd never look at me the same way again.

"Let's go," Josh whispers to Sarah, stroking her matted brown hair before steering her out the door. He looks back at me one last time while his wife sobs quietly and mouths the words *I'm sorry*.

Right, because I'm the one who deserves an apology. Because I'm the one who's truly been hurt. What happens if she never gets over this? I'll carry the guilt of what happened that night on my chest for the rest of my life.

Dad closes, then locks the door behind them before scrubbing his hands through his hair with a sigh. "What a terrible thing to happen. In any case, please don't for one second believe any of this was your fault."

Nodding, I brush the last of my tears away. "I know. I couldn't control the things he did when we were together, much less..." I can't find the words to finish the sentence.

Never in my life have I wished so much that I could tell the truth. The whole truth, too. Like the way Lucas tried to kill me with his car. The way he kidnapped me and tried to force himself on me. How he fell apart.

And the reason why he did.

"I think I need to go upstairs and lie down for a minute," I whisper, standing and steadying myself.

"Sure, of course, you do that. I'll clean up the kitchen. And if you need anything, just yell for me." I nod silently, then climb the stairs slowly. Those poor people. None of this was their fault. They didn't have the first clue what was happening with their son. I am not even sure they could have helped him if they tried.

Once I'm sure Dad is still in the kitchen, making noise as he washes up the pots and pans, I close the bedroom door and pull out my phone. I need support, stability. I need to know everything is going to be okay, even if it feels like it won't be.

Callum answers on the first ring. "Hey, there." He sounds happy but tired. It jumps out at me no matter how he tries to hide it.

And here I am, about to heap more steaming shit on him. "We just had a visitor."

"Explain." His tone is serious.

A minute later, he knows the whole story, and I'm left breathless and trembling. "What should I do? Do you think they'll make a big deal about it and try to start an investigation?"

"You have nothing to worry about," he assures me. "There's no chance of any of it being traced back to you."

"That's not what I'm worried about. What about you? Are you safe?"

"Absolutely. There's no reason for anything to be linked to any of us. You have nothing to worry about."

"I have everything to worry about." The memory of Sarah's weeping and Josh's anguish brings tears to my eyes all over again. They did nothing to deserve this, but I sat there and pretended and only added to their pain. "I'm worried about the person this makes me. I looked those people in the eye and told them I had no idea what had happened. Lied right to their faces."

"Which is a lot easier for them to deal with, I'm sure, than what truly happened. Would it do them any favors if they knew the truth?" His smooth, confident voice is like a soothing balm that eases my pain.

"No, it wouldn't."

"There you go. If anything, you're doing them a favor by letting them believe their son killed himself. He'll be their tragic little boy who lost his way instead of a man who tried to run you down, kidnapped you, and—"

"I know." I can't bear to hear the rest. Doubt he wants to say it all out loud, anyway.

Sinking onto the bed, I scrape together the courage to confess what's weighing heaviest on my heart. "There's more. We both know who's really responsible for this. I know Lucas made his own choices, but he didn't come up with all of this off the top of his head."

He snarls like I knew he would. "Amanda."

"What if she isn't satisfied?" I can see her in front of me, dressed to the nines like she was at the clinic. "I'm sure she still has it out for me." I'm absolutely certain of it, in fact.

Especially now, since she deduced I'm pregnant. No, I didn't confirm or deny it, but I don't think that matters.

"I'm not going to pretend you don't have a point. She could very well decide to try again. All she wants is to make me suffer."

"I don't feel safe," I confess, rubbing my stomach. I don't feel like either of us is safe.

"Then come home. Let me take care of you here. There's no way she can touch you while you're here, under my protection. She wouldn't dare."

He's both right and wrong. No, she couldn't physically hurt me, but she could show up again and raise hell.

Even with that knowledge, my body relaxes as soon as I hear the magic spell that his words weave. The tension that's almost locked my muscles in place drains away. My reservations about Dad's reaction drain away, too. This isn't about me, and it's not about him. My baby needs protection. It's like everything's coming into focus now.

That focus is what helps me get my things together before venturing downstairs, where Dad is finishing up in the kitchen. It makes it possible to stand straight and tall while he gapes at me in shock.

"You're going where?" He's so stunned, he didn't drop the sponge in the sink. Now he's dripping dirty water all over the floor, clutching it in his tightening fist.

"Be careful," I sigh, grabbing paper towels. "You'll slip and hurt yourself."

"Stop babying me." He snatches the paper towels from me and drops them on the floor. "Why are you going to Callum?"

"That's just where I want to be right now."

Because of course, I can't give him any specifics. I can't tell him about Amanda. He could end up getting himself hurt by putting himself in her crosshairs. It doesn't matter that he's a skilled detective who has dealt with people like her for years. I don't want to take any chances. Nothing stops her from hurting other people, specifically if it puts her ahead.

That's not the only reason; telling him about her would mean spilling all the beans. I can't do that. For so many reasons.

"Dad, please. It has nothing to do with you. I just really want to be there. I'll be fine. And it won't be forever—somebody has to come around and make sure you've eaten."

He tosses the sponge into the sink, muttering obscenities under his breath. "I don't like you leaving after you heard news like you just did. Is this about Lucas?"

"No, it's not." Not the way he thinks, at least. "I'm going to be fine. Callum's going to take care of me."

He turns his back to me, but my hand on his shoulder turns him around again. His eyes are getting red, and the tremor in his chin reveals the emotion he's failing to hold back. "And you know what else? He's trying to help us find out what happened to Mom. He really is. Because he knows it's what I want. We have to trust him, Dad. I need you to trust him. Can you at least try, for me?"

He barks out a sharp laugh. "You realize what you're asking?"

"All I'm asking you to do is let go of what you thought you knew. That's it."

Gripping the edge of the sink with both hands, he releases a pained groan. "If only it were that simple."

"I understand, but I believe you can do it, especially when you remind yourself that this is what I want."

I hate the way he lowers his shoulders and hangs his head in defeat. The last thing I want is to hurt him. "Right. This is what you want."

None of this is my fault. That's all I can tell myself as I kiss his cheek before carrying my bags to the car. None of this is my fault; I'm trying to do what's best for my baby. Our baby. Right now, Callum is what's best.

Callum will always be what's best. For both of us.

CALLUM

"Anything else you want to discuss with Costello when he comes in?"

"Hmm?" I barely heard Romero's question. He asked one; I know that much, though the substance was lost on me.

He only shakes his head, sighing softly as we emerge from the stairwell leading up from the gym. We're both showered and dressed after our morning workout. I can't pretend getting back into my routine hasn't done wonders for my mental state. I lost sight of the important things for a minute there, but I'm back on track. No more heavy drinking, no more feeling sorry for myself. The only way out of a mess is through action, not wallowing.

Though it seems my thoughts are still wandering, and of course, there's only one person to blame. The girl currently out to brunch with my daughter. I'd much rather have her in bed with me, the way she was when I woke up. By the time I was dressed for the gym, she was just beginning to stir after sleeping in on this fine Saturday morning.

"Costello," I mutter once I've caught up to his train of thought, abandoning memories of Bianca's sun-kissed skin for a moment.

"No, I think we're good. We'll be able to tell him things have been quiet lately."

"I wonder if he dropped a hint somewhere that he'd clued you in," Romero muses on our way down the hall. "That would explain why there's been no more trouble on our barges."

"Either that or Jack figures the message was sent. Let's face it, he doesn't have the manpower to defend what's his if I decide to declare war. There's only so far he can go. So long as we got the shipment back, that's what matters."

"And Sebastian Costello gets his piece," Romero adds with no small amount of bitterness, nodding to a pair of guards as we pass them in the hall.

"If it wasn't for him, we wouldn't have anything." He holds his tongue, his jaw working like it's a fight to keep his mouth shut. I understand why, whether he believes it or not. It was his quick thinking and the few well-timed phone calls that ended up finding those missing crates. I have no idea how he manages to hold so much information and so many contacts in his brain. The only thing I know is that he knew who to call once Costello confirmed it was Moroni behind the hijackings.

"Don't worry," I tell him once we enter my office. "You'll get what's coming to you. I don't forget the people who do right by me."

"You know I wasn't asking for anything special."

"No, but you deserve it." I groan and roll my eyes under his surprised stare. "Give me a break, would you? I'm trying to give credit where it's due."

"Then I guess I can't get on your case for spacing out in the middle of a conversation."

"What do you mean by that?"

"It's noticeable that the person you keep thinking about is the one who has you in this generous mood."

"No comment." He's right, of course, but we're not talking about my personal life right now.

The fact is, having Bianca here, under my roof has gone a long way toward helping me focus on what's been evading my attention lately. Nothing else matters more than my little bird, so knowing she's coming home to me at the end of the day goes a long way toward soothing the insatiable obsession. With my worries over her out of the way, I can steer my attention back to business.

"Which brings me to my next point." Before he says another word, he holds up a hand and goes to the door, glancing both ways up and down the hall before closing it to give us privacy. "I installed the software on all devices on the network yesterday, excluding Bianca and Tatum, as per your instructions."

"You're sure the girls weren't included?"

"I'm sure." I blow out a relieved sigh. No way am I dealing with the whole invasion of privacy and wrath of shit. "Only the men using the network got the download automatically pushed to their device."

I was hoping it wouldn't have had to come to this. However, some things are more important than what I was hoping for. Hell, I wish none of my guys were going behind my back in the first place. Wishes don't mean much.

"So any contact they have with Amanda..."

"We'll know about it right away, in real-time. There's no legitimate reason for any of them to reach out to her, after all." He takes a seat, tapping on his tablet. "And, of course, there's tracking involved, too. I tested it all out, and it seems to be working fine."

"I wish I could say I knew for sure whether I want something to come of this."

The concern in his eyes tells me he understands. "Whoever it is, the fact that they've gotten away with it for this long means they might get sloppy soon."

"Here's wishing." I'm sick of the suspicion.

I slowly sip the coffee, which Sheryl was thoughtful enough to leave on the desk—or perhaps Bianca may have dropped it off on her way out. She is always taking care of me.

Which makes me chuckle, though not out of warmth or fondness. If anything, I'm laughing at myself. "You know, I never thought I'd identify so much with Charlie Cole."

"What do you mean?"

"There he is, going around with all these suspicions without solid proof. I'm finally starting to understand how he must feel." That, and how Bianca seems determined to look after me—the way she does with him.

"Speaking of which, have you reviewed the list of names I compiled?"

If my head doesn't fucking explode, it will be a miracle. I walked into this room feeling good, energized, confident. All it takes is a catch-up session to remember how overwhelming the past few weeks have been. Bianca or no Bianca, I've got enough on my plate to make any man want to throw in the towel.

I made her a promise. I'm going to find out who killed her mother. I only hope she isn't in a hurry, since at least a dozen possible culprits could've had reason to send a message to Charlie.

"I scanned the names," I confirm. "And I'd like to set up meetings. Only this is touchy, so we can't make too much noise, or word might spread that I'm digging."

"You realize one of those names was Salvatore Costello."

"I'm not bringing it up to the kid today," I grunt, shaking my head. "That's not how Sal operated. We both know that."

"From where I'm sitting, it seems sort of obvious," Romero insists. "The first deal you struck with him was six months before that accident. He could easily have gotten jumpy, worried he was dealing with a man with a target on his back. Maybe don't dismiss it out of hand."

Even though I can't picture it, I see what he's saying. "What would Sebastian know about it? He was a kid, only a little older than Tatum. He wouldn't have the first idea."

"I don't see the harm in asking him to dig around, see if he knows anything. Approach it like you're asking a friend for a favor. Make him feel important, and feed his ego."

My phone buzzing couldn't have come at a better time, because otherwise, I'd have to remind him who's boss around here. He takes the opportunity to leave—the expression on his face tells me he's relieved.

Seeing Bianca's name on the phone immediately makes my heart swell. "Is everything alright?" I ask as soon as I answer the call.

Her gentle laughter soothes my worry. "And hello to you, too." Her slightly husky voice makes my cock twitch expectantly.

"I didn't expect you to call. Don't tell me they ran out of mimosas at brunch."

"Oh, you'd hear screaming in the background if that was the case."

"So what's going on? Is she alright?"

"Yeah, she just got up for a minute. I wanted to let you know she seems to be fine. We might go for a movie after this." Considering my daughter won't entertain the idea of going to a doctor to talk about her trauma, the best I can do is clumsily try to make her happy—and the same goes for her best friend.

"So long as she's enjoying herself. And thank you," I add. "She's been so much better these past few days, and you're the reason why."

"I pray you're right."

"When you get home," I murmur, "you should stop by my office. I didn't get to see you before you left, and I want to get a look at whatever cute outfit you're wearing right now."

"Why do I feel like you'd rather get a look at me without the outfit on?"

"The dirty mind on you," I murmur, chuckling, even though that's precisely what I had in mind.

"I better go. I think she's coming back." She ends the call before I have the chance to say I love her. I can tell her later. I have the rest of my life.

That list of names is at the forefront of my mind, and I pull up the file on my laptop while waiting for Sebastian to show up. I don't normally like taking meetings over the weekend—especially now that I have someone much more interesting here at home—but I have kept Sebastian waiting long enough. I do want to solidify our relationship. That means making good on my promise to give him a percentage of what we recovered, thanks to his helpful tip.

I remember every single one of these deals, and off the top of my head, I can't recall anyone being dissatisfied or even complaining about the grief Charlie was giving me at the time. I never considered him much of a threat, and it would surprise me to think any of these hard-bitten, experienced men balking over a single detective asking too many questions.

Stranger things have happened. Here I am, in love with his daughter. I couldn't have predicted that.

I'm arranging names in what I think is the order of their likelihood of being the perpetrator when Romero's footsteps ring out in the hall. "Henry called up from the gate. Costello's here a few minutes early."

"That's fine. Show him in." I stand and button my jacket, looking out the window in time to catch a glimpse of Sebastian stepping from his car. He has three guards with him, his driver included, all of whom make an imposing image clustered around the Maserati.

This smart ass. I see the way he looks up at the house while removing his sunglasses. Is he considering a place like this for himself one day? Or maybe this house in particular. Not that I want to give in to suspicion, but I recognize his hungry look. I need to be careful with this kid.

He's all smiles when he enters the room a minute later, extending a hand to shake. "Mr. Torrio. I was glad to hear you recovered your shipment."

"Thanks to you." I'm careful to avoid Romero's penetrating stare as I gesture for Sebastian to take a seat. "Would you like some coffee?"

"No, thank you, I'm fine." He unbuttons his jacket and makes himself comfortable. "I was hoping you'd given some more thought to the prospect of us working together."

"You've already proven yourself a valuable ally. And I was impressed with your prospectus. I think we could make this work." I hold out a hand, signaling Romero to bring me the agreement we compiled. "This is a counteroffer, if you will. Our terms work within the parameters of the terms you've already set. If you go over this and don't find any problems, we can move forward."

"I'll have my team take a look, but I can't see any reason there would be issues." I watch as he scans the information, his eyes moving over the page.

"I'm glad to hear it."

"So Moroni isn't a problem anymore?" Only his eyes move, lifting from the page and meeting mine.

"He hasn't shown his face."

"That's not what I was asking. Don't get me wrong," he's quick to add when my brows draw together, "whatever he brings, we can handle. If you need extra security on your barges, I can arrange that. We'll make this work. But I do need to know, you understand. What am I getting into?"

"It's handled." I hold his gaze, unblinking, daring him to fuck with me. I don't need him nearly as much as he needs me to give him a way to move his weapons.

"Good to know." He smiles—the quick, sure smile of someone who thinks they're untouchable. I would hate to see reality come crashing in on him someday. He's hot shit, sure, but he's untested. And he's already trying my patience.

I hear her before I see her, her voice filling the room all at once. "We decided not to go to the movie—"

Our three heads turn to find Bianca standing in the doorway, her eyes wide and face turning red. "I am so sorry," she whispers, backing away. "I should've known you were in a meeting, only the door was open."

And I didn't expect her back so soon. For lack of anything better to offer, I murmur, "Sebastian Costello, meet Bianca Cole."

He grins, standing, extending a hand. "I've been looking forward to making your acquaintance," he tells her, and unexpectedly his voice is much warmer than it was before. "I heard you're mighty dangerous with a fork."

Now her horrified flush is more like a nervous blush. "Not one of my proudest moments," she whispers, but a smile tugs at her lips.

"I would've loved to see it," he replies, oozing charm.

I wonder how long it would take to strangle him. It's irrational as fuck to be angry at another man for talking to her, but she is mine. Her voice and smiles should be saved for only me. He doesn't deserve to bask in her happiness.

"I'll find you when the meeting's over," I tell Bianca, who takes one more look at him before trotting away. Sebastian is still chuckling, shaking his head like he's impressed.

"You know, there was one other issue I wanted to discuss with you."

His attention swings back to me. "I'm all ears."

"We're looking into the death of a civilian, a woman. It took place, oh, fourteen years ago. We believe she may have been in the wrong place at the wrong time and that her husband—a detective—was the intended target. I know you would have no first-hand knowledge of anything that happened that long ago, but I was wondering if you'd ever heard any talk about that. Maybe you could ask around and see if anyone remembers."

"Are you asking me if my father had a woman killed? I think we both know that's not how he operated."

"Absolutely, and that was my immediate reaction, but that is roughly around the time I started doing business with your father, and if that detective was after me..."

"Say no more." He's frowning as he buttons his jacket like he's ready to leave. "I can't imagine that having come from Dad, but there's a chance someone on my crew knows about it."

"I'd appreciate any information you uncover. And in the meantime, I look forward to hearing from your lawyer. I'd love to sign a contract soon." His ready smile tells me he agrees, and Romero offers to walk him to the front door while I sink into my chair.

There's too much happening. My heart's pounding suddenly like it wants to burst from my chest. Moroni. Costello. The traitor in my crew. Amanda and the papers. Bianca's mother. My daughter. Everywhere I turn, more problems. More questions.

Every man has a breaking point. Until now, I couldn't have imagined reaching mine. That's never been me. I don't fall apart. I can't afford to. There are too many people depending on me, needing me. Decisions to be made, people to protect.

Somewhere along the line, it's all become too much. I see that now, sitting behind my desk, staring out the window while the world spins out of control around me. It's all too damn much. I've reached the point where I'm too overwhelmed to see the next step. Do I reach out to Amanda? Do I start making phone calls about a murder I'm sure the gunman forgot about long ago? Or maybe it's Tatum who needs my attention—I should go to her, spend some time with her. But Bianca needs me to fulfill my promise. And I need to protect what's mine, including my business.

In other words, I'm in the middle of a storm, and I have no idea which way to turn.

"I'm so sorry."

The sound of my little bird's voice reaches what little is left of my sanity. I turn toward her, soaking in the sight of her beauty. "You don't have to apologize," I murmur, gesturing for her to come closer.

Something holds her back, however. "No, that was super unprofessional of me. I saw the car outside, but since your door was open... I just wasn't thinking. I wanted to see you." She tucks a strand of dark hair behind her ear and bites her lip.

"I could never get upset with you for saying something like that." I hold out my arms, and she comes to me. Settling in my lap, her welcome weight provides me instant comfort. She settles against my body, winding her arms around my neck, and instantly all is right with the world.

"You look upset. Did the meeting not go well?"

"Actually, it went fine." I need to focus on what's working right now, and the deal with Sebastian is one of those things.

"What else is going on? You can talk to me. I want you to talk to me when things are bothering you."

"I'm a little overwhelmed at the moment, that's all."

"I'm sorry. Maybe you need to take a day off."

The innocence of youth. "You have no idea how much I'd like to, but I'm afraid that would only worsen everything. I have too much to deal with."

"Well, in case you were wondering, Tatum is fine." She places a gentle kiss on my cheek, then another closer to my jaw. The sweetness of it—I can't breathe, and now my heart is thumping. Not out of panic or being overwhelmed, but because I don't know how to handle what she does to me. It's like she shoves a hand in my chest and stirs up parts of my soul I thought were dead. The way she brings everything into crystal clarity without trying.

I deeply inhale the scent of her hair and skin. "You came back earlier than expected."

"The matinee was sold out, and we didn't feel like waiting around. Maybe we'll go out again tomorrow, and do a little shopping after the movie. As long as I can get her out of the house."

"She's lucky to have a friend like you." Just as I'm lucky to have her. She's become essential, what I need to survive. I wouldn't dare say that out loud for fear of overwhelming her, but the knowledge is there just the same.

"Can I ask you a favor?" I murmur, stroking her back, closing my eyes to soak in the wonder of her nearness.

"Anything."

"Don't ever leave me. I couldn't get along without you."

She lifts her head, wearing a sweet smile. There's nothing less than love shining from her baby blues, and I would happily drown in it as long as her loving gaze is the last thing I see. "That's something you never have to worry about," she whispers. "Because I'm not going anywhere. I'm afraid you're stuck with me for the rest of your life."

I must have done something right if it meant earning this. With that in mind, I can almost believe there's a way out of the seemingly hopeless mess life wants to dissolve into. So long as I have this and there's love at the end of the day, everything else will work out.

BIANCA

"*How* come you're not trying on any clothes?"

Damn it. I was hoping I'd get away with it.

We've been shopping for the past half hour, and only now has she thought to ask why I haven't picked out anything. I was kind of hoping she wouldn't pay attention. She's having a good time trying on skirts and dresses and jeans. Now she's frowning at me from the three-way mirror outside her dressing room stall. "Why aren't you shopping, too?"

I'm sure the response: *I don't know how much longer I'll fit into anything. It would be a waste of money to buy anything in my size when I don't have the first idea of how pregnancy will affect my body...* wouldn't go over well.

"I feel bloated," I groan, rubbing my stomach. "It's just not a good day."

"I'm sorry. Would you prefer we go back home?"

I like that she thinks of it as *home* for both of us. "No, I'm fine. I just know I would hate myself in everything I tried on."

"You always look great, if that helps."

"Thanks. And you look hot in that dress."

She does a little twirl in front of the mirror, hands on her hips.

The pale blue color goes great with her blonde curls and sun-tanned skin. "It's cute."

"I did not use the word cute. You'd be walking around setting off three-alarm fires in that dress."

For some reason, her smile fades. Instead of looking at her reflection with her usual confidence, she chews her lip—much more of that, and she'll split it open. "I don't know. Maybe not."

I never know the right thing to say. I know that whatever comes out will end up hurting her. It's like she doesn't care about looking nice anymore—like she would rather not even try.

Look at what he took from her. I haven't asked Callum about Kristoff, though I hope he's dead. It's the only thing he deserves.

"It's really pretty on you," I point out, trying to be careful. "I say buy it but leave the tags on. Try it on again in a week or two, and if you're still unsure, bring it back."

She runs a hand over the low-cut bust line, the thin straps over her shoulders. "Yeah. That's not a bad idea." She's looking at her body like she's never seen it before, as if she doesn't know what to do with it. I have to look at the floor out of panic that I'll start crying. The last thing I want is for her to think I pity her. I do, however. There's a burning pain in my chest that only spreads when I look at her.

"What about all this?" I gesture to the pile of clothes in the dressing room that she decided, for one reason or another, she didn't like.

"I don't want any of those." When I absently start picking things up, she scowls at me. "Stop. I can clean up after myself."

"I'll help you. It's not like I'm doing anything else."

"I feel bad. You should've said something about not feeling up to shopping today."

I didn't think of it until we were already at the store. The life growing inside me is at the forefront of my mind pretty much all the time. Oddly enough, I didn't give any thought to shopping with somebody who doesn't know I'm pregnant. I'm too practical to buy something for the sake of appearances, although that's what I should do if I want to keep her in the dark.

I have to tell Callum first. I wish I could find the right time. Only there's always something going on. He's in a meeting, or busy with Romero, or I have to go to work. He's been under so much stress lately, too. I still don't quite know how he will take the news. I don't want to ruin anything by telling him at the wrong time.

I hang up a couple of dresses and take them out to the rack where people leave what they don't want. I wonder if I'll ever look good in clothes like these again—form-fitting dresses, crop tops.

"You okay out there?" I jump, startled, when Tatum pokes her head out from the dressing room. "You got super quiet."

"Oh, I'm fine. Distracted, I guess."

"Worried about your dad?" she asks before closing the door again.

I wasn't until now after she mentioned him. "Yeah, a little, although that's nothing new."

"He hasn't gone back on saying he's okay with you and Dad being together, has he?"

"No. I can tell he's not thrilled, but he hasn't said anything." He sure will once he finds out about the baby. He'll have plenty to say. I just don't think I'll want to hear it.

"He'd better not if he wants to keep his balls."

"Tatum…" I have to laugh at how fierce she sounds. All she ever wants is to defend the people she cares about.

"Sorry, but it's true. You're obviously happy," she grumbles a little to herself, behind the closed door and out of sight. "With my dad. Which is kind of gross."

"Uh, I heard that." I tap the door with my knuckles. "I'm standing right here."

"I mean, gross in the way it's gross when you have to think about your parents as a person and not, like, a mom or a dad. It's not like he ever really dated before you two got together, so this is kind of new territory to me."

"But... you're okay with it? Right?" Asking a question like that is easier with a door between us. I strain my ears, wanting to hear anything she might whisper or mutter under her breath.

Turns out, I don't need to worry. She flings the door open just as I jump back to keep from getting hit then she wraps me up in a hug. "I'm okay with it," she whispers in my ear while squeezing me. "I don't want you to ever think I'm not. I'd feel so bad if I thought you were worried. All I care about is your happiness, and if you guys are happy together, so am I."

I wonder if she understands how important it is for me to hear that. "It's important we're still okay. You're the only one of my friends who bothered to stick around once..."

Her hold tightens, probably because she knows I'm thinking about Lucas and how he alienated me from everybody else in my life. Lucas, whose parents are half crazy with grief this very minute. Stop. You have to stop thinking about it.

It's like she can read my mind. "Do not blame yourself." When she pulls back and holds me at arm's length, wearing a stern little scowl, it's like I got my best friend back. Finally, with her eyes blazing and her cheeks flushed. "You hear me? I want you to say it. I do not blame myself."

"I do not blame myself," I whisper.

"Yeah. That's believable." She lets go of me and grabs the rest of what's left in the dressing room. "Come on. I'm starving. Give me a minute to buy this stuff and we'll have lunch."

"Sounds good." Even though I don't have much of an appetite; it's been touch-and-go the past couple of days. I know I need to eat, but the idea doesn't appeal to me. I wish I had somebody besides the internet to ask questions. I don't know if any of this is typical or if there's anything to make me feel better. I've read that peppermint seems to help, but my faith in it working is low. Everything makes me feel worse. *Gah, I miss my mom.* I wish more than anything she was here now to offer me advice. She would know what to do.

It's when we're in line at the register that the onset of sweating hits me. Suddenly I feel like I'm standing directly in front of the sun. "Is it warm in here?" I ask shyly.

"Not really." Tatum looks me up and down. "Are you feeling okay? You look a little green."

Once we move closer to the register, the feeling gets worse. Only once the girl behind the counter reaches for Tatum's clothes do I realize it's Tatum's perfume that sets me off. The stronger the smell, the sweatier and more nauseated I get.

"I'll meet you outside." Nothing in the world matters more than getting out of this store. The glass doors are my sole goal, and I walk toward them as calmly as possible, even as my insides start churning. Stupid me, thinking if I never got sick like this before now, I'd be one of the lucky ones who never had to go through it.

I burst through the double doors to the outside, sucking deep breaths into my lungs. The sunshine is so bright, glaring off the concrete, but there's an awning over the wide front window, and I take shelter beneath it. A few minutes pass, and the nausea seems to pass with every breath I take. *Shit.* Suddenly it occurs to me that I have a new reason to be nauseated. *What if she knows?* I can play it off, I think. I'll tell her I didn't have enough breakfast or something and started to feel dizzy.

"Hey!" Tatum's voice meets my ears as she comes out with a bag in each hand, a look of concern etched into her features. "It looked like you were going to barf all over the floor. Are you okay?"

No. Not with the smell of Tatum's perfume clinging in the air. The sickening floral scent suffocates me, making it difficult to breathe. Never mind the bile rising up in my throat.

I take off, lurching for the closest trash can and barely grabbing the rim with both hands before the nausea wins and I empty my stomach in the grossest, most public way possible. *Ewww.* Even as I'm gagging and retching, there's shame in the back of my mind.

Finally, it passes, and there's nothing left but a shaky, weak feeling left inside of me. Embarrassment tickles the back of my mind, but I shove it back. I can't be the only person ever to vomit in a garbage can at a shopping center.

Tatum comes up beside me, gently touching my back, which she rubs in slow circles. "I'll go to the vending machine and grab you a water. Wait here." She rushes off before I can stop her. Not that I want to. The taste of vomit clings to my tongue and I need to get rid of it now.

I can't bear to look at anyone as I sink weakly onto a metal bench next to the trash can. A few slow, shallow breaths of balmy air help clear the rest of the dizziness. Tatum returns, frowning as she hands me a cold bottle of water.

"Thanks," I whisper. "I'm so embarrassed."

"Nobody will remember it in five minutes," she assures in her typical no-nonsense way.

"Do me a favor, okay? Don't tell your dad. You know how he gets, all anxious and whatever. I'm sure he has enough shit on his plate." I play it off like it's not a big deal, but in reality, if he's even the slightest bit suspicious that there might be something wrong with me, he'll send me to a doctor before I can object.

"Yeah, sure. Maybe that bloated feeling was something else. It seemed to appear out of nowhere."

"Yeah. It did, but it's probably nothing. Just a bug."

I expect her to take the spot next to me, but instead, she folds her arms across her chest, the bags hanging from her wrists. "Hmmm, maybe. It's possible, yes, but the fact that you got sick that quickly after being okay all afternoon, and you don't want Dad to know."

Oh. No.

"You've been complaining that you're bloated," she continues. "And then yesterday, you didn't have a drop of alcohol at brunch."

"I didn't feel like drinking, so what" I whisper before taking another sip of water. My hands tremble. I can see the puzzle pieces clicking into place in her mind, each one moving strategically.

"Are you pregnant?" Tatum asks on a sharp laugh, like she doesn't believe the words but needs to ask anyway. A lie rushes its way to the tip of my tongue, ready to tumble off, but I don't have the heart to speak it. I'm tired of lying. She's going to find out eventually, and then I'll look like a hypocrite for trying to deceive her.

Damn it. This isn't the way it was supposed to happen. I didn't want her to find out like this—basically all on her own.

"Don't lie to me. Please." Her voice is low and flat, sending icy fingers of fear racing up my spine. "Are you? Or is there a possibility that you might be?"

My tongue is so thick I can barely speak. "I..."

Her eyes widen as a bright, red flush creeps onto her cheeks. "Fuck. Stop. Don't say anything else."

I press my palm to my clammy forehead. This isn't going well. Not at all. The fear of our friendship melting like snow in the summer terrifies me. I can't lose her. She's my best friend. "Wait, please. I didn't mean for this to happen, I swear. I've been taking birth control. It was an accident."

Her lips part, except nothing comes out. Every second that passes hardens her face a little more, until she might as well be wearing a concrete mask. I can't read her, and I hate it. "I... I need a minute to figure out how to feel about this."

"Please, don't hate me." My legs tremble as I stand, but not from nausea. This is so much worse than I pictured, even in my darkest, most fearful nightmares. I can visibly see her pulling away from me.

"I don't," she claims, but her shoulders pull up around her ears when I reach out, seeking to hug her.

My arms fall back to my sides. "You look like you do. I swear, I didn't plan for this. I don't even know what to do or how to feel. And he doesn't know. Not yet," I add in a rush.

She merely snorts. "Something tells me I would've known by now if you told him."

"Do you think he'll be mad?"

"How would I know?" My face falls, and her brows pinch together. "Sorry. I'm not..."

"You don't have to apologize."

She stares down at the concrete while I gaze at the water shooting out from the mouths of four metal fish in the center of the fountain. Kids are splashing and playing along the edges, and Moms are pushing babies in strollers with Starbucks cups nestled into carriers. How can they all walk past like everything's okay when my life is in the middle of falling apart?

"If you're worried that I did this on purpose or to trap him," I whisper, my chin quivering. "Please, tell me you believe me. It would kill me to know otherwise."

She blinks rapidly, shaking her head. "Never would I consider it. You're better than that."

"Thank you." I sigh with relief. There she was, telling me she was fine with us being together. I guess adding a baby into the mix makes it a whole other situation, in any case.

"Okay, let's just pause for a moment," she finally blurts out. "The whole thing is making me feel weird. I think we should go home. I need some time to think."

"Yeah, sure. Whatever you want." I have to bite my tongue before I can do something awkward, like ask her not to tell Callum. Something tells me I'd regret it if I did. That might be the final straw that breaks our friendship for good, if I haven't already destroyed it by confessing my secret.

Tendrils of fear snake up my back. There's no hiding the truth anymore. I must tell Callum before Tatum blurts it out—accidentally or otherwise. I should've known that I would never be able to keep this a secret.

All I can do during the long, quiet ride home is hope Callum meant it when he talked about having children with me. I can only hope he has it in him to be the man I need. The man we both need. The alternative is something I can't fathom thinking about at the moment. My only hope is that Callum and I can figure this out, and that my relationship with Tatum hasn't been ruined in the process.

CALLUM

"Patience," Romero advises, his eyes constantly moving as he scans the area around us while we stand beneath the covered stoop in front of his cottage. "Just because I haven't found anything yet doesn't mean I won't."

"It isn't you I'm frustrated with," I grunt, trying not to appear suspicious. There are no fewer than five guards within my line of sight, and I can't help but wonder if it's one of them.

The traitor.

"It's barely been two days since I installed the software," he reminds me. "Give it some time."

"I get it, but until then, I have to pretend I trust everyone equally, and that's frustrating as hell when you know one of your men is sharing information he shouldn't be."

"There is another solution. It's faster, if that's what you're looking for. You could just fire everybody and start over."

He recoils under the sharp glare I shoot at him. I know he wasn't serious, but I'm not in a joking mood. "I can't afford to lose my entire team at a time like this. Not with a new deal in the works and increased security."

"I know. I just wanted to ensure you knew all the possibilities."

What I don't want to voice, though, which he probably understands, is my hesitation in leaving the house unsecured now that Bianca is here. It's more important than ever to make sure there are eyes watching me at all times. I can't afford to throw away all of our security because of one bad apple. The frustration I feel mounts every day. The sense of betrayal. I almost wish Amanda would pull more of her shit in hopes somebody will slip up and reveal themselves as the one going behind my back to feed her information. She's been quiet—too quiet. So quiet that just the thought of it makes my hackles rise.

"I've been thinking," Romero murmurs, "what if we set a trap?"

"In what way?"

"We can come up with a made-up scenario. Divide the men into groups of three or four, get them all in a room together, then mention one of these fake scenarios."

"Such as what?"

"You're selling the house. You're moving to Europe. You're getting married."

Ahhh. Yes. "Something that would interest her," I muse.

"Exactly. If she comes back to you and throws it in your face, you'll know from whatever she tells you which story she heard. We can narrow it down to the three or four men who possibly gave her the information."

"You know, that's not a bad idea," I agree. "And those are the phones we can check, too, to see which of them made contact with her."

"It'll give us a direction to go off of."

"Yes, it will." There's a humming sensation rippling through my body, the buzzing of excitement, possibility. "I like this idea. I'll come up with a few stories I know will get under her skin, and you break down the men into groups."

The sound of tires crunching over gravel draws my attention, instantly wiping away all thoughts of Amanda when I catch sight of Tatum's car flying up the driveway.

Romero grunts in disapproval as we watch. "It's bad enough she refuses to have a driver," he mutters. "But does she have to drive like a bat out of hell?"

The car breezes past us before squealing to a stop in front of the house. The two of us watch, silent, as Tatum shoves her door open and jumps out, then reaches into the back seat for shopping bags which she yanks from the car almost violently.

"Tatum?" I call out, but my voice goes unacknowledged. She doesn't look my way, either.

"Great," I mutter, with Romero sighing in agreement. There I was, thinking everything was getting better.

What's worse, Bianca waits to open her door until Tatum is already stomping her way up the front steps and into the house. The worry in her voice when she calls out gets my legs moving without thinking. "Wait a minute, Tatum. Please?" Bianca goes ignored, too, which tells me whatever this is has to be serious.

"Bianca." The dismay on her delicate face draws me to her. Nevertheless, she's already hurrying from the car and up into the house by the time I reach her. *What the hell is going on?* I am chasing behind them both.

What could have happened? Fear knots in my stomach. Everything was fine when they left the house. So whatever it is, it must have occurred while they were out, and it upset Bianca enough that she ignored me in favor of chasing her friend.

Considering I'm already dealing with the bitterness of knowing I've been betrayed by one of my own, today is not the day to test if I'm willing to put a bullet in someone.

"Bianca!" I bark once inside the house. My angry bellow fills the air, echoing in the cavernous entry hall.

She peers over her shoulder, and it damn near stops my heart. I can't identify what's written across her face using any other word but fear. She's frightened. Immediately every horrible, terrible thought fills my head. Who hurt her? I swear to god I'll kill them, destroy them, make them wish they were never born.

"What happened?" I demand, marching toward her while she backs away, closer to the door separating Tatum's wing from the rest of the house. My daughter has already disappeared behind it.

"She's upset." Bianca peeks behind her to the closed door.

"No kidding. Why? That's my question. What happened while you were shopping?"

"I..." She shakes her head, shrugging, but her body betrays her as a slight tremble moves through her. "I'm not sure."

"Bianca, please tell me this isn't where we are again. Don't lie to me, because that's what you're doing, and you've never been any good at it. We promised to be honest with each other going forward, so I deserve to know. I don't like both of you being upset without knowing how to fix it." I reach for her and recoil with surprise when she flinches away from my touch. "What happened?" I demand. "I swear to god if I find out that someone..."

"No one did anything." She interrupts me before I can finish my thought. "It's just... I don't know..." Her chest begins to rise and fall rapidly, faster with every second. Her gaze widens, and she reminds me of a bunny in a trap. Now it doesn't matter if she flinches. I can't bear to stand by and watch her suffer like this, so I grab her by the arms and pull her close, holding her against my chest while she trembles against me.

"Whatever it is, you can tell me. We'll work it out. However, we can't if I don't know what we're up against." Deep down inside, I know too well that if she is afraid or hesitates to tell me the truth, it's no one's fault but my own. The way I treated her before, my moods swinging violently back and forth depending on how determined I was to keep her away from me for her own good. It's only natural she would still be afraid of me at times. That's a punishment I'll have to learn to live with as I earn her trust.

"Can we go sit down somewhere? Somewhere private?"

With an arm wrapped around her waist, I walk her to my office. Dread weighs heavier on me with every step we take. While in my head, I can't help but try to guess what's coming. It's a habit of being in my position for years; the effort to keep me and mine safe by foreseeing every obstacle and danger.

I'm in the dark now. There are too many possibilities, too many enemies.

Once we're alone, I sit her down, then close the door to give us privacy. "Do you need a drink?"

Her head swings back and forth. "No, not at all." She runs a hand under her eyes, sniffling. "I'm sorry. I didn't want it to have to come out this way."

Every fiber of my being is tuned into every move and breath she takes. I'm utterly helpless to everything that is her. She'll never understand how all that I am and all that I want is wrapped up in her. Some much so that I want to take her and shake her and demand answers—anything so long as I can vent this unbearable tension.

"I'm trying to be patient and understanding, but too many scenarios are running through my head. I'm going to need you to tell me right now," I grit out, and the way she flinches confirms the strain in every word.

Dropping to one knee before her, I cover her quivering hands with mine. "Whatever it is, I'm here. I want to help. Did you have a fight?" I ask, hopeful that it's something as meaningless as that.

"Not really." She stares down at our joined hands. "Although she is upset with me."

"Why? You know how she's been lately. I wouldn't take it personally."

"It's not like that. She's... I'm..."

"You're what?" *Leaving? Fuck, she's going to tell you she's leaving, because you never deserved her to begin with. She never wanted this. Who could blame her?*

The doubt in my mind is a terrifying reality.

"I was afraid to tell you," she whispers. "I didn't know how you would feel about it, so I didn't want to tell you yet. Only she figured it out, and now she's mad at me. The last thing I need is for you to be mad or upset too."

"Mad about what? For God's sake, talk to me. What would I be mad about?" Dear God, don't let it be what I think it is. Don't let her say she's leaving me.

"I'm..." She closes her eyes and exhales a deep breath from her lungs. "I'm going to have a baby."

It's like a bowling ball to the gut, knocking the air from my lungs. Except instead of pain, there's a rush of relief. I'm almost weak with it by the time I manage to take a breath which I release on a soft laugh. "Oh god, Bianca. Are you really pregnant? We're going to have a baby?"

"Yes." Her head bobs up and down, fresh tears rolling down her cheeks and dripping down onto the backs of my hands. "I know you said you wanted one, but saying and actually having are two very different things."

"Bianca. Shit." Gathering her in my arms to stroke her hair, I close my eyes and soak in the moment. She's pregnant. My little bird is carrying my baby. *Our baby.*

"Does this mean you're happy?" Her question is muffled against my shoulder, but I hear the anxiety in it just the same.

"Happy? I'm overjoyed! Are you kidding?" Laughing, I pull back to take her soft cheeks into my hands so I can stare into her dazzling blue eyes. "This is... it's everything. I told you I wanted children, and I wasn't lying. I want this. I want you. I can't believe you're growing our baby inside of you."

"I know, but it's so soon, and then I saw—" Her mouth snaps shut an instant before she averts her gaze, looking toward the window at my back.

"What?" I whisper. "Who did you see?"

"Amanda. She was at the clinic when I went to the doctor. We ran into each other in the lobby, and she said some things. I know she was just trying to get inside my head, and I was trying to remind myself that she's telling me these things because she hates you. Nonetheless, it didn't work."

"What did she say?" I nearly bark the question.

The look of heartbreak on Bianca's face makes me want to order a hit on Amanda at this very moment. "That you'd want me to get an abortion if you found out because you didn't want any more children. That the last thing you wanted was to be tied down again." The anguish in her voice slices me down to the bone.

I'll kill her. It's as simple as that.

How long have I told myself I must spare her pathetic life because she's Tatum's mother? She's never been a mother to her, anyway. I could have done Tatum and the world a favor by getting rid of her, but I didn't. Now it doesn't seem to matter if she's alive or dead.

"For one thing," I speak carefully so I don't spook her, "Amanda does not have the first clue on how I would feel about anything. She doesn't know me. You should know by now that she wants me to be miserable, which means making everyone around me miserable by association. Plus, she's herself, so I'm sure it must make her jealous, knowing you're going to have my child—a child I very much want, by the way. Just like I want you. I wouldn't have told you I wanted to be with you if I didn't want to be with you. Having a child is a bonus that comes with loving you."

This should be a joyful, blissful moment. The woman I love is telling me she's having my child. In its place, we're talking about my ex-wife and her snake-like tendencies.

"Tatum is upset," Bianca reminds me, and the worry lines between her brows make me want to wipe them from her face. "I don't know what to do or how to fix it. I can't lose her. She's my best friend."

"Yes, that's a little sensitive, though she'll come around. It's most likely the surprise factor that got her, but try not to let it worry you."

"Also, I threw up in a trash can," she grumbles. "When we were shopping, and well, she put it all together like a puzzle."

"She's observant," I agree, brushing her dark hair away from her face, my chest swelling with love and admiration as I peer into her eyes. A monster like me should never be given such a beautiful angel like her. "No matter what, I promise you, she will come around. We need to give her a little time and space, but she loves you. I know that much, and this won't change that."

Bianca nods, even as the harsh worry lines on her face don't appear to ease.

"I'll talk to her, too," I add. "I'll give her a few hours to calm down, then try and have a conversation with her. Don't worry," I insist when she gives me a skeptical look. "I just want to ensure she knows this isn't one of those situations where Dad forgets all about his first family now that he's got a new one. I would hope she'd know better than that by now, although who's to say?"

"I want to be happy about this," she frowns, her eyes searching mine. "I genuinely do."

"Then be happy," I tell her with a smile. "You deserve it. We deserve it. We're going to have a baby, and if you doubt at all the type of mother you'll be, stop right now. I already know you'll be amazing."

"I'm not worried about that. I was worried you'd be unhappy. That you wouldn't want me anymore." The relief in her laughter makes me hate Amanda all the more. Is there any low that women won't stoop to?

"I could never not want you. You're the air I need to fucking breathe, Bianca. If anything, that baby growing inside you makes me ten times more possessive of what I already know is mine."

"Wow, slow it down, caveman. I don't need you tossing me over your shoulder and carrying me back to your cave." She laughs, and that seems to ease the tension.

"Oh, you know damn well what I'm capable of, my little bird." I smile, "Now I have some questions. When are you due? And when is your next doctor's appointment?"

"The appointment is in a couple of weeks," she peers up at me. "The problem is, I'm not sure exactly when I ovulated, so I guess they'll be able to tell us the due date when we have the ultrasound. I've taken my pills religiously, except they must have failed at some point. I haven't had a period in a while."

"Is this also why you thought I'd be upset?"

"Well, yeah. Here you are, thinking I'm on the pill, and somehow I end up pregnant. That's pretty suspicious, if you ask me."

It would be, if I didn't have a part in it. Guilt eats away at my black heart. She thinks this is all on her, unaware of the switch I pulled with her pills. "These things happen." I ignore the nasty feeling growing in my gut and press a kiss to her forehead. "I'm not unhappy. I'm thrilled. This is a fresh start, and I can't wait to see what the future holds for us."

It's almost reverent, the way I drop a hand to her stomach, cradling her smooth belly. My child is growing inside her. Our child. Shit. I'm going to be a dad all over again. The final piece in my plan to keep her beside me is in place. "I swear I'll do right by you both. Tatum, too. There's more than enough room for everyone—not to mention anyone who comes after this, and believe me, I plan to make sure you're pregnant over and over again."

Ultimately, she laughs, swatting at my hand. "Slow down, one thing at a time. I just had my first bout of morning sickness today. Let me adjust."

I lean in to kiss her forehead again, then her salty, tear-stained cheeks. "I love you. Don't ever doubt that, and never let anyone tell you otherwise."

"I love you, too," she smiles through her tears. "I'm so emotional."

"That's to be expected." I stand, extending my hands for her to join me. "Come on, you look exhausted and need to rest."

"I don't need to rest," she shoots back.

I have to remind myself that telling her I'll tie her to the bed if she doesn't listen is not a favorable option, so instead I go with something a little less alpha-like.

"Do me a favor and rest because it makes me happy. You've had a lot of excitement today, and I can't fathom losing the tiny life we just discovered growing inside of you. I've never been pregnant before, clearly, but I can't imagine it's easy on the body."

Bianca sighs, her eyes twinkling with joy even as she rolls them. "If this is how you will be for the next seven months, I'm not sure I'll survive."

"Oh, little bird, if you think this is bad, just wait until you start showing. I can't be held liable for all the people I threaten simply for looking at you." I gently grab her by the back of the neck and pull her closer, brushing my nose against hers. "I've wanted to see you swollen with my child since that first night I saw you watching me on the patio. Now my fantasy is becoming a reality, and I'll do anything in my power to keep you this way."

She lets out a helpless groan before pressing her lips to mine. She's perfect, and everything that is mine. The mere thought of ever losing her again makes me crazy with rage. I won't ever let her go, no matter what happens. Even if she claims she doesn't love me. Even if she hates me. I can't live without her.

Nonetheless, to make certain nothing fucks with my plans, I need to make sure she never, ever finds out what I did to her pills or about the fertility shot. She's forgiven many things, probably more than most women would, but that? That's the kind of thing she might never forgive me for, and while I won't ever let her go, I'd rather have her love me than hate me. Because losing her or our child is not an option.

BIANCA

"Hey, what are you looking at?"

My heart just about jumps out of my chest as I quickly close my browser before turning in my chair to find Stephanie standing at the entrance of my cubicle. The way she lifts an eyebrow while folding her arms reminds me too much of my best friend—it hurts, since we haven't spoken all week.

I touch a hand to my chest, laughing. "You're like a ghost, I swear. How are you so quiet?"

"Maybe you were too busy looking at naughty things to notice me coming up behind you."

"Naughty things?" The idea makes me giggle, because she couldn't be further from the truth. It was dirty things that got me pregnant in the first place. Now, I am reading advice columns and googling baby names when I should be working.

"Nobody closes their browser that fast if they aren't looking at something they shouldn't be."

"Sorry to disappoint you, but I was reading junk on Reddit." At least it's a believable lie. "I don't want to get caught screwing around."

"Who cares?" she sighs. "It's Friday afternoon. Half the office is already gone for the day."

That's a good point, and the only reason I had the spare time to screw around on the internet. It seems most of the managers and their assistants schedule their time around Fridays in the summer, cutting out around lunchtime if they come in at all. "It is nice, the office being this quiet. I could get used to it." Even if I'd like to be one of the lucky ones who can sneak out with nobody minding. At least it makes the day easy and peaceful.

"Although come September, the good times are over." She leaves on that unhappy note, humming to herself as she sits in the next cubicle. I wonder why she interrupted me in the first place. Maybe she's bored. I'll have to be more careful with my time if she's going to be randomly popping over.

Soon enough, I won't have an option. Everyone will know. I smile to myself when I remember Alan walking me through the paperwork before I started, pointing out that I might be interested in their maternity leave policy one day. I could never have imagined I'd be interested in it this quickly.

Everything's happening so fast, yet I can't say I'm unhappy about it. Now that I know Callum wants the baby and is already planning on devoting a room to the nursery, it's simpler for me to look forward to the coming months. No, I still haven't told Dad, and I have no idea how even to begin broaching the subject with him—maybe once I have an image from the ultrasound, I can show it to him. It'll be more real, then. A picture of his grandbaby growing inside me.

Of course, the doubt trickles in. *What if he's never happy about it? If he can't accept it?* That would leave me with a difficult decision, but only one choice makes any sense. I have to choose me and the family I'm growing. If he can't love my baby because of who fathered them, that's up to him. I won't beg him to be a part of my life.

I'm still mulling this over when my desk phone rings. I sit up straighter, expecting somebody to chew me out for wasting work time; that's what guilt does to a person. It rings a second time, meaning the call is coming from outside the office. No chance of getting chewed out.

Tatum's number flashes across the ID. My stomach starts to churn while I reach out with a shaky hand to pick up the receiver. "Hey, What's up?"

"I..." Her voice is soft, low. "I'm sorry I've been such an asshole all week."

"You haven't been an asshole. Just quiet." Honestly, she's been avoiding me, but I'm trying to be understanding. "I'm not going to force you to see me or talk to me."

"I know. But I'm sorry, and I wanted you to know that. I've been thinking a lot this week, and I guess getting so upset on Sunday was childish. I'm sorry."

She has no idea how much I've wished to hear her say that. Aside from worrying about what Dad will think, her opinion has weighed heaviest on me. While Callum and I lie in bed talking about baby names, preschools, and colleges, there's always that twinge of guilt in my mind. The guilt of knowing Tatum is under the same roof we are, being miserable while we're so happy. Callum told me he tried to talk to her but, as I expected, she put up a brick wall between them.

"So long as you don't hate me."

"I told you before that I don't," she reminds me. "I meant it. I just needed time to figure out my feelings. And I guess I can accept having a brother or sister. It might even be fun."

"I sure need you," I whisper, blinking back tears. My emotions are all over the place lately. I guess I have to learn to get used to it while my hormones rage. "I can't do this without you. I'm scared and excited and worried and overwhelmed."

"I'm here," she assures me. "I can't wait to spoil that kid rotten. Can you believe it? A big sister, at my age?"

"That is sort of funny. Who knows? Maybe you'll find the right guy soon and have a baby, too. Their aunt or uncle will barely be any older than they are."

"Girl, slow down. Not everyone is in a hurry to birth children."

"I wasn't in a hurry," I remind her. "Believe me, I didn't plan this."

"I know. Sorry, that came out the wrong way. How about we go to dinner tonight and talk about it, and I can start planning the baby shower."

"Pump the brakes!" I'm caught between laughing and crying out of sheer relief. "There's a long time to go before we even have to start thinking about that."

"Do you think the best, biggest baby shower in the history of the world can be planned overnight? Get real. I'll meet you in the parking garage of your job at five with a choice of themes, colors, and menus."

The thing is, I wouldn't put it past her to do something like that. There are tears of relief welling in my eyes by the time I hang up. I didn't know until now how scared I was that she wouldn't come around. I feel whole again with the Tatum-sized piece of my heart back in place.

Before I forget, I send Callum a text to let him know.

Me: Guess what? Things are good with Tatum – she wants to go to dinner tonight, so I'll see you when we get home. She seems happy!

I know how much it'll mean to him, seeing that. Outsiders would never guess there's a big heart beating under that cold exterior. He might not always know how to express himself, however he loves as fiercely as he fights. Maybe more so.

Excitement for the future leaves me smiling like an idiot. I can't wait to get home tonight so we can celebrate.

* * *

"Five o'clock on the dot." Tatum grins, and I find her leaning against my car when I step into the garage. It's mostly empty, a mute testament to the way the entire building cuts out early on Friday. Everybody except me. "Bad girl. You must've left your desk a minute or two early."

"Nobody's around to care." And I spent the past few hours willing the clock to move faster so I could see my best friend again. It took sheer willpower to stay in my chair as long as I did.

"Where do you want to go for dinner?" She pushes away from the trunk, sliding her sunglasses up onto her head. Her flowered sundress tells me she isn't expecting anything fancy, but then again, neither am I.

"I'm up for anything." Dinner's not the important part. We could go to a drive-thru, so long as she talks to me.

"Maybe Italian?"

"Sure. Two cars?"

"Are you kidding?" she scoffs. "You're the designated driver for the next... how many months will it be until you give me a sibling?"

"Cute. You'll still have to pick up your car."

She shrugs it off, rounding the back of the car on her way to the passenger seat. "Or I could send Romero over here to pick it up. It's been too long since I've made him do anything for me."

"Yeah, I noticed you haven't been as hard on him as you used to be." I observe her over the roof of the car, curious to see her reaction.

I never get the chance.

Caught up in the excitement of seeing her, I didn't pay any attention to the black SUV with tinted windows parked next to my car. Not until the back door opens, and a pair of arms shoot out, wrapping around Tatum and pulling her into the car.

My brain shuts down at the sight of it. Like I can't handle what my eyes are telling me. Things like this don't happen. This isn't happening.

Yet before I can suck in enough breath to scream, a man dressed in black clamps a cloth over her nose and mouth. All I see is her wide, terror-filled eyes before she's pulled into the vehicle, feet kicking helplessly.

I'm frozen. It's like I'm watching from miles away, frozen in shock, refusing to believe what I'm seeing. It can't take more than five seconds before she's inside the SUV—then there's a man rushing me, clamping a cloth over my face. I know the smell. Lucas did the same thing to me when he took me from the restaurant. It's sweet.

How the fuck is this happening all over again?

Something snaps inside my head. *No, no, this isn't happening. Not to me. Not to my baby.*

Every self-defense lesson Dad ever taught me comes rushing back. I can't breathe in if I want to stay conscious, so I hold my breath while stomping a foot against his instep with all my might. He grunts in pain but doesn't release me. In my frenzy, I reach out, sinking my nails into any flesh I can touch, then I drive an elbow into his ribs.

"You bitch," he growls before slamming me headfirst into the trunk of my car. Everything goes dark and foggy. My body slumps when I lose control of it, and I can't help but breathe in.

My baby. My baby...

I don't lose consciousness, though. Not completely. It's more like being sedated; my brain still works. I hear everything, but I can't make my body move. I'm floating in a dream-like state, but this is all very real. A living nightmare.

"Get moving," one of the men snarls, shoving me into the car. I can't open my eyes. My head is pounding.

Tatum's body slumps against mine, heavy and unconscious. *Wake up. Wake up!* Her head lolls against my shoulder, and I want to nudge it, except I can't move. My limbs are useless.

"There wasn't supposed to be two of them."

"... be pissed..."

"He'll like it..."

Who are they talking about? I want to go to sleep. *No! Stay awake!* I

307

can't let the baby down. But there's nothing I can do. I can't fight if I can't move.

A sudden, sharp turn after endless driving jostles me out of my daze enough that I feel the SUV slowing down. Tatum moans softly but is still slumped against me by the time we come to a stop.

The doors swing open, and a second later, the one next to me also does. "Don't forget the pillowcase." That's the only warning I get before my head is covered by something that stinks of chemicals. A man wraps an arm around my waist and tosses me onto his shoulder. I feel every step my attacker takes, his shoulder digging into my ribs painfully.

Behind us, Tatum starts muttering indistinctly.

A musty smell tickles my nostrils, accompanied by a metallic scent. *Blood.* Is Tatum bleeding? Is it me? No, I don't think I'm bleeding. The smell fades away as we continue to walk, yet the remainder of that scent lingers. Someone is bleeding, or worse, dead.

I'm going to lose it. Once I start to panic—and I'm almost there—that's it. I might not come back. *Remember the baby.* The baby. I can't afford to lose it. I can't afford to lose my life or Tatum's. I need to remain strong.

"Leave them on the floor." I don't recognize the deep, male voice, but it's loud enough to cut its way through the frantic haze in my mind. "Why are there two of them? You were only supposed to take the one."

"She wasn't alone." The man carrying me drops me to the floor without warning, sending white-hot pain zipping up my spine when my tailbone lands against something hard. It's not concrete or flooring. Maybe wood? I can't help but suck in a gasp before crying out.

"What did you do to her?" Tatum's voice is thick and unclear. She's beside me. My back is up against a wall, it feels like. Everybody's voices echo—it's a vast space wherever we are.

"Shut up," a man grunts. "You're nothing but extra weight."

"Fuck you," she sneers.

"Don't," I whisper, lifting my head and trying to see through the cheap cotton hood. There's a lamp overhead, even though it doesn't cast enough light for me to make any details out.

That gruff voice rings out directly in front of us, so close he must be standing over where we're sitting. "You didn't bind their wrists? Are you an amateur here? What the fuck do I pay you for?"

Tatum scrambles next to me—she's trying to get up. I don't have time to reach for her before she grunts. The sound of her body hitting the floor fills my ears. "You asshole!" she screams. "I'll fucking kill you!"

"Oh, I know who this little spitfire is," the man observes with a cruel laugh. Suddenly a pair of hands grip my wrists, binding them with rough twine. "Tatum Torrio."

"That's right, fuckface," she snarls. "Which means you're either seriously fucking stupid or have a death wish."

"Shut up," the man sighs. "There's a time to shut up and a time to talk, and it's clear your daddy never taught you that. I could snap your neck like a twig and not even give a shit. Hell, you could fetch me a higher price, although I could also kill you to prove to your father how far I'm willing to go. If he wants the opportunity to meet his other kid, he's going to fall in line."

Bile fills my mouth before I catch hold of it. I can't throw up in this pillowcase. I can't let myself lose control. His confession is a bucket of ice raining down on me. This is all about the baby. They want to use the baby. Our baby.

Tatum's laughter is high-pitched, unhinged. "Oh, you think you'll get him to do what you want? You have no idea who you're screwing with. He'll tear your beating heart from your chest and toss it at your feet."

"I'm petrified."

"Tatum, stop," I whisper, inching closer to her. "You're going to get yourself hurt."

"Listen to your friend," he advises with a snicker. "She's a lot smarter than you, even if she did get herself involved with a stupid piece of shit."

"Keep talking, asshole," she snaps. "I can't wait to watch you die for this."

"Wait!"

My head snaps up at the sound of a woman's voice. Rapid footsteps fill the air—she's in heels, whoever she is. "What the hell is this? No. Not her! She wasn't supposed to be here."

"It's a little late for that. She's here now, so we'll make it work."

The woman comes to a stop in front of us. "No. It wasn't supposed to happen this way. She's not a part of this."

That voice. Even though she tries to whisper so we can't hear, I know that voice. It's too late. I've already heard her clearly—and that's not counting all the times I've listened to her taunts in my head.

Tatum realizes it too. "Mom? Is that you?" Suddenly she's a little girl, miles away from the cursing, snarling wildcat she was seconds ago.

"Tatum..." Amanda whispers.

"What is this?" she demands, her voice cracking. "What are you doing? Who are these people?" I can't find my voice, even if I would like to know the answers as well.

Amanda's shadowy figure shoves the man she's standing next to out of the way. "This wasn't part of the plan. You're not taking her. We only need this one."

"Amanda, you're exhausting," the man sighs. "And you seem to forget who you're talking to. This is my operation, not yours. You provided the information I needed. I'm grateful for that. Nonetheless, don't you dare get the idea that you're the one calling the shots."

"What are you trying to say?"

"I'm saying I do what I want, and I'm tired of your kid."

All hell breaks loose a split-second later. There's a sickening noise, like a punch but much worse. Tatum falls against me, limp and heavy like she was before. "No! Tatum?" I moan, nudging her. Her body moves helplessly, landing across my legs. "Tatum! Wake up!! What did you do to her?"

Amanda lets out a horrendous shriek. "You fucking bastard! This is over. I'm telling him everything, you son of a bitch."

The man laughs. "Funny, how fast someone can outlive their usefulness."

An instant passes before an ear-splitting crack makes me jump, yelping in surprise and fear. There's a heavy thud nearby, followed by the smell of sulfur as *gunpowder* fills my nostrils.

He shot her. Dead. Amanda. She's dead.

Tatum might be dead, too. She's not moving. I don't even know if she's breathing.

The air in my lungs stills. Panic grips me by the throat, suffocating the life inside of me. Something hard and warm presses against my temple. The world slows down, and every muscle in my body locks up.

This is it.

This is how it all ends.

How I'm going to die.

Every moment of my life plays on an endless reel in my mind.

Callum's face flashes before my eyes, followed by my father's.

I've let them down. I've let our baby down.

Tatum might be dead, and I'm next. Tears fall from my eyes, leaving cold streaks on my cheeks.

"Now," he murmurs. "It's your turn."

CALLUM

"You can tell summer's winding down."

I look up from the spreadsheet Romero insisted we compile—always organized, which I suppose I should be grateful for even if a Friday evening spent poring over spreadsheets isn't my idea of a good time. "What do you mean?"

"It's already starting to get dark, and it's barely past seven o'clock."

Sure enough, a look out the window confirms this. "I wonder how long the girls will be out."

"You know how it gets sometimes. Crack open a bottle of wine or two, and time melts."

"I don't think they'll be doing that tonight." When he lifts an eyebrow, I break the news I've been waiting all week to share. "This stays between us, but Bianca is pregnant."

Now both brows lift. "Oh. I... congratulations?"

I can't help but grin. "Yes, congratulations are in order."

"And she's happy about it?"

"You know. Things are still complicated." I'm trying to be kind toward Charlie for her sake, but I can't pretend his bias against me isn't a real pain in the ass at a time like this. My little bird should feel free to enjoy this monumental event, something that should bring her joy. Instead, she's too concerned about what he'll think. She thinks I don't notice how she sometimes drifts off, frowning, chewing her lip while absentmindedly stroking her belly. If only I could snap my fingers and take it all away.

"I'm happy for you." Though concern does touch his features before he asks, "How does Tatum feel about it? I assume she knows."

"It seems she's coming around. This dinner is a good sign."

Like magic, his worry lines smooth out. "Good. Nobody needs her throwing tantrums around the house. No offense."

"None taken. I don't like it when she loses her shit any more than you do." Clearing my throat, I turn my attention back to the list of names, every member of our crew. They're broken down by the shifts they usually take, then grouped into three's. Three seemed to be a manageable number.

Beside them are the stories we came up with. Moving to Europe, selling the property, getting married, and so on. I can already imagine Amanda blowing her top over each one.

"What about the pregnancy? We could use that as a lure. It'll drive her up a wall."

I shake my head. "No such luck. She already knows."

"Of course she does. She's a goddamn spider, sitting in the center of her web, waiting to strike."

"I've never heard it put so succinctly."

By the time we have everything in place, the clock now reads eight-fifteen. I check my phone, expecting something from Bianca, except there's nothing other than the text telling me they were going to dinner in the first place.

Me: Everything alright? Did you decide to make it a long night?

No, eight o'clock isn't exactly long, but it is when they had met up at five. Romero's right. Time can melt away, and I doubt Tatum would refrain from cracking open a bottle of wine just because

Bianca can't drink. Still, three hours seems a little excessive without a heads-up that they're doing something else.

"I'm going to the kitchen to get something to eat. Do you want anything?"

I'm tempted to say yes, but I stretch and rise from my desk instead. "I should at least take the trouble to walk down the hall." Otherwise, I'll sit and stare at my phone, willing Bianca to text me back.

We pass a window, and I see two of my men standing guard. I hate the way it feels necessary to play a game and act like nothing's out of order. All the while, I question their respectful treatment, willing myself to pretend the way at least one of them is. I can only hope there isn't more than one, or this plan with Romero will fall to pieces if Amanda gets conflicting reports from two different sources.

I force myself to push the concerns away while the two of us fix sandwiches using cold cuts from the refrigerator. Looking outside, I find myself admiring the effect the pool lights have on the patio, casting ripples over the concrete, the chairs, and the tables. Merely months ago, my little bird caught me out there with a woman whose name I can't remember. That night set me on the path I now walk.

And I want nothing more than to be in that pool with her, preferably naked, preferably sunk deep in her tight heat. She needs to get home soon, before the heaviness in my balls kills me.

The idea of her swelling soon, getting round and full thanks to the life I put inside her, only heightens my craving for her. She has no idea what she's in for as the months go on. I'm going to be insatiable.

We stand at the counter while we eat roast beef sandwiches, talking about nothing too significant for once. "I can't wait until football season starts," Romero mumbles around his food. "I miss having something to do on Sunday afternoon."

"You could always get a hobby," I point out.

He snorts. "Right. Since when do I have time for hobbies? I think you have me confused with somebody who doesn't work morning, noon, and night."

I'm about to suggest he take a little time for himself once the Amanda situation is settled when his phone goes off. An instant later, mine does the same.

It's almost shameful how quickly I pull the device from my pocket, my heart skipping a beat in anticipation of Bianca's reply.

That isn't what I find, though. "What the hell?" Romero mutters, reading his own message.

"Fuck around and find out," I mumble, dazed by the text message. "There's a crate waiting for you at your 8th Street warehouse."

"Mine says the same," Romero confirms. We look up from our phones, staring at each other for one breathless beat. Fuck. The inky feeling of dread consumes me.

I'm out of the room the next second, with Romero on my heels. His sharp whistle catches the attention of three men patrolling the halls, all of whom jog to catch up. "8th Street warehouse," he barks, directing them to their cars once we're outside. Meanwhile, I call Bianca and listen as her phone rings and rings. *Pick up. Pick up, damn it.*

Once her voicemail picks up, I have to wait for her cheerful greeting to end before being as careful as I can to not scare her if she is, in fact, sitting in a restaurant with Tatum. "Call me as soon as you get this," I speak softly while Romero gets behind the wheel with me in the passenger seat. "It's very important. Just please, let me know you're alright."

I call Tatum as we race down the driveway. Once again, I'm greeted by a voicemail recording. "Call me right away." It all feels so pointless. There's no way of knowing for sure the girls are involved, but instinct won't let me dismiss the idea.

Romero tears through the night, ignoring the speed limit, flying down residential streets at a speed that would curdle my blood under any other circumstances. *Now?* "Faster," I mutter, returning to that original text. *Fuck around and find out.*

Who the hell could this be?

When I try to send a text in response, it goes undelivered. The number comes up as *ID Blocked*. No surprise.

"I'm wondering if we should have brought more men," he grunts, swerving around a slow-moving minivan. A glimpse at the passenger side mirror reveals the car behind us, matching our speed, following Romero's every move.

"Between the five of us, if we can't handle it, then we have bigger problems."

"What if this is all a way of drawing us out? Whoever is behind this would know I'd come on the run."

"Do you want to take that chance?" He glances away from the road to stare at me for a moment. "We can always call for more backup."

"By the time they get there, what point would it make?" We're already halfway there as it is. "I don't want to wait for them."

Besides, this doesn't feel like an attack is imminent. It feels more like the attack has already taken place, I'm afraid. I don't want to think about what we might discover when we arrive. *Don't let it be Bianca. Don't let it be Tatum. Please, God, I know I haven't had much use for you in the past, but don't take out my wrongdoings on them. Don't take it out on my children, my love.*

Instead of calling for backup, Romero hands me his phone. "There's a contact in there for the warehouse. Call it. We always have guys guarding the doors." Of course. I'm so fucking beside myself I can't think straight.

The constriction in my chest only worsens with every ring that goes unanswered. Something is very wrong; I can feel it deep in my bones.

A handful of cars are parked outside the warehouse, and as we roll through the open gate, I recognize a few belonging to the men assigned to guard this warehouse. The others must belong to the guys who work down here.

He parks our car yards away, and we both arm ourselves, the second car full of my guys pulling in behind us. Romero steps out, standing behind his door for cover, gesturing for the men to check out the situation. All I can do is stare at the door leading into the warehouse while my heart pounds hard enough to drown out every other sound. I have to go in there, I can't wait, but I need to be smart, too. What if Bianca is in there? But what if she isn't, and she's left raising a child alone because I walked into a trap? *Think smart Callum.*

The men pass our car, their guns drawn, as two of them survey the area while the third steps up to the driver's side. He looks inside, then back at Romero. A slight shake of his head is all it takes to know he's dead.

"Fuck it. I'm going in." Romero calls out to the men to cover our backs while we approach the warehouse. With my Glock drawn, I kick the door open, Romero glued to my side.

There's a body at my feet, nearly blocking the door from being opened. Blood pools over the floorboards before congealing around him.

"Son of a bitch," Romero mutters, whistling for the men to follow us as we head further inside. The lights are on, giving me a clear picture of the massacre that occurred here. I count at least six bodies sprawled out across the empty warehouse floor. Blood spatters on the walls and the pungent odor of gunpowder still hangs in the air while we slowly make our way through the aftermath. From their positions, it's evident a couple of the men had drawn their weapons but weren't fast enough.

None of these things matter as much as the crate. It sits in the center of the floor beneath an overhead light. The pool of blood spread before it doesn't seem to have a source, yet the way it's smeared tells me a body was moved. I can hardly draw a breath, and almost every part of me knows I'm going to find something terrible inside it, the lid sitting beside it.

Nevertheless, I have to know. I have to face this. Every measured step I take is one step closer to my fate. To the fate that eventually befalls men in my world. *Fuck around and find out.* I've spent years fucking around, taking what's mine and stopping at nothing to protect it.

Now's when I find out what it indeed cost me.

I'm holding my breath as I step beside the open crate, forcing myself to gaze down at what awaits me. I've seen ugliness. I've been the reason for it many times. The sight of blood means nothing to a man who's shed the blood of countless others.

Only what I find in the crate wipes my mind blank. *Empty.* There's a moment when there is nothing in my head but endless darkness. No thought. Nothing but emptiness.

* * *

Subscribe to the J.L. Beck's Patreon for access to chapters from the next book before it's released alongside other exclusive content and don't forget to pre-order Empire of Pain. You can also check out her web store if you'd like to order signed copies or exclusive items.

ABOUT THE AUTHOR

J.L. Beck writes steamy romance that's unapologetic.

Her heroes are alphas who take what they want, and are willing to do anything for the woman they love.

She loves writing about darkness, passion, suspense, and of course steam.

Leaving her readers gasping, and asking what the hell just happened is only one of her many tricks.

Her books range from grey, too dark but always end with a happily ever after.

Inside the pages of her books you'll always find one of your favorite tropes.

She started her writing career in the summer of 2014 and hasn't stopped since. She lives in Wisconsin and is a mom to two, a wife, and likes to act as a literary agent part time.

Visit her website for more info: www.beckromancebooks.com.

To stay in touch with J.L., subscribe to her newsletter here. If you'd like exclusive, early access to ebooks, paperbacks, and other exclusive content subscribe to her Patreon. You can read the first couple of chapters of the next book there now!

facebook.com/AuthorJLBeck
instagram.com/authorjlbeck
patreon.com/AuthorJLBeck